HAUNTED BY AMETHYST

THE MYSTERY OF THE THREE GEMS, BOOK THREE

DEE ARMSTRONG

BiG DIPPER
PUBLISHING

Copyright © 2018 Dee Armstrong
All rights reserved.
Print Edition
ISBN-13: 978-1-949551-09-9

Big Dipper Publishing
PO Box 86
Garrisonville VA 22463
www.BigDipperPublishing.com

Cover design by Fiona Jayde Media
Author Photographs by Katie Lewis Photography

To my husband.
Who looked past my scars,
my rough ways, and my nutty ideas.
And loved me anyway.

————————

ACKNOWLEDGMENTS

As with everything in life, nothing worth having is created in a vacuum.

I would like to acknowledge the superstars in my life. They're my balcony people. The ones who believed in me when my own faith faltered. The ones who supported me with my dream of writing.

First and foremost, I would like to thank God for giving me such a great hunger to create.

My father, who when I told him that I wanted to write novels, treated me as if I was already a successful published author.

My mother, who gave me the love of reading and checks every page for errors that I've missed.

My husband, who has supported me unconditionally, pushes me for excellence and threatens to send me to the "cabin," if I'm allowing the silly stuff to get in the way of my writing dream. (Once, I rented a cabin to write in for a week. I was so lonely that I came home after one day).

My daughter, Kasie, who kept the light lit in the window and rejected the naysayers. One of my greatest cheerleaders.

My daughter, Lacey, my voracious reader. She read every

version and spread the word on my books. Another one of my greatest cheerleaders!

My son, Kody, who stuns me with his imagination and his natural story telling. One day my son, you too will write and the world will be better for it.

My Developmental Editor, Tessa Shapcott. She pushed me to write the best stories possible and, with her British wit, challenged me and allowed me to grow while lifting my spirits.

Copy Editor, Shannon Eversoll, who fine-tunes everything to a professional shine. Checking all those P's and Q's.

Fiona Jayde, who created my lovely covers. Setting them a notch above. Your storyboards are amazing.

This book wouldn't have been the same without each and every one of you. I have truly been blessed.

-Dee

ABOUT THE AUTHOR

 Since I borrowed my first romance book from my mom's nightstand, and read it under the covers with a flashlight, I've been a lover of romance.

Believe me, I've devoured my share of love stories!

I began my own fairy tale when a handsome Special Forces Green Beret decided to sit next to me. For a full year, we learned Russian together at the Defense Language Institute in Monterey, California.

While driving down Seventeen Mile Drive on his Harley with a 1940's sidecar, he knelt on the seat and proposed. My answer? "YES! Watch the road!" I've been giving him driving advice ever since. Almost three decades later, I still think he made the best decision to sit beside me because I'm crazy in love with him.

I am the proud mother of five children, four dogs, three fluffy cats and two crazy parrots. I was a Russian Linguist in the Air Force. I'm a Black Belt, a three time National Sparring Champion at the Black Belt level in TaeKwonDo, a gardening ninja and a DIY remodeling addict.

When not spinning stories, I enjoy walking with my hubby, jogging, kickboxing, collecting pets and attempting those impossible yoga poses.

I'm excited to focus full time on my secret passion—writing. I love the process of story telling, from the flicker of an idea to the birth of a new novel.

As you read my books, I hope the characters become your family and you fall in love right along side of them.

Please contact me, especially if you enjoyed Visions of Emerald. I love to hear from readers.

Happy reading,

🤍 Dee

dee@deearmstrong.com

WWW. *Dee* ARMSTRONG.COM

Dee's Blog

Ready for your next book? Go to
www.DeeArmstrong.com/shop

📘 facebook.com/DeeArmstrongAuthor

🐦 twitter.com/deearmstrongbks

📷 instagram.com/deearmstrongauthor

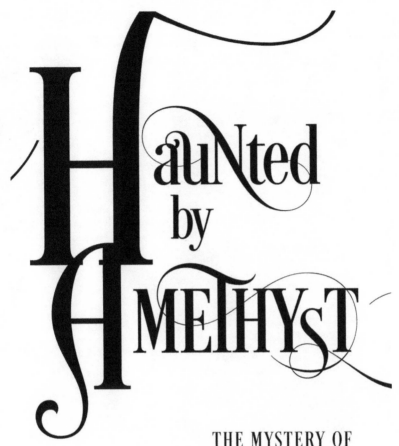

Haunted by Amethyst

THE MYSTERY OF
THE THREE GEMS, BOOK THREE
A TWIN SPRINGS TRILOGY

DEE ARMSTRONG

Part One

CHAPTER ONE

*D*ear junal
    Momys dead. izzys dad says we r a famly.
the twin springs famly he says izzy and ava hav to play wif me. Today we got fire flys. trapt them in a jar. izzys eyes glowd like the fire flys and my tumy fel warm and hapy i eat a fire flys and it roll and play in my tumy
    izzy make me fel good and hapy. i luv her. i want her to luv me to. i want to be dis happy forevr to play wif izzy forevr she maks me glow to
    niles

CHAPTER TWO

PROLOGUE

*F*or her eighth birthday, Diamond didn't wish for a pony, a Nintendo Gameboy or even to find out who her father was. She wished for one thing—to kill the Woman. But the Woman was already dead.

Diamond plodded a path towards Happy Springs Motel and avoided the worst parts of the cracked, uneven sidewalk, but stomped in each puddle of water. Rain soaked her long braids and the soggy paper bag of groceries she carried dwarfed her. She ignored the roar of the cars that passed her on Virginia's US Route 1 as she squeezed the bag closer to her flat chest. The red strands of her bangs blurred her vision and she blew them out of her way. "Couldn't even get one lousy wish," she grumbled.

A quick wipe across her face with the back of her hand only paused the raindrops that dripped from the brim of her hoodie and down her nose. She dug into her back pocket for the over-sized green key ring to hotel room 115. Home, at least for today.

Resentment churned in her stomach. She scrunched her

freckle covered nose and her eyes stung with unshed tears. She sniffled, rapidly blinked and shunned the weakness. Pushing hard on the door, she fumbled with the key. The rain swelled door wouldn't budge. She muttered under her breath, "Stupid hotel. Stupid door. Stupid wish."

Shoving her small shoulder into the door, she pushed with all her weight. With a groan, the door released, and she stumbled forward. The toe of her tennis shoe snagged on the crooked threshold and she fell heavily, scraping her knee through the already gaping hole in her jeans. She flattened the mountain of cellophane bags and a tall, lean jug of milk tumbled from the ripped sack. A giggle escaped her lips. "I'm okay, Mom. The Ramen Noodles saved me."

No response.

Her heart picked up its pace and thudded hard in her chest. She scrambled to her feet. A quiver of fear laced her voice, "Mom?"

Her panicked gaze searched the room. Sucking in a great breath of air, she prepared herself for what she might find. Raindrops, stale cigarette and pot smoke combined with the smell of lavender filled her nostrils. Immediately, she understood why her mother sat frozen on the bed, hugging her pajama clad legs with her head averted towards the wall. The Woman was here.

From the corner of her eye, she caught a glimpse of scraggily, long gray hair before the Woman's black and white form faded into the wallpaper. With a swoosh of air, Diamond released the breath she'd been holding. Relief flooded her limbs. Her mother was okay. Until the next time the Woman came.

Bending down, she filled her arms with the little square noodle bags and dumped them between mounds of half melted candles on the out of date wooden dresser. "Hey Mom! Got some grub." In the dimly lit room, her voice was overly bright and loud.

On the corner of the old dresser, a half full jug of milk laid in a bed of melted ice cubes. She dragged the milk out, twisted off the lid and sniffed. Wrinkling her nose, she replaced the lid and dropped the jug into a small, open trash can. Hooking her fingers through the handle of the new milk, she plopped it in the bucket. "Don't worry. I'll get more ice."

She tossed her wet hoodie on top of a small heap of clothes in the corner. Her gaze lingered on the TV and she longed to drown out the morning with an episode of Full House. Instead, she walked over to her mom, her purple Sketchers squishing with each step. Brushing aside the little bottles of pills that helped her mom get through her days and nights, she crawled up on the bed and snuggled beside her. Her mom was old. Almost thirty. Reaching up, she stroked her mother's once vibrant red hair back from her high forehead. Her mother felt cold to the touch. She had for years. Diamond assumed that was how the walking dead felt. Cold.

Her mother clutched her hand within her frigid grasp.

Diamond stroked her mother's bone thin fingers and then linked hands. The blue veins were easily visible through her sheer, pale skin. Like an opal, once blazing with color but now faded. "Whoever named you, must've had a magic eight ball or something. Opal fits you." *Unlike my stupid name.*

She stared down at her dirty jeans, faded to a light blue with holes and frayed bottoms. She owned two pairs of jeans from the Salvation Army, three t-shirts, plus her rocking Sketchers and a stupid pair of ugly, bright yellow rain boots that her mother had insisted she needed. Tossing one of her long, wet braids back over her shoulder, she brooded. "I'm not rich or shiny. Diamond's a stupid name."

Opal shifted on the bed and paper crinkled under her. Her voice cracked. "You're strong. Brilliant. Perfect name."

The crinkling sound drew Diamond's gaze. She tugged a piece of lined paper out from under her mom's butt and studied the huge brick building that her mom had sketched.

The building was long with arms stretching out to each side. A tall tower grew out of its body like a long neck with a shiny, bald head at the top. She snagged the pencil from behind her mother's ear and with quick, talented fingers, rounded off the top of the tower and drew in the face of a clock. "Right here, this is where the clock goes." She flipped the pencil around and scrubbed the eraser across the paper. "The columns aren't round. They're arched in curves like this." She glanced up and searched her mom's face for approval.

Opal's washed out green eyes filled with moisture until a single tear slipped down over the protruding bones of her cheeks.

Diamond caught the tear before it dropped and blinked up at her mom. They both had green eyes and red hair, but they couldn't have been more different. Her brows furrowed. *Why can't she fight? Fight the sadness for me?*

Quickly, she crumpled up the paper, the tear and the pencil together. She wanted to absorb her mom's pain and squeezed the small bundle until the sound of the pencil breaking popped within the silence. "Just a stupid building. Stupid. We can draw anything we want." She dipped her head and swallowed hard to press back tears. "How about the mountains? You love drawing mountains."

The scent of lavender flooded the dingy room. Opal stiffened and turned back towards the wall. "Why don't you go play? Grab something from the vending machines. Use the money from the dresser." With each word, her voice broke, as if it was difficult for her to pull the sounds through her clogged throat. "I just need time. Then we can draw."

Diamond couldn't see the Woman. Yet. But she smelled her. Felt her. Knew in her belly that she was coming. She grasped her mom's hand the best she could with her two small ones. "It's okay. I'll stay with you."

Her chin dipped to her chest and Opal shook her head. "Take your time. Light some candles and crack the window before you go."

Fury beat within her heart. She realized her mother was trying to wash out the smell of lavender, just like she tried to wash out everything else in her life. *Why couldn't she just tell the Woman to go away?*

She stomped over to her hoodie, pulled it over her head and struggled with the wet fabric. Her head popped out and she heard her mom furiously whispering. Dragging the rest of the hoodie down her front, she watched her talking to thin air. The lavender stench thickened within the room and gagged her with its overbearing weight.

Reaching over the dresser, she pushed the curtains aside and tugged the window wide open, not caring if the rain came in and ruined the ugly dresser. One by one, she lit her mother's candles and their various fragrances combated the reeking lavender scent.

She pretended not to notice the Woman taking full form. The hem of a long, ratty dress filled in with grays and fluttered without the help of a breeze. Bit by bit, the long length of her body and the rest of the tent like dress appeared and filled in. Her charcoal colored hair clung to her ashen face and cascaded around her shoulders. Only her glowing silver eyes and dark gray lips penetrated the mass of hair that covered her face. Leaning down, her lips brushed Opal's ear, and she urgently whispered.

Opal shook. She popped one of the bottle's lids and sprinkled her palm with the little pills before she tossed them in her mouth and swallowed them with a flick of her head.

Rubbing a piece of the broken pencil against her jeans, Diamond hesitated. "Mom, I'll get something later. Let's watch a show. I'll make you beef ramen. Your favorite. We might even have some hot sauce left. I can spice it up for you." Her heart beat faster and the Woman glowed in different shades of gray just like a character from an old TV show. "Please, let me stay with you."

Again, the Woman leaned down and whispered. Her mom slouched beneath the blankets and covered her head. It didn't matter. The Woman continued to speak.

Her voice muffled, Opal yelled from beneath her blankets. "Fine! I'll tell her. Wear your rain boots Diamond."

She studied her favorite shoes, not wanting to be parted from their pretty purple and white design for even a minute. "But, Mom," she whined.

"Do as I say." Her mother's voice slurred as the pills took hold. "Wear the damn boots."

Glaring at the Woman, Diamond kicked off her wet shoes. She shoved her feet into the stupid yellow boots and her bare skin skidded against the rubber insides. The boots came high on her knees and she felt like a complete reject. Turning back towards the dresser, she removed the striped birthday candle that she'd snuck out of the store and relit it on one of the candles. She closed her eyes and whispered, "I wish I could kill the Woman. I wish I could kill the Woman. I wish."

She blew hard, opened her eyes and looked back at the bed.

The Woman stroked the mound of blankets covering her mom.

Her heart felt like a heavy stone in her chest. She rammed cash, along with the green room key, the broken pencil and her mother's drawing, into her boot. Grabbing the door handle, she tugged hard to free the door. "Stupid wish," she muttered.

———

Rain dribbling from the overhang above, Diamond sat on the cement next to a vending machine with a bag of Cheetos and chugged down her second Pepsi. The heat and the soft hum from the back of the machine soothed her frazzled nerves. She licked her orange fingers before wiping them down the front of her hoodie. Her favorite meal, Cheetos and Pepsi. Tossing another Cheeto into her mouth, she sipped a little Pepsi and enjoyed the feeling of the pop snapping against the Cheeto until it became a soggy mess within her mouth. She munched it down and chased the Cheeto with another slug of Pepsi.

She scowled down at the stupid yellow boots. Reaching into her right boot, she pulled out the piece of notebook paper and smoothed it out on the cement between her spread legs.

Leaning forward, she added mountains to the background, a curved driveway and a pool off in the distance. Her quick strokes didn't hesitate. She'd dreamed about this building every night of her life.

Shading in the glint of the sun off the rows of tiny double windows that ran the length of the roof line across each arm of the building, she scarcely registered the smoke that tickled her nose. It wasn't until the wailing fire trucks screeched to a stop in front of the motel that she glanced up. She watched the firemen in their heavy coats. Her lids grew heavy from the warmth of the vending machine as they dragged long hoses from their trucks. Disinterested, she focused back on her drawing and hummed in tune to the vending machine.

Gradually, the Woman took form next to the soda machine. Dull as the world outside the hidden spot.

Diamond's small body tingled, warning of her approach. Her heart picked up and beat faster and faster. Her hands shook as she shoved the paper and pencil back into her boot. Once the Woman had fully formed, she understood and clambered to her feet. Awkward in the big rain boots, she raced from her hiding spot.

A fireman scooped her up before she charged head first into the gaping hole, blackened with smoke, that was once room 115. Over his shoulder, she noticed the owner of the dump pointing towards her and speaking to a young woman in a cobalt blue rain jacket.

The stranger popped open a golden yellow umbrella that looked like the sun shining. In high heeled shoes, she purposely picked her way across the parking lot, stepping over the spider web of hoses and mud puddles. She tapped the shoulder of the fireman, opened a folded piece of leather and showed a card to him. "Social Services. I'll take her from you."

Placed on the blacktop, Diamond's legs trembled beneath her.

The stranger bent down and the hem of her skirt trailed in a mud puddle. "I'm Miss Dodd. I'm here to take care of you." Her eyes were the color of a clear blue sky and swept Diamond up and down. "Nice boots. I should've worn mine. It's always good to be prepared." Her smile was prettier than any Diamond had seen. "What's your name?"

"Where's my mom?" she sniffled, guessing the answer but wanting the stranger to say it. Needing to be told what she feared.

Miss Dodd's eyes clouded and she gazed over her head towards the hotel room. "What's your name sweetie?"

"Diamond," she replied, wiping her nose with the back of her hand.

"What a beautiful name," she murmured in a soft voice. "What's your last name sweetie?"

She listened to the rain tapping on the top of the umbrella and watched as tiny drops flowed down the outside and dripped around them. Her throat thickened. Tears escaped from the corner of her eyes and blended in with the rain on her face. "Don't have one. It's just Diamond." Her voice careened high, until it was unrecognizable, even to herself. "I want Mommy."

Secluded in another world under the golden umbrella with Miss Dodd, she learned that her mother had finally escaped her pain. Diamond's birthday wish had finally come true. She'd killed a woman. Just the wrong one. Now, she was all alone in the world.

Alone with the Woman.

CHAPTER THREE

PRESENT DAY

*S*hoving another Cheeto into her mouth, JD Wolfe chased it with a swig of Pepsi. Her midnight black SUV blended into the darkened street. Raising her binoculars, she studied the exterior of a row of dilapidated townhouses and focused in on the end unit with its peeling, mud brown paint. Blood red sheets blocked her view through the upper two windows. The light, trying to escape from the upstairs rooms, cast an eerie glow onto the sidewalk below. Behind those windows, there was a ten-year-old girl. A little girl scared for her life.

Last week, on a brisk Tuesday afternoon, little Harmony Scott had walked home from school. She was counting the days until Thanksgiving break, like any other kid her age. But Harmony never reached the safety of her home, and quickly became one of JD's lost children.

Today, while other families gave thanks around a table and were oblivious to the outside world, Harmony's family spent it on their knees begging for their daughter's safe return. Fishing in her tall, black leather boots, JD tugged out a small, spiral notebook. She unwound the faded gray rubber band that strapped down its pages, flipped past the drawings she'd made from snippets of her dreams, to a penciled portrait.

She considered the sketch that she'd rendered using eyewitness accounts. A young man, early twenties, Caucasian. From outward appearances, he looked like a nice guy. The witnesses had said that he was incredibly thin with a clean-shaven face, short cropped, dark brown hair and an easy smile. Surveillance cameras from a gas station had shown him wearing clean clothes, a tucked in checkered button up shirt, dark waist coat, and dark dress pants. Witnesses had assumed that the young man was the girl's father or uncle at least. But the collar of his shirt had blown open in the wind and eyewitnesses swore tattoos of faces covered his neck. Tattoos of what had seemed to be kids' faces.

She didn't understand the so-called adults. She spoke to the face in her sketch. "If your tattoos had seemed odd, why didn't the witnesses say or do anything? Why did they allow you to take Harmony by the hand and walk with her around the corner?" She shook her head and glared down at the sketch, "But those odd tattoos, that's how I finally tracked you down, asshole. Found you right here at 'Looser Lane' in Alexandria, Virginia."

Lost and endangered children were her specialty. She not only understood how children thought, she understood the evil that preyed on them. Parents called White Wolfe Investigations and requested JD Wolfe's services when their child had disappeared and the system had failed them. Most parents assumed she was a man. But in the end, they didn't care. They wanted their loved ones back. She didn't know how the parents knew to call her, but they did. When asked how they came by her name, through tears and strained faces, they only replied, a friend of a friend.

As word spread, police detectives had begun calling and requesting a meet with Investigator JD Wolfe. In back alleys and coffee shops, they'd slipped her the case files of a child they couldn't find. Once she'd recovered the lost child, she gave the officer all the credit, preferring to keep her name out of the newspapers. She had one condition, however, that her oldest and only true, female friend, Miss Dodd, who since her marriage went by Mrs. Malloy, processed the children and ensured their safety.

That was how she and Rodriguez had truly started working together. He'd slipped her a tan case file with pictures of three little boys. She tried not to think about her first police case with Rodriguez and the boys that she'd found too late. The emotional devastation of that case and the press afterwards had proved Rodriguez was trustworthy. The one and only cop she'd ever come close to calling a friend.

Slipping the notebook back into its hiding place, she once again raised the binoculars. The sheets within one room fluttered and brightened, as if spot lights had hit them from within. Frowning, she froze and searched the red glow for clues. Her heart picked up a beat and she tossed the binoculars onto the passenger seat and dug under candy wrappers and empty Cheeto bags for her cell phone. Realizing it was in her back pocket, she snagged it and texted Mrs. Malloy, who's number was still under her maiden name of Dodd.

Her thumb tapped out a quick message. "Got a bad feeling. Need you now. What's your ETA?"

The dimmed screen flashed, "Twenty min, I-95 backed up."

Her gaze flickered up to the sheet covered windows. Twenty minutes was too long. A lot could happen to a little girl in a lot less time.

Her phone vibrated. Impatient, she glanced down at the text, "Did you call Rodriguez?"

"Of course, I did," she muttered under her breath and pressed speed dial on her phone. Rodriguez picked up on the first ring. "Where the hell are you?" she spit into the phone. She could barely hear Rodriguez over the sirens screaming in the background.

"On my way. A semi-truck jackknifed on 95. Having a hell of a time getting around drivers that don't know to keep off the shoulder during a traffic jam."

The sticky sweet scent of lavender filled her vehicle and her nose wrinkled up at the offending scent. The sick feeling of dread that she'd felt earlier dropped into the pit of her stomach and gnawed at the lining. She realized little Harmony's time was almost up. "Shit, shit, shit," she muttered under her breath before taking a deep breath in and steeling herself. An ice-cold thread entered her tone. "Gotta go, Rodriguez. Gotta go now."

He understood. "I'll call for back up. And let them know there's a friendly on scene."

"Get here as fast as you can. So I don't have to deal with the boys in blue." She hung up and refused to glance over at the Woman, but through her peripheral vision she saw that her transparent form now sat in the passenger seat.

She removed a hair tie from around the gear shift and secured her long pony tail in a knot on the top of her head, so the length of her red hair couldn't be used as a weapon against her. She replaced the notebook in her right boot, and verified her knife was accessible in her left. She drew the knife out and slid it back into its hidden sheath to make sure it wouldn't catch if she needed to wield its power. Leaning forward, she removed a Glock 42 from the holster in the small of her back. With a push of her thumb, the magazine popped out and landed in her palm. She checked the number of bullets before snapping it back into the well and raking the slide back to send a round into the chamber.

Her trigger finger lying on the side of the barrel, she laid the weapon on her thigh, cocked and ready. For a precious moment, her finger tapped the metal that was warm from her body's heat. Would the Woman ever leave her alone? Or would she drive her crazy, just as she had her mother? She continued to just show up and butt into her business. "Couldn't stay the fuck away could you?"

"*No,*" the Woman whispered, but her voice ricocheted within

JD's brain. From experience, she knew that only she could hear the ghost's cultured tones. Time to face facts—she'd never have a day without the ghost yelling in her head.

She knew there was no way to block her out, ignore her or push her away. She just had to deal with her. Anyway, the most import thing in her world right now was getting one little girl out of the townhouse alive. There was never anyone there to save JD. She knew how it felt to be helpless and without choices. Bottom line, the kid needed her more than she hated the Woman's presence. "Harmony's in danger?" she asked, but she already knew the answer.

The Woman nodded, and her glowing gray hair lit up the air around her.

The brighter she glowed, the more urgent JD knew little Harmony Scott's situation was. "Stay in the god damn car and let me handle it."

Behind the tangled screen of her hair, her face was drawn and there was a sad smile on her charcoal colored lips, but she nodded.

JD's gaze flickered up and down the street, before she eased her car door open and soundlessly latched it. In her black leather jacket and matching jeans, she faded into the darkness. Keeping her eyes on the windows for movement, she quickly crossed the street, the moonlight guiding her steps. Searching for a point of entry, she circled the townhouse. Her soft soled leather boots slipped sideways on slick ground. *Virginia weather,* she sneered. *Snow in the morning that melts into a muddy mess by afternoon and freezes into ice overnight.*

The rear windows of the townhouse were high and out of reach. The back stoop sunk sideways into the icy, uneven ground. A ripped screen door hung from the back door and flapped in the cold wind. The lower panel of the wooden door had been knocked out as a makeshift doggy door. Heavy construction plastic sucked in and out of the hole like a chest breathing.

Because of the massive size of the opening, her gaze searched for an enormous beast. She hoped that she wouldn't have to give away the element of surprise by shooting a charging mutt.

Across the yard, she spotted the owner of the doggie door. A sad excuse for a dog lay chained to a tree by a thick, muddy silver chain. Skin and bones, the once huge Great Dane lay sideways on the frozen ground. His belly was painfully bloated into a large ball. The heavy chain collar was ingrained into the skin around his neck. His white fur, spotted with black, glowed in the moonlight, though matted and caked with mud, along with a suspicious darker substance. *Blood.*

Either not willing or unable to, the dog didn't raise his head, only stared at her with flickering light blue eyes, so human it pained her. A low, pitiful whine rolled across the yard and reached her ears. The moon slipped behind a cloud and darkened the world between them. She raised a finger and pressed it to her lips. "I'll be back for you," she whispered, before crawling through the hole in the bottom of the door.

CHAPTER FOUR

*E*ntering a world of filth, JD plastered her spine back against a lower kitchen cabinet. Her Glock at the ready, she crouched momentarily in place and allowed for her eyes to adjust to the darkened room. The green glow of numbers from the stove emitted just enough light for her to survey the situation. It was four am kitchen time and the floor moved with hundreds of cockroaches, but no humans. Sliding her back up along the paneled cabinet, a roach crawled a path down her shoulder. *Disgusting boogers*, she thought, with a flick of her finger.

Reaching behind her, she carefully jiggled the knob of the door that she'd gained access to the house through. She unlocked it, allowing for a quick exit if needed. Not taking her gaze off the only other entrance to the room, she slid her hand up the door and searched for any latches that would prevent her and Harmony from getting away. Satisfied, her gaze continued to sweep the room. Sink filled with dirty dishes, half the cabinet doors missing, take-out boxes piled high on a small silver and teal Formica table, along with two aluminum and vinyl chairs in a mustard yellow. And, of course, an army of bugs searching the filth for their next meal.

She softened her knees into a ready stance. One hand palming the other, she held her weapon close to her body, ready. She stepped forward and cockroaches crunched beneath her boots. The sound rebounded off the walls. She paused, holding her breath deep in her chest. She listened for one heartbeat, then two. Satisfied she couldn't be heard, she purposely crunched her way across the kitchen and down a narrow, darkened hall. On her journey, she cleared a small bathroom, only finding more filth and crawling bugs before the short hall opened up into a living space.

Mounds of trash were piled throughout the small living room. The back of a long, putrid green couch almost touched both ends of the room, facing a huge flat screen television and the front door. Softly stepping over clothes and through rotting food containers, she mentally thanked her trusty boots for protecting her as she approached the couch. She was unsure if someone slept on the ugly sofa and she knew that she needed to clear the room or she'd end up trapping herself upstairs. Her forward momentum halted as she contemplated which side of the couch to move towards. If she picked the wrong side, a big enough man could sling her over the back of it. Then, she'd be in a world of hurt. And she wouldn't be doing herself or Harmony any good. *Fucking crap shoot.*

Quietly as possible in the mounds of trash, she made her way to the foot of the couch that she considered would have the least favorite view of the massive television. She steadied her hands, held her breath and rounded the couch. She expelled her breath in a soft swoosh of air when only little critters faced her. Shifting her attention to the open stairway, she squeezed around the couch and moved cautiously across the room. She released the lock on the front door and left the door ajar. Before she turned away, the wind moved the door ever so slightly. She reconsidered and eased the door closed but unlocked.

In somewhat of a crouched stance, she padded her way up the dirt brown, shag carpeted stairs. Quickly, she cleared another bathroom. Then, she hesitated, considering her options. From the layout of the windows visible from the street, she figured the top floor held two rooms, both of which had light illuminating from beneath the doors. Pick the wrong room and her element of surprise turned to shit. Scenarios raced through her brain and she decided on the far-right room. The one where the light behind the sheets had brightened unnaturally. Decision made, she moved determinedly forward towards her goal.

Suddenly, the Woman materialized and blocked the hallway. Unable to stop her forward momentum, she charged right through the Woman's transparent form. Fury exploded through her. What if she got ghost dust in her mouth? *Damn it!*

She raised her arm to wipe the offending concept off her tongue with the back of the sleeve of her leather jacket. Her arm froze only inches from her mouth, realizing she didn't know what filth was on her clothes from her journey through the house.

Pursing her lips, she wished that she could burn the ghost with the heat of her anger. But no, she wouldn't wish a fiery death on anyone, not even the Woman.

Raising her hands, palms up, the Woman shrugged. Glowing in her long ratty gown, she appeared right at home in the filth.

Calming herself with a breath, she silently mouthed, "What?"

Urgently, she pointed a gray finger towards the room she'd just prevented JD from entering.

Shaking her head, she mouthed, "No, shit." She turned and proceeded down the hall with her gun ready.

Again, the Woman appeared in front of her, hands raised and moving frantically in front of her semi-transparent form.

Completely giving up on her fighting stance, her weapon hung limply in her right hand. She pushed at damping the anger burning within her. "What?" she hissed.

Raising a finger to her lips, the Woman actually shook her head at JD. Through the charcoal colored strands of hair flowing down in front of her face, she gave JD a pointed look and tapped her bare foot on the carpeted hallway.

Her left hand squeezing into a tight fist, she wanted to scream at the Woman, jump up and down with her arms flapping and perhaps even shoot her. But Harmony needed her more. So, she calmed herself, readied her weapon and waited for the Woman to move.

A satisfied smile spread across the Woman's face and she nodded at JD like a proud mama.

Gritting her teeth, she stared heavenward before focusing back on the Woman's light gray eyes. "Gotta go." Soundlessly, her lips formed the words.

Brows furrowing over serious eyes, the Woman nodded and held up two fingers while pointing to the door with her other hand.

She nodded and mouthed, "Harmony." She flicked up her index finger, "Bad guy," and her middle finger joined, "Two."

Vehemently shaking her head, her monochrome curls fell around her face and she glowed even brighter in the hall. She held up three fingers. The word *three* rocketed from the Woman and through JD's brain.

Wincing with pain, her eyes flickered from the Woman to the door. "Three. *Shit,*" she whispered. "Two bad guys and Harmony. One guy, I could handle. Two, dicey." She hesitated, wanting to save the little girl. But, if things went to shit, then she might lose her.

The Woman's eyes widened and she glowed brighter, the brightest JD had ever seen. Her transparent form flew down and hall and she pointed at the door. Her gaze was frantic and intense.

JD realized it was now or never. "Time to go," she muttered.

Steadily, she moved towards the door. Her muscles tightened, and her gaze fixed on the target before her. Without hesitation, she pressed her lips together and traveled through the Woman's ghostly form before swiftly raising her boot and planting a hard push kick next to the door knob. The thin paneled door crumpled back against the interior wall and she entered, weapon ready.

Startled shouts bounced off the walls of the well-lit room. Taken by surprise, the occupants froze, dumbfounded by her presence.

Bright cylinder stage lights, supported by tripods, blinded her for a moment. From the brilliance of the lights, two black dots filled her vision and partially blocked her view of the room, and its inhabitants. She blinked rapidly and attempted to recover her full vision, losing valuable seconds.

Her gaze swept the room. She distinguished within the fuzzy dark dots a huge, older black man that was clad only in boxers with a large gut protruding over his elastic waist band. His jaw flapped open and closed and he stood sentry by a professional movie camera, complete with sound bar. Thick black wires lined the floor and traveled from the film equipment to a computer and wall plugs. Not pausing her forward momentum, she side kicked the large man back into the jumble of lights and cords and her gaze continued sweeping for Harmony.

In the middle of the room, stood a brass, four poster bed draped with a gauzy pink canopy and white satin bedding. In a demur, white cotton nightgown, that only just covered her bare bottom, perched little Harmony. Her slender arms were wrapped tightly around her bent legs, and the top of her forehead scrapped her bare knees.

Still as a statue, a skeleton of a man kneeled before the little girl. His pale, naked skin was luminescent under the bright lights. With his white cock proudly raised, his scrawny form was covered from chin to belly button with the tattooed faces of children. Boys, girls, black, white and brown were inked on his body for eternity.

JD's piercing gaze bounced from him back to Harmony. Her hair was pulled back from her face by a bright pink bow and curled into blonde ringlets that bounced with her sobs. She sat frozen in place, hugging her knees and JD's mind shifted to a time she never visited in her past. To a crappy hotel, where her mom had sat frozen on a bed, hugging her knees. Only one thought rebounded through her mind and scratched deep grooves through her consciousness. *No more lost children.*

Her roar filled the room and she brought justice in the form of a swift round kick that slammed hard into the base of the skeleton man's skull. He crumpled in a heap, knocked out cold.

Turning, she pivoted her weapon to the other man left in the room. Having regained his feet, the man held his hands up in front of his face, the fat under his chin jiggling with his movements. "Don't shoot."

"On the floor!" she yelled. Anger raged through her veins. "Face down. Now!" She leveled her weapon towards the man's crotch. "Or I shoot your dick off." She wanted more than anything to pull the trigger.

Amidst broken bulbs and wires, he dropped face first on the floor, his bald head reflecting the remaining lights in the small bedroom.

"Lace your fingers behind your head. Now!" Cautiously, she approached. Grinding her boot down on his face, she held him in place. She holstered her weapon in the small of her back, removed a zip tie from her back pocket and reached down to secure the man's hands.

Suddenly, the man's thick hand snaked out, grabbing her heel and jerking her foot high.

She was propelled backward and landed hard on her back. The holstered gun slammed into her spine and the back of her head hit the dirty carpet, rattling her teeth. The force of her fall expelled the air from her lungs.

Moving extraordinarily fast for his massive size, the fat man was on top of her, grappling for the gun behind her back. His huge belly nailed her to the floor. Raring up, she caught him with a swift elbow to the jaw, before slamming her palm into the soft underside of his nose. Blood spurted and instantly covered both of them.

The fat man howled in pain and stanched the flow of blood with his hands.

She reached down, withdrew the knife from her boot and sliced the man's side.

Recoiling as if burned, he pulled back. Knowing it was now or never, she surged her hips upward and over, flipping him over. Now, she straddled his massive stomach. Crawling up the gigantic bastard, she pinned one of his wrists to the floor with her knee and positioned her other shin on the side of his neck where his carotid artery pumped oxygen to this brain. Pressing her leg down with all her weight, she cut off the blood flow. Her knife at the ready, she watched until the bastard's eyes fluttered closed and he no longer moved beneath her. She slapped him on the back of his bald head. "Have a good nap, asshole."

Breathing heavily and covered in blood, she rolled the fat bastard over and secured his hands and ankles with zip ties. Gaining her feet, she wobbled for a moment from the rush of blood to her head. Sighing deeply, she walked forward and secured the skeleton man and tossed him on top of his partner before turning to Harmony.

For a moment, JD just sat on the edge of the frilly bed. Leaning forward, she propped her elbows on her legs and allowed her hands to dangle while she calmed her breathing. Harmony was still crying into her knees and JD envisioned her mom. She couldn't help her mom, but she could help this little girl. "Harmony."

The girl stiffened and sniffled.

She rubbed her tired eyes with her knuckles and shifted more towards the little girl. "Harmony, I'm sorry there're bad people in this world. But right now, you're safe. I won't let them hurt you."

The girl raised her head. A thick foundation coated her skin that was shades darker than her china doll complexion. Florescent pink lip gloss was lacquered to her lips. Heavy electric blue eyeshadow weighted down her lids and her once child-like eyes brimmed now with grown-up tears. Stained with black eyeliner, tears dribbled over, running thick tracks down her still chubby cheeks and dripping off her chin.

JD lifted her hand and wiped some of the eyeliner away with the pad of her thumb. "Did they put this makeup on you?"

She nodded, her hair springing around her.

Snorting and twisting her features into a funny face, she declared, "Well, they suck at it."

A giggle escaped Harmony's lips. She studied the stranger before her, judging her and weighing her trustfulness. Her chin trembled, then she launched herself at JD. Wrapping her skinny arms around her neck she sobbed hard into her shoulder.

She hugged the little girl tight and let her cry. Brushing the curls on the back of her head, she wished she could erase everything the girl had endured. Once her tears settled down into hitching breaths, she asked, "Do you want to help me take out the trash?"

Harmony lifted her head and confusion filled her gaze. "Trash?"

Thumbing her nose at the two men piled on top of each other, she raised a brow and considered the little girl. The choice she made now would determine her future course. Would she remain cowered on the bed and allow the past to rule her future? Or would she take action and set her own destiny. She waited. Only Harmony could decide her path.

Stiffening, the young girl considered the two men. Tremors shook her body and her chest hitched with her suppressed emotions. Turning back to JD, her painted lips squished into a thin line. "Take out the trash."

A proud smile spread across her face and she hugged Harmony tight. She too had experienced the powerless feeling of being a child at the mercy of an adult. "That's your first step in taking your power back. You just showed how strong you are. Resilient. You're going to be just fine."

Intensely, Harmony gazed up into JD's eye. "Do you think so?"

"I don't think so." She removed her leather jacket and helped Harmony weave her arms within the warmth. "I know so."

Off the floor, JD snatched up and shook out a pair of jeans the little girl's size. She handed them to her before grabbing a pair of purple and white sneakers. "Cute shoes," she said with a wink.

A tear slipped from the corner of Harmony's eye. "My mom and I bought them."

Crouching down before the girl, JD leveled her gaze, "I know people who will take care of you. Get you back to your parents. They're on their way. Let's take out the trash until they arrive. You get dressed and I'll take care of the fat bastard. Then we will pull the skeleton down together."

Looking at the two men trussed up on the floor, she nodded. "He does look like a skeleton. An ugly, mean skeleton."

JD did just as she promised. After taking care of the fat bastard, together they dragged the skeleton through the filthy house and out the back door, depositing them in the snow beside the dog. Sirens wailing in the distance, they released the dog and used the heavy chain to wrap the two men to the tree.

Later, JD sat in the front seat of her SUV. She watched the boys in blue, Rodriguez and Mrs. Malloy handling the situation. Noisy neighbors shivered in the cold, unwilling to miss any of the excitement so they could gossip. She waved to Harmony. Bundled up in a blanket and sitting in the back of an Ambulance, the girl's blue eyes stared at her. Little Harmony was lucky—she had parents at home anxiously waiting for her. Some didn't.

JD's childhood path had been different. She never knew her father. Her mother, well, she'd killed her when she left candles lit in their motel room and the window open. The cheap curtains had caught on fire and set the whole motel room ablaze.

For three years, she'd lived within the system, moving from

group home to group home. She understood the law of the land. Only the strong survived. If it weren't for Mrs. Malloy sending prospective families to the orphanage, she never would've found a real home and a real family.

She'd be a statistic just like the girl before her. She knew in her gut that she'd be a fatal statistic if Milton Wolfe hadn't come to the home searching for a little girl for his wife and a sister for his son, Jaxon. They'd brought her into their pack, given her their last name, and had protected and loved her. It was then Diamond had become Justyne Diamond Wolfe.

Through the family company, White Wolfe Investigations, she'd found her life calling. Tracking down and helping as many children as she could. Giving them the justice they deserved. The job paid decently, but it wasn't about the money. She stashed away every penny so that she could one day give the other kids what she found with the Wolfe's. A home, a true home. A place where lost souls would have a chance to heal and gain their power back.

A whine from the back seat of her car caused her to reach out and turn up the heat. Not too much heat, too fast. The dog's frozen body needed to adjust gradually to the changes in temperature. She and Rodriguez had a hell of time getting the huge mutt into her car. "What am I going to do with you now?" she asked the dog, studying him from her rear-view mirror.

Gradually, the Woman materialized in the back seat and filled the car with lavender. Settling in, she sat with the dog's head in what would've been her lap, but was just empty air.

Hoping to gain relief from the awful smell, JD cracked a window. The phone in her boot buzzed and she dug it out. "Hey, Jax. What's up?" she murmured absentmindedly. The sun rose above the townhouses, warming the earth with its rays. The neighbors faded way, either going to work or losing interest in all the early morning excitement.

"Hi, JD. Heard you found the boy and were already on a new case. Got a minute?"

She inched the window down a little more and turned up the heat to compensate for the cold air rushing in. "Just painting my nails. What do you want?"

Her brother's deep voice hummed across the line. "Well, as you probably know I'm working an insurance fraud case in the Blue Ridge Mountains of Virginia."

She snickered under her breath. "Yeah, Lee said you screwed it up. Scuttlebutt is you need a woman to finish the job. Not like you Jax. Getting lax in your old age? Lax Jax. That's what the Geezers will call you." She could almost hear Jaxon grinding his teeth over the phone before continuing. She bit her lip to keep from laughing at his obvious discomfort. "Lee wanted to send me in but we got the call to find little Harmony."

"Is that the case you're on? Did you find her?"

A smile spread across JD's face as wide as the freckles peppering her nose and cheeks. "Yes, Mrs. Malloy and Rodriguez assure me that she'll be back with her family by lunch time. Harmony Scott might have missed Thanksgiving, but she'll have Christmas."

"You're amazing. There isn't a better tracker in the States. Hell, probably in the world. Don't know how you do it, but I'm glad you do."

Jaxon's pride flowed over the phone, warming her. A part of her enjoyed his praise but she pushed away the weakness. Glancing up to her rear-view mirror again, her light green gaze clashed with the Woman's gray one before bouncing away and focusing in on the dwindling crowd. "Don't go getting all misty on me," irritation laced her voice. "What the hell do you want Lax Jax?"

He stuttered.

She frowned and rubbed the back of her neck where the muscles had relaxed and released the tension of her hunt. "Spit it out."

"I'm going to ask a woman to marry me," his breath whooshed

in her ear. "There, are you happy? Couldn't let me just say it in my own time."

Listening to her brother grumble across the phone, she felt like a piece of her was being ripped away. Of course, she knew he'd one day marry but the thought of losing him hurt. "No shit," she whispered. "Do the Geezers know?"

"God, I hope not. Look, JD, can you come out?"

"Don't know what to do with a woman, huh? Perhaps Lee can help you out. I'll dial him right now. We can conference call. Get you fixed right up. If we can't help you, then," she paused for drama, "we'll have to go to the Geezers."

Her brother's voice was low and deep and promised repercussions. "Fuck you, JD. Fuck you."

Busting into laughter, she pounded her palm on the steering wheel and wiped the moisture away from her eyes with the back of her hand. "Isn't that the problem, Lax Jax? You're lacking in that department."

An ominous growl came through the phone, causing her to laugh harder. "JD, stop the bullshit. I need you."

Instantly, she straightened, and the laughter faded from her lips. Her brother never needed her. Never. All business, she replied, "Okay, Jax. Whatever you need."

A long, drawn out breath escaped him. "The woman I want to marry owns the hotel I was sent to investigate. It's all on the up and up. They aren't filing fraudulent claims. But the damage that was done to the hotel has created a financial burden. Bookings are down, and until the insurance money comes through, the hotel needs to draw in more guests and the revenue they bring. I was hoping you would—," he paused.

She waited for him to continue, but silence stretched between them. "I would what, Jax?"

"It would be a huge boon to the hotel for the artist DiWolf to display her works for the first time at my fiancée's hotel. The first ever meet and greet with the reclusive artist."

Revulsion rolled down her spine. She felt exposed when connected to the raw feelings that she'd inked onto paper with her art. Each piece, a glimpse into soul. Into the dreams that haunted her. It was easier just to let others handle the sales of the pieces she dared to part with. "Are you fucking crazy? A meet and greet? You want me to parade around, shake hands and actually talk with people over four feet? Do you want me to wear a damn dress too?"

Her brother backtracked. "No, no, JD. Okay, so it's a lot to ask. Maybe not a meet and greet. How about just displaying your artwork? Please, Diamond."

Sitting quietly, she brooded about her brother's request. He never called her Diamond. She looked over the scene before her and Harmony waved goodbye from the ambulance. She returned the little girl's wave with a little two finger salute. She wanted more than anything to help lost children like her. Perhaps her artwork was the way. Perhaps it was time to turn her back on the past and use her artwork to help others. Others, who unlike Harmony, didn't have a family waiting at home to love them. *Damn it. If I'm going to deal with strangers, then I might as well go all the way and hold an auction to finance my dream of opening a good home for children in need. Anyway, adults are just tall children. Aren't they?*

Silence stretched over the phone until Jaxon spoke. Defeat laced his subdued voice. "Don't worry about it, JD. But I still need you to come out. There's a painting here you must see. No one will need to know you're DiWolf."

Ignoring her brother's comment, her thoughts ran full steam ahead. She could do it. *Slap some palms, smile for a camera. That kind of shit.* "I'll do it. A meet and greet. Plus, I'll auction off some pieces. Ten percent of the proceeds go back to the hotel."

He sputtered over the phone, "You don't have to—"

A long, low whine emitted from the back and she stopped listening and glanced up. In her rear-view mirror, the Woman stroked the dog's matted fur and began swaying as she hummed a song within JD's head. Furrowing her brow, she glared at the ghost, who returned her look with a bright smile. Snarling, she mumbled, "Gotta go," and hung up on her brother mid-sentence.

Putting her car in gear, she absentmindedly waved to Rodriguez and Mrs. Malloy. As they became pin pricks in the distance, the Woman also faded from sight, confirming what she knew in her heart. She'd never marry and have children. Kids were for other women. Women who didn't see and talk to ghosts. Women who couldn't pass the insanity gene on to their children for them to be tormented. She'd never do that to her child.

She'd endured years of being tormented and teased because others couldn't see the Woman she talked to. The system had tried to help by sending her to their psychiatrists with all the fancy letters following their name. But nothing could help her. Not the therapy, not the drugs they prescribed and not the hypnosis. She rubbed her temple where they'd placed the leads of their torture machine. Sure as hell not the shock treatments.

She'd been committed to the loony bin for six months, before she was dragged out by Mrs. Malloy and placed in the orphanage. During that half year, she'd learned a hard lesson. If you don't want to be strapped down, drugged, and have experiments done on you, then don't let people know you see and talk to a ghost. But Mrs. Malloy and the Wolfes had saved her. From then on, she'd learned to keep her mouth shut, her boots on and her weapons ready.

CHAPTER FIVE

Unlike the families celebrating Thanksgiving at Twin Springs Hotel and Spa, Logan Oakes didn't spend the day stuffing his face with turkey and all the trimmings. He was holed up in his hooch. The parachute material was a sorry excuse of a shelter. Barely kept the cold away. Nevertheless, he couldn't stand the thought of being trapped in a building. Like his team.

What if fire snuck up on him? Again. Or worse, trapped him in a building?

In his mind's eye, he pictured Amethyst Fairbanks' portrait. Her beautiful, green eyes, full of kindness. Red hair framed her sweet face and made her skin appear milky white. Pure. "I'm pitiful," he groaned. Drawn to a dead woman like a moth to a flame. "Perhaps it's because she also experienced the wrath of fire before she died."

Like her, a sea of flames had extinguished any chance of love. He'd never experience it for a day, an hour or even a second. Not like the passion his friends enjoyed.

He continued talking to himself, anything to keep sleep away. The flashbacks away. "How quickly love grew between Isabella and Theo. Between Ava and Jaxon."

First hand, he'd witnessed a love powerful enough that it enabled a man to traverse freezing water or run into a burning building to save his soul mate. "It's humbling." His lips curved into a slight smile. "They deserve it."

Still, a searing pain for the loss of something he'd never felt and would never experience, pierced him. Willingly, his battered body absorbed the additional agony as he pushed buds deep into his ears and flicked his music on loud in a futile attempt to mute the ringing in his brain and drown out the memories. "Better to live in a tent than to fail my friends again. Besides, animals belong in the woods."

He chuckled and mocked himself. "I fooled myself," he stared into the dark. "Thought I could walk among the living." However, living in the human world was too painful and fate had proved him wrong. "Face it asshole," he condemned himself, "no one will let you forget how disgusting you look. You're unfit for human eyes."

He rubbed the beard on the left side of his face, the untouched side. "At least with my beard hiding the man I once was, no one will question what I've become. An animal. The beast fire forged.

"Half man, half beast, no one wants you."

Pulling his poncho tighter over his head, Logan attempted to ignore the biting cold and meld with his music. The ringing in his ears had abated but the cold had seeped deep into his bones. "Too damn cold for November," he grumbled and blared his music even louder.

"What does it matter if I freeze to death? During the day, the world can't stand the sight of me. At night, I can't stand the thought of my sleep being infiltrated by the memories of what turned me into a monster." He lay there, staring into the dark, ignoring the wind penetrating the tent and fighting the sleep attempting to overcome his resolve to stay awake.

"Don't close your eyes. Don't fall asleep." He stretched and found a sharp rock beneath him. Ground his back into the rock.

Pain renewed his strength. "Stay awake. Otherwise the dead will come." Will play out behind his lids. He'd be back with the ghosts of his team or watching Director Hollingsworth stumble from the barn, his body engulfed by flames, his death screams filling the air until the only thing that remained was white silence and burned flesh. "Screw that."

However, memories of smoldering death had plagued him way before the Director's fiery end. It was that memory that hunted him. The one where the putrid stench of burning flesh wasn't only his own, but that of those he loved. Respected. That was the dream he feared.

Pushing back against the heaviness of his lids, he pulled his eyes wide. "Maybe if I hold sleep at bay long enough, then when exhaustion finally over takes me the dream won't register. My brain will be too exhausted to remember it." He blinked to help the dryness. "Maybe."

Little by little, his lids lowered, and his body slumped. A deep slumber filled his body, eased the tension from his muscles, weakened him and left him vulnerable to the deep recesses of his brain. Shuffling in his sleep, he fought the inevitable and the nightmare overtook him. . .

. . .Normally the dry desert air stifled Sergeant First Class Logan Oakes but, after eighteen different missions in the sandbox, he'd learned to ignore it. Today the air lay eerily quiet.

Through his night vision goggles, the world around him was cast into shades of green. He adjusted his stance and raised the tip of his M-4 rifle up, ready. Long barrel today. Just in case he needed to take out a shooter on a roofline.

He scanned the flat roofed, ugly gray building to his left, then the hulled-out hospital that his fellow Americans had built on his right. No movement. He never understood why the locals had stripped the hospital bare of anything of value after the allies had left, but they did. Down to the pipes and electrical wiring.

Something was wrong. He checked the muted face of his watch. He *felt it. All was quiet, too quiet. Rolling his shoulders, he attempted to push off the feeling. Quiet was also good, though. Get in, grab the head of a new terrorist cell plus his right-hand man and get out before the city woke for morning prayers. That was the plan.*

The rest of his team had already entered the squatty building and he was covering their six. In his mind, he followed his team through the building and waited for confirmation that they'd connected with Tango one and Tango two. Taking them alive was the mission. Plus any intel. Still, his headset was silent.

Had the cell bugged out? Maybe it was bad intel. Naw, Wolfeman had verified it. If Wolfeman said the intel was good, it was spot on. He was never wrong. His instincts had saved their asses more than a few times. He resisted the urge to glance up at Wolfeman's sniper perch in the upper right window of the hospital and give him away.

Logan checked the target pack on his wrist. The area photo showed a picture of the two story building. Each side color coded. They'd entered through the green side, as planned. Still, something didn't sit right. His headset was unusually quiet. "Sixty seconds till exfil," he murmured into his throat mic.

No reply.

Like a dog with a prize T-bone, the bad feeling sunk its sharp teeth into his bones and chewed relentlessly. He paused at the door, studied the area and searched for something. He didn't know what.

Suddenly, his headset went nuts. A jumble of voices sounded off. The whole team was sounding off over each other and chopping the line into unintelligible gibberish. A shout reached out from within the belly of the building. Then another. The bad feeling sunk its teeth in and ripped at his bones, no longer a suspicion but fact. His team needed him.

Ready and willing to sprint inside and join the fight to defend his brothers, he jerked the door open. A creaking sound to his left distracted him. Immediately, his head turned to confront the added threat. Across his headset the code word "Avalanche" was shouted. BOMB. Too late.

The sand trembled beneath his boots before a whoosh of air wrapped an invisible fist around his body and dragged him inside the open door-

way. Just as quickly, the blast of air expelled him, spitting a rolling ball of flames over his body and propelling him back twenty feet through the air.

Screaming pierced the air. Horrible screams. Death screams. Engulfed within a terrible heat, he staggered to his feet. He must help his brothers. Through a fiery glowing haze, he observed one, then two of his brothers spilling from the building, now an inferno from hell. An inferno ate at their camo uniforms and illuminated the horror melting on their faces. The gut wrenching screams continued to puncture the air and combined with the screams of his brothers-in-arms, branding his brain with their agony.

Collapsing onto his knees, Logan rolled in the tan dirt and pebbles. Feverishly, he attempted to kill the flames that licked at his right side. Rising to his hands and knees, he inched forward. The smell of burning flesh smothered him as he crawled. Dirt caked the smoldering wounds on his body. Smoke scorched his lungs. A single mantra tattooed a mission within him, "Regain my fighting position. Aid my brothers. Get everyone home alive.". . .

Logan rolled over in his poncho. He'd made it through another night. "Damn it."

Rubbing his fists against his eyes, he attempted to grind away at the memory filled dream. He laid back and stared unseeingly at the top of his tent, blinded to the fact that the snow from the previous night had partially collapsed his hooch.

Even though the nightmare was no longer reality, a foul taste coated his mouth. The flavors of a banked fire, smoke and burned flesh mixed with great loss and failure. His dry tongue rolled around within his mouth in a vain attempt to dispel the nauseating combination.

He smacked his lips, swallowed hard and thought about his last mission with his Special Forces team. It wasn't until after the mission, when he laid in the hospital, wrapped in loose gauze bandages, and reported a haphazard bedside debriefing that he'd realized the screams filling the desert air that day were not only his brothers, but his own.

Cold air penetrated the tent and seeped into his bones. He welcomed the freezing temperatures. It banked the fire, cooled his heated memories and froze the pain of his failures, past and present. As usual, the dream had increased the constant ringing within his brain. He massaged his right ear, where it melted into his skull. He didn't try to fool himself. He understood why he'd pitched his tent in Virginia's Blue Ridge Mountains during the dead of winter. "I'm a worthless piece of shit."

The snapping of the tent's door being thrust back didn't register through the heavy metal music that blared in his ears. The flash of late morning light, shining through the olive-green para-chute material of his poncho, brought him on high alert and tensed his muscles. Before he could react, hands grasped his ankles and dragged him out of his make shift tent, poncho and all. He threw off the binds of the material and his muscles tensed when his mind commanded his body spring up into a fighting stance. Partially upright, pain seared through his hip. His leg crumpled beneath him and he collapsed backward. Unable to pull himself up out of his muddy position, Logan raised his fists and prepared himself for the beating that would follow when he lost the fight.

CHAPTER SIX

"*Y*ou look like shit."

Unfiltered by his tent, daylight blinded him, and Logan blinked until his brother came into focus. Samuel Oakes's seventeen-year-old frame seemed even taller when you were laid out on your back. Logan ignored his Army buddy, Jaxon Wolfe's, grunted agreement and lowered his fists. With excruciating slowness, he rolled over onto his hands and knees and raised himself up out of the mire that was now his life. He rubbed at his bad right hip, where his movements burned a hole of unending misery. "Who the hell cares, kid."

Jaxon's golden gaze raked over his skin. "Good morning, sunshine," he growled and shoved his hands into the pockets of his jeans. "I agree with the kid."

Logan refused to glance down at his filthy Van Halen shirt. He knew the print on front was muted more by days of sweat and dirt than age. He scratched at his blonde hair, darkened with filth, matted and plastered against his head. Ignoring the grime and oily build up beneath his fingers, he shot back, "Sorry my locks aren't as pretty blond as yours, princess."

He hoped the comment would get a rise out of the kid. The

only fun he had left in this miserable life was poking at his teenage brother. He rubbed at a patch of whiskers that bloomed within the florid, razed skin on the right side of his burned face and waited for a response.

His brother's body hummed with anger. "I'm glad Mom didn't come with us and witness her son living like a pig. Someone has to care for her, protect her heart. You're sure as hell not. Damn it. I'm sick of hearing Mom cry." He thumped his fist against his thigh. "Tired of her hiding her tears because worry's eating away at her. Worry for you, jackass."

At the truth within his brother's words, Logan froze, and a sharp pang of shame seeped into him, soiled him. Not the rise he'd hoped for. His gaze twitched over to his brother, on the cusp of manhood. Looking every bit their father's son in faded blue jeans, white t-shirt with a thick green work shirt over top. The morning sun shone off the gold and bright blond streaks in his light hair. His skin was smooth and untouched by pain or cursed by flames, only plagued by the occasional blemish. His brother was the mirror image of the carefree boy he'd once been.

His gaze shifted to one of the few survivors from his Special Forces team. Jaxon Wolfe, known as Wolfeman, and the human lie detector to the men on the team. What the hell did these two know about being an outcast? About living with the face of an animal? "Assholes," he muttered under his breath.

"You coming into work today?" questioned Jaxon, his voice deceptively soft.

Bending down, supporting the majority of his weight on his good leg, he scooped up his now wet poncho from the snow compacted by their footprints. "Nope."

Zipping up his scuffed leather jacket against the freezing temperatures, Jaxon crossed his arms and leaned against a tree. At Logan's answer, he raked his fingers through his gunmetal black hair. "Why the hell not? You have a tower to finish."

Tossing the poncho into his home, he didn't bother to glance up at his friend when he replied. "Anybody can finish the Tower."

Watching Logan for a moment, Jaxon's mind chewed on his words. "Isabella's hoping to have her wedding in the Tower. She feels it will bring the General's Gems full circle."

Logan whipped around and his blue gaze flashed. He rubbed at the added pain his quick movements had caused in his hip. "Look, Dad and the kid," he jerked a thumb at his brother, "have it under control. Leave me the hell alone."

Sam's breath came hot and fast, visible in the cold air as anger bubbled beneath his skin. Hands curling into fists, he watched his older brother limp around his crappy campsite. "What about Mom?"

"What about her?" The space where Logan's right eyebrow used to lay puckered and attempted to rise with the question.

"What about her?" Sam demanded, fury stuttering through his words. "What about her? Mom was afraid she'd lost you to the 'curse' when your Army Doc called. She wept with relief when she found out that you were alive. She wanted to fly out and be with you in the hospital but what did you say? No! You told Mom no. And when you came home, alive, she continued to cry. Why? Because of your stupidity. You're the asshole, Logan. You came back alive. So, out of the two of us, you'll live. Just like Dad."

Logan evaluated Sam's words, thinking of the supposed Oakes curse where every generation two sons were born, and one always died tragically early to be buried by the remaining brother. "It's all bullshit, Sam. There's no curse. You dumb shit. Just bad luck. But don't worry, little bro," he reached out and tussled his brother's hair with the three fingers left on his mutilated hand. "I didn't come back alive, only half alive. We broke the curse." He turned, ducking down to enter the hovel he called home.

Anger burned within Sam, vibrating his body before it exploded in a roar that echoed off the trees and scattered birds from their perches. With a rush of speed, he tackled his brother, rolling the two of them into the tent. The makeshift room collapsed around them. He climbed on top of his brother, straddled him. His fists connected with the flesh covering his brother's face before Jaxon dragged him back by the collar.

Still shaking with the feelings that rushed through his teenage frame, he shook his fist at Logan. "You're breaking Mom's heart, asshole. You'll finish the damn Tower for Theo and Isabella. Not only because you promised, and Oakes don't break their promises, but also because Mom wants you to. She needs to see you making something of yourself."

With the tip of his boot, Sam kicked snow in his brother's face. "Show up for work tomorrow or I'll drag your ass in. Make Mom cry again, and I'll kill you myself," he spat, before spinning around and stomping off through the woods.

Sitting amidst the churned up frozen earth and his collapsed tent, Logan spit dirty snow and blood out of his mouth. He wiped the rest of the muddy wetness from his face with the tail of his t-shirt. Thoughtfully, he rubbed his jaw and watched the man leave, who once was his little brother.

"If you don't watch it, he'll become a better man than you." Jaxon pulled his gaze from Sam's retreating back.

"He already is." Logan's brain gnawed on his friend's comment. "Maybe he always was."

Jaxon leaned back against a tree and studied his friend, sitting with his heels dug into the snow, his arms resting across his bent knees. "He needs you, you know."

"Bullshit. Why would he need the help of half a man? He's got Dad. Hell, he has you. There isn't anyone better. You saved my sorry ass." He paused, failure burning a hole in his gut. "Saved Ava."

Ava Fairbanks' beautiful face flashed before his mind's eye. Her soul lifting laugh. Rich, ebony hair. Jaxon was a lucky son-of-a-bitch to have the love of a woman like her. Emotion clogged his throat, but he pressed the words through. "Ran right into the barn through the black smoke and searing heat. Didn't care about the flames. The destruction." He tapped his clenched fist against his thigh, fighting the emotions consuming him. "What did I do? Fell to my knees and cried like a fucking baby. I couldn't even save my childhood friend."

In agony, he rubbed his hands over his face. The burn scars flowing from his right temple, across his cheek and down his neck were like a Braille tale of misery and defeat beneath his palm. He wiped his hands off on his jeans. "Even though I know first-hand the devastation of fire. The great destroyer of lives. I couldn't save Ava from the Director who was trying to kill her or the fire. But you could."

He shook his head and refused to meet his teammate's gaze. "I'm a coward. I can't help anyone. Not Sam. Not Ava. Least of all myself."

Jaxon grabbed Logan by the front of his t-shirt and jerked him up out of the muddy snow and into a standing position, until they were nose to nose. "Look, I don't want to hear any more of this crap. Ava needs to know you're okay. Isabella needs you to finish that damn tower. Hell, you heard your brother, even your mom needs to see you living. They're our new team. They're our comrades. Now, pull yourself up by your boot straps damn it and move out. Or I'll sock you one in the mouth myself." He released his strangle hold on Logan's shirt. "You heard the kid, get your ass into work tomorrow morning."

CHAPTER SEVEN

*I*n the back seat, JD leaned her head against the headrest and swallowed hard. The movement of her SUV climbing and twisting around the mountainous path through the Blue Ridge Mountains caused her mouth to fill with saliva. She despised the back. Cracking her window, she admonished her father, Milton Wolfe. "Slow down!" She gasped, "I'm going to blow chunks."

Her father's gaze met hers in the rear-view mirror. "Don't you have a puke bag back there someplace?" He addressed his brother, riding shotgun. "You'd think she'd be more prepared."

Casting a look over his shoulder, Clifford Wolfe offered his advice. "Shove your head between your legs, girl. That'll help." He shook his snowy white head and ribbed his brother. "It's your fault. You never allowed the girl to gain her sea legs. You'd think as a Navy man that would've been your first priority. At least I hooked her up for her first accelerated free fall from twenty thousand feet. Of course, an Army man needed to cover your ass."

Her head rolled to the side. She ignored the banter from the front and cracked open an eye. Trees sped past her window. Groaning, she squeezed her eyes shut and realized what a terrible mistake she'd made allowing the Geezers to take control of her vehicle. Sweet lavender seeped into the car and her hand shot out, pressing the button to fully open her window. *Great, fucking great,* she brooded. *Now I'm going to throw up potpourri chunks but only I can smell the potpourri.*

"You'd better slow down, Milt," stated his brother Cliff. "She's looking green around the gills."

"Check," he replied, lifting his foot from the accelerator. "Only a few clicks to go."

Springs, vibrated through her head. She leaned forward and covered her ears to block out the sound. Without opening her eyes, she knew the Woman sat beside her because she screamed one word over and over within JD's skull. *Springs! Springs! Springs!*

The Woman's voice grew so loud that JD began humming and rocking herself in a vain attempt to block the sound out. The concern of barfing was driven from her mind, only to have one word jackhammered relentlessly within her head. *Springs! Springs! Springs!*

The Woman's single word vocabulary grew louder than ever before in JD's life. *Why can't she shut up, give me some peace? No! She keeps repeating the same damn phrase.*

Mentally, she envisioned wringing her invisible neck. Instead, her hands balled into fists and she glowered at the Woman happily bouncing beside her. A growl germinated deep within her chest and exploded out of her mouth. "Shut the fuck up!" she screamed.

The two brothers shared a look but remained silent and pretended nothing out of the ordinary had happened.

Springs, the Woman whispered. Her hands were clasped eagerly in front of her chest. A single, silver tear escaped and rolled down her cheek, only to fade away into thin air as it fell. *Springs.*

"I don't have a fucking drink of water!" she shouted. "Leave me the hell alone," she added, just as a water bottle flew through the air. It sliced an arcing path through the ghost before bouncing off the seat and landing at JD's feet.

Realizing the scene that she'd just made, she stilled. Embarrassment filled her and coated her mouth with its bitter taste. It had been years since she'd lost her composure in front of her family, or anyone else for that matter. Bending and scooping up the bottle, she reigned in her emotions. Her voice unusually soft, she tossed a "Thank you," back to the Geezers.

Twisting the cap off the bottle, she swigged a gulp of water. Before her eyes, the snow topped mountains opened up into a gorgeous valley. A patchwork of town buildings and streets were laid out amongst trees and rolling hills. Railroad tracks stitched a jagged path around the boarder of the valley and veered diagonally across the middle. The town's crowning glory was a redbrick hotel with its arms open wide and a shiny tower shooting up from the base.

The same hotel from her dreams. The one her mother had always drawn with the town and the mountains nestled along the border.

Leaning forward, she could make out the pool. She knew exactly where the stables laid, the back way to the ski slope and the path to the falls. The best places in the river to fish in the summer and the safest places to ice skate in the winter.

She felt a funny sensation in the pit of her stomach. As if she'd just fallen through the rabbit hole and the imaginary world of her dreams had become reality. A feeling of relief washed over her. It was real, all real. Not sure if she wanted to laugh or cry, she took in big gulps of fresh air and attempted to tamp down the feelings that were overwhelming her. In wonderment, she gaped at the Woman beside her.

Happily, she nodded, and tears cascaded down her translucent face. She softly murmured in JD's head, *Springs*.

Was this what the Woman had been trying to say all those years? Finally starting to understand, she repeated, "Springs."

"That's right, JD," answered her father from the front. "Twin Springs Hotel and Spa. The hotel where your brother compromised himself and White Wolfe Investigations." His eyebrows were still wrinkled together from observing his daughter's episode. Noting the return of color to her face, he muttered to his brother. "Can't wait to meet the little lady who turned my son inside out and caused him to forget his duties."

Completely ignoring the Geezers' conversation, she pointed out landmarks as the car slowed to a stop before continuing through the streets leading to the hotel. "That building used to be an ice house. The power house was to the right and the Railway Express Agency was across the street. And see that building?" she now also bounced up and down in her seat. "That old run-down building used to house the employees that worked within Twin Springs. I can't believe it. Someone ripped the porches off the front and removed the domed viewing area from the top of the bay windows." She gazed in wonder at the dilapidated, four stories high, dirty white Victorian building. "I always thought it would be a wonderful place to live."

Bits and pieces of dreams that she'd forced from her memory flooded back. She remembered names that she'd assumed were fiction of her childish, sleeping mind. After her stint in the mad house, she'd shoved the memories of her dreams so far back into her subconscious that she'd all but forgotten them. Only the paintings and sketches she made to quell her dream-state imagination had remained.

She rambled on, "It was once a hotel too but the smoke from the train station seeped into it and turned away the guests. But the," she searched her memory banks for the name she'd made up as a child, "the General housed his servants there and had the tracks moved. Didn't want any competition for Twin Springs from some rinky-dink hotel that was snuggled up beside the

Grand Dame. Instead, he added a row of cottages behind the hotel for guests to enjoy a more private retreat. I can't believe that I dreamed of a real place."

Her brows furrowed. Her mother had also drawn pictures of the hotel. Was she cursed with the same dreams? JD didn't understand it all. Yet. But she knew who was responsible. The Woman.

Why did the Woman want her to know about Twin Springs?

Circling up and around, for a moment the SUV paused at the crest of a hill with the glory of Twin Springs spread out before the occupants. Digging in her boot, she pulled out her small notebook and flipped to the back where a tiny, folded piece of notebook paper was tucked. She unclicked her seatbelt and eagerly leaned forward between the two brothers. She unfolded the paper and shook it out in front of their faces. "See, it's Twin Springs. The picture my mother drew is of Twin Springs!"

The pieces clicked into place within her mind and she rambled uncontrollably. "All this time, I thought we were nuts. Mom dragged me from motel to motel always with the word Springs in their names. My mom searched for this." She pounded the paper with her index finger. "The Woman wanted Mom to find Twin Springs." For once, she wanted to share her happiness with the Woman. She turned back to the seat beside her. But she was gone.

The two brothers glanced at the pencil drawing and back to the brick building sprawled before them. In unison, they said, "I'll be damned."

CHAPTER EIGHT

ands shoved in his pockets, Logan ignored Isabella's offer of tea and stared up at his woman in the portrait. Half listening to everyone convened within the General's office, scratch that, now Ava's office, he rubbed at his hip. Two days ago, Jaxon and his brother had dragged him out of his tent.

It still pissed him off. They wanted him to work? To finish the Tower? Fine! He'd finish the tower. Not because his brother had found his balls and became a man but because Ava and Isabella Fairbanks had stood by him when he returned from the battlefield. The sisters hadn't shunned him, screamed or cringed away at the sight of his monstrous face.

Ava's African Gray parrot chomped on his apple slices and stared at him with knowing eyes. He still couldn't believe their childhood friend, Niles Porter, Twin Springs' Security Manager, had kept the bird trapped in a tiny cage and living in a cavern beneath the hotel. Never would he have thought that Niles was capable of trying to murder Isabella by holding her under the water either. Even though he knew Niles had deserved to drown and was swept away by the river, a part of him still felt badly for the boy he, Ava and Isabella had grown up playing with.

The bird chomped and squawked before he switched the apple slice out for a piece of mango with his large, gray claws. His gold eyes pinned Logan and he lowered his head and growled.

Growling back at the parrot, Logan's ears perked up with Jaxon's mention of DiWolf's paintings and the artist coming to Twin Springs. Of course, he'd heard about DiWolf. Everyone knew about the artist's works, but no one knew anything about the artist. He thought about the piece he owned. A pen and pencil drawing of a little girl. She sat beside an old vending machine with rain boots up to her knees, her jean clad legs spread. Her long braids scraped the floor as she hunched over a piece of paper with a broken pencil clasped in her tiny hand. Something about the determined look on that girl's down turned face had spoken to him. "I have one of DiWolf's pen and pencil's. Dropped a month of my hazardous duty pay on it."

Their conversation hummed in the background and his gaze shifted back to the painting. Reluctantly, he glanced over to the two sisters talking with Maddy, Jaxon and Theo about the little scraps of paper he and his father had found stashed in the walls of the tunnel where they'd discovered Ruby's remains.

Had it only been a week since Ava was trapped in the stable? A week since he'd helped his father and the coroner with the General's daughter, Ruby Rockwell's, remains. For him, the last seven days felt like a lifetime. Unwillingly, he sniffed the air. Even the roses within Ava's office couldn't cover the fact he reeked from living in the tent. Rolling his shoulders, he pushed away the feeling of embarrassment that crept up his spine. They wanted him, they'd have to take him the way he was, stench and all. Perhaps the smell would keep everyone else away. Make sure that no one mistook who he really was—a monster. A mutilated, mean, monster.

He rolled his eyes at the women when they went all gooey eyed over the ruby and diamond headband that had been found with Ruby's bones. He muttered under his breath, "I'll finish the damn Tower, but they'll take me as I am."

Reluctantly, the left side of Logan's lips curled up when the women squealed in distaste for Theo's logical idea of selling the headband to fund the repairs for Twin Springs. He glanced up at the beautiful carbon copy of his childhood friend in the painting. The similarity of Ava to the General's daughter, Ruby, was amazing. Just like the similarity of Isabella to the General's other daughter, Emma. Only the General's oldest daughter, Amethyst, remained alone and without a present-day twin.

The General had adorned each woman in the portrait with a very valuable gift. Emerald, who Isabella had insisted that her family had called Emma, wore a gorgeous necklace. A huge cushion cut emerald, surrounded by diamonds, dangled from it. Everyone had thought the necklace was lost in the great fire of 1928 with the General's Gems—his girls. But Emma had given the necklace to Theo's ancestor Jean Claude Flamme. He had converted the pendant of the emerald necklace into a ring and had cherished the gift for almost a century before Theo had proposed to Isabella and slipped the emerald onto her ring finger.

Begrudgingly, he admitted that the diamond and ruby headband was spectacular. The way the jewels caught the light and glittered as it was passed from Ava, to Maddy, to Isabella and was gushed over. The women were right. The gems were their heritage and a part of the Grand Dame. It was a shame they'd never find the long necklace of amethysts and diamonds that was draped around the General's last daughter, Amethyst Fairbanks, Ava and Isabella's great grandmother.

Their heritage should remain within Twin Springs for future generations. He groaned beneath his breath when an idea came to him of how to display the notes and headband for the family and public to enjoy. *Great, more work for me before I can return to my woods and be left the hell alone.*

He dug at the dirt in his beard before speaking up. "I was

thinking," he said. "What if we carve out a space in the Tower for a museum of Twin Springs? We could finally chronicle the timeline of the Grand Dame. We could have a section highlighting the letters found in the tunnels that document Twin Springs' role in the Underground Railroad."

Of course, Theo's little sister, Maddy, flew with the idea. Her enthusiasm allowed him to once again study the portrait. He sympathized with Amethyst, alone and without a double. He felt alone too. As if he had lost his own double, the man he used to be. He muttered under his breath, "I'll finish the Tower for Ava and Isabella and for the General and his Gems. I'll bring Twin Springs back to her former glory. But that's all, damn it."

The room erupted with excitement. *Did they hear me?* He shifted uncomfortably. *No. I'll be damned. Jaxon just proposed to Ava.*

He zeroed in on her excitement and grunted with satisfaction. He slapped Jaxon on the back and whispered in his ear, "Take care of her or I'll kick your ass."

Jaxon's golden eyes scrunched up at the corners and he laughed. He pumped Logan's three fingers in a firm handshake. "You can try," he replied, before a serious glint entered his gaze and he nodded back. His face was firm with resolve. "I'll protect her with my last dying breath."

Logan nodded. "I know you will." He returned to his position, taking up sentry beneath the portrait, ignoring the racket of everyone celebrating and the happy squawks from Ace. Everything was secondary to his time with Amethyst.

CHAPTER NINE

*H*er eyes transfixed on the hotel, JD didn't realize the vehicle had come to a complete stop. Repressed past visions from her dreams were filtering through her brain. Her door opened. Cold air rushed through the car and snapped her out of her trance. She cast a distracted smile at the valet, one word vibrating through her brain, *home*.

The valet gawked at her, his mouth opening and closing. She grabbed her backpack, the only bag she'd need for the weekend assignment, and slung it over her shoulder. Her attention was completely filled with the sprawling brick building before her as she gave the valet a distracted, "Thank you."

She rounded the car and climbed the white steps to the veranda that stretched across the front. With each step, a ghostly apparition materialized and played out in an un-living black and white movie. Walking forward, she entered a silent film of sepia and gray actors. Their movements were stark against the present day, colored backdrop of the red brick walls. It was as if her paintings had come to life. Just in black and white. And that was when she realized, she'd been drawing dead people, not just snapshots from her dreams.

Damn it. This confirmed her suspicions. Her dreams weren't dreams at all, but visions the Woman had placed in her head. Visions of dead people, who were walking and talking ghosts. She grumbled under her breath, "At least I can't hear them. Unlike the constant buzzing of the Woman in my head."

She passed a tall, slender man. Circular wire spectacles framed his eyes. A square box camera hung from a strap around his neck. Looking down, as he fiddled and fumbled with the switches of the camera his slicked back hair tumbled into his eyes. Unconsciously, he brushed his bangs back on his head. With the tip his finger, he pushed the eyeglasses back up on his nose.

A burly man waved his arms impatiently in front of the other ghostly figure. He shouted silent orders to the trembling man with the camera. The older man commanded the space with his huge form and towered over those around him.

The General, whispered through her mind.

A man to the General's right stood straight as an arrow. A sneer twisted his lips. His hair was also slicked back but stuck to his skull. Clothed in thick wool pants, bloused into his tall polished boots, and a starched white shirt that was stiff beneath a three-button wool jacket, his demeanor screamed past military experience.

Two women with lace caps and black and white maid uniforms stood three steps back and to the side. The one with her head cast downward and her hands demurely clasped in front of her grasped the end of her necklace between her palms. The other maid's arms were unable to reach around her large stomach. Instead, she rested her clasped hands on her pregnant belly and broadly smiled for the camera.

Three young women stood to the left of the General and embraced each other for the picture. Soundless laughter escaped their black and white forms as they shuffled together for the picture. In the middle of the joyful trio stood the Woman. Just as JD closed the distance enough to see her face without the scraggly strands of gray hair blocking it, the Woman turned her back and addressed one of the maids behind her. Even without seeing her face, JD knew it was her. The other two ladies, dressed in 1920's finery, waited for the Woman to turn before they looped their arms behind her and posed for the camera.

As the Woman turned, her immensely huge belly protruded between the trio and JD stumbled on the steps. She couldn't take her eyes off that belly. She was pregnant. JD hadn't ever considered that the Woman she'd hated all her life could've been a mother.

As the black and white scene played out before her, the real world continued around her in a full spectrum of colors. Cars continued to swing through the circular drive. Bellhops rushed about with luggage and guests chattered to each other. Behind her the Geezers argued with their bellhop about not needing assistance with their bags and admonished each other for packing more than needed.

Ignoring their banter, she continued up the steps, her gaze grounded on that huge belly. Holding her breath and squeezing her lips and eyes tight, she stepped right through the dead's left-over essence and continued through this new version of the Woman, her belly heavy with child. Releasing her breath, she blinked and pretended nothing out of the ordinary had happened. From past experience with the Woman, she knew no one else would be aware of the silent movie that played out on the wide steps of the hotel.

An elderly doorman, in a black suit with dark green trim, grasped a circular brass doorknob in the middle of a massive glass door and swept it wide for her to enter. He turned to greet her, the ready smile on his lips slipping into a shocked slack jaw stare as his eyes bulged. He stuttered out, "W-w-welcome to Twin Springs Hotel and Spa." His intense stare never left her face.

She bristled. Sweeping through the open doorway and into the hotel from her dreams, she muttered beneath her breath, "What a perv."

The hotel reeked with the smell of roses and vanilla. The combination drenched her senses, choking her and causing her to halt in her tracks. She gasped to catch her breath.

Her father and uncle trailed behind her and also quickly stopped. "Whoa, girl! Give some warning if you're gonna come to a full stop," said her Uncle Cliff.

Ignoring him, she surveyed the Lobby that was different, yet the same, as in her dreams. She absorbed the length of the long Lobby. The same extraordinarily tall ceilings that hovered over the wide expanse were anchored on both ends by balconies that led to the floor above.

As in her dreams, guests mingled around the tall, double rows of alabaster columns that lined the Lobby. Instead of the area rugs that should've been covering a wide, planked wooden floor, her feet sunk into thick, wall to wall carpet. The Lobby was lined with comfortable groupings of stuffed chairs and couches instead of hard wooden and wicker chairs surrounded by ferns and small fountains. Even with all the changes, the bones were the same. "The Grand Lobby," she whispered.

"What's that? What's that girl?" Uncle Cliff questioned, turning to his brother. "Didn't you teach the girl to speak up?" His voice grumbled but his concerned green gaze scrutinized his niece's every move.

Milt shrugged and pulled his brother aside. "She's been acting odd since the episode in the car."

Cliff grunted and gave an affirmative nod. "Well, the similarities between the hotel and the picture are uncanny. Odd."

Milt rubbed the back of his neck. "The expressions on her face remind me of the little orphan I brought home. She's struggling with an issue. Something big."

"Her eyes seem glazed over. I hope she doesn't fall into another fit in the middle of the Lobby. It would embarrass her terribly."

Milt nodded. "I wonder why she's having episodes again." He released a long, drawn out breath. "I've always worried that I should've gotten her help. Professional help."

"Negative," his brother replied. "You did the right thing. She threatened to run away if we took her to any psychologists. It was better that she was with us, than a pawn in the broken system. Better that we kept her fits to ourselves. Remember that middle school counselor? She raised one hell of a ruckus when she caught JD yelling at a wall. How did you get her to back off?"

Milt's cheeks glowed cherry red. "She was having an affair with the gym teacher. I, um, slipped her some pics I'd snapped and told her I'd keep quiet if she did. By high school the episodes seemed to stop."

They glanced over at JD muttering under her breath and acting odd.

"At least until now," Cliff replied.

"Or she just figured out how to hide them." Concern knitted Milt's brows together into a worried line. "If she has another one, we'll handle it. Can't have her heart hurt."

"Roger that," replied Cliff, his voice gruff. "She's our girl."

Raising his voice, Milt called to JD, "Hold up here, while I ask where to find Jax." He strode away to the counter and quickly returned. "They said he's in the General's Office. Gave me this map. The office is directly over—"

Her gaze cleared. She raised her hand and pointed towards two, massive double doors directly across the Lobby. "That's the General's Office."

"How do you know that?" demanded Uncle Cliff. His gaze collided with his brother's, but he kept his tone light. "That girl's got one hell of a compass inside her head." He elbowed his brother, "I taught her that."

She felt her father's attention heavy upon her, even as he addressed his brother. She didn't want to worry him. However, she couldn't control the knowledge in her head. Placed there by the Woman. *Fucking bitch, now bringing my father more worry and pain.*

"You didn't teach her shit," muttered her father, causing an argument to erupt.

Ignoring the Geezers, she crossed the room to find her brother. Their argument grew heated in her ears and she pulled open the office door. She'd had enough of their rivalry for one morning. "Shut up," she ordered and rubbed her temples. Lowering her voice, she implored, "Please."

CHAPTER TEN

A ruckus exploded from the Lobby as deep male voices and a woman's voice reached Logan's ears. Reluctantly, he pried his eyes away from the portrait.

"Crap," Jaxon muttered, rubbing the stubble on his chin with the back of his knuckles. "The Geezers have arrived."

Enjoying his friend's discomfort, Logan chuckled under his breath. Before being mutilated by fire, he'd looked forward to meeting Jaxon's father and his uncle from the stories his buddy had told of the two men's careers in the military and their antics as private investigators. He wondered if straight laced Theo was prepared for the chaos that Jaxon's family would bring.

"Yeah, the Geezers are my dad and uncle." Jaxon added before a woman's loud voice told the two men beyond the doors to, "Shut up."

Jaxon's gaze fixated on him and an uneasy feeling crept down Logan's spine.

"It sounds like they brought my sister, too."

Logan's one good eye widened with surprise. Wolfeman's stories of his sister were just as legendary as the Geezer's antics had been with their Special Forces team. No way in hell, would he deal with Jaxon's insane sister. "They forced me out of my tent to finish the Tower not to deal with a crazy woman," he muttered. He moved to slip out the secret passageway that had been discovered behind the bookcase in Ava's office wall, but he was grasped by the collar of his t-shirt and pulled back. "You rip my Van Halen shirt, I'll pound your face," he muttered to his Army buddy.

"Promises, promises," replied Jaxon, chuckling beneath his breath. "Don't you want to meet my family?"

Ace squawked, "Get the fuck out," above the booming voices.

Growling under his breath, he turned to face the two legends entering Ava's office. The room exploded around him when the woman from the portrait trailed behind. Living flesh and blood. Her gorgeous, crimson red hair was loose around her shoulders and curled just below her breasts. In her heart shaped face, her iridescent green eyes were alive with an inner light. Freckles were sprinkled across the milky white skin on her nose and cheeks.

Involuntarily, he took a step forward towards the living vision before him. She was a carbon copy of Amethyst Fairbanks, the dead woman he'd secretly lusted over and loved. An ache exploded in his chest, forbidden hope flooding in as his heart expanded at the sight of her. Then, the living angel from the portrait spoke.

"What the fuck is that? A parrot? I like him."

CHAPTER ELEVEN

*I*gnoring everything around her, another loud squawk reached her ears and drew JD's attention across the General's office. "Is that a parrot?"

"I'll be damned," said her father, scratching his peppered hair. "Yep, it is."

She couldn't believe her eyes. A large, gray bird sat on top of a massive, black wire cage. The parrot's claw lifted to his mouth and he ate a hunk of a walnut. *A damn bird,* she mused. The crazy parrot shook his tail at her, displaying the beautiful red tipping his feathers. Pleasure filled her at his cute antics. "I like him."

Tearing her attention from the parrot, she examined the room surrounding her. An exact replica of her dreams. Unlike the movie that had played on the Veranda, this scene was real and in full, panoramic color. The General's massive mahogany desk dominated the right side of the room. His wife had picked it out for him. At the time, he'd pounded his chest and declared it was a woman's desk because of the curves and carvings within the dark red wood. He shouted that it wasn't appropriate for his manly office. But, his wife, with her soft ways, had always won any war with the General. Behind the desk the glass shelving enclosed little knick-knacks that had also been placed lovingly by his wife. The only piece of furniture Mrs. Rockwell had allowed her husband to select was a heavy coffee table with black leather inlay across the top and eagles carved into the legs. Her gaze swept downward, looking for the short table, but it was missing, a tea cart standing in its place.

Lost in her own thoughts, she continued her assessment of the office. Across the back wall ran a long, waist high bookcase. As her gaze followed the length of it, she noted the framed black and white photos above the wall that traveled straight to the huge, metal cage. Now, the bird, he was never in her dreams.

On one of the General's leather couches sat a young girl. *Mid-teens,* she thought. Light ebony skin, her hair twisted into tight, cork screw curls. Eyes the most unusual shade of light gray, almost silver with a dark ring around the outside. Exquisite.

In JD's experience girls with that kind of beauty were natural targets for sick men. She hoped her family was prepared to protect her. Her gaze swept the girl from head to toe. The teenager was dressed too old for her age in a long blue skirt and white, long sleeve, silk shirt cut low, sending off all the wrong signals. She shook her head with disappointment. Obviously, the parents had lost control of their daughter. Immediately, she became one of her lost children and she vowed to watch over her while at Twin Springs.

Beside the teen sat two women. One, a tiny little thing with thick, sun-kissed blonde hair that was pulled back into a ponytail. She looked comfortable in her skinny black jeans and white tank top. The other exuded a natural sensuality. Her glossy, jet-black hair was cut short and sharp against her jaw. Elegance and beauty described the woman perfectly in her mint green, silky shirt and black slacks. Both women stared at her. Their matching ice green eyes were wide with shock.

JD's heart picked up a beat and pounded hard in her ears. Both women were colored replicas of the two monochromatic ladies posing with the Woman on the steps out front.

In the corners of her consciousness, she registered her brother and another man standing by the door. Her dreams were forming within the living world around her. Panic clenched her throat. The Woman didn't bring her peace by coming to Twin Springs. Instead, JD was surrounded by ghosts. Now, in the living, breathing, full color world.

If it wasn't for her brother and the Geezers, she might have embarrassed herself and their good name by running screaming from the room, tearing her hair from her head. Perhaps she was asleep and all this was a dream. Cautiously, she reached out and touched the General's desk with the tips of her fingers. It was firm. Real.

She wasn't sure if she wanted the hotel to remain in her dreams, so that her own world remained safe. Or, if she wanted the hotel to be real, thus giving her the possibility of being sane. If the hotel was real, then her mother was sane all along. Could Twin Springs hold the key to unlocking her past? It must hold the secret of why the Woman was connected to her mother and now to her. Unless nothing was real and she was stuck in a nightmare of the Woman's making. Unsure what else to do, she pinched herself. She felt numb and the pain barely registered. So, she reached out and pinched her brother too. Just for good measure.

"Damn it, what was that for?" Jaxon growled, rubbing his arm.

"Because you're there," she grumbled back. It was real. Everything was real and in full color. She clenched her fists until her nails bit into the soft flesh of her palms. They weren't ghosts. Just mirror images of the dead. The thought brought a foul taste to her mouth. She couldn't think of anything worse than being a carbon copy of the dead.

"Everyone, meet my sister JD. The pincher." Jaxon returned his sister's glare before continuing. "My father, Milton Wolfe, and his brother, Clifford."

She felt the women's gazes. The two technicolor ladies and the young girl's mouths still hung open. She ignored them. Some women were judgy and she didn't play stupid female games. Besides, the female race spoke a language she didn't understand, even though she was born among them.

Moving further into the room, she registered another man within the General's Office. At the sight of him, the carpet shifted under her feet and the floor tilted at a crazy angle before righting itself, for standing stiff amid her technicolor living dream stood a man, half monster, half human and marked by the heat of fire. Ignoring everyone else, she moved towards the bird cage and kept an eye on the half-melted man before her.

Leaning in, she pretended to examine the gray parrot, while covertly eyeing the burnt man. Only his brilliant blue eyes moved. His gaze followed her advance but he continued to stand stock still, like a bronze statue the artist took a blow torch to one side of in a vain attempt to destroy his creation. Her fingers itched to take out her notebook and quickly sketch the man. Even with the scars that crisscrossed a torrid path across half his face before traveling beneath his collar, he radiated a contradiction between strength and desperate need.

That need reached out to her. Clutched her heart. Half of the man screamed out for her to understand, to protect, to guard and to bring him within her arms for comfort. The other half challenged her to come close and promised retribution by fire if she dared to peek beneath the scars. At the same time, his stance, the way he held his shoulders back, the way his gaze traveled her slender frame, emitted power and an incredible heat. A heat for her.

He shifted his weight. She averted her eyes and noticed how the minor movement tightened the already stretched and taut skin around his eyes with pain. This man had experienced Hell. And returned. Her breath caught in her chest with the agony that he must have endured. Her mother had crossed over the same throes of anguish in order to find peace. But the suffering her mom had endured had been caused by her daughter's careless actions. Her actions.

No one spoke. Time lapsed into an uncomfortable silence. She stiffened and her mind exploded with a horrific conclusion. *My God, he's just like the Woman! Another ghost to haunt my days and dreams with a never-ending need.*

What if he didn't return from Hell? Perhaps she'd just entered the Devil's den. Unsure what else to do, she reached out and pinched the beast. A great roar resounded from deep within his chest. But she knew from experience that only she could hear the fury of the dead. She raised her chin, ready and welcoming him to charge.

CHAPTER TWELVE

*F*rustration rumbled deep within Logan's chest, but he refused to rub the flesh on his pec where her fingers had ripped at his skin. He forced words through his clenched teeth. "Wolfeman, get your sister under control."

Relieved that all eyes had swung to Jaxon, he rolled his shoulders back and glared at his teammate's sister. She was clothed from head to toe in black, from the roughed-up leather jacket, to the jeans clinging to her long legs and down to the boots that placed her at his eye level. When she'd first entered, he could've sworn that she was his woman from the portrait in flesh and blood, his to have and hold.

For the briefest moment, he'd had hope. Hope that the woman before him would be the one. That she'd see past his scars. The one to calm the beast. And then she spoke with the mouth of a bloody pirate, complete with tall boots. He'd winced at the words that had flown from her mouth. *Why wouldn't she like Ace? The bird's vocabulary matches her own.*

From the stories Jaxon had told in the team room, he knew she was trouble. With her foul mouth and damn boots, she was nothing like his woman in the portrait. The woman who filled his dreams. Disappointment hit him deep and caused his whole body to shudder with an unfilled need.

"You alright, son?" The pirate woman's father asked.

His gaze shifted to Milt Wolfe. The flecks of green in his golden-brown eyes pierced deep into his soul. An uncomfortable thought entered his mind and he shifted his weight uneasily under the possibility that Jaxon's father would detect the coward he hid beneath the gore and filth. *Is he a human lie detector like his son?*

Glancing around the room, he realized everyone's attention had moved back to him. The two Geezers had marched up to him and quietly studied him. Standing side by side, the brothers resembled each other. Uncle Cliff's head was completely silver. His brother's dark hair was salted with gray and not far behind. Where Milt's eyes were gold with green flecks, his brother's were completely green. Wearing the typical off duty look for a military man of jeans, leather belt and a button up shirt with the sleeves folded up and exposing their muscled forearms, each man stood uncomfortably close to him and assessed him from head to toe.

They only saw the side of him ravaged by fire. The muscles in his neck bunched into cords of steel. Why did people keep calling him back to the land of the living? Just to gawk? Poke at the beast? He glared back. If everyone wanted to stare at the animal that he'd become, then that was what they'd get. The beast. "Like what you see?"

He jerked his t-shirt up and revealed the torrid scars that covered his chest and flowed over his abdomen. A growl built in volume, like an avalanche of wrath, and rolled across his voice. With his free hand, he grasped the clasp of his belt and harshly continued, "I have more scars down here, if you want to stare at them too."

Three of the women within the room exclaimed out loud. Ava jerked to her feet. Maddy sat eyes wide and Isabella's fingertips covered her mouth. Only JD failed to respond to the disgusting scars that he'd revealed. The last spark of life left in the ashes of his heart wrenched at their reactions. But he doused the budding flame, telling himself that it didn't matter because the agony of their pity would be too great. He must reject them first. Hurts less. After all, if they saw only the beast, then they wouldn't ask for more than he was able to give. He clenched his teeth and took solace within the pain.

Jaxon entered the fray. "Dad, Uncle Cliff, this is Logan Oakes. My Army buddy from the Unit. He's the one I told you about. The only survivor of my last mission."

The two Geezers squinted their eyes. Gravely, they examined him, gauging and weighing the burnt man before them. "You can stop showing off your badges of courage, son." Milt's head swiveled towards his brother and he rambled on. "Typical Army man, thumping his chest and showing off his medals. Now son, if you had any sense about you, then you would have joined the Navy like a real man."

With difficulty, he followed the crazy turn of the conversation. *The stupid old men blew off my wounds.* A red hue inched its way up Logan's neck and he lowered his shirt. "Your son's an Army man," he shot back.

Milt shook his salt and pepper head sadly, "The one huge disappointment of my life. The day my son joined the Army instead of the Navy, the oldest and most distinguished branch of the service."

Slapping his brother on the back, Cliff hooted with laughter, "That's the day your son became a real man. Not a pansy ass deck swabber."

"Dumb grunt," mumbled Milt back towards his brother before he addressed Logan. The green flecks in his eyes glowed. "Scars mold a man. Show his mettle. Badges of courage displayed for the whole world to view the fortitude, strength and character within. True grit, son. Shows you've got balls." He clasped him by the shoulder and pulled him forward to whisper loudly, "Besides, chicks dig scars." Eyebrow raised, he nodded his head towards his daughter.

Surveying the new trio before him, he wondered, *What the hell was Jaxon thinking, bringing his crazy family to Twin Springs? Badges of courage? Bullshit. Obviously these men have never experienced women cringing in disgust and turning away from the sight of their mutilated skin. Chicks dig scars?* His gaze bounced off JD and back to her father. *What the hell did they know about a woman's rejection?* The skin where his right eyebrow once laid rose. He crossed his arms over his chest and grunted, "Bullshit."

Ace screeched out behind him and flapped his wings wildly, "Bullshit, bullshit."

The two Geezers crumpled with laughter and nudged each other as they moved towards the cage. Quieting down, Milt whispered to his brother, "Definitely an Army man, stubborn headed as a mule."

"That so? Then the bird's a Navy man," shot back his brother. "All he has to say is 'bullshit'."

CHAPTER THIRTEEN

*L*ogan wasn't a ghost after all, but a man who'd battled the fires of Hell and returned. Pity closed up JD's throat and she didn't trust herself to speak. Not even to defend the burned man that the Geezers had offended with their lighthearted banter. Even though he'd lowered his t-shirt, she couldn't erase the sight of the hills and valleys of Logan's muscled stomach trenched across one side by an unholy fury of scars. Tears pricked at the back of her eyes and she blinked away the sympathy that consumed her. She'd glimpsed the pain he'd held back with his clenched jaw and ridged stance. She stepped forward to apologize for the embarrassment her family had caused but an authoritative voice reached out from across the room and halted her uncharacteristic actions.

"Gentlemen."

The man her brother stood beside unfolded himself from his spot against the wall. His ebony hair was clipped close to his scalp, his light black skin and the sharp angles of his cheek bones over powered by the glint in his steel gray gaze and purposeful stride. She pegged him as one of Twin Springs' owners.

"Name's Theo Beaumont." Intent on bringing the situation

under control, he continued, "Let me make proper introductions. This beautiful, blonde woman is my fiancée. Isabella Fairbanks, and Twin Springs' Head Executive Chef. Her sister, Ava, is our Group Sales and Special Events Coordinator, here at the hotel."

"And my future wife," piped up Jaxon. He moved towards the exquisite woman with glossy black hair and put his arm around her.

The Geezers shuffled over to each woman and shook their hands. "So, this is the woman who compromised both your assignment and White Wolfe Investigations," stated Milt, firmly shaking the beautiful woman's hand.

"Ava didn't compromise me," his son replied. "Did that well enough on my own. Didn't realize Logan lived in the area and my cover was blown when he recognized me."

Milt acknowledged the statement with a nod. "Good to hear. Welcome to the Wolfe family."

Ignoring the by play, JD examined the technicolored versions of the two women from the Veranda. The blonde was child-like in size. In comparison, her sister was everything that all women craved to be. Sexy, tall, slender and drop dead gorgeous.

Theo continued the introductions and gestured towards the young girl with expressive gray eyes. Her long black curls bounced around her small face and reminded her of Harmony. "This very impressionable young lady is my little sister, Maddy."

"Isn't anyone going to say it?" demanded the teenager. Excitement vibrated through her body and caused her to squirm in her seat. "Jaxon's sister is an exact replica of Amethyst Fairbanks." She turned and pointed up to a portrait above the fireplace.

All gazes rose towards a large oil portrait. For once, the Geezer's quieted. Then, they muttered simultaneously, "I'll be damned."

For there, in vivid oils, were three women frozen in time. Dressed as if from the 1920's, were Isabella and Ava. Around Isabella's neck hung a necklace with a huge emerald surrounded by diamonds. Ava wore a headband with ruby and diamond encrusted roses. Next to the two women, the artist had painted JD's face!

The details were astounding. The artist had captured her perfectly. From the delicate handling of light on the waves of her flaming hair as it framed her face, to the authoritarian way she held her head, and down to the glint in her gaze when she assumed she was right. But the artist had dressed her richly in an antique two-piece dress from the twenties. Painted around her neck was a double looped, long necklace. The amethyst stones of the necklace were separated at different intervals by gold links and tiny diamond balls. Even in the oils, the necklace sparkled and made a dramatic impact on the viewer.

The scent of lavender filled JD's senses. Out of the corner of her eye, she saw the Woman's black and white body forming beside her.

Along with everyone in the room, the Woman studied the portrait. She turned. From behind the scraggly hair hanging in front of her face, a translucent silver tear rolled down her cheek and dripped off her chin. Just like before, the tear faded away and disappeared before dropping to the floor. For the first time in JD's life, two words were spoken by the Woman and vibrated through her brain. *Thank you.*

Her long, gray dress fluttered in an invisible wind and she rose up towards the painting. Gradually, her form changed. The monochrome tips of her hair reddened. The crimson color traveled up the shafts until her whole head blazed. Her long hair fanned out around her, before snaking in, and twisting into curls at the nape of her neck. Her ashen skin warmed to a strawberries and cream and her silver-gray eyes flickered and lit to an iridescent, light green. Every part of the Woman colorized and changed until she blended in with the portrait. And they became one.

The lavender smell thickened, filling her throat until it choked her with its sweet scent. JD couldn't believe her eyes. The woman who'd driven her mother insane, and haunted her all her life, was the spitting image of herself. The artist had captured the Woman and, at the same time herself, for all time on canvas.

She glanced at the living faces within the room and saw all the dead women from the portrait. Isabella. Ava. And, now, herself.

The scent of roses, vanilla, and lavender combined together and overwhelmed her. She felt lightheaded and her stomach rolled. The General's room spun and she swayed on her feet. Knees buckling beneath her, the floor rushed up to greet her. She was going to perform a face plant right at Logan's feet.

Powerful arms wrapped around her and held her tight. Encircled within Logan's embrace, his heat seared her through his t-shirt, but she was protected by his strength. She felt safe.

For the first time in her life, she leaned on another human being and allowed him to support her shaking limbs. Still, the light seemed overly bright in the room and a great heat washed over her and combatted with the fragrances that assaulted her senses. Gazing up into the incredibly blue eyes of the beast, her head spun. "I'm going to puke."

"Whoa! There she goes again," bellowed her Uncle Cliff. "Shove her head between her legs. That'll bring back her color."

Instead, Logan hooked his arm under her legs and easily carried her over to the couch. "Move over Maddy," he ordered, grumbling under his breath, "Of course, the sight of my ugly mug makes you want to vomit."

Before he could dump her onto the couch, she went limp in his arms and slipped into a dead faint.

CHAPTER FOURTEEN

*A*rguing voices filtered into the edges of JD's fuzzy brain. *The Geezers.* She focused in on the booming wordplay of their animated voices. Her lashes fluttered against the brightness of the outside.

Liquid splashed across her face and drenched her front. She sputtered and jerked to a sitting position. "What the hell?"

Eyes wide open, she took in her surroundings. She was the only one on the couch. Someone had removed her leather jacket and everyone in the room stood gawking down at her. An empty tea cup dangled from her Uncle's thick pinky finger. She held her damp shirt out from her chest. Tea dripping from her lashes, she glared up at her brother. "You couldn't stop them?"

The room erupted into a torrid of voices, all wanting to know how it was possible for her to look exactly like Amethyst Fairbanks. Everyone but Logan. He stood back from the crowd, his arms crossed, scowling down at her. But all she saw was the strong planes of his face, the strength of his jaw and the hurt deep in his gaze. His words vibrated in her brain, *Of course, the sight of my ugly mug makes you want to vomit.* Her lips parted, but she couldn't find the words to soothe his pain.

"Enough," Theo's voice cut through the buzz. "Obviously, this has been a great surprise for JD. Everyone calm down and let's fill her in on the history of Twin Springs and the General's Gems. Isabella, why don't you begin."

JD tore her gaze from Logan and wiped the tea from her eyes with the tips of her fingers. She glared up at the Woman in the portrait and suppressed the spark of hope that she'd never have to deal with the bitch again.

"I guess we should start with Dad's death." Isabella glanced at Ava and the brunette nodded. "Our father passed away recently."

At the news, JD sat a little straighter. "I'm sorry."

Isabella's tiny lips spread into a sad smile. "Thank you." She rallied and continued. "Unbeknownst to my sister and me, Dad had sold Theo's parents half the shares of Twin Springs years before. When we returned for Dad's funeral, we found out that there were a lot of strange accidents at the hotel that were draining us financially."

"That's why Jaxon was called out. We were hired to investigate the insurance claims," inserted Milt. He shoved a hankie to his daughter.

JD felt her father's gaze. Evaluating her. Assessing her. Not wanting him to worry, she tilted her head to the space left on the couch.

Immediately, he sat beside her and pounded her back with reassuring pats.

Jaxon interrupted. "The accidents were really sabotage by their Security Manager, Niles Porter. He was cooking up moonshine in a cavern under the kitchens of the hotel. Once his operations were discovered by Isabella, he attempted to kill her by drowning her in an underground river that runs beside the cavern tunnels. Instead, she hit him in the head with a rock and he was swept downstream."

"Grisly business," muttered Cliff.

"Yes," replied Isabella. "It was terrible. One of Niles' sabotages resulted in the hotel room above this space being flooded. The floor gave way and revealed this room."

"The General's Office," murmured JD, wiping her face.

"Yes. The General had three daughters. Emerald, Ruby and Amethyst. They were called the General's Gems. All three of his daughters died in the Great Fire on New Year's Eve, 1928."

JD's hands shook. She bunched the hankie up into her fist and willed herself to stay strong. But her voice cracked when she asked, "They were all named after precious stones?"

Isabella nodded. "Yes. Unusual, I know."

"Not to me, it isn't," she replied. Her voice grew in strength. "My mother's name was Opal and my middle name, the name my mother gave me, is Diamond."

The room hushed as the information was absorbed. Isabella turned to Milt. "Your wife's name was Opal?"

Shaking his graying head, he grasped his daughter's hand. "You're cold," he muttered and rubbed her fingers to warm them up. He glanced up. "My daughter's adopted. Her name was Diamond when we brought her home. But she didn't want that name, so we made it her middle name. She picked Justyne for her first name and Jaxon started calling her JD as a kid."

Pulling a silver pen from his pocket, Theo rolled it between his fingers. Contemplating the women before him, he asked, "What was your last name before you were adopted?"

She shrugged. "I didn't have one."

Maddy gasped and plopped down on the other side of her. She took over rubbing her hand from her father. Milt rose, clasped his hands behind his back and paced the space under the portrait. "You didn't have a last name? You have no idea about your family?" Maddy implored.

Backed into a corner, Logan glanced away from the portrait and asked, "You all own an investigation agency. Your team didn't try to find her roots?"

At Logan's question Milt paused. "I tried. My wife believed

that, one day, JD would want to know where she came from. But I hit a dead end. I still have a file with the information I unearthed. Cliff's son, Lee, sent the file to Jaxon."

"I still can't believe you had a file on me," she pulled her hand from Maddy's grasp. "Like I was a missing child." She growled, "I knew who my mother was."

"This doesn't make any sense," injected Isabella. "Before, there was a correlation. Emerald, or Emma as I knew her, spoke to me in dreams so that I could find out how she died. So I could reunite her with her lost love. While trying to help Emma, I fell in love with Theo, the descendant of her lost love, Jean Claude Flamme."

"The same happened with Ruby and myself," added Ava. "I located Ruby's remains and discovered how she died. At the same time, I discovered that your brother, Jaxon, was the direct descendant of Ruby's lost love, Guy Wolfe. Showing a connection between Twin Springs, Ruby and the Wolfe family. But how does that connect with you?"

JD's gaze flickered to Logan. "I suppose you're related to— What was Amethyst husband's name?"

"Everett," whispered Maddy, again patting her hand.

"I suppose you're related to Everett and I'm her mirror image. So we are supposed to..." Her voice trailed off and she felt heat rushing into her face.

"Wow," said Maddy. "The freckles on your cheeks and nose look like little angry dots when you're embarrassed."

JD loved the honesty of children. "Thanks, kid." She tugged her hand free again and suppressed a smile. Couldn't help but like the girl.

"No way in hell," Logan replied, thumping his mutilated fist against his jean clad leg. "You're nothing like the woman in the portrait. Nothing like Amethyst Fairbanks."

Ava linked her arm in his, calming him. "No, Logan isn't related to Everett Fairbanks. But he is related to Twin Springs.

His family, the Oakes, are the original owners. The General purchased the hotel from his ancestors."

"Also," added Isabella, "our great great Grandmother Amethyst never lost her great love. Her husband, Everett lost her in the fire but the connection was never lost between the two of them. He's buried next to her in our family plot."

"Emma and Ruby spoke to both of you?" she asked, but didn't look anyone in the eye in case they guessed her secret. "As ghosts?"

"I know it sounds crazy," replied Isabella. "Emma didn't really speak to me, but she communicated with me in my dreams. I was lucky, Ava's experience was much more intrusive."

Swallowing hard, she didn't want to ask but she needed to know. "How so?"

"Since my teen years, I've battled bouts of sleepwalking," answered Ava. "I would wake up in crazy places, not sure how I got there."

"Once I arrived," Jaxon spoke up, "the sleepwalking intensified. Ruby took over Ava's body and transported her back to 1928 in visions."

Again, she swallowed hard to moisten her dry mouth, so she could speak. "Like a movie? A silent movie?"

Ruby laughed, and the twinkling sound lightened the mood in the room. "I wish. No, I sleepwalked. In my mind, I was having a dream. I felt everything as if it was happening to me. I wasn't in my bed when I woke. Usually, I'd find myself in some very embarrassing situations."

"Perhaps it's the necklace," declared Maddy, releasing her hold on JD. "Maybe this time is like a treasure hunt. In the portrait, you can see each of the General's Gems owned an expensive piece of jewelry. Isabella and Theo found Emma's emerald and diamond ring. Ava and Jaxon uncovered Ruby's diamond and ruby head band." She turned to Ava and Isabella. "Do either of you have Amethyst's necklace?"

The sisters shook their heads.

"See!" Her eyes gleamed with excitement. "It's a treasure hunt."

Theo spoke up. "Calm down Maddy," he warned. "I don't want you tearing through hotel rooms or digging up the bushes hunting for Amethyst's lost necklace."

Burrowing herself further down into the couch, the teen crossed her arms and buried her chin into her chest. "Fun sucker," she muttered under her breath.

Milt spoke up, "What does all that have to do with my little girl?"

JD rose and examined the painting. It was exquisite. Deserved to hang in a museum, instead of in an office. She admired the delicate handling of light and shadows. The subtle, yet skilled, use of colors that blended together and brought the three sisters to life. All the proportions were on target and balanced. The details were exact, down to each freckle and the fine hairs tickling the neck of the subjects. The painting was a labor of love. Each stroke of the brush cast with care. Lightly, she traced the pads of her fingers across the artist's signature. Everett Fairbanks. The husband of Amethyst. "So," she whispered, "your name was Amethyst and not Bitch. Who knew?"

Her father's question hung in the air. Jaw set, she stubbornly lifted her chin. "I don't know, but I'm going to find out."

She paused and gazed at the portrait. Isabella and Ava had endured similar hauntings to hers. Except, they had each other to lean on. A glimmer of hope filled her. Perhaps it was time. Time she tested the waters and let these two women have a glimpse at her inner most secrets. Perhaps they held the key to escaping the Woman's presence.

Taking a deep breath, she found courage that she didn't realize she possessed and bared her soul to the strangers in the room. Her voice was low, but steady. "Since I could pick up a pencil, I drew pictures of this hotel, as did my mother. I dreamed of this hotel that you call Twin Springs." Bending down, she pulled the folded-up piece of notebook paper from her boot and smoothed it out for everyone to see.

Shocked gasps filled the room. Jumping up, Maddy snatched the paper from her hands in order to get a better look. "It's Twin Springs!" she declared, handing the paper to Ava to be passed around.

Their excitement built within JD. A clue. The painting was a clue to find out where she'd come from. Where her mother had come from. Why her mother had possessed a desperate need to locate the place where she belonged. Such a strong, tangible pull that she had searched for a spot to call home, even though she never understood what a home was. "My mother drew that picture the day she died. It was only one of many though. Repeatedly, she drew different pictures of this brick building. All from different views and times of the year. I added the extra details around the hotel."

She watched her most prized possession traveling from hand to hand. She must find out how she was tied to this old hotel and Amethyst in the portrait. If she discovered the connection, then perhaps the Woman would stop haunting her. And she wouldn't go crazy just like her mom. She gazed up at the portrait and into the eyes of the Woman she hated since, well, forever. Determination joined the hope that grew within her. The fact that her face was a carbon copy of the Woman in the portrait was her first good clue. Wasn't that what she did? Her specialty? She tracked down leads to discover the truth. She wouldn't fail, no matter what. Perhaps then, she'd finally be free.

The thought of living a life without the Woman propelled her forward. "Walking into Twin springs, I already knew this office belonged to a man called the General." Her voice gained in strength. "I dreamt it. Because of my dreams, I know things I shouldn't about a hotel that I've never read about or set eyes on before in my life. Such as, the General's wife was a slightly different version of you, Isabella, and obviously of Emma. All three of you were tiny women. There is a short cut to the hot springs through a hall that runs directly under the Grand Lobby. Tea Time is served promptly every day at four."

Identifying Theo as the leader of the group, she spoke to him directly. "I don't understand why or how I know all this, but I do. With your permission, I'd like to stay and find out. For me, the treasure is much greater than jewelry. The treasure is knowledge." *And freedom. Freedom from the Woman.*

Theo nodded. "I realize you'll pursue those answers with or without my permission. But I appreciate you giving me a choice. By all means, you're welcome."

The Geezers grunted with satisfaction.

Theo headed them off before they asked. "As are the rest of your family. We'll have rooms set aside for as long as you need. Not only to help you find your answers, but also because you are now family. Even though Ava and Jaxon are engaged, your connection to the family was well established a century ago. Your family's heritage is connected to Twin Springs through Ruby's connection to Guy Wolfe."

Theo continued, the glint within his gaze hardening. "But let me lay down the rules while you are visiting Twin Springs. This is a place of business and our home. As such, I expect you to conduct yourselves properly. We do not use four letter words in the Grand Lobby. We watch our language around the ladies. And," his gaze swiveled to the older two men, "we speak at a normal level."

JD didn't give a damn about his rules. Only her mission.

Logan listened as Theo read the Wolfe family the riot act. He removed a baseball cap from the back pocket of his jeans and placed it on his head, pulling it down low over his burned face. He jerked open the door and addressed the room. "I don't want any part of your so-called treasure hunt."

Firmly, he slammed the door in their surprised faces. But he couldn't so easily shut away the part of his mind that recalled JD's creamy skin. Velvety smooth beneath his palms. Her soft curves as he held her in his arms. And her scent. The sweet perfume of lavender. It fueled his lungs better than air, blew heat into the cinders of his heart and ignited the ashes.

He dragged the brim of his cap down further as two young girls zoomed past him. Ice skates hung from their shoulders. Happily, they chattered to each other. "Close call." Neither noticed the monster before them. "Almost didn't cover my face in time," he mumbled. What would the Geezers have said if they'd started screaming? "Chicks dig scars. JD sure as hell didn't. Could hardly stand the sight of me."

He gnashed his teeth. A growl built deep in his chest, where his heart used to lay. Who was he fooling? Just himself. "No woman wants an ugly ass beast in her bed."

He picked up his pace down the Grand Lobby, past the area that he'd recently finished renovating into Still Waters Bar & Grill, behind a gigantic Christmas tree and into the east wing of the hotel. Instead of ducking behind the white barriers and into the Tower's belly, he passed the roped off area that declared 'Excuse Our Mess.' He went directly across the hall and through a nondescript white door that lead up through the wing's four floors and to the newly created upper portions of the Tower.

He skipped the elevator and climbed the stairs. Pain shot up his right leg and into his hip. He welcomed it. Each agonizing step reminded him of why he needed to keep his distance. Not just from the living, but from the flesh and blood version of the woman he loved and longed for.

Loving a woman in a hundred-year-old portrait was safe. JD wasn't. Getting close to her and flirting with the fire of her rejection, that was something a burnt man would never do. Mind made up, he decided to stick to the shadows and keep a wide distance. His voice echoed eerily within the empty stairwell. "I'll fulfill my promise to finish the Tower." His boots thudded against another steel tread. "For Theo's and Isabella's New Year's Eve wedding. Then I'll retreat back to my forest." He paused at the threshold of the Tower Restaurant. "Where I belong."

CHAPTER FIFTEEN

"*J* can't believe you dreamt of Twin Springs!" Maddy double stepped to keep up with JD's long stride. "I had hoped that one of the General's Gems would appear to me. Just like they did with Isabella and Ava at my age."

JD pulled her thoughts from the burned man, who with a slam of a door, had declared his thoughts on Maddy's quest to find the Woman's jewels. Even harder, she dragged her thoughts away from the haunted look in Logan's gorgeous, sky-blue eyes and the hunger that emanated from them.

Glancing around the Grand Lobby, JD shrugged into her leather jacket without missing a step. She couldn't help but compare the reality before her to her dreams. Ivy wallpaper no longer lined the back wall, but the Bellhops Stand was still in the same place. A huge, fat Christmas tree stood exactly where the General liked it. Somehow, she knew the General would freak over a bar in his Grand Lobby.

JD spied the heavily pregnant black and white version of the Woman. Refusing to acknowledge her presence, she watched Amethyst from the corner of her eye. Her monochrome figure stood eerily out against the multi colored background of lobby.

The General's daughter in the portrait, JD now knew as Ruby, sashayed up to the Woman. She observed Ruby powdering her face in a compact before bending down, lightly grasping Amethyst's gigantic belly by the sides and shouting silent words at the mound. She placed a kiss on her sister's large stomach. Lifting her face, Ruby laughed up at her sister.

Averting her gaze, JD addressed the young teen walking beside her in the real world. "Be careful what you ask for."

"What do you mean?" Tilting her head to the side, the teen's silver gaze sharpened to an uncanny resemblance of her brother's.

Hmm, mused JD, used to working with children. *Better be careful with this one. She's quick.*

She searched for a topic sure to pull Maddy away from her current train of thought. Spreading a wide smile across her face, she raised her voice an octave and imitated a teen's excitement, "I love your shoes."

Swelling with pride, Maddy glanced down at the straps of gold with spiked heels. "Aren't they awesome?" Glancing over to JD's boot clad legs, she contemplated the soft black leather and thick, comfortable heel. "I like your boots, too."

"They get the job done." JD leaned against the Front Desk counter and trailed her fingertips along the granite surface. *I wonder why they replaced the white marble top.*

A girl working at the counter glanced up. Not quite Maddy's age, her hair was home dyed to a midnight black, showing glimpses of silver blonde roots, that contrasted with her milky complexion. Weariness prematurely wrinkled the youthful skin at the corners of her unusual turquoise eyes. Dark circles curved under her eyes and a good wind could've knocked over her rail thin frame. With JD's scrutiny, the young girl's smile faltered, but she rallied and plastered it back on her face. "Welcome to Twin Springs Hotel and Spa. Checking in?"

Maddy grinned and her dimples twinkled her amusement.

"Diana, this is Jaxon's sister, JD. I know, I know she resembles the woman in the painting in Ava's office." She rolled her eyes and patted JD's hand. "You're going to get a lot of strange looks because of the resemblance." She leaned forward towards Diana. "We'll need to comp three rooms for her party. Place them in the east wing near the rest of the family's rooms."

Absentmindedly, she thrummed her fingers on the counter and listened as the teen handled her check in. *They hire them young here.*

The teenager's attention swiveled from Diana to her. "Do you think your father and uncle want connecting rooms?"

"Might as well, the Geezers will be back and forth between each other's rooms anyway. It'll cut down on traffic in the hall."

"If you want, I'll take the keys to them. And once they've finished playing with Ace, I'll show them to their rooms," offered Maddy.

Distracted, JD's gaze swept over Diana's attire. Black skirt, white starched shirt. Something was off. She could sense it. Smell the fear.

The girl's clothes gave nothing away. Not the usual attire that a teenager would wear, but Maddy's outfit didn't match her age either. Besides, it was her uniform. Her nails though, they were bitten down to the quick. Focused on the fidgeting girl, she replied, "I'm sure they'll appreciate it. Thanks."

A little boy dashed up to the counter and distracted the young Diana.

JD glanced down at the boy. He struggled to contain his energy enough to wait his turn behind her. Dressed for the pool, his still damp, baggy swim shorts reached down past his pale, knobby knees. Superhero figures hung out of the elastic waistband of his trunks. She assumed more toys were shoved into the already full navy-blue backpack, monogramed with double M's in bright red, that weighed down his shoulders.

Her gaze zeroed in. She gauged his age to be between six and eight. Glancing behind him, no mother or father was hovering in the background. Nothing pissed her off more than negligent parents. JD decided to tease the little guy. "Nice dolls."

The boy's head whipped up and his eyes narrowed, piercing her with their green-blue intensity. The wet locks of his white-blond hair stuck to his chubby cheeks and neck. "They're action figures," he sneered back. "Superheroes."

Crouching down in front of the little guy, she held back a chuckle and cast him a serious smile. "Superheroes, huh. I suppose you've got Batman and Superman in there."

Rolling his eyes, the boy shifted his weight. "They're for babies. I have real superheroes, Wolfman and The Blue Flame. And," his voice lowered, "a villain. The Dark Shadow."

His tiny eyebrows crinkled, "What happened to your shirt?"

Her lips spread into a wide smile. "My Uncle Cliff threw tea on me. Saved me from the evil Woman's spell and falling into a deep, deep sleep."

His eyes wide with wonder, the boy breathed out, "Cool."

High pitched and tight, Diana's voice rippled down to them. "Bruce, your mom said to wait here for her while she ran up to your room." Her confident smile wavered as she addressed JD, "I have your room ready. Here's a map of the property."

"Don't worry about a map." Maddy looked knowingly over at JD. "She doesn't need one. Besides, I'll walk with her."

Taking her time as she rose out of her crouch position, JD's gaze flickered back and forth between the boy and Diana. She froze. Just for a millisecond. Something was off. She sensed it. Taking the credit card sized key from Diana, she slipped her room key into her boot with a flick of her fingers.

Covertly, she scanned the area behind Diana and honed in on a torn, dirty black backpack that was bursting at the seams. The tip of an action figure's foot poked out from the side pocket.

Her mind drew the pieces of the puzzle together. Young girl. Too young to be working. A nondescript black backpack. At reach and on the ready. Young boy. No parents. Also, with a backpack at the ready. Both children with matching turquoise eyes. Connecting the pieces together, her heart sped up and she knew. *Runaways.*

Keeping her eyes from meeting the young girl's, in case she bolted, she smiled brightly and replied, "Thank you."

Reaching down, she mussed the young boy's hair, "Have fun swimming with your superheroes."

"Your room is this way," directed Maddy. "But I guess you knew that. Or did you?" she asked, tilting her head.

Not willing to explain to the teen how little she knew or even understood about her new reality, she answered, "Don't worry about me. I'll find it."

An odd clicking noise sounded behind her. Turning, JD bumped into a solid chest and was grasped by two firm hands.

"Excuse me," a man muttered.

"Dr. Ottoman," exclaimed Maddy. "You look great. Rest and relaxation at Twin Springs has done you wonders."

JD gave the tall man a once over. His flip-flops were the culprit of the odd clicking sound as they slapped against his bare feet. Dressed comfortably in exercise clothes, the man's thin neck was cushioned with a rolled up white towel that dangled down from his shoulders. His skin was chalky under the rounded collar of his blue exercise shirt. His clothes were a couple sizes too big and appeared to be straight from the packaging, due to the creases that still hung from his large, gaunt frame.

Speechless, he stared down at her. His deep, dark blue gaze swept her from head to toe, lingering on her face for long, uncomfortable moments.

The teen's head swiveled from JD to Dr. Ottoman and back.

JD felt her face warming under the stranger's intense stare and wanted to punch him in the gut for making her feel uncomfortable. Her hands balled into fists. But Theo's warning sounded in her head and she relaxed. Instead of pounding on him, she stepped back out of his embrace and extended her hand, "Dr. Ottoman."

"Pardon me," purred Maddy. "Let me introduce you two. Dr. Ottoman, this is JD Wolfe, the sister of our Security Manager. JD, this is Dr. Ottoman, a guest here at Twin Springs. He has been recuperating from..." Her voice trailed off. "What did you tell me? Oh yeah, extreme exhaustion. He's a doctor who's just returned from Africa. He helps children."

Her hand engulfed by the man's large one, JD filed the information away. She linked his unfitting outfit to a man who was used to purchasing clothes one size and hadn't yet adjusted to his new reduced form after losing a large amount of weight. His intense gaze was still scanning her features and she tugged her hand from his grasp. "Nice to meet you."

Taking the end of the towel, he mopped a sheen of sweat from his brow. "Please, call me Clay," he replied, his voice a low, deep whisper. He continued wiping sweat from his short, cropped, blond hair. "Forgive me, perhaps my time at the spa and my walk around the hotel was not such a good idea. Too soon. Are you visiting Twin Springs for pleasure or work?"

Unwilling to share her situation with anyone, she answered, "Just visiting with family."

An uninhibited explosion of loud voices interrupted them as the Geezers exited the General's Office. Bemused, JD watched her father and Uncle Cliff mess with the staunch Theo before slapping him good naturedly on the back.

Even straight-laced Theo was no match for her Geezers. "I guess they're done playing with the bird," she muttered to Maddy.

She shared a smile with the sick man. "That's my family. You might want to keep your distance. They can be overwhelming."

She turned towards Maddy. The teen gaped at the Geezers

joking and ribbing her big brother. She patted the younger girl on the shoulder. Laughter laced her words, "Go save your brother. Take the Geezers their keys. Show them around Twin Springs. Perhaps your tour will wear my father and Uncle Cliff out a little. Think of them as two rambunctious toddlers and you'll be fine."

"Okay. Two toddlers," Maddy's voice whooshed out. "Two toddlers high on sugar!" She rushed over to the men.

Chuckling under his breath, Clay quietly replied, "Looks like they're a handful."

Her lips spread into a wide smile. "Yeah, but they're mine. It was nice meeting you, Doctor. Hopefully, we won't need your services due to my family."

"What? I'm sorry, I missed what you said. When you smile, your face lights up. Something about helping your family if needed?"

Uncomfortable, she shifted her weight. Her hands curled again into fists but she refused to beat up an ill man.

Placing his hand over his heart, he begged forgiveness. "So sorry. Now, your face is bright red. I've embarrassed you."

JD unclenched her hands and rubbed her palms on her black jeans. In her peripheral vision, she kept a watch on Diana. The girl had leaned over the counter and was whispering furiously to the little boy. Her turquoise gaze shifted and scanned her surroundings as they spoke. She'd rattled the girl and she wanted to bolt. Time was short.

She didn't know what the kids were running from, or running to, or why. But they were lost. Alone. She'd sniff out their secrets. They belonged to her now, were hers to protect.

He mopped at his brow with the towel. Unsteady, he swayed.

Shifting her attention back to the sick man, she braced herself to catch him in case he fell. But he steadied. "Maddy said you help children? How so?"

"I'm a pediatric doctor."

"Oh," She glanced over to the kids. "That's nice."

His gaze traveled from her to the boy and back again. "Not just that. I work with the authorities on child trafficking."

"Really," she turned her full attention back to him. "I'd love to hear more. How do you help? Do you have a line on how the trafficking is perpetrated in Africa? Do you know how that differs from in the States? Or even world wide."

The corners of his lips inched up into a smile. "I've worked all over the world with such cases. I'd be glad to fill you in. Would you like to meet for tea?"

Usually, she brushed men off, but this time she hesitated. His knowledge could help her in the future. "Sorry, I have to handle a matter right now. But another time. Sure."

"Another time," replied Clay.

She felt not only the doctor's gaze following her as she walked away through the Grand Lobby, but also another's. Diana's worried gaze bored a hole into her back.

Ducking out of view, JD leaned against a pillar next to the Christmas tree. She enjoyed how the pine scent washed out the stench of lavender around her. Already dismissing the doctor from her mind, her thoughts shifted to the children.

She'd spooked the girl. Fear had oozed from her pores and coated the air around her like a cheap perfume. Reaching down, JD dug her cell phone out of her boot, pressed quick dial and raised it to her ear.

Immediately, her cousin's gruff voice filled the line. "Leeland here."

Pinning the phone to her ear with her shoulder, she gathered her flaming red hair up into a ponytail and secured the long length with a hair tie from her wrist. "Have a case. A couple of lost kids. Runaways, I'm thinking. Female, five feet, four inches. Caucasian. Black hair, dyed. I think originally a light blonde. Blue eyes. Age thirteen to fourteen.

"Traveling with a boy. Looks like her brother. Caucasian, four foot-two. Same blond hair and blue eyes. Six to eight years. Going by the names of Diana and Bruce. The girl's scared shitless. I think I've spooked her. Time's short."

"I'm on it." The clicking of key strokes filled the line.

"Thanks. Let me know right away," she replied, already distracted by the job ahead.

"JD?" Lee's voice was unusually sweet. Soft.

Distracted by her surveillance of the kids, she mumbled, "Yeah? That's all I have."

"No, that's not all!" shouted Lee over the phone. "Can you explain to me why the hell I came home last night to a damn dog in my kitchen?"

"A dog?" she questioned. Damn, she'd forgotten about dumping the Great Dane before she'd left.

His voice erupted with anger across the line. "Yep, a fucking huge dog."

She held her cellphone away from her ear, as his voice exploded over the line. Forcing a half smile at the guests whose heads turned towards the sound of Lee's voice shouting, she replied using a fake happy voice, "A big one, huh?"

"Yes, JD." His voice returned to the deadly soft tone. "One huge dog, ugly as shit, sleeping in the middle of my bed."

She snuck a glance back over her shoulder, to the Front Desk. Clay was speaking with Diana and keeping her attention occupied. "I'm on a job. Man up Lee. Take care of the mutt. Feed him, take him to the vet and I'll figure out what to do with him when I get home."

Lee spoke slow. Deliberate. His words pierced the line with his anger. "I. Don't. Like. Dogs," he spit out the words one bite at a time. "Have you forgotten? I sure as hell don't like them sleeping in my bed. The damn thing wouldn't move. Had to sleep on the couch."

"Shit," she whispered under her breath, when she remembered. The Geezer's wives were at the beach. That meant Lee had to care for the dog. Damn it, she never would've forced him to care for a dog. Not since the small dog had attacked him when they were kids. Had bitten him in the crotch and down the inside of his legs. The silver and purple scars were still visible.

Shifting her weight, she stared down at her feet and a sensation of guilt crept up her spine. She cleared her throat. Opened her mouth to apologize. But the safety of the kids was more important than Lee's fear of dogs.

She shook off the unpleasant feeling and replied, "For God's sake. Grow a pair. Put on a cup if you have to but take care of the dog until I return. I'm dealing with Jax, runaway kids and the Geezers. You can handle one damn dog. He can barely stand anyway."

She paced and considered the situation. "Or if you want, I can send the Geezers home to dog sit. Just waiting for you to come home every night until my job's done. You guys can bond. Watch the History channel together."

The line grew quiet. "Fine," he growled. "Finish the damn job ASAP. I'll get your intel. But you get the hell home and take your damn dog."

Knowing better than to laugh at a man when he was down, she replied, "Wilco," and pressed End on her phone. Slipping her phone back into her right boot, she studied the two kids and the doctor at the Front Desk of the building that had haunted her since birth.

Maybe finding Twin Springs was an opportunity for a new life. A life without the Woman, without the dreams of a time gone by. A life she could finally control and mold to her needs. Perhaps Maddy was right. The Woman wanted her jewelry found.

Rage boiled within her at the thought of her mom's fragile mental state that had ultimately been destroyed because of the Woman's constant haunting. Was it all over some stupid, sparkly necklace?

She added the new mission to her list of jobs. All she needed to do was find the damn necklace. Then, she'd be free. Unshackled from the Woman and released from the dreams. She again glanced back at Doctor Clay Ottoman. Maybe even free enough to give a soft-spoken man a chance. He'd be safer than the beast whom burned her with his gaze and tugged at her heart with his need.

CHAPTER SIXTEEN

*H*er heart throbbing in her throat, Parker Reinhard glanced at JD talking on the phone. "She knows," she whispered to her little brother. "I have no idea how she figured out our secret but the redhead over there knows." She pointed across the Grand Lobby.

Colton glanced over. "No way. She just likes superheroes."

A form shifted in the peripheral of her vision. Dr. Ottoman. She'd forgotten that he still stood at the Front Desk. Relief flooded Parker, seeing the doctor's back was turned towards her instead of his steady gaze. It seemed JD had also distracted him. She cast a concealed glare at the redhead before the guest turned. Parker stuck her receptionist smile on her face and regained her position at the Front Desk, "Dr. Ottoman, may I assist you further?"

The moments stretched out as the doctor stared at JD. Watching her little brother fidgeting, Parker tried again to gain the attention of the tall, thin man. "Dr. Ottoman?"

The doctor tore his gaze from her new nemesis and Parker was a little amused despite herself.

"I think you can." His midnight blue eyes narrowed thoughtfully. "How much advance notice would you need to book me a private table for two in the Tasting Room."

Her eyes flittered between the doctor and JD. Speaking with her professional adult voice, she replied, "If it's not already booked, only a couple hours."

Using his towel, the doctor mopped up beads of sweat from his forehead. "Good to know. I'll give you a ring when I'm ready."

The unsure gleam in his gaze reminded her of Colton. Touched, she smiled, "That would be great. Consider it done."

She watched him walk away. Once the elevator doors shut behind him, she glanced over to make sure that her brother hadn't run off to play.

No one had realized that the small boy shuffling his feet in front of the reception desk was her little brother. Until now.

Parker shook her head, then waved him over and whispered, "She's connected the dots. Somehow she knows we're together." She leaned further over the desk. "Worse, she's the Security Manager's sister!"

She itched to grab her brother, her backpack, and run. Instead, she glared at the redhead. "Why did she come here? Things were going so well."

For the past eight months she'd worked at Twin Springs. Under the name of Diana, she'd started working in the kitchens. Head Chef Dubois hadn't cared about her background. He had his own secrets to hide.

Resentment burned in her belly. "I didn't volunteer for every position available, work my way from the kitchen, to maid service and finally to the Front Desk for her to ruin it all."

Her brother's gaze lit up. His voice rose with excitement. "Let's go back to living in the attics! It was cool up there. Fun."

"Shush!" She considered the idea. "The problem with living in the attics is sneaking the food up and not getting caught using the showers in the locker rooms."

"Awe," whined Colton. "We can do it. I'm super-fast."

"Twin Springs is the perfect hiding spot, remote in the mountains. I didn't think anyone would find us here. It gives us everything we need." She rubbed her temples.

"I thought I had it all worked out." Working at the Front Desk enabled her to slip Colton passes to the different amenities the hotel offered. During the summer, while she worked, her brother had swum, attended fishing and hawking lessons, played video games in the Arcade, and watched movies in the Theatre.

As the leaves fell from the trees and the mountain air cooled and then froze, Parker would keep her brother busy with the indoor spring fed pool, ice skating, and ski lessons. The ideal spot for two runaway siblings to hide.

"There are even kids here for you to play with." Friends, whose parents were not around long enough to ask questions. "Most of all Twin Springs is safe. Was safe. Perfect until the nosey redhead checked in." Her eyes stung with unshed tears as visions of her brother being ripped from her played in her head. "She ruined everything!" She smacked her fist onto the counter. "No!"

Horrified that she might've drawn attention to them, she lowered her voice. "As long as I can keep my job at the Front Desk, I can move us from hotel room to hotel room. Hopefully, I can keep us one step ahead of the Night Auditor. And her. Or we'll have to leave."

"I don't want to leave Twin Springs," he cried. "I like sneaking into the hot springs late at night."

Hatred built up within her and she scowled at JD. "I don't want to leave either," she mumbled. "When we had a real family, Twin Springs was my favorite place to vacation. It's full of wonderful memories."

Sometimes, if she tried hard enough, she could pretend she was still part of a true family. Daydream into a world where her mom and dad were still alive, and they were vacationing. Dad would order a tree for their suite or slip a small package under the enormous tree in the Grand Lobby. Just like he used to. Or her parents would sit at the fire pit and wave to her and her brother as they ice skated. Or laugh when she swooshed a spray of ice shavings into her brother's face. "Memories of Mom and Dad."

But those were stolen memories and daydreams. Real life was no place for fairy tales. She shook her head. "Look, no matter how much we want things to be as they were when our parents were alive, they won't be. Not ever. Nothing will ever be the same again. We can't let anyone find us. They can't guess you're my brother. Understand?"

Colton nodded, his gaze serious. "I'll keep quiet. Even if they hold my feet over burning coals, I won't tell. Even if they—"

She ignored his ramblings and continued reasoning out the best places to hide. "Perhaps we could live in the abandoned hotel down by the train station." She stepped back and brushed her backpack with her foot. Just to make sure it was still there. The old white building with its lacy trim along the arched rooflines, and cone shaped turret jutting up one side, could be an alternative to Twin Springs. Looked like no one had stepped foot within its peeling facade for decades. "That might work."

Her brother made a swooshing sound and smashed his fist into the palm of his other hand. "—Even if they try to smash me with a chandelier. Even—"

But at Twin Springs, they were safe. The Grand Dame watched over her and her brother. She liked working with Isabella in the kitchens and at the Front Desk with Theo and Ava. Yes, she even enjoyed working with crazy Maddy. Her gaze washed over the older girl, coveting her beautiful clothes and easy confidence while working with guests. Maddy owned everything Parker had lost. Theo and Isabella would be her parents, she dated, kissed boys, and went to school.

"—Even if they burn my body like the Blue Flame—" Colton rubbed his hand down the right side of his face.

Never in a million years would Parker have considered she'd miss school. But she did. She missed the thrill of wearing a brand-new outfit on the first day. The butterflies in her stomach when a boy stopped by her locker and flirted with her. This would've been her freshman year. The loss tied her stomach up into knots.

She'd never graduate from high school or go to college, like Maddy. But her little brother would. She'd make sure of it.

She'd never be a regular, teenage girl again. Her aunt had stolen that when she became their legal guardian after her parents died. Loss threaded her voice with a husky tone. "If they find out, then they'll send us back. To her."

Her brother's mouth fell open. He pulled one of his action figures from his swim trunks and squeezed it hard within his fist. "I don't like her."

Thinking, he chewed on his lower lip. "What about the cops?"

"We tried that. Remember?" She'd learned an important lesson. "At first, they nodded their heads and patted the back of my hand." Remembering, she chewed on her lip. "I thought they were going to save us." She shook her head. "But then they looked at each other knowingly over my head and one left the room. They had pretended to be nice. Gave me a soda and a candy bar. But then *she* walked in with her fake tears. That's when I realized the police had ratted on us and we couldn't trust anyone."

"I wish you'd used your truth lasso on her. Then she'd tell them what happened."

Parker shook her head. Her brother hid his pain within a fantasy world where superheroes saved the day. She pressed down the urge to yell at him and tell him to stop with his dumb stories.

Going quiet like his sister, Colton hugged his superhero. "She was really mad."

Pissed was more like it, she thought, reliving the painful lesson her and her boyfriend had inflicted upon her back side. "Yeah."

"She locked you in your room for a full week."

"Yeah." Parker swallowed back the remembered taste of fear that she'd lived with for seven full days and nights. Not knowing if her brother was alright or not. Her aunt yelling at her, threatening to take her brother from her if she didn't behave. Then she'd send in her boyfriend and punishment under his hands had almost broken her. She made sure her brother never saw the bruises.

Parker had no choice, her and her brother's lives depended on her keeping them safe and hidden from their aunt. "We had to run."

He puffed out his chest. "I'll protect you."

She gave his scrawny, little boy body a meaningful look. "What about her boyfriend?"

"The Crusher," he whispered under his breath and glanced around. A tremor of fear rolled through his body.

She felt terrible and wanted to chew back the words. Only the fear of being caught prevented her from rushing around the counter to hug him. She searched for something to say to reassure him. Anything. "I'll use my powers over the weather and electrocute him with a lightning bolt."

He rolled his eyes, "That's Storm. You don't have that superpower." He gnawed on his lower lip. "Maybe Wolfeman or the Blue Flame can help us."

She leaned over the counter and ruffled his hair. Normalcy, that's what they needed. To pretend life was normal. "How about we sneak into the Main Dining Room late tonight. Have a family dinner."

Head tilted to the side, he considered the idea. "With a seat for Mom and Dad too?"

Her heart wrenched. "Of course." Swallowing hard, she forced words from her clogged throat. "I'll sneak some leftovers from the kitchens."

She pulled a pass out from behind the counter and handed it to him. "Good for an hour of games in the Arcade. Go. Have fun."

He snatched the ticket. "Cool."

He rushed through the Lobby and past the redhead, but JD seemed distracted, yelling into her phone.

Parker adjusted the maps and folios behind the counter. She just needed to come up with a story, a great excuse for why the little blond boy kept stopping by the Front Desk for assistance, until JD left.

She'd realized their living at Twin Springs wouldn't last forever but she'd hoped it would last until she saved enough money and they could find another place. A place of their own.

Four years. It seemed like a lifetime, but it was all she needed. Then she'd be an adult, and no one could take her brother from her. "Perhaps everything will be okay."

Pinning back her shoulders, Parker's thin, fourteen-year-old frame accepted the burden for the responsibility, care and safety of her energy filled little brother. Even if Colton was a wild child and had a mind of his own.

There was nothing she could do but keep watch, be ready and, if necessary, grab her brother and run. The little booger was all she had left.

CHAPTER SEVENTEEN

JD enjoyed the first day of December, leaning against a pillar in the Grand Lobby and watching kids line up to sit on Santa's lap. Mrs. Clause snuggled into one of the high back, rounded chairs with a white lace cap on her head, knitting away. The enormous Christmas tree twinkled in the background. An elderly man, decked out in a black tux, played holiday tunes on a long, black piano.

"Amazing," she muttered. "How do they do it? They've pulled out all the stops and provided Twin Springs' guests a holiday season to remember. Picked a damn good Santa. Real beard and all."

She scrutinized her own outfit. Dressed head to toe in black, from the leather jacket, to the t-shirt, to her jeans. "Not quite the usual holiday attire. But we never had anything like this where I grew up."

She shrugged. "My new case is more important than my clothes."

From under her lashes, she verified that Diana was still working her shift at the Front Desk. Satisfied, she scanned the Lobby. "Damn it. Where's Bruce?"

She abandoned her post to hunt down his current location, her long legs eating up the length of the Lobby.

"JD!" Jaxon hollered, his voice resounding through the Grand Lobby. "Hold up!"

Guests' heads swiveled, and the piano man's fingers stumbled across the keys.

Matching her brother's long stride, Theo shushed him. "No shouting," he admonished.

"Sorry, I forget when I'm around my family."

Planting her boot clad feet wide, she waited for the two men. Jaxon appeared ready for anything in his black t-shirt and tan tactical pants. Theo, the epitome of a business man in a dark gray suit with a white shirt open at the collar. "What's up?"

Coming to a halt in front of her, Theo flashed a smile, showing brilliant white teeth that would've melted a lesser woman's resolve and brought her to her knees. "Jaxon just informed me that you're DiWolf."

Immediately, JD slapped her palm over the man's mouth. Lifting her hand, she hushed him and bore holes into his body with her sharp glare. She grasped him by the upper arm and dragged him into a secluded seating area in front of one of the many large fireplaces. The fire warming her back, she scanned the immediate area. Her panicked gaze searched for someone who'd heard Theo's declaration. "I swear, men are worse than women. Can't keep a secret to save your ass, Jaxon."

"What the hell are you talking about?" At her glare, he raised his hands, fingers splayed in surrender and defense against her anger. "You agreed to host an art show and auction to help bring an influx of business to Twin Springs."

"Shit, shit, shit. I forgot about your meet and greet." She shuddered and rubbed her eyes with her fists. She'd have to come to grips with the vulnerability of people connecting her with her art. With a deep sigh, she wiped her palms on the front of her jeans. "Yeah, I said I'd do it. I've already asked Lee to ship my pieces."

Theo's smile deepened. He clasped her slender fingers within his grasp and brought her hand up to his lips. Frowning a little at the bruises and scrapes across her knuckles, he kissed the back of her fingers. "Thank you. My family thanks you. The Grand Dame thanks you."

Completely taken aback, a hot flush crept up her face. She just knew her freckles were standing out against her ruddy skin. Jerking her hand back, she wiped the back of her fingers off on her jeans. "Do that again and I won't," she grumbled.

Shaking his head, Jaxon mocked his sister's behavior, and muttered to his friend, "My sister's just a pretend girl. Be careful."

In the blink of an eye, JD brought her fist back and slammed it into her brother's solar plexus. "Asshole."

Jaxon buckled beneath the force of her punch. Gasping for breath, he sputtered between deep breaths, "See," and raised his hand up apologetically.

Theo grabbed them both up by the elbows. He led them past the Christmas tree, the gourmet shop called Independence Place, and around the white dividers and red velvet ropes that cordoned off a construction area. He ducked down under the ceiling to floor sheets of plastic visqueen before reading the Wolfe siblings the riot act. "We do not hit or punch each other in the Grand Lobby."

Rubbing his stomach, Jaxon chuckled. "Good to know you can still take care of yourself, sugar."

"I'll be sure to give you another lesson if you ever doubt it again." Arms crossed, she tuned out the rest of his words and glanced around the room they were renovating. Even though it was still under construction, dark wood gleamed in the light, backdropped by a wall of windows. The floor was lined with a sheeting of brown paper to protect newly laid floors. A rough table created from sawhorses draped with a painter's tarp and a plywood top was covered with blue prints. A man leaned forward poring over them. Through the windows curving across the back wall, morning sunlight streaked his blond hair with golds and bright blond highlights. JD's heart swelled within her chest. His name escaped her lips with a sigh. "Logan?"

The blond man's head rose, and her breath caught in her throat. His sky-blue gaze connected with her light green. She scanned his features, the high cheekbones, smooth planes and strong jaw. An easy, welcoming smile spread across his face, and his gaze lit up when he recognized the men behind her. "Hi Jaxon, Theo. Did you guys come to check our progress?"

Blood roared through her ears and her gaze cleared. The man before her was not only a teenager, but a snapshot of who Logan was before his last mission. A glimpse into the carefree man he would've been. Should've been. Her heart burned with pain for the beast she'd met earlier. "You're not Logan," she whispered.

Crossing the room, Theo clasped the younger man on the back. "Not today. I'm here to show the space to Jaxon's sister. She's agreed to hold an art show and auction in the Tower." He turned to introduce them. "JD, this is Sam, Logan's younger brother. Sam, this is the artist DiWolf."

Cringing at Theo again associating her with her art, she held out her hand. "Sam—"

A crash sounded behind her and she flipped around, ready to meet the threat.

Standing over a pile of boards he'd just dumped on the floor, Logan glared at her from under the brim of his grungy baseball cap. He wiped his hands off on his clothes, wearing the same band shirt and jeans that she'd seen him in for over a week. "No way in hell, are you DiWolf."

Lips curled in disgust, Logan scowled at her. Distain dripped from him and she hated it. It made her feel unworthy. Like she'd felt every time a family came to the orphanage and picked another child. *Damn him.*

For the first time, she decided to take true ownership of her artwork. *Why not? He obviously finds me lacking anyway.*

She crossed her arms and leaned back against the makeshift desk. "Sorry to burst your stinky, fangirl bubble, but I am."

Glowering at the crass excuse of a woman before him, Logan shook his head in denial. "There's no way this wanna-be-man gave birth to the poignant passion and vulnerability of the artwork of DiWolf." The art he coveted. "No way."

A breath hissed out from between JD's pursed lips. "I'll show you a wanna-be-man." Swiftly, her fist shot out, aimed for Logan's nose. But, her brother hooked an arm around her waist and the punch fell short.

Lifting his struggling sister up and away he placed her closer to the table. "Please," he whispered in her ear, "Don't give Theo an excuse to kick our family out of Twin Springs."

She stilled, gazed into his eyes and settled within his embrace. "Okay. I'll try."

He kissed her on the cheek before releasing her and raised his voice, "Believe it or not, Logan. My sister is DiWolf, the reclusive artist."

Squinting his unburnt eye until it matched the sliver of the other eye, pinned down in the corner by the scarred skin, he raked JD with his gaze. "Bullshit."

It pissed her off that he mocked her. Branded her unworthy of feelings. She sneered, "Sorry to steal your lollypop, but I'm DiWolf." An ill feeling flowed through JD when she announced the words out loud for anyone to hear. "Deal with it." She told him and herself.

"Logan," Sam warned. His hands squeezed into fists as he glared at his older brother. "Cool it."

An animalistic gleam emitted from Logan's gaze. Determinedly, he limped towards the table.

JD braced herself for his assault.

Stopping just short of bumping into her, he tossed a rectangular box of ten penny nails on the table behind her. "You're in my way," he said gruffly.

"Tough shit," she grumbled back, noticing where the molten tissue flowed under the rounded collar of his t-shirt. No man pushed her around. "Get over it."

"Actually," interjected Theo, "Maddy came up with a great idea. She thinks that the completion of the Tower would progress faster and smoother if the two of you worked together."

JD and Logan's heads swiveled to Theo.

"No way," snarled Logan.

"What?" barked JD.

"Of course, she did," muttered Logan, staring down at the second rate hologram version of the woman he'd admired from the portrait.

"It's a great idea." Jaxon added, "Come on JD. We're running out of time and you'll be a great help to Logan and his crew. You have a gift, insight into how the hotel looked in the past. With your help we can bring the Grand Dame back to her original glory. Everything rides on the Tower finishing, Theo and Isabella's wedding and an influx of funds from the art show."

Stepping back, Logan circled the table to stand beside his brother. "I don't need some foul mouth little girl helping me."

Why couldn't this asshole cut her a break? Wrath filled JD and spewed from her lips. "Fuck you."

Logan raked her body with his disgusted gaze. Displeasure bubbled within him as the dream he'd created gazing at the portrait faded further and further from the reality standing before him. "Honey, every time you open your mouth, that possibility gets lower and lower."

Raising her fists and stepping forward, JD visualized slamming the heel of her palm into Logan's nose until blood spurted all over his stupid hair band t-shirt.

Grabbing his sister by the arm, Jaxon dragged her hard against his side, muttering in her ear, "They need your help. I need your help. Don't let him get to you. Please, Diamond. "

Elbowing her brother in the side, JD hissed, "Don't call me that."

Staring at the half man before her, she tamped down her irritation. Helping Logan would permit her to search for clues to her past and allow her to keep an eye on her lost children until Lee's information came through. Perhaps she'd even find out why a stupid necklace was so important to the Woman that she'd found it necessary to follow and torment her mother, driving her to a life of drugs, poverty and death. Something that was so significant to the Woman, that she had then continued to follow the next generation. Follow JD. "Fine, I'll help him, even though he's a butt faced jerk."

Leaning over the desk, JD said, "Let me see what you've got." Reluctantly, she admired the bones of Logan's Tower. How the Tower flowed into Twin Springs until they became one. "Am I standing on the ground floor of the Tower?"

"Yep." Logan hooked his thumbs into the loops of his jeans, rocked on his heels and mocked, "I can see how well this is going to go. She doesn't even know where the hell she is."

Straightening, her green gaze flashed. "Dumb shit! The Tower wasn't originally here. It was above the kitchens."

"How did you know that?" breathed Sam.

Ignoring his brother, Logan elbowed JD over, grinding his teeth when the lavender fragrance of her hair reached his nostrils. "I know, but this location is more central to the activities within the Grand Lobby and the shops on the Promenade. The guests won't have to walk down a long hall to reach the main body of Twin Springs. The proximity to activities and the uniqueness of booking a room in one of the twelve luxury suites within the first three levels of the Tower will allow Theo to charge top dollar for the suites."

She hated to admit it but the benefits of moving the Tower made sense. JD scanned the rest of the blue prints. She approved of the design's clean lines and beauty. Picking up the long, flat pencil, she altered the exterior view of the Tower. "The top is domed, not square" she said, sketching out the changes with talented fingers. "The columns supporting the dome are arched, and a clock face is inlaid in the dome, here. Under the arch was a sitting area, with trellises, ivy, urns of flowers and a gigantic fountain in the middle."

Floored by her talent, hard reality slugged Logan in the chest. The crass woman before him and the artist whose work had touched his soul were one in the same. "Shit."

"I'm sure it's an easy fix." Her talented fingers continued on to adjust the level directly below the dome. "There were awnings here. Dark green and white stripes. This was the General's level."

"How does she know that?" asked Sam.

Ignoring his brother, Logan snatched an eraser from the table and, with his three-fingered hand, quickly erased her drawings on that level.

"Hey!" she shouted. "What the hell?"

Wiping the eraser crumbles off the prints, he plucked the pencil from her fingers. "This level is a restaurant, offering a panoramic view of the mountains surrounding Twin Springs." He flipped the blue prints to a floor plan of the level. "With its own kitchen here, a late-night menu and large dance floor. This is where your art show and the wedding will be held."

Their eyes met, anger and resentment sizzling between them, snapping in the air around them.

Theo's calm voice flowed between them, "I'm sure the two of you will work out a compromise between then and now. We're pressing to hold the art show and auction on the afternoon of December 31st. That evening will be my wedding and we'll celebrate into early morning, since it is also New Year's Eve. Do you think we're on target with that date?"

Trying to ignore the scent of the woman before him, Logan calculated the time needed in his head. "Without any unforeseen circumstances." His gaze pointedly swept JD's slender frame. "It should be fine."

"That's it." Her voice was soft. Deadly. "I'm going to beat the shit out of him and carve my initials in his ass." Growling deep in her throat, she reached down into her boot and palmed the handle of her knife. "I'll show you unforeseen circumstances."

Roaring with fake laughter, Jaxon gathered his sister up in his arms and hugged her hard. "You're so funny, sis. She's such a teaser." Leaning forward he whispered in her ear, "Be good." Bodily handing his sister over to Theo, he pushed the two of them towards the plastic covered opening. "Theo, why don't you help JD understand what you want in the Tower? I need to talk with my Army buddy for a minute."

CHAPTER EIGHTEEN

*A*rms crossed, rolling back on his heels, Logan reveled in the sight of staunch Theo wrapping his arms around JD's waist as he hustled her from the room. *Good. Piss her off. Push her away. Good game plan.*

Kicking out and shooting glares in his direction, JD gave one last snarl before dipping under the plastic visqueen divider.

"Wow! She's—She's—," stuttered Sam, his blue eyes sky wide.

"A pain in the ass," filled in Logan. But he was in awe of JD. Of her passion.

Sure, her passion had raged to kick his ass but she'd come alive. Her cheeks were flushed in her creamy skin and her eyes sparkled brighter than emeralds. And damn it, those freckles. His heart picked up and slammed in his chest. It might be worth the ass beating to have her all over him.

No, he'd build a wall around his heart. A firewall. One she could never penetrate. Mentally, he continued building the wall, one brick at a time.

Sam sighed and tucked his hands into the front pockets of his jeans. "She's awesome."

Holy crap, Logan removed his baseball cap and slapped it on his thigh before tucking it into his back pocket. Couldn't have his little brother falling in love with JD. She'd eat him alive. He snorted. "Yeah, just awesome."

He cuffed his brother on the back of the head. "Get a clue. Look past the beauty boy. She's all legs and trouble."

Slowly turning, Jaxon rubbed the back of his neck and gazed off into the distance.

Smoothing his blond hair back into place, Sam glowered at his big brother. "She's got spunk. Mom would love her."

Horror flowed over Logan's features. If his mother took JD under her wing, he'd be doomed. He reached for an excuse, any excuse, to keep the two women separated. "No way in hell will she taint Mom with her foul mouth. You hear me?"

Jaxon cleared his throat. "You know Logan, you're one of the few men I've trusted with my life. Would trust with Ava's life."

Suddenly uncomfortable, Logan shuffled items on the table. "Okay."

His voice hushed, Jaxon continued, "I understand JD can be difficult."

Letting out a sharp snicker, "Difficult," Logan jeered, "Your sister's crazy, Wolfeman."

Shaking his head, Jaxon looked up and scorched his comrade-in-arms with his gaze. "Crazy? No." His level stare pinned Logan to the spot. "Dedicated. Passionate. Driven. Protective. That's JD. There isn't another woman in the world like her."

Feeling the weight of Jaxon's intense gaze, Logan rolled his shoulders. Unwilling to let his friend's words penetrate, he placed another brick in the wall. He rolled up a blue print and sneered, "That's a relief."

Logan swore the hackles rose on the back of Jaxon's neck and his nostrils flared.

"Woody, you don't know shit about her."

Sam studied the floor.

"Let me give you the mission brief on JD." Jaxon splayed his hands on top of the plywood and leaned in.

"My parents tried for years to have another child. Mom yearned for a girl. Someone she could dress up and go shopping with. After leaving the military, Dad and Uncle Cliff decided to resurrect the family's investigative agency and Mom said she needed some balance in her world."

Jaxon paced in front of the small worktable. "After a couple of years of trying for another kid, my parents decided to adopt.

"I went with Dad to the orphanage." He stopped and raked his fingers through his black hair, rattled. "I had no idea other kids lived like that. The orphanage's director told us to go out to the courtyard within the middle of the large, cement block building and pick a girl. Kids ran wild. It was like a free for all. Imagine school recess on steroids.

"Dad and I stood at the top of a set of cement stairs and stared out at the melee. Suddenly, my father shot off down the stairs and the kids parted before his long stride. I rushed to catch up and couldn't believe what I saw. In the middle of the yard, a little girl, no more than eleven, held off a boy twice her size with a butter knife."

"Was it JD?" asked Sam.

Shocked more than he could admit, Logan hid his emotions beneath a sneer and shored up the wall around his softening heart. "Of course, she carried a knife at eleven."

Caught up in the past, Jaxon continued as if he hadn't heard either man. He thunked his Army buddy on the shoulder with the back of his hand. "You should've seen her. Her hair in braids like frickin' Pippi Longstocking, all bruises and legs. Her green eyes huge, through a mass of matted red hair around her scalp. Scraped up yellow rain boots up to her knees. The teenage boy lunged at her. Took her out at the knees. She rolled in the dirt, fighting for all she was worth. All for a raggedy spiral notebook" he held out his hand, "No bigger than my palm."

Picturing the scene, Logan felt a tug in his chest and a brick tumbled from the wall around his heart.

"The boy had scrambled to his feet and held the notebook high above her head. Just out of reach. He strutted around her with his prize. Then, I guess she'd nicked him with the knife because the game of keep away suddenly turned mean."

Logan straightened and listened intensively.

Jaxon's voice thickened with remembrance. "I'd jerked forward to help her, but Dad pulled me back by the shoulder. Told me, 'Let's see how it pans out. I think she can take him.' Together we watched, waiting for the outcome of the scuffle."

"You didn't stop them?" asked Sam.

"Negative," Jaxon replied. "A couple more times, I lunged forward to intervene, but Dad held me firm. Each time he whispered things in my ear like, 'She won't thank you for fighting her fight, son. Don't worry, we won't let her get hurt. What would happen if I fought all your fights for you at school, or with Lee? There won't always be someone there to save her. She needs to know how to protect herself.'"

He rubbed the black stubble along his jawline. "Just then, JD swiped the boy with her foot, bringing him to the floor, and he landed hard on his back. In the blink of an eye, she'd scrambled on top of him, pressed her knees into the soft skin under his upper arms and tacked him to the dirty blacktop. Her butter knife was pressed to the side of his nose. And she asked," he stopped and chuckled to himself. "She asked the teen how close he wanted his shave."

Logan laughed despite himself and the mortar holding the wall together cracked.

"Can you believe it?" Jaxon's gaze twinkled with shared amusement. "How close he wanted his shave. I heard the director's feet pounding towards us. Immediately, JD sprang to her feet and concealed her knife and notebook in her boots. Wide eyed and innocent, she stared at the director expectantly."

Logan pressed his lips into a firm line to keep from smiling at Jaxon's description.

"The director started yelling at the little girl, named Diamond, and my father moved in. Hooting with laughter, he clamped the female director on the shoulder and pronounced, 'We'll take her.'"

"Her name was Diamond?" questioned Sam, intently listening to Jaxon's story.

Nodding, he answered, "Yep, Dad told her she could keep the name, or pick another. She selected Justyne for her first name but kept Diamond for her middle. The director was so relieved we were taking the little girl off her hands, she bundled up JD, pointed to where my father should sign and bustled us out the door."

"She kept the boots?" asked Sam.

Jaxon chuckled under his breath. "I've never seen her without boots of some sort on."

Pretending he wasn't interested, Logan organized the top of the worktable. "What was in the notebook?"

Shaking his head, Jaxon replied, "It took years for her to allow me to peek into her notebook. There were drawings. When I first came to Twin Springs, it all felt so familiar to me. I knew that I'd seen this building before. It was the notebook. JD had drawn sketches of Twin Springs over and over within its pages."

Drawn in by the story, Sam moved closer to the table. "She'd been here before?"

"No. I'd asked her about the long building that she drew, and where it was. She had no idea. She just drew the vivid images in her mind."

Sam rubbed his forehead. "How can that be?"

Jaxon shrugged. "She didn't know anything about her family's history. Not even the name of her father. She couldn't seem to stop drawing. It was her outlet, I think.

"At first, her pictures were drawn in whatever medium she had access to. Usually a ball point pen or a pencil. For Christmas,

Uncle Cliff gave JD a box with little square pallets of colors. Once JD discovered watercolors, she found her true love."

"And DiWolf was born," mumbled Logan, struggling to accept the new JD before him.

"To my mother's disappointment, JD gravitated towards the men in the family. Life wasn't easy for her. She grew up playing with Lee and myself. We're a rough and tumble bunch. We play hard, but we love hard too.

"Kids used to tease her because she talked to thin air as if someone was there. Her tough demeanor scared off the other girls. Not to mention, how she dressed. Mom tried to turn her into the sweet girl she'd wanted but JD lived her life on the edge. As if the bottom could drop out at any moment. She never shared her drawings with anyone other than family."

Still rubbing the creases of worry and confusion from his forehead, Sam asked, "Then how was she discovered?"

"One summer, I entered her drawings into a contest. She was pissed. In retribution, she poured honey over me while I was sleeping and released red ants in my room."

"As a kid, I'm sure that seemed like a type of justice," murmured Sam, his face grave.

"A kid?" Jaxon grunted. "She was seventeen. I was home on leave. But it was all worth it. That contest launched her career." His eyes glazed over, "When I saw my sister's reflection in the portrait, I knew that I had found a clue to her past."

Shaking the fog from his head, he continued, "Yes, she's tougher than nails. She cusses just like the men in my family and she'll knock out a man twice her size. But she has a heart of gold. Once she sees you as part of her pack, she'll protect you with her life."

Logan squashed the yearning that churned within him to be a part of her pack. A part of her life. "Couldn't imagine being a part of her pack. She'd rip you to pieces."

Sam slugged his brother in the arm. "Quit it."

Jaxon just ignored him. "At the Agency, her skill is finding the lost. Mostly missing children, but occasionally a wife or husband that has disappeared. I don't know how she does it, but she tracks down the innocent. She takes on the cases the police have given up on. All the while never knowing where she and her mother came from. Never knowing her own heritage."

"She doesn't know anything about her family." Sam shook his head. "I couldn't imagine not knowing where you came from."

"She knew who her mom was," inserted Logan.

"Yes. Her mother died in a fire. That's how she became orphaned."

Gut punched, air hissed between Logan's lips and bricks tumbled.

"She doesn't know anything else about her lineage." Jaxon's voice grew firm with resolve. "Until now. I owe this to her. To help her find out about her past. How she connects to Twin Springs. To her doppelgänger hanging in the General's room."

He leaned forward, towards his Army buddy.

And Logan leaned back at the fire within his gaze. Deep down he knew what was coming and he knew he couldn't refuse Jaxon. The man who had saved him from fire's deadly kiss.

"I need to see her happy before I move forward with Ava. Finding out about her past is a gift I—No, we, can give my sister by allowing her to help on the Tower. If I know JD, she'll ferret out how she's connected to Twin Springs. Just like on that crumbling blacktop, she'll come out on top. She needs to heal. Damn it!" His fist impacted the plywood table and it shuddered. "Let the Grand Dame heal her."

Jaxon searched Logan's scarred face that was twisted into an unforgiving mask. "Woody, she deserves happiness. All I'm asking is for you to give her a break and put up with her helping on the Tower while she finds those answers."

"You of all people should understand," inserted Sam. His lip curled up in distain towards his older brother. "Don't be so stiff and unbending. We've put up with your grumpy ass and all your bull. Cut the girl a break. She seemed nice until your started treating her like crap."

Glaring at his Army buddy, Logan considered his limited options. But he understood not fitting in. He understood being judged by the monster on the outside. Was he guilty of treating JD just like strangers treated him? Judging her on the outside, not willing to look past her foul mouth and crass actions.

Could he work with her every day and still hope that the wall around his heart would hold? All he wanted to do was retreat back to his woods and be left alone. Hide from the world. Hide from JD because, if she breached his wall and turned away in horror, then her rejection would destroy what little resolve he had left to live in this world. Her rejection would drag him back to the dark place where screams and fire lived.

But his best friend was asking his help. He owed Jaxon his life but in payment would he lose his soul? Or worse, his heart?

The table between the men jiggled and a small tennis shoe stuck out from beneath the tarp.

Surprised, the men watched the shoe disappear back under the table. Leaning down, Jaxon snagged a foot and pulled a young boy out. He scooped up the little blond-haired boy by the nape of the neck and secured him, "Whoa, what do we have here?"

Logan glared, showing his displeasure at the kid hiding within his worksite.

"What should we do with him?" questioned Jaxon. He looked from the kid to his Army buddy and back. Then started laughing.

"What's so damn funny, Wolfeman?" Logan asked, glaring.

Lifting the boy by his blue backpack, Jaxon held him out at arm's length and firmly within his grip. The boy dangled from the straps of his backpack, clothed in swim trunks and a batman t-shirt, his feet a good three feet off the ground.

Jaxon chuckled, "Look at him. With his curly blond hair and

innocent blue eyes, he's a dead ringer for the boy angel smoking a cigarette on your Van Halen t-shirt."

Glancing between his shirt and the boy, Logan grunted with agreement. "Better not catch you smoking. Fire kills." Putting on his meanest face, he squatted down before the boy and growled.

"What are you doing in here?" questioned Sam. "This area is off limits."

"Nothin'," the boy continued to squirm for his release.

Gaining his full height, Logan advised, "Let him go. Kids explore."

As soon as his toes touched the floor, the boy spun around, stomped Jaxon's foot and high tailed it out of the room.

Watching his tough Army buddy rub his offended toes, Logan shouted after the boy, "Come in here again, and you'll have to face me."

The boy slipped under the plastic and escaped.

Still rubbing his shin, Jaxon asked, "So what do you think? Will you work with JD? Help her out?"

Logan turned and stared out the curved bay windows lining the back wall. The morning sun blinded him, but it didn't matter. All he could see was a little girl with braids. All alone. A sprinkle of freckles across her nose. And the wall around his heart crumbled. "Damn it. I'll do it."

CHAPTER NINETEEN

*B*ent over the Tower's blueprints with a colored pencil in her hand, JD sketched out changes. She glanced up when the plastic sheeting separating the room from the rest of Twin Springs lifted. Unsure how to work with Logan since their last encounter, her heart thundered in her chest. "Oh, it's you."

Ava's gorgeous laughter filled the air. "Sorry to disappoint. Who were you hoping for?"

Glancing up, JD took in how perfect Ava looked in a bright red dress that molded to her curves. She didn't even have to look down to remind herself that she was covered from head to toe in black. With a shrug of her shoulder, she averted her eyes back to the blueprints, "No one."

Placing her elbows on the makeshift table, Ava leaned over. "Maybe a doctor? I hear the two of you made quite the connection. He wants to ask you to dinner."

"Shoot me now," groaned JD. "Why are men so difficult."

Ava lifted a brow. "The doc seems pretty even keeled to me. Not that I've had a chance to really speak with him."

"Sorry, you're right. The doctor seems . . . nice."

Tucking her glossy, jet-black hair behind her ear, Ava gave a throaty laugh. "You mean safe. How boring. Where's the passion in safe?"

Afraid Ava would guess her secret, JD continued sketching out room designs for the Tower. "I'm not looking for passion. I've got better things to do right now." She ticked off a list in her head: get rid of the Woman, save two runaways, help give the new Tower some of the old Tower's splendor and avoid Logan as much as possible.

"Hmm," murmured Ava. "So, is it another man that's putting your teeth on edge?" She leaned in further and her voice lowered to a husky, conspiratorial whisper. "Maybe one with eyes the color of the ocean on a summer day?"

JD snorted. "Please." Even though she secretly agreed, she added, "I've never noticed the color of Logan's eyes."

Ava gave a roguish grin and her green gaze twinkled. "Then how did you know I was talking about Logan? He used to be quite the flirt. Made all the women's hearts go pitter patter."

JD groaned and tossed down the pencil. "Logan's a pain in my ass." She crossed her arms and dared the other woman to disagree.

The plastic parted and Logan limped into the room in a baseball cap, faded jeans and a ZZ Top band t-shirt just visible through his open work shirt. Through the windows lining the back wall, the morning's rays shone over him and lit up the displeasure on his face. "Well you're no Suzy Sunshine." He looked down at the table. Colored pictures were sketched all over his plans. "What the hell have you done to my blue prints?"

"Only what Theo told me to do." JD braced herself for a fight. "Help you make the Tower represent the Grand Dame."

"Look, just because I promised your brother that I'd put up with you, that doesn't mean you can use my blue prints like a coloring book."

"Put up with me," JD sputtered, feeling as if he'd just thrust a knife into her chest. "Bullshit. Theo told you that I had insight into how the Tower should look. You have to work with me."

"He didn't say that you could bring in your crayons and color all over my plans." He snatched the blue prints up and rolled them into a tube. "You're like working with a child."

JD hissed and looked at him through a blood red haze. "I'm going to kick your ass."

"Whoa," Ava gave a nervous laugh and raised her hands up between the two. "You're going to have to learn to get along." She turned towards Logan. "I'm surprised at you. What happened to southern hospitality? Your mama would be embarrassed to hear you right now."

"Mama's boy," muttered JD.

Ava turned. "Look, JD, this is Logan's space and we need him to finish the Tower in time for Isabella's and Theo's wedding. New Year's Eve is just around the corner. Work with him, not against him."

Shame filled JD and she hated it. "You're right. I'm here to help." How could Logan make her heart thunder with desire and her blood boil with anger, all at the same time? Besides, the last thing she wanted was to get kicked out of Twin Springs and never be free of the Woman. "Sorry I drew out my ideas on your plans. I should've used a sketch book."

Like a good southern boy, Logan touched the brim of his baseball hat with his two fingers, as if to tip his cap. "I apologize for being rude." He placed the blue prints back on the table.

"Now that wasn't that hard." Ava's lips curved into a sensual smile. "I wouldn't call Logan nice or safe," she declared.

"Thanks, Ava," Logan replied dryly.

The gorgeous superstar leaned in towards JD and whispered, "But passion? He's got that in spades."

Heat rushed to JD's face.

Logan raised his eyebrow, "Secrets don't make friends, Ava." His gaze met JD's. "Wanna share?"

"She said that—" Her mind searched for a safe answer. "You love wallpaper."

Logan snorted. "It's just dreamy," he mocked.

Her hands trembling, JD grabbed the blue prints. "Do you mind?" With his nod, she opened them. "On this level, I think the Tower rooms should have an ivory wallpaper with little tiny birds and flowers. Just like," she paused, and swallowed the words, 'it had before', before they escaped. He'd think that she was nuts again.

"You've got to be kidding me," Logan shook his head.

"I know it's girly, but it reflects the Grand Dame in her prime."

A rumble sounded in Logan's chest. "No way."

"Well, then," she paused, thinking of her other ideas. "What do you think about a fountain up on the Tower Terrace?"

"Are you nuts?"

She picked up a pencil and threw it at him.

He caught it in his hand. "Nice try, but I grew up with a little brother. Let me show you." He flipped through the blue prints. "We'd have to add additional beams into the ceiling of the Tower Restaurant to support the weight." His finger drew two lines across the diagram. "Here and here."

"Great!" Excited, she snatched the pencil back and drew in the fountain. "It will be beautiful."

He growled at her.

She growled back. "We **have** to put a fountain up there. Covered by a huge gazebo. Arched. With a clock face in the dome."

"You guys are so much fun," Ava called over her shoulder. "I love the passion. Keep it up! Can't wait to see the results." She ducked under the plastic sheeting, her laughter trailing behind her.

CHAPTER TWENTY

*W*ell into the second week of December, JD's raised voice penetrated the hushed voices within the Grand Lobby. "Logan Oakes, you get back here!"

Logan gritted his teeth. Guests' heads rose from enjoying their tea, searching for the man that the tall redhead was calling out. Him, damn it. Everyone stared at him. Fury roared in him as JD continued her fish wife antics. He couldn't do it. He couldn't do what Jaxon wanted when his hands itched to throttle his sister.

"Get your stinky ass over here and face me like a man," she bellowed, thundering forward. Her boots thudded on the lush carpet spread throughout the Grand Lobby.

Halting between two pillars, Logan rolled his shoulders and deliberately turned to face his enemy. A fiery, crimson headed wench with green eyes from the seas of hell, named Justyne Diamond Wolfe, his nemesis and his siren. "And now part of my construction crew," he grumbled.

Unwillingly, he commanded the avid attention of every guest and employee within hearing range of JD's voice. A rumble sounded within his chest. *Everyone wants to draw the monster out of his woods and torment him,* he brooded. "You want to stare at the monster?" he growled low and stepped out from the protection of the pillars. "Fine!"

The afternoon sun shone down on Logan, spotlighting him in the middle of the Grand Lobby. He whipped off his hat and turned in a slow circle allowing every eye to soak in its fill of his grotesque form.

The sun's rays shimmered off the sandy stubble in his beard and cast deep shadows within the razed skin. Baring his teeth at the indrawn breaths and the gasps of horror, he turned towards JD.

Squinting, his gaze rolled over her luscious, long hair caught up at the crown of her head and spilling down her back in a long, thick braid. Her tight, black, mock turtleneck skimmed the swell of her high breasts before nipping in at the waist of her black, form fitting jeans. Legs spread, hands on her hips and the voice of a shrew, her body called to his. Thankfully, the ringing in his ears, and her crass manners, prevented him from answering her call and crashing into the rocks at her feet.

Lifting his mutilated right hand, he beckoned her with his three remaining fingers. His blue gaze pierced the distance between them and his gravelly voice penetrated the silence. "Want to know if I'm a man? Come close little girl and find out."

Exclaims escaped the lips of the families relaxing in the Lobby. Maddy and Diana cast tight, polite smiles to the new families checking in and rushed to distract them from the scene playing out.

Exiting her office to see what the commotion was about, Ava's normally unruffled composure jolted in disbelief. She smoothed the waist of her green dress, tucked her dark hair behind her ears and slid into her role of Group Sales and Special Events Coordinator. She began soothing guests, working her way down the Lobby to the feuding couple. Her feline grace and sensual beauty captivated the crowded room and distracted the guests. When she reached JD and Logan, they were in a nose to nose standoff.

Behind a sensual smile, she hissed between clenched teeth, "Come with me. Both of you."

"No way," grumbled Logan under his breath. He stepped back, ready to bolt. "You're not trapping me in a room with her."

With an exasperated sigh, Ava curled her fingers into the sleeve of his denim jacket and prevented him from leaving. "You guys are going to work this out. Or I'll call Theo and have him deal with both of you."

Slapping his baseball cap against his leg, Logan limped down the Lobby. He waited to the side and allowed JD to pound past him and into Ava's office.

"See what you caused!" she taunted, body checking him.

He inhaled deeply as she passed and closed his eyes. His anger had absolutely no effect on her. Why was that? When just her presence, her lavender scent, rocked his world. He gritted his teeth and followed.

Ava cast a roguish grin at the audience in the Lobby. "Lovers," she gave a saucy wink and closed the door behind them.

"What?" roared Logan.

Ace squawked, flapping his wings while his eyes pinned the humans. "What," he squawked.

"Look at what you caused." JD thrust him aside and moved further into the room.

Ignoring the bird, Logan jumped back into the fight. "What I caused?" His hands opened and closed into fists at his side. "I'm not the one screeching across the Grand Lobby for all the guests to hear."

Legs spread and arms crossed, JD glared at the disfigured man before her. "I wouldn't have to yell, if you'd just—"

Her enraged words hung in the air. Out of the corner of her eye, a large man, monochrome in color, rose from behind Ava's desk. Leaning on the desk, his palms spread upon the surface, his face darkened with emotion. He addressed a materializing black and white ghost that resembled Ava. But the woman perched on the corner of his desk wasn't Ava. That beautiful raven-haired woman stood just inside the double doors.

Even without sound, JD understood that the General was mad as hell and he vented all of his anger towards his exquisite daughter, Ruby Rockwell.

Her mind raced to catch back up with her current argument with Logan. But her voice had lost its furor and she ended her sentence with a soft, "listen."

The fragrance of roses seeped into the office and Ava stiffened. Her light green gaze scanned the room. She stepped forward and captured JD's hand within hers. "You're pale. Are you okay?" she whispered.

"Listen?" exploded Logan, entangled in his own anger. He hobbled around in a circle and scowled up at the portrait.

"Can you see them?" whispered JD.

"No, but I can smell her."

"That's all I do, is listen." Mocking her, he raised his voice into a high pitched shrill. His face twisted into a bizarre, half bearded mask in his feeble, mannish attempt to imitate JD's facial patterns. "You should have the walls papered with this pattern. The floors should be this way. Damn it, you're worse than Maddy."

Ava squeezed her hand and JD felt an unusual feeling of solidarity with another woman. Even with the sideshow of the ghosts, she attempted to rally, keep track of her argument with Logan and rejoin it, but then the General grabbed Ruby by the back of the neck and rubbed her lips with a hankie and their fight riveted her attention. Silent words flew from the General's lips and Ruby stormed from the room.

She rounded on Logan. "I don't give a flying f—" Feeling the squeeze of Ava's fingers, she modified her words, "farg about what you think of me. I'm trying to do what Theo asked and return Twin Springs back to her former glory."

One eye on the General, her heart thundered in her chest. *And then, maybe, the world of the past will stop haunting me.*

A sly smile pulled at the taut skin around Logan's mouth. "Sure Diamond, let's make the Grand Dame look like an old maid. Out of date and non-relevant."

Her blood boiling, JD released Ava's hand and shot forward to rip Logan's tongue out of his mouth. Her upper lip curved up into a snarl, "Don't you ever call me that."

The General's massive fist slammed against the wood of his desk and the sound of the dead rocketed through her brain. Her forward momentum staggered. She lurched forward and then back. Her steps faltering, she came to a standstill. For the first time, the sound of the world long dead and her own reality swapped in her head. Her knees buckled and a monochrome version of herself collapsed to the floor in front of the desk.

A black and white Logan rushed over and cradled that version of herself, held her head with his palms.

But JD felt nothing. Not his hands sweeping back her hair, or his arm supporting her head. She flipped around. In horror, she watched as the wood beneath the General's fist glowed to a polished mahogany stain and the flesh covering his hand filled in with caramel freckles and a ruddy hue. Vivid coloration flowed up his tan sport coat, up his black vest and filled in the shiny brass buttons upon his chest, until color exploded through his gray tinged russet hair. Colors swept up and out from his body's massive form and filled in the world around him.

The two contradicting worlds around JD had switched. Today's world was cast into a silent, slow motion video of blacks, whites and grays. While the General's world had flooded into full, living technicolor.

This time, it was she, not the Woman, who stood as a ghost and watched as events unfolded.

CHAPTER TWENTY-ONE

"What the hell just happened?" JD's mind reeled. She stood stock still and evaluated her environment.

The General had calmed himself. Now, he shuffled his papers and shifted in his chair.

She squeezed her eyes shut, then cracked open one eye, hoping that her world would've rightened itself. But the General was still there. He removed his jacket and laid it across the back of his chair. All in color.

She glanced down at her body. She was gray, just like the Woman. "No way. I can't be. Can I?" Her body tingled and her breath came in panicked puffs. "Oh, God."

She rushed over to her other body, lying on the floor with her head cradled in Logan's arms. Her heart racing, she scrambled into position and attempted to lay down and press herself back into her own body. Nothing happened. She closed her eyes and tried again. Willed herself back into her body. Nothing.

She opened her eyes and gazed up into Logan's. So blue. So frightened. He was talking to her, but she couldn't hear him. Instead, in her panic, she spoke to him. "Will I ever be able to get back? To be with you? To touch you? To piss you off?" Bitterness laced her laugh. "I was scared of your fire. I was afraid to get burned. Sometimes I'm so stupid."

When he smoothed the fine hairs back from her face, she couldn't feel his touch. "But now I'm afraid I'll never feel your heat again."

Her heart ached with the loss. She raised her hand and laid it along his scarred cheek. "I wish I could touch you. Soothe your pain. Heal your heart.

"But now I'm no good to anyone." She stared at the ceiling. "I'm sure as hell not going to haunt you like she did me."

She sprang up and stormed over to the General. She growled deep in her throat before shouting, "I don't belong here!"

Lashing out, she push-kicked the desk but her foot went through the wood and she ended up in the middle of the General's lap, staring at him. Hastily, she backed up.

A tentative knock sounded at the door and she jumped.

The General tugged at the midnight black tails of his buttoned-up vest and the cuffs of his starched, white shirt before calling out in a deep, commanding voice, "Enter."

A man with his eyes down cast, dressed in a billowy white shirt and caramel trousers spattered with specs of paint, slipped into the room. His brown hair had been slicked back with some kind of a gel, but his bangs had escaped and dangled in front of his eyes. JD gauged him to be the same height as the General, but his athletic build appeared slight against the breadth of the General's massive shoulders.

Moving between the two men, she waved her hands before each of their faces. Filling her lungs with air, she expelled a blood curdling scream that should've rocked the walls.

Instead of acknowledging her presence, an exasperated sigh escaped the General. He slumped into his chair, propped his elbows on his desk and leaned his forehead into his palms. "What do you want Everett?"

"Hello, Everett." She addressed the brown haired, shy man in front of her. "You're the brilliant artist who created the portrait of the General's Gems." She glanced up at the wall to compare the artwork with its creator, but a large, rectangular mirror hung in the portrait's place. Surprised, her attention shifted back to the two men before her.

Flecks of paint speckled the back of his hands. Nervously, he smoothed his pencil thin, tan mustache with the tips of his fingers before replying. "Sir." He cleared his throat. "I have almost finished my surprise for Ame. I know my wife's time is nearing and I have worked around the clock to finish the painting before we gift you with your first grandchild."

Concentrating back on his papers, the General grumbled, "You know I hate the pet name that you gave my daughter. Her name is Amethyst, damn it."

Absentmindedly picking at the paint on the back of his hands, Everett peered up at his father-in-law. Behind the round, wire frames of his glasses, he blinked twice. His eyes appeared large and owl like. "Yes, sir." His voice was as gentle as his demeanor and he pushed his bangs back. "Amethyst's time is short. I hope to have her gift ready before the birth. I have left space in the portrait for you. If you could just pose for an hour or two."

Lurching up, the General roared, "An hour or two!" He plopped back down. "I don't have time to sit around for you to paint me. Unlike you, I actually have a job. Ensuring the prosperity of Twin Springs."

Eyes wide, Everett blinked and cleared his throat. "Please. Sir, your image in the portrait would mean the world to Ame." He stuttered and restarted. "I mean, Amethyst. She would love having a portrait of her family. It's my gift to her for bestowing me the honor of a child."

A panel in the wall behind JD moved and an overly slim man emerged from the darkness, his back ramrod straight and his pace clipped and rhythmic. Tall and thin, his tweed pants were bloused into tall, black polished boots. A matching tweed jacket hung from his shoulders. Beads of sweat dotted his forehead and kept his blond hair slicked back from his wide forehead. A dark shadow of evil dwelled within the blue depths of his gaze and focused intensely on the reserved man.

Unconsciously, JD stepped in front of Everett. "Who the hell are you?"

His eyebrows arched up. "Didn't you give her the gift of a child with your seed? Or is she really the man in your relationship?"

Chuckling at the man's joke, the General gestured the tall man forward with a flick of his hand. "Lieutenant Porter, explain to my son-in-law that some men actually work for a living and don't flit around playing with paints."

Scoffing, the Lieutenant removed a pristine, white handkerchief from his pocket and mopped at the sheen of sweat on his brow. Settling himself on the couch, he mocked the man before him. "Men like Everett here were born to luxury. They do not understand fighting for what you want or for those you love."

Brushing back his wayward bangs, Everett stepped forward. "Sir, may I remind you, I served my country in the Great War."

Huge guffaws emitted from the General. "You captured snapshots of the war, not the enemy. If the efforts I have perceived are of any consequence, then you were piss poor at your duties."

Keeping his voice light and calm, Everett glanced down at the floor and replied, "Sirs, many War Correspondents and Photographers went behind the front lines with the soldiers."

"Yes," smoothly replied the Lieutenant, lounging back against the leather cushions of the couch and crossing his legs. "But did you, Everett? Did you ever go within five hundred yards of the front lines?"

Everett picked at the flakes on his hands. "My post was in DC as you are already aware."

"That's right," replied the Lieutenant. The evil in his gaze glowed brighter. "Your rich family insured that you remained on this continent."

"That's enough," barked the General. His brows furrowing, his light green gaze raked the form of his son-in-law before dismissing him. "I'm not going to lounge about for your silly portrait. Get out of my office and remain out of my sight for the rest of the day."

A florid flush seeped up Everett's smooth cheeks. "Yes, sir," he replied, spinning around and exiting the room.

The words of his father-in-law accompanied Everett through the doorway. "I can't believe that while I was away fighting the war, my wife married Amethyst to a coward."

The General's fist again slammed against his desk, covering the soft click of the door latching behind Everett. "I'll be damned, if Ruby or Emerald will make such terrible matches."

"I heard the scuffle between you and Ruby all the way to my office," replied the Lieutenant.

Throwing his beefy hands in the air, the General addressed his right-hand man from the Great War. "She wants to sing. Dance. And be in the talkies on the silver screen, as she calls it. Doesn't want to marry any man." He reached into his desk and withdrew two, short, crystal shot glasses. Removing an illegal bottle of brandy, he poured two fingers for both himself and his comrade-in-arms. Leaning forward he passed a glass off. "As you know, I returned from the Great War to the Blue Ridge Mountains of Virginia to pay my respects to the widow of the bravest man I knew. Samuel Oakes."

JD observed the Lieutenant, head bent, sneer into his drink. "And purchased his family's inheritance right out from under them," he added.

His voice commanding agreement, General Rockwell amended, "And gained his widow freedom from the daily trials of running Twin Springs."

"Of course," acquiesced the Lieutenant, raising his glass in a mock salute. "Releasing the little woman from her burden. Only a genius would have seen the possibilities within this pile of bricks."

Lowering his voice, JD barely caught the Lieutenant's mumbled, "Oh, wait, that was me."

"I set up Private Oakes' widow with enough land and money for her and her two boys to farm for generations. At the same time, I give his widow not only a place to sell her wares, but I ensure that she receives top dollar. It's the least I could do for her sacrifice."

General Rockwell's chair squeaked as he inclined back, staring off into the distance. "I wish you could have been with us that day. Oakes strapped a piece of tin from a roof to the front of my vehicle. He whooped out a hillbilly yell and drove us straight into the enemy's front line." Sipping again, he gritted his teeth as the alcohol burned a path down his throat. Feeling alive at the expense of the hero he admired, General Rockwell added, "God bless Private Oakes, and God Bless the United States of America." He slammed his empty glass down on the desk.

"Oakes?" questioned JD. She glanced down at Logan. He had shrugged out of his denim jacket, rolled it up and placed it under the head of her passed out form. "You're talking about Logan's ancestor?"

The Lieutenant snuck a peek at a gold timepiece from his pocket. Half-heartedly, he repeated the General's toast, his voice sounding remote and tin within the office.

Bending forward, Rockwell refilled his glass and lifted the bottle in question towards his friend.

He waved him off.

Shrugging, General Rockwell topped off his own glass. "You know, Porter, when I moved my family to Twin Springs, along with my new son-in-law, I thought my days of fighting were over. Instead, I returned home to a war with my three girls. A conflict where the rules are fluid and ever changing. A battle front where the enemy possesses weapons that can unman a soldier and leave him bare.

"Why can't they be just like my men and follow orders? It seems the harder I push, giving them orders, the more they pull away and distance themselves from me. Amethyst, Ruby and Emerald are all I have left of my darling, soft wife." He stared down into his glass before rallying. "I must ensure their future by marrying them off to strong, wealthy men."

A slyness lit up the other man's blue eyes. "I told you that I would marry Emma."

The General shook his head. "Emerald will fall in line. She has a sweet heart, just like my dear wife. God rest her soul. Even Everett, that yellow belly of a man, loves my Amethyst and she him. It's Ruby, I must attend to."

Watching the scene play out before her, JD noticed that the General's face had flushed with anger.

"All Everett wants to do is fiddle with paint. Tell me, who is going to care for my Gems when I join my wife in heaven? Who?"

Squaring his shoulders, the Lieutenant piped up. "I will ensure they are taken care of."

The burly man shook his head, "I appreciate it, but that's not your job. I must fulfill my promise to my dear wife by ensuring all my daughters' and their heirs' futures. Somehow, I have to turn my current son-in-law into a real man. A strong husband to care for Amethyst. Make her happy. I vow," his fist pounded on the table, causing brandy to swish over the sides of his glass. "I will never allow one of my daughters to marry another man of his piss poor caliber. Damn it, those girls are my greatest accomplishment." He gazed sadly down into his drink.

JD witnessed the gigantic mountain of a man, who'd earned the Medal of Honor by fighting valiantly for his country, grumble into his drink. "I love my Gems. More than life."

"Do you? Do you really?" The Lieutenant studied the General over the rim of his glass.

Face downcast, the General nodded, watching the amber liquid twirl around in his glass as he rocked it. Suddenly, he rallied, pinning back his shoulders and lifting his chin. "Since only I know what is best for my girls and what will make them happy in the end, I need a firm plan of attack." He slammed back the last of his drink and turned the now empty glass face down on the leather desk blotter. "It's time to wage a new war on my girls."

CHAPTER TWENTY-TWO

*T*he firm rap of knuckles sounded on the General's door. "Father, may I come in?" a cultured voice requested.

The General's head swiveled from the door back to the Lieutenant. "It's Amethyst," he whispered. "Swing it back, man. I have to hide the evidence." Urgently, he motioned for his Lieutenant to bring his glass.

JD's mouth hung open. Within seconds, the General's whole demeanor had changed. Getting comfortable for the show, she plopped down onto a chair and propped her boots up on the coffee table between the two chairs and the couch.

The Lieutenant emptied his glass and handed it off.

"Up man, go, go, go." Ame's father waved his hands at the Lieutenant, motioning for him to exit back through the hidden door in the wall. Cupping his hand, General Rockwell expelled his breath in short bursts into his palm and sniffed the results.

"Damn it, man, move!" he loudly whispered and dug around in the top drawer of his desk. With a grunt of satisfaction, he popped a peppermint candy drop into his mouth.

The Lieutenant stood, tugged on the hem of his jacket, clicked his boots, gave a mock salute and marched through her inert body and Logan's head.

Logan's face was the mask of a soldier. He held her wrist, checked her pulse and turned to Ava kneeling beside him, just as the wall hissed closed behind the Lieutenant. Silent words left Logan's mouth. Ava nodded and jumped to her feet.

"Come in, darling," the General called out. His usual booming voice mumbled around the hard candy filling his mouth. Immediately, he gained his feet and waited for his daughter to enter.

JD's head swiveled towards the door. Framed in the doorway was the colored version of the Woman she'd hated as long as she could remember. Draped in a silk dress the color of lavender with pearl encrusted collar and cuffs, the Woman smiled warmly.

"Was this you?" JD's gaze narrowed, and she leapt to her feet. "Are you the reason I'm here?"

The Woman stepped into the office as a transparent Ava rushed through her form and out the door.

The sweet scent of lavender flowed around the Woman and permeated the room.

Legs wide, arms crossed, she glared at the woman who'd messed up her whole life. "What the hell are you playing at?" She swore a blue streak that should have burned the walls with her hatred. "What the hell have you done? Who will help the runaway kids?"

Resentment ate at her insides. Consumed her. Ame had everything; a home, a family that loved her, a man who put up with a boat load of shit from her father. Everything she'd never allowed JD to possess, never allowed her mother to possess. Her fist clenched. Low and deadly, she whispered, "You did this to me."

Without warning, she charged the Woman, passed through her form, out the door and staggered to a stop in the Lobby. "Damn it."

She flipped around and, out of habit, reached for the knob but only grasped air. Growling in her throat, she marched through the closed doors and back into the office. Her chest heaved. Angry tears fell from her face and disappeared once they dripped from her chin. As usual, the Woman was the one person she couldn't stop. "Take me back. NOW!"

Nothing. The Woman didn't flinch or reply. Instead, she murmured, "Father dear," and waddled over to her father.

"Father dear." Mocked JD, imitating her. She plopped down onto a chair and propped her boots up on the coffee table. "Bitch"

The General opened his arms wide, waiting for his eldest child.

She slipped into his warm embrace and his long arms reached around her massive girth for a hug.

Sniffing the air, Ame hesitated. She leaned back and smiled up at her father. "A little early, isn't it?"

Hemming and hawing, the General released her and shuffled back to his desk. "I'm not one of the ladies who read your etiquette and manner pamphlets, my dear. Been having a bit of a cough. Needed something strong to fight off a cold." He lifted his massive paw of a hand and gave a weak cough into his cupped palm. "Just a little medicine to make it through the day," he added, sitting heavily into his chair. His gaze settled anywhere but on his eldest daughter.

Her eyes crinkling at the corners, Ame's bemused smile greeted her father's anxious gaze. "You do understand that alcohol is illegal. Even here at Twin Springs."

"Stupid law," he grumbled.

Bending forward over her stomach, she straightened the ornate black phone on his desk and adjusted the leather blotter before mopping up the circle of liquid with a tissue from her sleeve. In a soft voice, she inquired, "Father, why was Everett in your office moments ago?"

Adjusting his weight in his chair, General Rockwell sighed deeply. "The man wanted me to pose for the gift he's painting you. Good God, woman. Sit? For two hours? He must be mad."

Stroking her stomach, she chuckled and moved around the room, straightening knickknacks as she went. "He does love to paint."

Her father harrumphed behind her.

Shoulders stiffening, Ame continued straightening her father's office. "Father, he is a good man and I love him."

The General bristled behind her. "I'm sure you do. It's men's business, Amethyst. Don't worry yourself."

Quickly whipping around for how massive her belly was, JD's eyes widened when the Woman marched up to her father's desk and planted her palms on the wooden surface. She leaned as far forward as her unborn child allowed.

"Anything to do with my husband is my business. He's not bold like you, he's a gentile man. A man of the arts. A man of great passions for his creations. As such, it is up to you and me to protect him. To support him in his endeavors and to accept him for who he is."

"I'm just looking out for your best interests," said the General, patting the back of his daughter's hand. "Don't stress yourself my dear. Think of your child. We need to keep my first grandson happy and healthy."

Rubbing the undersides of her belly, she leaned back and studied her father. "The way to keep your grandson happy is to treat his father with respect and courtesy. That will bring both myself and my son great happiness."

"I want what is best for you my dear. Just need to help your husband become a man. Take responsibility. After all, he might one day run Twin Springs."

Ame's laughter chimed like church bells and flowed over her father.

With the musical sound, the corner of his lips curled with joy. Emerald might have the size and coloring of his dear wife, but his Amethyst encompassed her spirit. "You laugh just like your mother."

"I know, Father," bending down she kissed him on the forehead. "I miss her too," she whispered before straightening. "Let my husband follow his passions. We all know you will live forever."

JD ground her teeth. She wanted to hate the Woman and the innocent baby she carried but, damn it, she respected her. She'd just read her father the riot act and the man loved her for it. Why didn't that work on Logan? She pushed away the errant thought.

Turning to leave, the General's relieved voice reached Ame. "I thought you were here about Ruby's temper tantrum."

Halting just shy of the door, Ame swung around to face her father.

JD noticed a ruddy hue sweeping up his neck.

"Ruby? What did you do?"

Her father's fist slammed against the desk, rattling his papers and pencils. "She refuses to marry the man I picked for her. She wants to be an actress and sing on stage." The General grumbled deep in his chest. "A Rockwell? Treading the boards? Impossible."

"I know. But she's a passionate woman, just like my husband."

Grumbling under his breath, the General reached down to grab his stash, before thinking twice and halting. "That's right, they are both women," he mumbled, rubbing his hands on his thighs.

Ignoring the hushed comment, Ame tucked stray hairs into the bun at the nape of her neck. Letting out a long sigh, she gazed heavenward. "Ruby's too much like you. That's the problem. You butt heads. I'll speak with her again."

A sly look entered her father's gaze and he surveyed his daughter. "Perhaps you are the best one to handle Ruby. My secret weapon," he softly murmured.

"No Father, I'm not your secret weapon. I'm the luckiest girl in the world. I have you as my father and," she twisted the knob, opening the door, "Everett as my husband."

While the General sputtered and coughed, pounding his chest with his fist and watching his eldest depart, in JD's real world, Ava returned with Maddy, Theo and Isabella. The women dropped to their knees around JD's inert form.

"Oh! And, Father dear," Ame paused in the doorway. Her russet hair glowed in the light seeping through the door. Giving a pointed look over her shoulder, she said, "I'll send someone in to clean your whiskey glasses before they start to stink up your drawer."

JD stood and pushed up the sleeves of her black turtle neck. "Now that I'm in your world, I'll have a better chance to find out what the hell you want." She gave a passing glance at her own grayscale body collapsed on the rug, now surrounded by all of the Twin Springs owners and Logan.

They circled her, their lips forming silent words. Logan scooped her motionless body up in his arms and gently laid her out on the couch. Each of the people in her world moved in slow motion like a silent film at quarter speed.

"Since I'm here, I might as well give you some of the hell you've given me." With a half glance back at her own world, she followed the Woman into the Grand Lobby and into the past.

CHAPTER TWENTY-THREE

ollowing Ame through the door, JD stopped dead at the opulence within the Grand Lobby. The hardwood floor glistened in the sunlight streaming through the rectangular, stained-glass windows running along the ceiling of the long room. Thick wallpaper coated the walls. Reaching out, she attempted to run her fingertips along the green leaves on the cream paper, but her gray fingers faded into the wall. "Looks like velvet."

Ame half turned, pausing as if she'd heard JD's comment, before she continued waddling at a speed walk down the Grand Lobby.

"Can you hear me?" Immense satisfaction coursed through JD's veins. A huge smile spread across her face. "That's right, bitch! Sucks to be haunted."

Soaking in her surroundings, in order to shove Logan's stupid plans for Twin Springs down his throat, she admired the thick, oriental carpets under groupings of wicker and wooden chairs. The room was alive with plants and large urns exploding with an abundance of flowers. Balancing trays on their out stretched hands, an army of servants, clad in black and white garb, attended to every need of the guests. Seated at a long, glossy black piano, a man plucked a snappy tune on the black and white ivory keys, while guests grouped around tables laughing. Some were shuffling cards or playing chess. Others sipped tea, enjoying each other's company.

She walked through a smiling group of guests garbed in furs, cloche hats and thick coats. Dressed to the hilt, all the guests seemed to adhere to an innate sense of style. Secretly, she envied the women's clothes, since her style never evolved from black on black. Jeans and leather.

Inspecting the lobby, she was taken aback by how carefree and happy everyone was. The General had created an opulent getaway in the mountains for his guests.

Gazing ahead, JD increased her pace in order to catch up to Ame. She passed between the Front Desk and the Bellhop Stand, exiting onto an enclosed patio with fountains and more ferns. Long, wicker lounge chairs were covered with pillows and ornate, iron chairs circled tables. "Damn, people liked their plants in 1928." She peered at a large fountain with baby cherubs pouring lemon scented water from tilted cups. "And their fountains."

Following Ame to the right, she entered a huge ballroom. "The Crystal Ballroom," she breathed. Men in thick cargo pants passed through her body. They scurried around, working an intricate rope system. Following the ropes with her eyes, she realized that they'd just removed a huge chandelier, dripping with crystals, from the ceiling and were replacing it with a large, black, iron version. "Damn, you're an ugly sucker," she muttered. "I guess not everyone had splendid taste in this decade."

The Woman rushed up to a man and two maids arranging roses in a massive vase. JD immediately recognized the two maids from the scene she'd observed playing out on the front steps of Twin Springs when she'd arrived. The man turned towards Ame and JD's eyes widened with shock. A crisp white shirt stretched across his wide shoulders. His black pants were bloused into tall, black boots and held up with suspenders. Even though the man's coal black hair was cut sharp to the sides of his head and slicked back from his brow, he held a stunning resemblance to her brother, Jaxon, from the strong jaw, down to the golden eyes with green flecks. She gasped in awe, "Guy Wolfe, the revenuer who'd retired and founded White Wolfe Investigations."

She studied her adopted family's ancestor. According to her brother, Guy had been undercover at Twin Springs as the General's chauffeur. She examined his wide shoulders, steady gaze, and powerful stance. "There's no way people could've mistaken this man as anything other than a man of action," she grumbled. "Unless they were just plain stupid."

Reaching the group, Ame cast a welcoming smile at Guy and the two maids. Plucking a stray red rose from the table, she clipped the end with a pair of sheers and inserted the stem into the vase. "Has anyone seen my sister?"

"Yes," said Guy, about to place a rose in an empty space. "She's in the Theatre."

"I should've known." Ame released an exasperated sigh.

"I'll fetch her for you," he volunteered, jogging off through mirrored, double doors with the rose still in his hand.

A small groan escaped from the pregnant maid's lips. Pausing in her duties, she arched her back and attempted to rub the small of her back with her fingertips.

"Betty," admonished Ame, "Why are you up on your feet? Who told you to prepare this room for tonight's Tea Dance?"

"M-M-Mrs. Ame," stuttered Betty, her bow lips curved with a little smile. "You sound just like your sister."

"Well, we need to take care of you." Ame leaned in, tucked a strand of the maid's honey brown hair behind her ear and whispered, "If you share with me who the father is, Betty, then the General and I can help you. We will make him marry you."

"Oh M-M-Mrs. Ame, I c-c-canna do that. He would not be happy if I did. But don't you w-w-worry," she patted Ame on the back of her hand. "He p-p-promises to take care of me. Make a grand Lady just like you and Ruby. He promises that we will marry, and h-h-he and I will run a gr-gr-grand hotel together. Our child will in-in-inherit everything."

The other maid carelessly tossed the last of her roses into the vase and clutched the large, wooden cross hanging from a leather string around her neck. "Don't listen to him, Betty. He speaks with a devil's forked tongue. Doesn't he Mrs. Ame? He's taking advantage of the fact that she is a sheltered mountain girl. The bible says…"

JD listened to her quote from the bible and rub the wood of her cross.

Placing her fists on her hips, Betty's skin took on a ruddy glow. "J-j-just because I st-st-stutter, doesn't mean I am slow in the h-h-head, Gabby," shouted the pregnant maid.

JD's head swiveled between the two pregnant women. One draped in luxurious purple silk with pearls at her throat and wrists. The other draped in sturdy black cotton, with white lace at the cuffs and collar. "See Ame! See how lucky you are? You have a husband and her poor child will be born into poverty."

In a full lather, Betty struggled to force the words out of her mouth as fast as her tongue could form them. "My ba-ba-baby's father is a p-p-powerful man. He j-j-just wants me to give him time to set things up right for us. I love him, and he p-p-promised to take c-c-care of me."

"Do you think you are the first of us servants to be wooed by a powerful man?" inserted Gabriella, wagging her finger at the other girl. "You might not be stupid, but you are a fool."

Now only half listening to the conversation, JD was using her hands in an attempt to measure and compare the width and depth of Ame's and Betty's baby bellies. She hooted with laughter, "Damn Ame, you're huge! You should be the one stuck in a bed."

Rubbing her ear with her fingertips, Ame tried to calm the two women. "Ladies, I want to help you. Help you both. But I need you to trust me." Pausing in her discussion with Betty and Gabriella, Ame twirled around and stared straight through JD's head.

Freezing, JD waited. "Can you really hear me?" She pumped her fist in the air and hooted. "Yes!"

After a few seconds, Ame turned back towards the servants and tried again. "Betty, tell me who the father is. Gabriella, give me the name of the man bothering you and I will speak with the General on both of your behalf's."

The sound of an angel singing flowed out of the Theatre. All movement halted within the Crystal Ballroom. Everyone, men and women combined, turned towards the mirrored doors and listened. Entranced by the melody of the song. The voice rose to a crescendo, releasing joy, beauty and piercing emotion within a single final note.

The silence felt heavy after the feelings released by the song. Broken from the trance, the flurry of activity resumed within the Crystal Ballroom. Men hauled the iron chandelier up to the ceiling. Gabriella wiped tears from her face with the corners of her white apron. "Miss Ruby's singing touches your soul."

Absentmindedly, Ame nodded in agreement. Her gazed was fixated on the Theatre doors. "Yes, she does. I wish my father felt the same way." Focusing in on the maids in front of her, she issued orders like a general, "Gabriella, I want you to make sure Betty rests. I am putting you in charge of her."

The maid huffed and crinkled the stem of the rose in her hand. "But, I'm your personal maid. The General will fire me if I am not close by for your time of need." Her other hand rubbed her cross with her distress. Gabriella argued her case with Ame. "Please, the General scares me."

Ame adjusted the small white piece of lace on Gabriella's auburn hair. "Don't you worry, I'll send Everett to fetch you when my time comes. The General will never know." She squeezed her maid's hands, before again bending in towards Betty, "Trust me, I can help you. I just need his name. My happiness depends on yours."

Silence stretched from the Theatre and drew Ame's attention. Contemplating, she rubbed her stomach. "I wonder what is taking Guy so long to fetch Ruby?" Torn between pressing her maid for information and worry over her sister, she hesitated before hurrying off towards the Theatre. In her rush to check on her sister's well-being, she left the mirrored doors propped open as she entered.

Right away, the maids began to bicker.

"You should have listened to Miss Ruby when she told you to take it easy," grumbled Gabriella. "My salary puts food on my family's table. If I get fired—" she left the threat open.

JD paused to listen to the two maids. She understood being poor. The ravenous hunger spread by the fear of not knowing where your next meal came from.

Her eyes wide and fearful, Betty clutched a rose to her bosom. "Don't worry, my man w-w-will take care of y-y-you too."

Tapping her fingers on the cross, Gabriella berated the other girl. "Don't you think I want the fine clothes, a loving husband, a real house, not a slap shanty? Do you think I want to end up like all the other mountain girls? Pregnant with seven kids before twenty-five?

"I've worked hard these past five years here at Twin Springs and where has it gotten me? Us? I make my own clothes from the Butterick patterns, but they will never be as fine as the Rockwell sisters' dresses. If I continue on the path I am on, the only softness around my neck that I will ever feel, will be from the rabbit my brother skins for me and not a fox like the Rockwell's. A powerful man also chases me. He promises me the good life but only if I do things against my God."

She lifted her gaze heavenward. "But the bible says, 'What? Know ye not that your body is the temple of the Holy Ghost which is in you, which ye have God, and ye are not your own? For ye are bought with a price: therefore, glory God in your body, and in your spirit, which are God's.' So sayeth the Lord."

Quickly, Betty crossed herself and repeated, "So sayeth the Lord."

Without pause, Gabriella continued to berate the pregnant maid. She pressed the cross between her open palms as if in prayer. "You'd better hope this man proposes or you will end up in poverty just like your mother and her mother before her.

Pinching her lips together, Betty fumed at the other woman. She quivered from head to toe and a strand of curly brown hair escaped from under her cap. "The b-b-bible also says, 'h-h-help comes to those who h-h-help themselves,'" stuttered Betty.

Squeezing her cross tight within her fist, Gabriella lowered her head. "You are such a dolt. Benjamin Franklin said that, not the bible." She stared at her pregnant friend, the glow pinned to her cheeks and the abundance of hope she exuded. "But perhaps you are right, Betty. I will pray about it. Maybe, the gentleman wooing me is my path to a better life."

Green eyes wide in her pale face, Ame rushed back out the doors of the Theatre. She spread her arms wide across the opening and announced, "No one goes in there."

The two maids surged to Ame's side. "Is M-M-Miss Ruby alright?" asked Betty.

Smoothing the fabric over her belly, Ame nodded her head. "She just needs a moment."

Curious, JD strolled straight through the gaggle of women and into the darkened Theatre. There, on stage, illuminated by bright lights stood Ruby Rockwell, the earlier version of Ava. Her silver dress shimmered and reflected the light. She was tipped back within the arms of Guy and he was busy ravishing her mouth.

"Damn, I love the 1920's." Turning to give the couple their privacy, JD noticed that Ame's human barrier hadn't lasted long. A handful of male workers, the maids, Everett and the Lieutenant were also enjoying the show on the stage.

CHAPTER TWENTY-FOUR

he Lieutenant sneered at the couple on the stage. Clapping his hands, he announced. "Everyone out and back to work."

The workers scattered at his command.

Standing behind his wife, Everett rubbed her shoulders. "Ame, Betty is exhausted, and you should also rest. Why don't the two of you go rest in the Tower?"

Her head swiveled between her husband and her sister. "But what about Ruby?"

The Lieutenant sniggered behind them. "See, Fairbanks!" he declared with glee. "Can't even command your own wife or a maid. The General's right, you're a lost cause."

Ame's gaze narrowed into an icy glare cast towards the Lieutenant. Dipping her head, she meekly replied, "You're right Everett. Betty and I could use some rest. Thank you." She kissed him on the lips, grasped Betty by the elbow, and together they waddled out the door.

Everett rounded on the Lieutenant, his hands balled into fists at his side. "My wife's and my relationship is none of your business, Porter," he stated. Dismissing the man, he turned to handle the couple on the stage.

His thin lips twisting into a sneer, the Lieutenant called after him. "Your wife thinks you are a wimp just like her father does."

JD could tell by the stiffening of Everett's shoulders and the slight pause in his step that the Lieutenant's barb had hit home. Lengthening her stride, she followed the quiet man to the stage.

The taps on the bottom of the Lieutenant's boots clicked with each of his steps and caught JD's attention as he departed. "What an annoying noise." She returned her attention back to Everett, curious how the gentle man would handle the kiss that she was sure rated the level of a major scandal in the twenties.

Skirting around the side of the stage, Everett took the small staircase two treads at a time. "Guy." He nodded to the tall man who was no longer attached to his sister-in-law's face. "Ruby, may I speak to you?"

Taking her time, Ruby powdered her lips and face with a silver compact of powder. "Nothing to talk about," she purred, painting her lips blood red before she pressing them together. Gently, she rubbed the lipstick between her full lips and then blew an air kiss towards Guy. "We were just caught up in the moment. Nothing special."

"Looked pretty damn special to me," shouted JD, lounging in one of the crushed red velvet seats. Her boot clad feet were propped up on the wrought iron seat in front of her. "Wish I had some popcorn. It's getting good."

"Guy would you excuse us?" asked Everett, pushing his round glasses back up his nose.

"Ruby?" Guy questioned. His golden gaze remained steady on the brilliant woman before him.

"Oh, how sweet, he wants to protect you, Ruby," hollered JD up at the couple on the stage. "You go, Guy! Don't kiss 'em and leave 'em."

Flipping her head back, the streaks of blue in Ruby's glossy black hair sparkled under the lights. "Gentlemen, it was just a stage kiss. Don't make more of it than it was."

Tilting his head with acknowledgment, Guy turned his back on Ruby and exited the stage.

"Ruby, you're a chicken shit," mocked JD. "That was a hell of a lot more than a stage kiss."

His hands clasped behind his back and head slightly bent, Everett watched Guy leave, until just he and Ruby stood on the stage. Once the Theatre doors closed and Everett was sure they were alone, he rounded on his wife's sister. "My God, Ruby, the General's going to get in a lather when he hears about what transpired on this stage."

Ruby's musical laughter rang out and bounced off the Theatre's pressed tin rafters. "Don't worry about the General. I can handle him."

JD noticed him studying the General's daughter before him. She could tell he was thinking hard, coming to a decision. "Get off the pot, Everett. Get out whatever's rattling around in your brain."

The tall man stepped away from his sister-in-law and stared out into the darkened Theatre. Suddenly, his shoulders drooped, and he sat down on the edge of the stage. His legs dangling over, elbows on his thighs, he held his head with his paint speckled hands. His slicked back hair fell around and forward, between his spread fingers.

Despite herself, JD felt for the man. "Damn Everett, nothing's that bad."

All the gusto drained from Ruby at the sight of her brother-in-law brought low. She settled down beside him and placed an arm around his shoulders. "It's the General, isn't it?"

"He thinks my art is a worthless occupation of a man's time."

Squeezing his shoulder, she replied, "Don't worry about him. Ame adores your artwork. Your paintings give her joy."

"In the beginning, all I wanted to do was paint the world around me and love my wife. I lost myself for hours bringing to life the pictures in my mind. Life was simple. My world revolved around palettes of color and discovering the landscape of my wife. I realize now, that isn't enough. Painting gives me joy, but Ame," he paused, swallowing hard. "She gives me life. She provides the canvas and medium necessary for me to survive. My talent as an artist is nothing compared to becoming the strong man she needs. The man she deserves."

Rubbing his face with the palms of his hands, he added, "I need your help. I'm a failure of a man. My wife's embarrassed by me. The Lieutenant and the General constantly mock me in front of her. I want Ame to be proud of me. I don't want our son to be ashamed of his father. But I have no idea how to be what they need. To be what the General wants."

"Everett, your wife loves you just the way you are. Believe me."

He pushed the frames of his glasses back up his nose. "I feel that she does. But over time, will our love be enough? Day after day, incident after incident, where she is publicly shamed by my actions. Or rather, my lack of actions. Will Ame come to resent the fact that I cannot be like the great and powerful General?"

Throwing her arms out before her, Ruby declared to the invisible audience, "The General is a horse's ass." Her voice raged, projecting harshly through the Theatre. "He pushes people into molds that they don't belong in. He tries to cast those around him into a role that he considers proper. Ignore him. I do."

"I tried that. At first the General's barbs were in private, but now, he treats me with unveiled contempt and dismisses me out of hand. In time, his powerful opinion will wear Ame down. I need to be strong like you."

Rocking backward, Ruby's infectious laughter filled the stage. "Like me? That's rich."

Everett turned towards his sister-in-law, his speech picking up in tempo to match his fervor. "I need your assistance. You're on your way to becoming an actress. Teach me how to portray myself as the man the General wants, the man my wife needs. A strong man. More outspoken, confident and outgoing." He considered her for a moment. "Aggressive."

He grasped her hands within his. "Just now, in the General's office, I tried to fight back. To defend myself, but failed miserably. I've listened to you sing on stage. You project confidence. Teach me how to project confidence."

Wrinkling her nose up, Ruby scoffed, "Confidence is a mirage. It's what is in here," she tapped on his chest, where his heart laid beneath. "It's the passion, the love, that matters. You have that in spades."

Lifting his glasses, Everett rubbed his eyes, like a little boy, with his paint splattered knuckles. "I can't fail. The General already believes that I'm half a man. A coward. The thought of Ame being embarrassed by me—" His voice broke and lowered to a husky whisper with suppressed emotion. "I realize that I'm not worthy of a woman of her caliber. If Ame also comes to believe that I am half a man," he paused, clearing his throat before continuing. "It would destroy me to lose her love, to not be the man she needs. Help me. Please. Help me to become a man my wife will be proud of."

JD regarded the quiet man, humbling himself on stage. All for the Woman. "She's not worth it, Everett," she whispered over the lump stuck in her throat. Sickened by the Woman destroying yet another person, she bounded from her seat. Her wide strides ate up the long aisle between the rows of theater seats.

CHAPTER TWENTY-FIVE

*Q*uickly, JD caught up with the two pregnant women waddling their way through the Jefferson corridor. At the end of the hall, a private elevator led directly to the Tower.

Anger pumping within her veins, JD yelled after the Woman. "You're such a fucking bitch! Ruining lives. It doesn't matter if you're alive or dead. You have a wonderful husband. All he wants to do is paint. Can't you understand that? Or are you too full of yourself to see past that huge belly you're sporting?"

Coming to a complete stop, Ame paused, canted her head, listened. Stopping beside her, the maid imitated her actions. "Do you hear anything, Betty?"

Shaking her head, more curls escaped from under Betty's lace cap. "N-n-no ma'am."

Shrugging her slender shoulders, Ame wove her arm through Betty's and continued down the hall. "I've been hearing the most irritating buzzing sound lately."

Balling her hands into fists, JD stalked after the Woman. "I'll buzz you."

Shuffling beneath the weight of her unborn child, as she

walked beside her employer, Betty glanced up at Mrs. Fairbanks from beneath her lashes. "M-M-Mrs. Ame, does your baby move a lot?"

"Oh, yes." Pleasure curled her lips. She rubbed a hard lump that might have been the baby's foot or elbow. "It seems he's constantly fighting for space within his room."

Betty softly replied, "M-m-mine is quiet. He doesn't seem to m-m-move much at all."

Ame stumbled to a halt in the middle of the hall, causing JD to plow through them.

"Can't you give some warning?" grumbled JD.

Leaning forward, Ame grasped her sister's personal maid by the shoulders. "What do you mean? Does the baby not move at all? Not late at night or early in the morning?"

Unused to the attention, nervousness hampered Betty's speech. She struggled to pass the words through. "S-s-sometimes early in the m-m-morning."

Her gaze lit with concern, Ame asked, "Do you have any idea of when your time will come?"

Casting her gaze downward, Betty replied, "I t-t-think soon. A f-f-few weeks, no more."

Ame patted the girl reassuringly, "I will speak to the General. We'll need someone by your side to call for the doctor when your time comes."

Leaning her head back, Ame rubbed her temples, thinking. "I know. We will move you and Gabriella out of the employee housing and into the old quarters for the guests' servants in the attics. We'll place her in a room next to yours in the attics."

Warming to the idea, she continued, "In fact, we will move you to the larger room at the end of the attics for this hallway. Perfect! I'll have it cleaned out right away. It is big enough for a crib and a bed. Lay down a large rug for a little guy to play on. The room has two doors, one leading to the hall where Gabriella's room will be, so she can assist you, and one leading to an elevator that comes out near the Front Desk." Ame's light green gaze glowed with ideas. "If Gabriella is next door to you, she will hear you call out in the night. Plus, you will have the convenience of using an elevator instead of the stairs."

Betty's brown eyes widened with surprise. "Th-th-thank you Mrs. Ame. You are so kind."

JD rolled her eyes. "Yeah, right. She's just a patron of generosity. To quote Logan, 'Bullshit.'"

Ame hugged the maid close, laughing as their bellies bumped. "You are a part of the Twin Springs family. Let me assist you, Betty. Tell me who the father is."

"That's right Ame, stick your nose in further. Maybe she doesn't want your help," JD grumbled. Lounging back against the wall, she reached down into her boot and drew out her knife. She practiced flipping and catching the knife by the handle while waiting for the women to stop yammering. "You'd think that with your bellies so distended and pressing all your organs up and out of the way, you wouldn't have enough air left to talk so damn much."

Twisting her hands above the mound of her stomach, Betty hesitated. Looking up and down the hall, she shuffled closer to Amethyst. "You're right M-M-Mrs. Ame. He's a rich man. A p-p-powerful one too." Her brown eyes brimmed with tears. "There are r-r-rumors that he has another lady. I've even heard that he wished to m-m-marry one of your sisters."

With her words, JD understood what was happening. Betty was scared of her lover. Instinctively, she held her knife at the ready. Betty might love him, but he scared her shitless and she felt the need to protect both the girl and unborn child.

Ame scoffed, "Who's this man that thinks the General would allow him to marry one of his Gems?"

Blanching, Betty replied, "I c-c-canna tell you, M-M-Mrs. Ame." Huge tears slipped down her cheeks. "I don't w-w-wanna raise my child alone. G-G-Gabby is right. My child will starve without a f-f-father, a f-f-family."

She wiped the tears away with the end of her apron. Her gaze earnest, she added, "B-b-but a lady l-l-like you could help me. Teach me how to be a lady. A w-w-woman of culture, like you and y-y-your sisters. Then I w-w-will become a wife he desires."

Attempting to cross her arms over her belly, Ame replied, "He sounds like a rummy. Perhaps you'll be better off having us as your family. Your son can grow and play with mine."

Sniffling, Betty wiped the back of her nose with her sleeve. "H-h-he's not a drunken bum. P-p-please, Mrs. Ame. I love him. H-h-he makes me feel s-s-special and loved. He p-p-promised to care for me, but m-m-more as a servant than a w-w-wife. But if you help me, then he w-w-will see me as a lady. If you help m-m-me talk like a lady. You speak s-s-so pretty. Not st-st-stuttering like me. Gabby is making me fine lady clothes."

Betty pressed Ame, "With your h-h-help and Gabby's clothes, people will not look at me as a servant. P-p-perhaps then he will see me as a l-l-lady and ask m-m-me to marry him. M-m-my son will be born with the protection of his name and a father. And h-h-he will be proud to have m-m-me on his arm as we walk down the Grand Lobby."

Pressing her fingertips to the bridge of her nose, Ame studied the woman before her.

Brandishing the blade of her knife, JD pushed back from the wall. "Find out who the bastard is and kick his ass. You're always snooping in other's lives!" she shouted, circling around the couple. "Betty deserves better. The child deserves better."

A swift kick under her ribs brought Ame out of her reprieve. "Certainly, I'll help you. In fact, my sister will help too. No one can control their voice better than Ruby. We will begin in the morning."

Squeezing Betty's wringing hands, Ame added with a glowing smile, "I will speak to the General right now about moving you and Gabriella to the attics on this wing. For right now, go rest in my room in the Tower."

Her gaze alight with excitement, Betty leaned over their bellies and squeezed Ame tight. "Th-th-thank you," she whispered, before twirling around and heading down the hall.

Ame watched the young woman walk away. Noticing Betty headed to the stairs she called out, "No more stairs, take the elevator. You hear me?"

"Y-y-yes ma'am," Betty answered. She doubled back and called for the Tower's private elevator.

Flipping around in the other direction, Ame speed waddled down the hall.

Stashing her knife back in her boot, JD quickly followed, easily keeping time with the muttering woman. "Didn't know you talked to yourself." Stepping up her pace, she moved in close to overhear.

"Bastard is taking advantage of women within Twin Springs. Who could he be?" Ame rubbed her temple. "Someone with enough social standing to assume the General would accept him as a son-in-law. I'll search the records for the names of guests who lodged at Twin Springs nine months ago. Compare that list with our current guests."

Reaching the opposite end of the hall, Ame called for the public elevator. Pressing her palm against the wall, she struggled over her belly to reach her shoes. Wobbling on one foot, she wrestled with the small metal buckle to loosen the bands of her t-straps. Accomplishing her goal, she sighed with relief.

Noticing the Woman's feet were swollen and off color in the tight shoes, JD swore. "Your feet are awful."

Attempting to adjust the other shoe, Ame wobbled and almost toppled over.

Lunging forward, she attempted to grab hold of the Woman and prevent her from falling, but her gray arms swiped through Ame's body. Frustrated, she hissed, "Be careful."

Righting herself, the Woman sighed, "That's much better."

"You should've listened to Everett and laid down." JD's nostrils flared. "But no, you're a selfish woman. You don't care if you endanger your child. You don't care about the consequences of your actions. You're not helping Betty out of the goodness of your heart. You're doing it because it makes you feel good. Makes you feel powerful."

Ame continued to mutter out loud, "Men are exploiting the naivete of the women under my care. Not only Betty, but also Gabby. This will stop. Even if I have to trick or threaten them, they'll tell me the names of the men taking advantage of them. Once I find out who they are, they will do the right thing by them."

She smoothed the fabric over her belly. "Father will know what to do. I don't know who this man thinks he is cavorting with the women of Twin Springs, but General Rockwell will take care of him. No one is more powerful and deadly than my father."

Stepping across the elevator's threshold with the pregnant woman, JD shouted, "Why can't you just leave people alone! Stop meddling in other's affairs."

$\mathcal{H}$alf jogging down the Grand Lobby behind Ame, JD shouted, "For a pregnant woman, you're a pain in the ass to keep up with."

Double timing it, she tried to maneuver around the guests within the Lobby. Growling deep in her throat, she muttered, "Screw this," and plowed through them. A tingling sensation traveled through her body each time.

Without knocking, the Woman flung open the door to the General's office and charged through full steam ahead.

Leisurely, JD shadowed the Woman. "Damn, she's pissed."

"Father!" Ame called out. Coming to an abrupt stop, she expelled a deep breath and deflated before JD's eyes.

"Where is he?" mumbled Ame.

To the Woman, the General's office was empty. But for JD, her world had continued to slowly play out silently in black and white. Walking over to her other self, she stared down at her body laid out upon the sofa. Her vibrant red hair was now a dark shade of gray. In her new monochrome form, her resemblance to the Woman she hated growing up was remarkable.

For a moment, she watched. Maddy sobbed in a chair,

clutching one of Isabella's handkerchiefs in her grasp and dapping at her tears. Intently, Theo spoke into his cellphone. Her beautiful, arched brows drawn, Ava kneeled next to JD's body and pressed a compress to her head.

Leaning down and touching her gray-scale forehead with her finger tips, JD felt a coldness and a pull deep in her chest, between her transparent form and her body on the couch.

Logan paced behind the couch, constantly smacking his three-finger fist against his thigh.

Isabella entered through the door with the Geezers in tow and everyone glanced up with expectant looks on their faces.

JD cringed at the worry lines creasing her father's brow. "Great, just great."

"Great, just great," repeated Ame, drawing her attention. "I'll just wait." Moving over to the couch she laid down directly on top of JD's black and white form, blending the two into one. Propping her feet up on the arm of the couch, the pregnant woman groaned and rubbed her belly with her palm. "Feels so good to be off my feet." Looking down at her baby belly, she questioned, "Don't you think?"

Lifting her hand, JD placed her palm on her own belly and felt the replying kick of the child now nestled within her transparent form. "Holy shit," exploded from her lips. "Amazing."

Jaxon exploded into the room through the same secret passageway in the wall as the Lieutenant earlier.

"Hmmm, what's in there?" She slid through the open doorway. There was a long, skinny hall lit by scones. To the right, shelves lined one side of the wall with bottle after bottle of hooch. JD murmured, "Damn General, one hell of a secret stash. Tsk, tsk. Illegal in your day."

Undecided whether to go left or right, the sound of voices pulled her left. Thick, red carpet softened her step. Sticking only her head through the wooden door at the end of the hall, she noticed men lounging in leather chairs with pipes in their mouths and newspapers spread across their laps. A din of smoke hung in the air. "The Officers Hall in the 1920's," she muttered. "Today, it's the Presidents Hall."

Quickly, she pulled her head back and walked through a door to her left. Six women sat on benches that lined the room, three on each side. In black dresses with rounded white collars, they spoke into mouth pieces that extended from the wall, holding a small black telephone receiver up to their ears that was shaped like a cone.

With polite, fake voices the women spoke into the mouth pieces, pulling and reconnecting a jumble of thick gray wires to plugs in the wall. Strained voices rose above the din of the six women speaking. Continuing forward, she passed through the wood of another door.

In a tiny room stood the Lieutenant and Gabby. Green curtains were drawn closed across a wide window on one wall, next to another door. "Must also lead to the Officers Hall."

A thick, wooden shelf ran under the window. On top sat three, small, golden machines with knobs and gears, each resting upon a mahogany box and covered by a glass dome. Ribbons of thin white paper that had been expelled from the machines covered the table and spilled over in white streams onto the floor. One of the machines started clicking and spitting out more long, white paper. "Ticker tape machines for the rich guests to check their stock portfolios," breathed JD in wonder, before the couple in the little room drew her attention back to them.

"Gabby," the Lieutenant held the maid tight, placing kisses down her throat. "Do this for me and I'll take you away from here. Leave the filth and poverty of the mountains behind."

Gabriella drew away, separating herself from the Lieutenant's grasp. "I don't think I can." Vehemently, she shook her head side to side, her lace cap falling to the side of her auburn hair. "To separate a child from his mother. A baby, no less." She raised the dark wood of her cross up to her lips and kissed it. "Please don't ask me. It goes against God's will."

"God's will? God's will?" bellowed the Lieutenant, grasping the leather chain of her cross in his hand. "Is it God's will that your mother died from pneumonia, caring for you and your eight siblings?" Deliberately winding the length of the leather around his hand, he dragged Gabriella closer and closer and lowered his voice to just above a whisper. "Is it God's will for you to be at the beck and call of the Rockwells? Serving their every whim for the piss poor wage they grant you?" He adjusted his voice, soothing her with a velvet tone. "You deserve more, Gabby. Let me give it to you. Let me take you away from all this. Save you from serving the General's spoiled girls."

He tipped her chin up, brought his face closer and closer to her until their lips were just a breath apart. "I'm not asking much. Just for you to keep an eye on Ame and when her time comes, bring the baby to me."

He nipped at her bottom lip, before soothing it with a kiss. "Then, together, we'll leave Twin Springs behind. The General will pay anything to get his precious grandchild back. We will both get what we want. You, great riches. Think about it. You'll never have to make your own clothes or bow low to serve another. While I, finally break the Great General Rockwell. I'll drain him of every penny he owns. Then, when he thinks he has paid enough to ensure the return of the future of his line, I will make sure he will never see his grandchild again."

Instinctively, JD reached down into her boot and palmed her knife. "Don't listen to him." Realizing she was powerless to help the maid, she slipped her knife back and leaned in close, placing her lips against the maid's ear as she saw the Woman do with her mother. "Tell him what he wants. Then back away and get help."

"No, I won't do it," said Gabby, straining away from the Lieutenant. "I'll tell the General."

His nostrils flared and his face twisted into a mask of anger.

With a flick of his wrist, he jerked Gabby up and twisted her necklace tight against her throat. The leather strained against the white collar of her uniform and limited the supply of air to her lungs. "Who do you think the General will believe? The man who stood by his side during the Great War, or you? A whore. I'll tell him that you seduced me with your body, and he will turn you out. Isn't your little sister a laundress here at Twin Springs? Your brother works in the Stables? Do you think the General will keep them on if I expose you as a slut and tell him your plans to steal Ame's child?"

"My plans?" wheezed Gabby.

"Of course, they're your plans. After all, I'm the General's most trusted confidant. He would never suspect me," he sneered. "Or you can do as I say. Then we can leave this shit hole to live a life of luxury."

Her liquid brown eyes pleaded up at him. "Please. Please don't ask this of me," she begged.

JD shouted in the maid's ear, "Go to Everett, Gabby. Tell him. He can help you."

Suddenly, JD's translucent body jerked, and she stumbled backward. Warmth pressed against her lips, tingling them. She lifted her fingertips and brushed them against her mouth. The tugging intensified within her chest, dragging her away from the couple. The sensation increased in strength until she felt herself flying out of the tiny room, through the outer room and back through the passageway and to her body. The world around her spun and her chest compressed. Once, twice, three times. Again, lips pressed to hers.

"Where the hell's that doctor?" shouted Logan high above her. His lips sealed around her's and he pushed air into her mouth.

Air flowed between JD's parted lips, causing her to choke and cough. Her chest rose and she filled her lungs with fresh air. Her lashes fluttered. Slowly her eyes opened and she was greeted by Logan's sky blue eyes, directly above hers.

Reaching up, she cradled the burned side of Logan's face with her palm. Her fingertips traced the shriveled and scarred skin where it stretched the corner of his eyelid down to his high cheekbone. "Can you see me?"

Logan searched JD's light green eyes. The caress of her fingers blazed his skin and he answered her strange question, "Of course, I see you."

Pressing the pads of his fingers against the base of her neck, he felt the steady beat of her pulse. Relieved, he sat back on his heels and allowed the others within the room to swarm her. Everyone spoke at once, ensuring her health for themselves. Only half listening to her reassure everyone that she was fine, Logan glanced up at the General's three Gem's staring down on the occupants of the room.

He'd been shocked when she'd passed out and wondered if she was playing a prank on him. When she didn't come to, he wanted to call 911, but Ava said a doctor had checked in. So, he sent her to fetch him.

Staring at JD laying there, with her eyes closed, he'd felt like he was visiting the painting. Just as he had every night since they'd discovered the portrait. Seeing her silent and still for the first time, the resemblance between her and Amethyst Fairbanks had pierced his heart.

Then, her breathing had become labored and her face more and more pale. The longer she remained still the more he worried. He went from wishing for her to wake up, to yelling at her to wake, to begging for her to screech at him in that obnoxiously loud voice that she loved to use.

As time ticked on, her breathing had shallowed until no breath escaped her lips and his heart leapt into his throat.

In an attempt to breathe life back into her, he pressed his lips to hers. It was then he understood. No matter how loud of a foul mouth and pain in his ass she was, she made him feel alive. Somehow, she didn't care about his scars and ugly mug. She gave him shit, yelled, ranted and verbally sparred with him about anything and everything.

He snuck a glance at her. The Geezers were taking turns between patting her hand and squeezing her tight with hugs. "Okay everyone, back up and let her have some room."

JD was still so pale that the only color on her face was her tiny freckles. "Where the hell is that doctor?" he repeated.

"You have a secret passageway from this room?" asked JD.

Stunned, everyone looked at her.

"Yes, we do," answered Ava. "How did you know? You were out cold when Jaxon came through the opening."

"I guess I heard him enter from that direction," she answered, a secret smile on her lips.

She's lying, thought Logan. He watched the tell tale signs. What could have made her heart slow to a stop? His gaze met Jaxon's and he raised an eyebrow in question.

The General's door flung back against the wall. Maddy rushed in, pulling Dr. Ottoman by the hand. "She's here. Get out of the way, Logan. Let the doctor get to JD."

Pacing the long perch within his cage, Ace's screech pierced the room. He stopped, hanging his head low. His gray feathers puffed out and he growled. Between snarls, his feathers quivered, and he breathed deeply.

"Quiet the bird." Taking a kerchief from his back pocket and mopping his brow, Clay Ottoman asked, "What happened here?"

Hands on her hips and stamping her foot on the floral rug, Maddy glowered at Logan. "He yelled at her and she passed out."

"Is that so?" muttered the doc, kneeling down beside his patient on the couch.

Logan squirmed under the gazes of everyone in the room. He

opened his mouth to reply but couldn't think of one damn thing to say. He had been yelling at her.

"No, no it's not," replied JD. Her cheeks pinkened and she searched her mind for an excuse for her behavior. "I think I forgot to eat today."

Maddy gasped and covered her mouth. "Are you pregnant?"

"Fuck no," shot back JD.

"And she's back," mumbled Logan, taking his baseball cap out of his back pocket and shaking it out. Relief flooded his body and he hid his smile by ducking his head.

Green sparks shot from JD's gaze. "Screw you, Logan."

His blue gaze flowed over the woman before him. Her athletic build, her high, beautiful breasts, full lips that he'd felt beneath his. Fire burned a path through him and his body hardened in response. Even her damn boots were kind of growing on him "If you keep offering, I might just take you up on it."

The women in the room gasped and Maddy rushed over and kicked him in the shin. "You're just being a mean jerk."

He growled in the back of his throat and refused to rub away the pain.

Theo hauled his sister up by her arm, pinning her to his side. "Say sorry. We don't resort to violence."

The mutinous teen crossed her arms and refused to even look in Logan's direction.

Everyone's attention shifted as the doctor lifted JD's wrist by his thumb and two fingers. Watching his digital watch, he asked her, "Are you pregnant?"

"No, not a chance. I don't want kids." She glared up at Logan. "What if my kid ended up—" She shook her head. "Negative, not happening. I can't have any."

Tugging his cap down over his head, Logan didn't reply. He hunched his shoulders. Covertly, he glanced around the room. The condemnation of everyone's gaze burned his skin.

Dr. Ottoman rose, holding her hand within his. "I prescribe

rest for the next couple days and food. Lots of food." He paused, "Can't have my patients not eating. How about dinner with me? We can talk more about the children. How to help them. Protect them. Not just here, but world wide."

Having her family and Logan listening in, heat rushed into her face. "Yeah, I guess." She shook her head. "No, you're right. I'd love to have dinner and talk more. Nothing is more important than the children."

Watching the tall, smooth skinned doctor slather all over JD, Logan felt the urge to punch him in the face. "What kind of a doctor has a digital watch," he mumbled beneath his breath. Deciding he couldn't take any more bullshit, he didn't wait for JD to accept the doctor's offer. He slipped from the room and closed the door behind him.

CHAPTER TWENTY-SEVEN

Two days later, JD tracked Bruce, catching up with him just in time to spot his sneakers disappearing through an opened window. She glanced up at the old Victorian building that used to be called Soda Springs Hotel and felt genuine lust. She rolled her eyes, "Great. I'm not just consumed with thoughts about a burned man but now I'm lusting over an old derelict building."

Even though the morning sun warmed the front of the building, mold covered the once white boards. It was a shame what time had done to the facade. From her dreams, she knew that the street must've been raised because the two-tiered, covered white porch that had run the length of the building was now gone. Instead, pavement ran right up to the window lined brick base. It was through one of those old windows that her runaway had disappeared.

She slipped her hands into the pockets of her black jeans and strolled along the sidewalk, offering a smile and good morning to a couple walking arm in arm. Under her breath she muttered, "Didn't see the boy sneaking into a boarded-up building, did you? Adults. Oblivious to the world around them."

On the right corner of the abandoned hotel, a curved tower used to house the Mercantile Store. That would be her entry point. As she rounded the building, she glanced up at clear blue sky instead of walking under the covered platform that had once jutted out. It was a shame that the platform with the wooden benches was gone. Even though the railroad tracks no longer ran along the right side of the building, the shaded area would've been a beautiful place to sit and watch the sun rise over Twin Springs. She shook her head. "Damn it, the Woman has filled my brain with memories that don't belong to me. Knowledge that I shouldn't have."

Back on mission, she focused on a door at the back where the railroad engineer would go to fill his thermos with coffee before pulling out and heading towards Charlottesville. Pulling a lock pick set from her tall boots, she pushed up the sleeves of her thick, black sweater, squatted down and quickly worked the lock. With a glance over her shoulder, she silently slipped inside.

In the distance, she could hear the soft footfalls of a little boy heading upstairs. Carefully, walking on the slanted wooden floor, she followed.

The floorboards squeaked behind her and a hand clamped down on her shoulder.

Immediately, she spun. Raising her arm as she turned, she broke the hold and trapped her assaulter's arm. Without a pause, she palm-heeled him in the face with her other hand.

"Jesus!" roared Logan, covering his nose with his free hand.

"What the hell are you doing here?" Her face was inches from his and she stared straight into his gorgeous eyes. His scars faded into the background and for a heartbeat, she lost herself within his blue gaze.

"Damn it woman, I think you might've bloodied my nose."

Instantly, she released him. "Don't sneak up on me again!" She socked him in the shoulder.

"What am *I* doing here?" Logan roared. "I could ask you the same question." He pulled his hand back to check for blood. Not seeing any, he scooped up the baseball cap that she'd knocked off and pulled it down low over the right side of his face. "That was one hell of a punch. You're obviously feeling better."

In the distance, feet pounded down a back staircase.

"Someone's in here," Logan pushed her behind him. "Vagrants. Stay back. I'll take care of this."

JD shook her head and pushed past him, heading towards the back of the building. "Please."

He grabbed her by the shoulder and she spun around.

Holding his hands up in front of his face, he muttered, "Look, let me handle this."

She looked him up and down and huffed. "I've got it. Stand back."

A door opened and slammed shut.

JD threw her hands up with frustration. "Look at what you've done! Now, he's gone."

Leaning back against the doorframe, Logan crossed his arms. "Do you have a habit of making all men feel small and worthless, or do you save this treatment just for burned men like me?"

Her jaw dropped. "I—I—" Her brows furrowed. "I'm not the one who blew our cover, asshole."

"Nice." The puckered lip on his burned side attempted to raise into a half smile. "Keep it up and I'll think you actually like me."

"Fuck you."

"Now I know you definitely like me."

Her hand curled into a fist. "Dream on, jerk." If he were her brother, she would've taken him down and rapped her knuckles on his chest until he cried mercy. Instead, she concentrated on the room around her. A soft sigh escaped her, "God, I love you."

His breath hissed in and his heart thundered in his chest. "What did you say?"

She walked into the middle of the room and turned in a circle. "I love this room. Look at the tall ceilings." She shouted up, "Hello!" and her voice echoed. "The moldings, original door. And the space!"

His heart settled down. "Sure, lovely." Prying his eyes from her glowing face, he glanced around. "All I see is cracked plaster, floor boards that are rotten in places, dust and cobwebs. I see work."

"Look at the shelving that curves along the side walls. Sturdy oak. Those are original. They used to hold goods for sale when this was the Mercantile Store. Good old Virginia Ham, in cloth sacks, used to hang from those hooks." She spread her arms wide. "Right here was the cash register."

"How do you know all this?"

She let out a long breath and moved over to the windows. "I have vivid dreams."

Walking around the room, he tried to see it as she did. Stopping next to her, he replied, "Don't we all." He gazed unseeingly out the dirty window. "I wish my dreams were about what buildings used to look like."

She rubbed some of the dirt from the window, creating a clean spot. "What do you dream about?"

He shrugged. "Fire and death."

She absorbed the information. If he'd been a little boy, she would've wrapped him in her arms and held him, assuring him that everything would be alright. But Logan wasn't a little boy who believed everything that adults said. He knew better. "I'm sorry."

He glanced up, surprised, and smiled, "Yep, you like me." He joked to lighten the mood. "Maybe I should sweep you up into my arms and kiss you."

Shaking her head, she rolled her eyes and continued into the building. "You wish."

"Yeah, I do," he whispered under his breath. Catching up to her in the next room, he asked. "What are you doing here anyway?"

Her eyes glowed as she took in the wide-open room. "I

thought I saw a boy. Small build. Jeans, t-shirt. Curly blond hair. Came in through a window. How about you?"

"Well, I know I saw a woman. Tall, slender build." Sexy, his mind added. "Black shirt and pants. Red hair in a ponytail. Picked the lock and entered through a side door." He mimicked her, clicking off a description.

She laughed. "Sorry, it's habit."

"Your brother told me that you find lost kids. Do you think this boy is lost?"

"I know he is. He might be living in here with his sister." She glared at him. "Hopefully, you didn't scare them off and now he and his sister are back on the run."

Raising his right hand, he twisted two of the remaining three fingers left. "Finger's crossed."

When she focused in on his burned hand, he shoved his hands into his jean pockets. How could he forget that he was burned? Somehow, around her, he felt like he used to. A man who could banter with a woman. Flirt. What a fool. He focused in on finding the kid. "Let's look around and see if they left any evidence that they're living here."

She held her hand over her chest, feigning disbelief. "You don't mind the fact that we're breaking and entering? Trespassing?"

"Naw," he chuckled, thinking of the owners—his parents. "I don't think anyone will mind."

"Wonderful." She rubbed her hands together. "I've been dying to see inside this building."

"Why?"

She hesitated. Sharing wasn't her strong point but something about Logan drew her out. Made her want to blabber all her secrets. "For a long time now, I've had a dream of creating a home for lost kids."

"Don't they have homes to return to?"

"Sometimes. More often the kids are lost because their home

life is so crappy. Dysfunctional. Even dangerous. They need a safe space to call home. To grow in."

"Isn't that what the foster system is for?"

"Spoken like a man who's never had to live with strangers."

Logan remembered Jaxon's story of how he'd found JD. Her yellow boots and butter knife. Fighting for what was hers. Shame flowed over him. He reached out and placed a hand on her shoulder, rubbed her arm. "You're right. I've never had to live with strangers."

JD glanced down at his hand. He snatched it back, but she felt like she'd lost something, when she wanted nothing more than to lean into him and let him soothe her pain. Instead of punching him, she smiled. "Don't worry about it."

Distracted by the little freckles spreading across her nose, Logan had the distinct urge to kiss each and every one of them. Hold her tight and keep her safe. He shook his head, what was wrong with him? Focusing on anything but those damn freckles, he said, "So, tell me, what do you think about the old girl?"

JD expelled the breath that she didn't realize she'd been holding. "Well, the space is wonderful. This room, which used to be the dining room for the hotel, would be a great multi-purpose room. Fill it with tables where meals could be served. Then games played."

Logan nodded. "I can visualize it. A huge screen TV over there to keep the kids together and bonding."

"Exactly." She continued on up a wide staircase. "Look at all these bedrooms," she murmured, opening doors on each side of the landings as they wound their way to the top. On one of the landings was a large area with six oval windows. "This spot would be a great library or reading room." They continued on, searching the building.

"Well, at least it doesn't look like the kids are living here," stated Logan as they headed down a back stairway.

"No, that just worries me more. They're staying someplace and

I'd rather it was in this dirty old building than out in the woods. Living like animals. That would break my heart."

Logan didn't reply.

At the bottom of the stairs, there was an outside door and a swinging door. "I guess this is where he exited."

"Looks like it. Do you still think this old hotel would be a great place for your lost kids?"

"It's perfect," she replied over her shoulder as she walked through the swinging door and into a large room.

She came to an abrupt halt and Logan bounced into her.

Steadying them both, he took in the room over her shoulder. "Wow."

The excitement fled from her body. "This used to be the kitchen." But now the room had a huge hole in the floor where slow water leak had gone unnoticed. "Damn."

Logan rubbed his chin. "I guess no one has been keeping up on things here." His face reddened. He'd have to let Dad know. "Didn't realize it was this bad."

"How could you? It's going to take a bucket load of money to fix this." Under her breath, she murmured, "Don't think selling my little paintings will come anywhere close."

"Don't worry, Dad and I can fix it. Just focus on what you'd do with it."

"Well, we'd need a huge fridge and stove. Industrial size dishwasher. Lots of counter space."

Visualizing the picture she'd created, somehow Logan kept seeing himself standing by her side. And he liked what he saw.

"A long, wide island with stools for the kids to pull up to. At least 15 feet or twenty feet."

The dream she was creating with him crashed at his feet. "Good God woman, how many kids are you planning on saving?"

Confused, she turned, her eyes wide. "All of them."

"Whoa, back on up the bus." He rubbed the back of his neck.

He felt a panicky feeling deep in his chest as he added up the costs and calculated feeding that many mouths. "Are you crazy?"

Immediately, she saw red. "Crazy? Who are you to call me nuts? I've spent my life having people think I was wacko." She tapped him on the chest with her index finger. "I'm as sane as you are. I didn't ask you to dream with me. You invited yourself along, asshole." She shoved past him.

"Wait," he called out.

"What?" She flipped around. "Do you want to mock me more? Spit on my dreams?"

"No." He couldn't stand the hurt in her eyes. The pain he'd caused with his careless words. "Do you really want to save every single lost child?"

She marched up to him and dared him to argue. "Yes, every single one."

Laying his hand on his heart, Logan made a promise. "Then that's what we'll do."

CHAPTER TWENTY-EIGHT

For days, snow had twirled around Twin Springs, trapping a bored little boy inside. As the sun set behind the mountains, Colton Reinhard rummaged in the bottom of his blue backpack until his small fingers brushed against the cool metal of the lighter. His fingers curled around the prize and a satisfied grunt emitted from between his lips. Deep in the back of his mind, he heard his dead mother's voice warning him about the dangers of playing with fire and he hid the lighter under his shirt.

Even though he knew most of Twin Springs was enjoying a late dinner or dancing in the Crystal Ballroom, he still hugged the lighter close to his scrawny chest while he searched the shadows of the attic room. "Guests never come up here," he reassured himself. "If they do, I know the drill. My name is Bruce. My parents are having dinner in the Main Dining Room. It's their anniversary and they don't want to be bothered."

This room was his favorite hiding place. Even his sister didn't know about his secret lair at the end of the slanted, attic hallway. There were so many treasures within the room. He'd found his ultra-cool blue backpack here. He figured the two M's stitched on the backpack stood for Mighty Man, but his sister had said it was closer to Mickey Mouse.

When he'd found the backpack, he'd dumped the laptop and small notebooks that were inside it behind a stack of boxes and refilled the bag with his superheroes. His sister, Parker, didn't care where in the attics he'd found the backpack, just as long as he hadn't stolen the bag from a guest.

A tingle of fear and unease soaked into his chest and he brought the lighter out from under his shirt. He flipped the gold cap up with a flick of his thumb and back into position with a click. It was a good thing his sister didn't know about it, or that he'd stolen it from the bad man. But the mean man had hurt Ava, so Colton thought it was okay.

Parker was still mad about him bugging her at the Front Desk with so many people around. Afterwards, with his small hand in the air, he'd solemnly sworn to his sister, "No matter how much they torture me, I will never reveal our secret identities."

Living at Twin Springs was the best. He loved discovering new secret hallways, roaming the attics and swimming in the pools. Plus, no school. Only the easy peasy lessons Parker forced on him.

Even though he wouldn't say the words out loud, he loved his sister. He used to think having an older sister sucked. But now, she was all he had left. Criss-crossing his legs, Colton placed the lighter on the thread bare carpet. He dragged the sleeve of his shirt up over his shoulder and held his skinny, seven-year-old arm out. Grunting hard, he flexed the muscle of his bicep and quickly measured the results between the thumb and forefinger of his other hand. Proudly, he examined the results. "I can protect Parker," he announced. "She doesn't understand how strong I am. I'm super-fast too. Just like a superhero."

Dragging his backpack closer to the padded seat in the dormer window, Colton pulled out his favorite two action figures and a redheaded Barbie that he'd found by edge of the indoor pool.

"You're now Wolfeman's sister. I heard Logan breathed life back into you."

Envy burned deep within Colton. "Maybe if I follow Logan and Wolfeman around, then they'll teach me how to become a real superhero. Just like them. I just need to gain their trust." Studying his toys, he whispered, "My parents wouldn't be dead, if I was a real superhero. I could've breathed life back into them."

Grasping one action figure by the waist, he deepened his voice, "Wolfeman saved Ava from fire and brought the Blue Flame out of the woods." He dropped Wolfeman onto the padded seat, grasped his other action figure in one hand and flicked open the lighter's lid with his thumb. Hesitating, he chewed on his lower lip, kneading it between his teeth. His heart thundering in his chest, he rolled the pad of his thumb on the tiny metal wheel.

And the lighter sprang to life.

Transfixed, Colton gazed at the gold and blue flame, sensing the power.

Holding the flame to the right side of his action figure's face, he watched it lick and eat at the features. The plastic melted and branded his new hero. His nose twitched at the pungent smell of plastic burning and he forgot about moving his thumb away from the metal spikes of the little wheel. The fire bit the pad of his thumb and he flung the lighter across the room. Soothing his finger by sucking his thumb, he examined his toy. Backdropped by the darkness of the night sky in the window, he held the action figure high above his head.

The full moon illuminated the freshly melted side of his action figure and fueled his imagination. Using his storybook voice, he declared, "And the Blue Flame was born, sparked to life by the power of the fire. Hidden by the darkness, the moon their only guide, the Blue Flame and Wolfeman band together to fight the dark evil hiding within the shadows of Twin Springs."

CHAPTER TWENTY-NINE

*S*hifting and slipping off her shoes behind the cover of the Front Desk Counter, Parker rubbed the arch of her foot across the top of her other foot. After working the dinner shift in the Main Dining Room last night and a double shift today at the Front Desk, pain radiated through her legs and into her feet. Fatigue seeped into her bones and she fantasized about slipping into an empty guest room and sleeping for days. But she no longer had the luxury to crash, as she did as a child. Now, she needed to safeguard her brother by keeping a watchful eye.

Through her eyelashes, she tracked JD marching down the Grand Lobby, dressed as usual in a black t-shirt, skinny jeans and her boots. Monitoring her enemy's advancement out of the corner of her eye, she spread a welcoming smile across her face and diverted her attention to an elderly couple checking in.

While her husband handed over a credit card, Mrs. Elliot brushed a stray strand of her silver hair back into her elegant chiffon updo. Eagerly, the elderly woman perched herself up on her tippy toes and leaned into the counter. "I understand DiWolf will be making a personal appearance at the art show."

On strict orders not to reveal JD's identity to the guests, Parker's gaze flickered towards the General's Office where JD's movement had abruptly halted. "Yes, ma'am. The artist will not only speak about each piece, but will be taking pictures with the patrons purchasing the artwork from the auction."

Mrs. Elliot vibrated with excitement and elbowed her husband. "We've wanted to purchase one of DiWolf's pieces for years, but they rarely come up for sale."

Yeah, well wait till you meet her, mused Parker. She monitored JD pacing in her tall black boots and scowling at whomever she spoke with on the cell phone.

"Diana, is it?" asked Mrs. Elliot.

Glancing down at her name tag, Parker replied, "Yes, ma'am."

The elderly woman slipped a folded-up C note across the granite counter, "Perhaps you could place our room next to DiWolf. Or maybe even jot down his room number."

"Now, now, dear," added the husband, squinting at her from behind thick rimmed glasses. "Don't put her in an uncomfortable situation."

Parker's turquoise eyes widened with the offer. She stared at the money beneath the woman's manicured fingers. Deeply tempted to add the cash to her emergency fund, words stuck in her throat. *What would it hurt putting the couple on the same level as JD? No one would need to know and an extra hundred dollars could mean an extra week of food on the run.*

But she would know. Parker had sworn not to fall to the level of her aunt, whose greed for money had created a dark abyss within her soul. "I'm sorry, Mrs. Elliot. Even the staff doesn't know the identity of the artist DiWolf."

Shoulders slumping, the elderly woman slipped the bill back into her purse. "Oh, well. If you do find out," she left the offer hanging in the air.

"Please enjoy your stay with us, Mr. and Mrs. Elliot," replied Parker. Fixing her "welcome" smile on her face, she handed the couple their key cards. Peering between the couple's shoulders, her gaze clashed with JD's and an oily feeling rolled in her gut. She realized her time at Twin Springs was short.

Cell phone to her ear, JD paced in the Grand Lobby. She kept an eye trained on the young girl working at the Front Desk. "What the hell do you mean, you don't have a lead on the kids? How many missing brother and sister combos are there?"

"Don't give me any shit, JD," growled Lee over the phone. "I'm up to my ass in dogs here."

Her brow furrowed. "What are you talking about?"

The anger in Lee's voice bit into her ear. "The damn dog."

Coming to a standstill, she bit back. "The dog? Get over it."

Lee's voice boomed across the line. "Get over it? You dumped the dog on me, not the other way around."

She flipped her long ponytail over her shoulder and tracked the couple Diana checked in. Ignoring the guilt weighing down on her shoulders, she traced the toe of her boot in the carpet and muttered, "Pansy ass," under her breath. She snickered over the phone, "Oh yeah, how you two boys getting along? Sleeping in your bed yet?"

"No," Lee's voice grated across the line. "I'm still sleeping on the floor."

JD hooted and her face lighted up with laughter. "Lee, you've got to grow a pair. Kick the dog off your bed. Show him who's alpha male."

"That's just it, JD." His voice slowed as if talking with a child. "I'm alpha male. But your dog's an alpha bitch who just gave birth to twelve puppies."

"Puppies?" Squeaked JD, realizing her cousin would make her pay dearly for this one.

Lee's chair creaked and she heard his boots slam on the floor. "Yes, twelve puppies. Did you hear me loud and clear? Tweeelvvve puppies. I'm sleeping on the floor next to the dog and her litter. I split the puppies into two groups of six. I have to alternate the groups every four hours for feedings. I haven't had any sleep for days."

She flushed. "Jeez, I'm sorry, Lee. I wasn't paying much attention to the sex of the dog that night." She paused, thinking, her eyes sweeping over Diana working the Front Desk. "I can't come home to help you."

Lee growled over the phone.

Unconsciously, she splayed her hand out in front of her. "Not yet," she added. "Somehow, this hotel holds the secret to my past. Plus, I have to protect the siblings until we find out who they are hiding from."

Silence stretched between them until Lee sighed deeply, "I understand. I'm still searching for the identities of your runaways, but no one has reported a brother and sister missing. Are you sure they're siblings? Perhaps cousins?"

Her eyes met Diana's. "There's no doubt in my mind."

CHAPTER THIRTY

*A*round the corner, in a shoebox room called the Security Office, Logan leaned against the door jam and tried to ignore his brother monitoring his every move. "What?" he muttered to Sam.

"You know it's safe to actually go all the way in," his brother mocked. "A fire isn't going to sneak up on you and bite you in the ass."

"Bite me," Logan grumbled. "What the hell do you know about fire."

Against his will, he inched further into the room. When his brother blocked the door with his body, panic almost smothered him. He sucked in long, deep breaths and impatiently waited for his Army buddy to sit. "Damn it, Jaxon. How do you work in here? It's like being in a coffin."

Settling himself into his chair, Jaxon tilted back precariously onto two wheels and crossed his ankles on the edge of his desk. "What's up? I feel like we're having a team meeting."

Sam scooted further into the room.

Reluctantly, Logan shuffled over so his little brother wasn't blocking the exit. "Why didn't you tell me JD had a medical condition?"

Instantly concerned, Sam pushed even further into the little room, where he could easily hear both men. "What medical condition?" he asked, his blue gaze searching his brother's. "What happened?"

"A couple days ago, JD passed out in Ava's office. She stopped breathing and I had to give her CPR."

"Yeah, right," scoffed Sam. "You just wanted to see if the redhead tastes as good as she looks."

Pitching forward, Jaxon's feet hit the floor hard and he scowled at the younger Oakes boy. The green flecks in his brown eyes glowed eerily within the room. "That's my sister you're talking about, Sam. Be careful. I am very protective of her." He turned his attention back to Logan. "The Geezers told me all about it."

Logan pulled his hat off and thunked him in the chest with it. "It's not a joke." He rolled up the dingy baseball cap and shoved it into his back pocket. "At one point, I didn't feel a heartbeat and had to apply chest compressions. I'll admit, it scared the shit out of me."

"Me too," replied Jaxon. "My dad said nothing like that has ever happened before. Sure, lots of other strange things happen around her. She's had what we call her fits. But that's just been outbursts. Never passing out cold."

Glancing between the two men, concern laced Sam's voice. "What do you mean?"

Rubbing the black stubble on his face, Jaxon added, "Never anything medical. Sure, Diamond, I mean JD, sometimes talks to walls or an empty space next to her. She has an uncanny ability to know things she shouldn't and a talent for finding lost things and people. But the Geezer's don't remember her ever passing out before and needing to be revived. This is something new. A new symptom added to her previous condition. I'm really concerned that I never should've asked her to come."

The thought of never having met JD almost floored Logan. She was a pain in the ass, sure, but made him feel like he was one of the living. Not an animal living in the woods. In a hushed tone, he asked, "Why did you?" almost afraid to hear the answer.

Taking a small ball from his pocket, Jaxon squeezed it in his fist before replying. "You've seen the portrait. How much she resembles Amethyst Fairbanks. The portrait must be a clue to her past." He thought for a moment, tossing the ball back and forth between his hands. "Perhaps Twin Springs isn't good for her."

Rolling his eyes, Sam inserted, "That's just stupid. How can a building not be good for someone?"

Unwilling to admit it, Logan feared that Jaxon might be right.

Ignoring the boy's comment, Jaxon pumped the ball within his fist. "Look at what happened to Isabella. And to Ava. Maybe I've placed JD's life in danger by asking her to come here."

Remembering when JD'd trapped his arm and smacked him in the face, the unburned side of Logan's mouth curled up. "She seems pretty damn tough to me. Tough enough to take care of herself and not need a man to protect her. Besides, the Grand Dame didn't attempt to kill Isabella and Ava. Niles and Director Hollingsworth did and they're both dead."

Again tossing the ball back and forth, Jaxon replied, "I know, I know. I just feel uneasy. My gut's telling me something's wrong. We missed something."

Shifting his weight back onto his good leg, Logan asked, "What could we have missed? There hasn't been any more sabotage since the Director died. Bookings are growing. Things are looking up."

The ball stilled and Jaxon looked up and asked, "How's the Tower coming?"

He shrugged. "Going well. If your sister doesn't keep sticking her two cents in, I think we'll finish on time."

A wide grin spread across Jaxon's face and his teeth gleamed against the black stubble on his face. "Thanks for letting her trail around after you. I really appreciate you putting up with her."

Uneasy, he shifted, and a ruddy hue spread across his face and seeped under the scars. *Keep cool. Don't let them guess how much you care about her.*

He tossed out a nonchalant, "Don't worry about it." Noticing his brother's intense gaze, he switched the subject. "Since we're talking about younger siblings being under foot, what about you Sam?"

"What about me?" asked Sam. He leaned in and sniffed his brother. "You actually smell . . . not bad. Tell me, big brother, is there something between you and the gorgeous redhead?"

Ignoring the question, Logan feigned anger and asked, "Why the hell are you still under foot?"

Brows furrowing, Sam bristled at his brother and puffed up his chest, "I'm not underfoot. I'm helping you like Dad asked."

Logan straightened and took a menacing step towards his little brother. "What the hell are you talking about? I don't need you to help me. I'm not an invalid. Go back to the farm where you belong."

"You're such an asshole. Never thinking of anyone but yourself."

"Settle down everybody," Jaxon tossed in. "Nobody thinks you're an invalid. Maybe Sam wants to help."

Stepping even closer, Logan grumbled, "Bullshit, you hate being indoors. Don't you have cows, chickens or something to tend to at home?"

"Alright," muttered Jaxon, "I guess you're going to have it out in the middle of my office." But neither brother heard him.

At his brother's words, Sam's eyebrows shot high in his forehead. "Are you saying I'm not smart enough to help with the Tower?"

"Here we go," muttered Jaxon, and he leaned back to watch the show.

Sam stepped closer and bumped his brother with his chest.

His brother's nose inches from his, Logan knew they looked two sides of a coin. One, scarred, considering his life over. The other, on the cusp of manhood, his whole life ahead of him. "Don't be an idiot."

"You think I'm stupid? Who's the one living in the woods like an animal? Maybe I should tell JD that you can't even sleep one night indoors. What do you think she'd think about that? You're a coward."

Recognizing that tempers were about to blow, Jaxon bounded to his feet and pulled the two brothers apart. "Cool it, pull your heads out of your asses or I'll get the Geezers to deal with you." Feeling the threat wasn't enough, he added, "No, I'll get Theo. Or should I call Mrs. Oakes. Dale says she can whoop both of your butts with one arm tied behind her back."

Feeling the full impact of his words, the brothers broke apart.

Alarms squealed through Twin Springs.

"What the hell is that?" demanded Sam.

"Fire," whispered Logan. Blood drained from his face and he froze.

"Fire!" yelled Jaxon, rushing over to examine the large red panel on the wall of his office. Examining the blinking dots, he turned, grabbed fresh walkie talkies from the line on his desk and tossed one to each of the brothers.

Lifting a newly placed fire extinguisher from the wall, he rapidly spoke into his walkie. "Theo, we've got a fire in the attic above the Bellhop Stand. I'm heading up. Call the fire department." Jaxon pushed the two brothers aside and rushed from the room.

Startled, Sam gazed after Jaxon, then, he glanced over at his brother. "Why are you just standing there? We've got to go help."

Logan willed his body to move but nothing happened.

"Come on," Sam urged him. "Let's go."

Again, he willed his body to move, but still it refused to

comply. Even his throat had closed up and he couldn't mutter a word.

A sneer of disgust crossed Sam's lip and he shook his head. "You know, you were my idol growing up. Now I'm ashamed to call you brother." He sprinted from the room and didn't look back.

Unsure how long he stood there, the disappointment on Sam's face burned into his brain. Disgrace and dishonor seeped through Logan, as his heart slammed against his rib cage.

His mind clicked back to his teammates, stumbling from the squatty, flat roof building. Flames licked at their bodies. He remembered his oath. "Regain my fighting position." His foot inched forward. "Aid my brothers." He bent down and picked up the walkie talkie. "Get everyone home alive."

CHAPTER THIRTY-ONE

*a*larms piercing the air, JD shouted over the phone, "Gotta go, something's up!" She hung up and slipped her phone into her boot.

At a full sprint, Jaxon and Sam tore up the stairs between the Front Desk and the Bellhop Stand. Sam shouted over his shoulder, "Fire in the attics!"

Rushing to help, JD and Parker almost collided at the bottom of the stairs. She placed a hand on the girl's arm. The teen's face was twisted with angst. "Diana, listen to me. You're needed here to calm the guests and direct the fire department."

Her face pale, Parker clawed at JD's hands holding her back. "Let go of me." Her voice rose to a fevered pitch. "My brother's in the attics."

At the slip, JD's grip tightened. She understood that terror had overwhelmed the girl and she didn't realize what she'd just revealed. Leveling her gaze, she ordered, "Stay here, I'll get him and bring him back to you."

Parker's body shook uncontrollably within her hold. She squeezed her eyes shut and shook her head. "I can't. He's my responsibility."

When her eyes opened, they were wild. Terror controlled the teen. "He's all I have left." She tore from JD's grasp and dashed up four flights of stairs, pushing guests out of her way as she went.

JD sprinted after her. At the top of the stairs, a black and gray fog filled the crooked corridor so that distinguishing the skinny doorways was almost impossible. Illuminated by small lights from above, the foul smoke cast an eerie glow down to the short end of the hallway and beckoned those foolish enough to enter.

Undaunted, Jaxon and Sam plowed through the gray smoke, just steps ahead.

Coughing on the noxious fumes, Parker doubled over, bracing herself against the wall. Seeing JD, she surged further down the hall.

Catching up with the teen, JD grabbed her up in a bear hug and lifted her off her feet. "Sam!" she called out. The young man's form jogged back out of the black smoke to her. "Hold her back," she demanded and shoved her into his arms. "Don't let go of her."

Face serious, he nodded. His strong arms circled Parker and pinned her arms to her sides.

Kicking, Parker yelled, "Let me go!" She strained within her binds, but he held her firm. "Colton!" she screamed, her voice traveling against the dense smoke in the long hallway. "Please, let me go," she begged. "Colton!"

Grabbing her by the chin, JD pulled her face up. "We don't have time for you to act like a child. Stay here and shut up. Jaxon and I will bring your brother back."

JD flipped around and dashed into the smoke, joining her brother. "There could be a little boy up here."

His golden eyes gleaming in the smoke, Jaxon acknowledged her with a nod.

Seamlessly, the siblings fell into their search and rescue pattern. Operating as one, they systematically examined each room off the narrow hallway, feeling the doors for heat and checking for smoke under them before entering and clearing the room.

The smoke thickening around her, JD pulled the rounded collar of her t-shirt up to cover her nose and mouth. Puffs of smoke billowed out from under the last door on the left. The once white door was now gray with soot and smoke. She ignored the stinging in her eyes and tested the door by laying her palm on the aged, wooden surface. Warm, but not hot. "Over here!" she shouted.

Crouching low, she cracked open the door and scanned the room through the thick smoke. A fireball of flames rose from an artificial Christmas tree, blackening its limbs. Coughing and choking, a boy used his backpack to beat back at the flames. Thick, gray ash and black soot discolored his hair and coated his face and skinny arms.

Undaunted, the flames leapt to the ceiling over his head and traveled to the window, blackening it with heat.

Consumed with his feeble efforts, Colton was oblivious to the flames forming around him and inching a path of destruction towards him. The fire consumed everything before it, licking a fiery path down the yellowed curtains, twisting the dry fabric into ashes as it went.

Within the blackened window, JD flashed back to another motel room. The gaping hole of what once was room 115. The room where fire's kiss had stolen her mother from her. Emotions clogged her throat and tears wet her eyes, but she blinked back the weakness and charged. She scooped up the boy, backpack and all, and whisked him away from danger.

Jaxon rushed past her and used the fire extinguisher to lay a white layer of foam over the tree, across the ceiling and window. Using a sweeping motion, he smothered the fire.

With the boy held tight against her body, JD spotted Logan in the hall. His limping gate ate up the distance between them as he surged forward with another fire extinguisher. His pale, scarred face was twisted into a mask of determination.

"Sam!" she shouted down the hallway. "Help Jaxon and your brother. Make sure the fire's out. Once the Marshal inspects the area, open some widows to clear the smoke," she ordered.

Immediately, Sam released Parker and jogged down the corridor.

Set free from his hold, she rushed forward and ripped her brother from JD's arms.

Hugging her brother's soot covered body tight within her arms, Parker slid down the wall and leaned back against the peeling wallpaper. She held him in a death hug, then pushed him back and ran her hands all over his arms, face, legs, checking to see if he was burnt. "You scared me!" she yelled, her voice still laced with tremors of fear. "How stupid—," she choked up. "I love you. Thank God you're alright."

His face alive with wonder, he looked up at her. "You should've seen it. The redhead and Wolfeman—"

"Shut up." She hugged him tight again. "Just shut up."

He squirmed within her hold and mumbled from the depths of her clenched embrace. "You're super strong."

She sobbed into the crook of his neck, smearing soot all over herself in the process.

In the distance, JD heard her brother report in to Theo over the walkie as he walked down the hall. "Fire's out. When the Fire Marshal arrives, I'll go over the scene with him. Doesn't look like sabotage this time. A little boy playing with a zippo lighter. Didn't realize that if you don't close the lid, the flame continues to burn."

Turning towards her brother, confusion lined her forehead. "You thought it might be sabotage? Why?"

Logan limped out of the charred room holding a smoldering, blackened lighter in the remains of the aged yellow and fire blackened curtain. "Thought I warned you about smoking," his voice was unusually calm. A muscle vibrated on the side of his neck when he displayed the lighter. Through clenched teeth, he addressed the boy clutched in Parker's arms. "Told you that you'd have to deal with me, if I caught you." Progressing down the hall, he stalked a direct route to the boy. "People die in fires," he snarled. "They're left mutilated for the rest of their lives." Logan's gaze sparked blue flames aimed at Colton.

Calm and focused, JD placed her body between the burned man and her lost kids. She braced herself for a fight. With a flick of her wrists, she secured her ponytail in a top knot, tugged at the jean fabric covering her thighs for more kicking space, and easily settled into a fighting stance. "Back off, Logan."

"He's right, JD," inserted her brother. "We've had a lot of fires here at Twin Springs. I thought it was sabotage, but perhaps just a kid who doesn't realize the destruction fire can cause."

Parker stood, her stance rigid, and pushed her brother behind her. "You can't hurt him. He's little." Her whole body shook, but she stood firm and shouted, "None of those fires were my brother's fault!"

"He's your brother?" questioned Logan. Stalking the boy, he added, "The timeline fits. The fires started after you started working at Twin Springs." He growled deep in his throat, "A man died in the fire at the stables. His whole body was engulfed with flames. Do you know the agony of dying by fire? I do. Ava almost died, too." His face a mask of fury, he continued forward towards the boy peeking out from behind his sister, his gray curls sticking to his face and neck with sweat.

Striking out with her front foot, JD push kicked Logan in the chest and he stumbled back a few feet. "I said, stand back. These kids are my responsibility."

"JD, Logan," warned Jaxon, now surging forward to enter the fray.

His face flushing purple, Logan charged.

JD prepared herself for his advance and shifted her weight to her back foot. She shot off a side kick, full force to stop him.

Sidestepping and scooping her foot with his arm, Logan jerked her leg up and she landed hard on her back. Following her to the floor, he knelt on a bent knee beside her, his thumb and the two fingers on his right hand pinning her shoulder to the ground. "Look close, JD," he growled, his face mere inches from hers. His eyes never left hers as he canted his face, baring the right side fully for her inspection. "See the damage fire causes."

Her gaze flowed over the taut and raised skin stretched across his face. The agony he'd suffered was evident in every crater, hollow and sinkhole created by fire's kiss. Softly, she spoke, the pent-up emotions deepening her voice to a husky whisper. "I know the damage fire causes. My mother died in a fire because of a stupid little girl's actions." Tears formed in the back of her eyes. She blinked them away, adding, "My actions." Covertly, she slipped her knife up between them and held the tip against the soft skin at his throat. She didn't want to hurt him. He'd suffered enough pain. But she must protect her kids. "I also know the damage caused by adults on children. Now back off."

Breathing heavily, Logan worked to suppress the anger raging through his body. "People could have died. People I love." *You*, he thought, but didn't have the courage to voice.

Relaxing beneath him, she dropped her arms and the knife rolled from her hand. She gazed deep into his eyes, into his soul and whispered, "You promised to save every child. Even stupid boys and girls that play with fire."

His body shuddered and he closed his eyes. Leaning his forehead against hers, he whispered back, "You're right."

"Enough!" Theo's voice vibrated down the corridor and pierced the smoke and tension.

Behind him, the Fire Marshal stood with his mouth hanging open. A helmet in one hand, the reflective strips of his thick yellow jacket and brown pants glowed eerily under the light. His wide-eyed gaze took in the sight of the soot-covered couple on the canted floor. "Was she holding a knife to the throat of the Oakes' older boy? I'll be damned."

The tone within Theo's voice froze everyone in place. "I've had enough." His voice whiplashed through the hall. "Logan, get off her. Now! JD, if I see your knife out of your boot again, or hear you cussing up a storm in the common areas of this hotel, I'll personally kick you out of Twin Springs."

With difficulty, Logan lifted himself off JD and helped her to her feet. He attempted to rub away the pain shooting down his leg.

Pristine in his dark blue suit, Theo jerked at the knot of his tie, loosening its hold, and his steel gaze raked everyone in the hallway. He scooped the little boy up and shoved him towards Logan. "The boy's your responsibility. Meet me in Jaxon's office, then help him get cleaned up."

"But—," Parker spoke up.

"Diana, you and JD go down to Ava's office. I'll send Isabella and Ava to meet you there. You'll tell them what you know about this fire and any other fires at Twin Springs."

His steel gaze touched on each and every face in the hallway, scorching them with the molten glow. "I'm warning all of you, put the needs of the Grand Dame before your own selfish agendas. Twin Springs is our home. Our legacy. If you can't understand that, then get the hell out."

Part Two

CHAPTER THIRTY-TWO

*D*ear Journal,

 Mrs. Fairbanks saw me slip out of my great, grand-father's secret room in the attics. At first, I didn't know what to do. Then, she paused at the top of the stairs. She didn't think anything of me calling out her name and waited for me with a fake smile on her stupid lips. She'd discovered my secret. Forced me to take action. Why was she even in the attics?

She didn't believe I would hurt her. All it took was a little push. Her blue eyes widened. I watched her wobbling on the edge of the top step, her arms flapping out beside her. Unable to catch her balance, she realized she was going to die. For a brief second, her eyes met mine before she tumbled. I felt ill afterwards, worried that Izzy would find out what I did and hate me. But Mrs. Fair-banks died before she could tell on me.

I left Ava a rose and Izzy a mason jar of fireflies, to say I was sorry. But Ava didn't care. And Izzy didn't notice the jar and one by one, the fireflies died. Their lights going out one after the other.

I can help Izzy with her pain. But she keeps pushing me away. Izzy and Ava stood over their mother's grave, crying and holding each other. While I had to strain to see over the shoulders of the adults surrounding them. The warm sun on her face, Izzy turned to her sister.

I thought I loved Izzy. But she's a bitch. The only joy I have left is tripping her and taunting her with her clumsiness. My heart swells with joy when she shakes her fists and yells at me for calling her Dizzy Izzy. I tried teasing Ava the same way. But the look she gave me, made me feel like dirt. Like I wasn't a man, just a bug at her feet. I'm glad Ava hangs out with Logan.

But Izzy, I have tried over and over to become her friend. She'd rather hide in the kitchens with her imaginary friend than me. I almost punched her in the face when she told me to leave her alone. The desire was so strong my hands curled into fists, but I stopped myself. I just couldn't believe it. How could she choose someone more invisible than me?

Somehow, I want them to pay for how badly they treat me. I hate them. Sometimes I get so mad that I feel like my brain is boiling inside my head and my whole body turns hot. I want them to feel the heat I feel.

I want to be strong like my ancestor. Then, I'll be in charge and they'll need me. I'm going to fulfill my great, grandfather's dreams and take over Twin Springs.

It will take time to destroy the Fairbanks and have the revenge he deserved. I'll have to hide my room so that no one else will discover my secrets, my true birthright.

Still, I feel utterly alone. Except when I read with my great, grandfather in his journals. The stories warm me and remind me of what I must do. Wait in the shadows, covering the pain that festers and grows within my soul with silence until the right time comes.

Niles Porter, the rightful owner of Twin Springs.

CHAPTER THIRTY-THREE

*F*rom beneath her lashes, Parker watched JD pacing underneath the portrait in the General's Office. Her face was smeared with soot and twisted into its usual scowl, but showed none of the emotions swirling beneath the surface. She must've felt her gaze because she paused, spread her boot-clad legs into their usual stance, placed her hands on her hips and studied her. Sitting on the couch, Parker refused to squirm under the pressure of her gaze.

"You're going to have to talk to me, Diana. I can't help you if you don't."

Mutinously, Parker clamped her mouth shut.

JD growled deep in her chest.

Parker's gaze slid to the dark-haired woman lounging in the leather chair. Her make-up was perfect and her silky, ebony hair thick and full at her jawline. Even with the late hour, Ava could've walked the red carpet and outshined any movie star. Would she be the first to kick her out once she found out that she'd lied?

JD drew Parker's attention when she mumbled to Ava, "Why are you here? I can handle this by myself."

Shrugging one of her graceful shoulders, Ava's full lips spread into a smile and she smoothly answered, "Because Theo said so."

Parker's head lifted and her eyes lit up. Theo was the key. She wished she could talk to her brother. How could they get Theo to allow them to stay at Twin Springs?

She glanced at the teenager sitting beside her. Not wanting to be left out, Maddy had inserted herself into the situation. For once, she looked sixteen, with her face scrubbed bare, curled up on the couch beside her in pink fuzzy pajamas. Perhaps, Maddy could help.

Isabella backed into the room, rolling a tray laden with cookies, hot cocoa and tea. Maneuvering the cart into the middle of the room, she accidentally bumped JD with her hip. The petite woman smiled at everyone, "Sorry."

Throwing her hands up in the air, JD complained, "Are we having a sleep over?" She shook her head and moved out of the way. "This is serious."

Isabella shrugged her shoulders and said sheepishly, "I thought everyone could use a snack."

Gracefully, Ava leaned forward in her chair and began serving the two girls on the couch. "Wonderful idea."

Leaning against the fireplace mantle, her arms crossed, JD asked, "Now that we all have milk and cookies, can we get down to business?"

Against her will, Parker's hands shook. She fumbled with her cup and it clattered against the saucer. Quickly, she shoved the weakness out of sight and hid her hands beneath her legs.

JD perched herself on the corner of Isabella's armchair. "Let's start with your real name."

The young girl's gaze slid between the three women before her and the portrait above the fireplace. They were lined up just like in the picture and they didn't even realize it. She whispered, "It's Diana."

Feeling Isabella's attention on her, she studied the chocolate chip cookie on her plate. Perhaps if she escaped the redhead, she could sneak a couple cookies to her brother. Isabella was so sweet and made the best chocolate chip cookies. Just the right balance of chocolate and cookie dough. She must've just baked them. They were still warm.

She'd be a wonderful mom. Parker's heart warmed with the idea of the small blonde woman taking care of her and her brother. Slipping into a dream world where wishes came true, she traced the pattern on the dessert plate with her fingertips. Lace winged butterflies and plump ladybugs weaved in and out of the flowers circling the edges of the plate. The fat bodied bumble bees on the tea cups were her favorite. The dishes brought back memories of when her family was whole and having tea in the Grand Lobby. Gut wrenching loss radiated through her body and snapped her out of the dream, tears welling up in her eyes.

Leaning forward, JD coaxed in a soft tone. "Come on, I need you to talk to me. I can't help unless you start being honest with me. Your brother's name is Colton, not Bruce."

Ava's infectious laughter filled the room and Ace immediately joined in copying her.

JD stiffened. "You're not helping."

Glad their attention was diverted onto each other, Parker wiped the tears away and glanced up at Ava.

Amusement glittered in the beautiful woman's gaze. "Don't you get it? Diana and Bruce."

Parker's heart beat hard in her chest.

At everyone's blank stare, Ava added. "Diana Prince and Bruce Wayne?"

"Wonder Woman and Batman," gasped Maddy.

Grabbing the cookie and shoving a huge chunk of it into her mouth, Parker shrugged. "My brother has a thing for superheroes."

Sliding another cookie on the young girl's plate, Isabella cajoled, "So your brother's name is Colton, and your name is. . ."

"Parker. It's Parker, okay." She shoved the plate away from her and glared at the redhead. "All of this is your fault. I should've grabbed Colton and booked it the first day you showed up. You've ruined everything. Always hanging around, sticking your nose in where it doesn't belong."

"And your last name?" asked Isabella.

Parker folded her arms across her chest, bent her head and frowned at the plate. She'd messed everything up. She should've changed her brother's hair too. Once they start searching for a missing brother and sister, her brother's white blond hair will give them away and their aunt would be called.

"How about your real age," prompted JD. "You're not twenty-two, as your application states."

"Next time Colton won't get to pick the names," she grumbled. All she needed to do was buy time, until she could grab her brother and run. They'd hide somewhere. Once it was safe, she'd change their names again and move on. "Okay, I'm seventeen and a half. Please don't make us leave. My birthday is only a couple months away. Just give me until I turn eighteen, then I'll have legal guardianship of my brother."

"Where are your parents?" questioned Isabella.

"They're dead," her voice was flat and final. Grief flickered across her face before she gained control of herself. Thinking, she glanced over to Maddy. "They died in a car accident."

"Oh no," Maddy flung her arms around Parker. "Just like my parents." She squeezed Parker tight. "Of course, Theo will let you stay. I'll make sure of it."

"How did you end up at Twin Springs?" prompted Ava.

Relaxing into Maddy's embrace, Parker replied, "We used to vacation here. At least once a year. My brother and I had explored every inch of the hotel. I've always felt safe here. Happy."

Huge tears slipped down Maddy's face and she wiped them away with the backs of her hands. "I completely understand."

Rising from the chair's arm, JD looped her thumbs in her front pockets. Legs spread, she looked down at Maddy hugging the crap out of Parker. "Well that's the first honest answer out of your mouth."

"What do you mean?" snuffled Maddy.

"Parker's feeding you a line of bull and you're falling for it hook, line and sinker."

Maddy scowled up at JD and her hold on Parker tightened. "You're so mean. What do you understand about losing your parents? Of the pain of having someone who loved you with their whole heart, die?"

"Maddy," warned Isabella.

Shaking her head at the scene before her, JD replied, "She's not twenty-two, or even seventeen." Looking Parker up and down, she evaluated the bad dye job and slight pudge in her cheeks. "She's no more than fourteen."

"No way," gasped Maddy, pulling back. "You're two years younger than me? But—but—you've held jobs all over Twin Springs. You've ordered me around."

Hate emitting from her turquoise eyes towards JD, Parker's back stiffened and her voiced hardened, "Fourteen and a half."

Maddy pushed away from the younger girl. "You're a liar. You're probably just a spoiled brat who didn't know how good she had it and ran away."

Rage and the unfairness of Maddy's statement coursed through Parker's belly and she trembled with anger. Pointing a finger to her own chest, she spat, "I'm a spoiled brat?" She poked Maddy in the chest with her finger. "What about you, in your silk shirts and nice clothes? Ordering everyone around like you're royalty or something."

Her voice pitching, Parker lifted her chin, rocked her head side to side and mimicked the demeanor of a Princess. "What did you demand everyone call you when you first arrived?" Her eyes brightened. "That's it, Jacqueline. Princess Jacqueline," she mocked. Twirling a lock of her dyed black hair around her finger, she imitated the older teen. "I'm Princess Jacqueline and you must do as I say."

"Shut up!" yelled Maddy, pushing the other girl backward. "That was my mom's name. I bet your parents aren't even dead."

Hands dropping to her lap, Parker thought back to the day she'd discovered her parents lying in bed. "I found them. Their bodies stiff, eyes closed as if they were still sleeping. Their faces pink like cherries. But no matter how hard I shook them, they wouldn't wake. They were dead." She pushed away the pain and lashed out. "What do you care? You have two sets of parents now. Theo and Isabella, plus Jaxon and Ava. Do you know how much I wish I had someone who cared watching out for me and my brother? Do you know how hard it is to work and keep an eye on a little boy?"

Her world breaking apart, tears filled Parker eyes until they over spilled. She rubbed her eyes hard with the heels of her hands. Her voice lowered, laced with defeat. "You're spoiled Maddy. You have everything. People to take care of you. People who love you. People to keep you safe."

Crouching down before the young girl, JD said softly, "I understand how it feels to take care of someone else at a young age. The weight of the responsibility pressing down on your shoulders, dragging you down. You don't have to carry the burden alone anymore. I can help you."

Her chest hitching, the young girl stared at the redhead. She sounded sincere. Did she really know how it felt? Did she really care? A thread of hope in her voice, she asked, "Can we stay at Twin Springs?"

JD's eyes never wavered from the young girl's. "I can't make that promise. I don't belong here. Just like you."

"You don't belong here?" Anger pierced her heart. Parker

couldn't believe the bald-faced lie that she'd just told her. She couldn't trust her. She couldn't trust anyone. Not with her brother's life on the line. Passion flowed through Parker, raising her voice to a fevered pitch. "You don't belong here? Can't you see?" She pointed up to the wall behind JD. "That portrait proves you belong here."

At a loss for words, JD glanced up and into the Woman's painted eyes. "I don't know where I belong." She clasped Parker's hands between her own. "I spent my childhood not knowing my father or even my last name. Traveling with my mom from one place to another. Never staying long enough to call anywhere home. My mother wasn't able to take care of herself." Pain clouded her gaze. "I took care of her, not the other way around. Let me help you and your brother. Trust me."

The sincerity in her voice flowed over Parker and her heartbeat picked up in speed. Did she dare trust the redhead? The thought of staying at Twin Springs, being able to go to school and return to some type of a normal life, made her mouth water. She swallowed hard. "Can you promise my brother will be safe? No matter what?"

JD released one of Parker's hands and raised her right hand. "I promise on my life that I will keep you and your brother safe," she vowed.

Clearing her throat, Parker asked, "And together?"

A wide smile spread across the redhead's face, stretching out the freckles sprinkled across her nose and cheeks. "And together, I promise."

Parker gazed deep into her light green eyes. She wanted more than anything to trust her. To once again be a regular teenage girl. "Okay."

Maddy bounced in her seat. "This is great! But, I have to tell you, my brother will make you go to school as long as you're here. He feels an education comes first."

Hope spread through Parker's chest, warming her. The corner of her lips twitched. Suppressing the smile, she twisted her lips into a sneer and rolled her eyes. "I guess I can do the school thing." She gave a half shrug of indifference. "If I have to. As long as Colton has to go too."

CHAPTER THIRTY-FOUR

*R*ising to her feet, JD smiled at the teenagers. She would've killed to have a friend growing up. But she was the nutty girl arguing with herself in the corner.

"Why don't you girls go and block out two connected rooms for Parker and her brother. Make it close to Maddy's," suggested Ava.

Shooting to her feet, Parker gasped out, "I'm supposed to be holding down the Front Desk till the Night Auditor comes in. Who's tending the Grand Dame?" She moved to rush from the room.

Grabbing her by the hand, Ava prevented her from sprinting out the door. "Theo and I can handle the Front Desk. Go get a room. Maddy can lend you some clothes until we can go shopping. Relax. Have a bubble bath."

Moisture pooled in the young girl's eyes. "Are you sure?"

"I'm sure."

Maddy squealed, jumping up and down next to the younger teen. She tugged Parker by the hand, pulling her to the door. "Let's go."

"Wait," said Isabella. "Theo wanted me to speak with you about the previous fires at Twin Springs."

Pausing by the door, Parker held one hand in the air and placed her other palm over her heart. "I swear, my brother and I didn't have anything to do with the other fires."

"Do you know who set them?" questioned Ava.

Shaking her head, she replied. "I assumed Niles or Director Hollingsworth. But my brother and I didn't."

All eyes pivoted to JD. Surprised at the attention, she was shocked for a moment, before she realized why. "She's telling the truth."

"Wonderful," answered Ava. "Well then, off with you two."

Lacing her fingers through Parker's, Maddy pulled the girl out the door. "Let's run by the spa, soak in those huge teak bathtubs, and give each other pedicures."

"Don't do anything that Theo wouldn't approve of!" Isabella's shout flowed over the girls' heads as they rushed out the door. She settled down on the couch, grabbed a cookie and broke it in half. "Between the kids, your dad and uncle, Theo's going to have his hands full."

Leaning forward, Ava picked up one of the cookies and munched on the corners. "I caught," she paused, "what do you call them?" She snapped her fingers. "Oh yeah, the Geezers in here one morning trying to teach Ace new words. What does fubar mean?"

Feeling uncomfortable, stuck in the office with the two beautiful women, JD shuffled towards the door. "You don't want to know."

Longingly, she gazed at the exit and mumbled, "They seem to be having a great time, here at Twin Springs." She inched her way closer to the doors." Don't worry, their wives will call them back soon."

Isabella sighed, "Hopefully, they can stay until after our wedding."

"Be careful what you wish for." Pausing, her mind shifted gears, and she remembered her brother's claim of sabotage. Realizing she couldn't escape the room yet, she added, "I know Jaxon was sent to Twin Springs to find out if you were filing fraudulent claims. When he said you were in the clear, I didn't realize there were more fires. Or that they were fires set by two different people."

Isabella shared a look with her sister. "We should've fully explained. Niles was our Security Manager. He grew up with Ava and me. Over the years, something changed within him. He sabotaged Twin Springs in an attempt to destroy the Grand Dame. He told me so. When he tried to drown me. Instead, the power of the water sucked him down stream and he drowned."

Ava added her own story. "After I returned to Twin Springs, my old boss followed me. He was a crazy man. We think he started the fires here after Niles died."

Gazing up at the portrait, JD absorbed the new information and took a moment to process the data. "I think tonight was a little boy playing with fire. I don't think he meant to burn down the hotel."

"I agree," stated Ava.

The two sisters shared a glance and Isabella shifted to the edge of her seat. "You know, Parker was right, you do belong here."

Uncomfortable with the women's support, an uneasy feeling rolled down her spine and she moved closer to the door. "Let's not go getting all warm and fuzzy. I'm not going to paint toes together or something."

Delighted with her reply, Ava laughed. Not willing to miss the opportunity to chime in, Ace copied the sound.

"You're family." Ava patted the couch cushion. "Sit with us. I won't touch your feet. I promise."

Isabella snorted. "Don't believe her. Ava loves to make people over."

"Girl stuff. Um, thanks." She rubbed her moist palms on her

jeans and inched away from the sisters. "I know Jaxon is marrying Ava and you all feel that makes us family." She shuffled closer to the door.

"No, it's more," replied Ava. "Go ahead and tell her."

Isabella's cheeks flushed. "Kind of embarrassing," she muttered. "I guess, I should start at the beginning."

JD suppressed a groan and reached for the knob.

"You see, I had an imaginary friend growing up. Emma, she taught me how to cook. When I reached my teens, I started having these dreams. Dreams that I drowned. At the time, I didn't realize that my dreams were really Emma communicating with me. I think she wanted me to find her."

JD halted and whipped around. "Emma was a ghost?"

"Yes, the ghost of Emerald Rockwell."

"Tell her about the smells," prompted Ava, watching JD's reaction.

"There was a strong scent of vanilla every time Emma tried to communicate with me."

"Vanilla?" JD's legs shook beneath her weight. Moving away from the doors and back towards the sisters, she sank onto the couch.

"Yes," replied Ava, bending forward. "With me, things were different. I started sleepwalking in my teens. I would wake up in strange places and not know how I ended up there, or what I did while sleeping. When I recently returned to Twin Springs, my sleepwalking also returned. But now, I remembered everything from when I was sleepwalking. Ruby would take over my body and give me clues to what had happened to her. That's how we found her body dumped at the opening of a tunnel. Until then, everyone thought she'd died in the Great Fire of 1928." Ava pinned JD with her gaze, "I smell roses, when Ruby's around."

"Roses," repeated JD weakly. She couldn't believe it. These women's stories were so close to her life.

"You smelled it too, didn't you?" questioned Ava. "Before you passed out, you smelled the roses in here. Did you see Ruby?"

"I—" began JD, but the direct stares from the sisters stopped her. Did she dare share her deepest secret with these women? What would be the worst thing that could happen if she did? They couldn't lock her up in a looney bin. "Yes, I could smell roses."

"I knew it," exclaimed Ava.

"Knew it," repeated Ace, pacing his cage.

Her eyes earnest, Isabella leaned in. "Have you always smelled roses or vanilla?"

Over the blonde sister's head, JD stared into the painted eyes of the Woman. "No, lavender."

"Lavender?" Isabella's brows wrinkled. An odd expression flowed over her face before she stilled, and then leaned forward. "Of course, lavender! I've always thought Twin Springs smelled of vanilla, roses and lavender. The fragrance of home."

"The fragrance of home?" repeated JD, her heart slamming against her chest. "For me, lavender was the stench of hell. It meant the Woman was coming. For me, the Woman, you call her Amethyst, wasn't a friend. She tormented my mother until she turned to drugs and alcohol to mute her presence. My mother begged for the Woman to leave her alone, until finally her mind broke. When Mom died, the Woman haunted me. I hate the scent of lavender."

Isabella reached out and laid her hand over hers. "I'm sorry. It must've been terrible."

Pulling her hand back, she shrugged. "I dealt with it."

"What else?" asked Ava. "Why did you pass out?"

Bounding to her feet, JD resumed pacing in front of the fireplace. She wanted to tear down the painting and rip it to shreds with her knife. But the need to lessen the burden she'd carried for so long propelled words from her reluctant lips. "The Woman always appeared to me in black and white, like those old movies on TV. My first day at Twin Springs things started to change. I saw images, like movie clips from a silent black and white film, playing out before me. The first time I entered this room, the Woman transformed from black and white into full color. I never knew her hair was red, like mine. Or that her face matched mine, because it was always covered by strands of her gray hair.

"She thanked me and merged into the painting. You were all here in the General's Office but none of you said you saw her."

Isabella's breath caught. "I didn't but, other than me, no one has ever seen Emma. Not even Ava."

Speaking in a flat voice, she continued, "It doesn't' matter. The day I passed out, the scenes flipped. Our world became silent and I entered the world of the past, in full technicolor. I followed Ame through a day in her world. I was the ghost." She told the sisters about her journey.

Ava absorbed her tale. "Why do you think Ame is coming to you and so vividly now?"

Pivoting, JD's light green gaze met the sisters'. "You tell me."

Shaking her head, Isabella replied, "It can't be to find out how she died. We know she died in the fire. Ame's body was the only one found."

Ava spoke up. "Do you think Maddy's right? Ame wants JD to find her necklace?"

Feeling their acceptance of her experiences, she walked closer to the sisters. "I don't know. Seems like a lot of interference for a piece of jewelry."

Surging to her feet, Isabella piped up, "Perhaps showing you a piece of her life, was Ame's way of thanking you for bringing her home."

Also rising to her feet, Ava reached out and grasped her sister's hand before also linking her fingers within JD's cold hand. The three women created a circle. "Whatever it was. We're in this together. We'll figure this out."

CHAPTER THIRTY-FIVE

*H*olding the kid by the collar, Logan opened the door of the Security Office and pushed the seven-year-old pyromaniac inside. "Sit," he commanded.

Colton climbed up in Jaxon's chair, shoved his hands under his dangling legs and gazed at his sneakers. One of his laces was loose and draped to the floor.

Trying to control the emotions surging through his body, Logan paced within the compact room. He flexed his hands and suppressed the urge to throttle the kid. *Just wait for Theo and Jaxon,* he chanted as he paced the four steps the room allowed, turned, and rubbed at the pain in his hip. *Keep your cool and wait.* He paced another four steps before turning and repeating the process over again. *What if the alarm didn't go off? What if the fire had spread?* The questions piled up and he paced faster and faster, soothing the pain with his fist until finally words exploded from his mouth, "What the hell were you thinking?"

The kid lifted his shoulder and refused to look him in the face.

"You didn't think." A molten spray of rage flowed through his voice. "Admit it."

He shook his head. Then Colton's chest started heaving, holding back his tears, and he mumbled a reply.

His unintelligible answer just pissed Logan off more.

"You didn't think, did you? What if the fire had spread?" He pounded his fist against his leg. "Do you know the destruction fire causes?"

Colton burrowed his small body further into the chair.

"Look at me!" Logan's voice reverberated through the tiny room.

Shaking his head, the boy refused to look up.

A red haze clouded Logan's vision. "You want to play with fire and you can't even look at me?" Getting on his knees before Colton, he jerked his face up by the chin. "Look at what fire causes. Can you see how it shriveled my skin, ate away at it? The pain of fire's bite was unbearable. Agonizing. I screamed so loud that I didn't even recognize my own voice. Then I cried like a baby. Balled up in the dirt." He shook the kid's chair. "What if the fire had spread? You saw your sister in that hall. What if it caught her? Ate at her skin. What if she now looked like this!" He smacked the burned side of his face with his deformed hand.

"How would you feel then? It doesn't matter because after her face was destroyed there would be nothing—" He squeezed the arms of the chair, his throat clogged with emotions, but he continued to rant, his voice hoarse with fear. "Do you hear me? There'd be nothing you could do about it. She'd look like this." He glared at him out of his half-melted eye. "And you'd be powerless to fix it."

Tears and snot streamed down the kids face. But Logan refused to care. The what-if's stabbing his heart, he whispered, "What if she died?"

Colton's face crumbled. He threw his arms around Logan's neck and squeezed. "Sorry." He sobbed, tucking his face into the crook of Logan's neck. "I'm sorry. I didn't mean to burn everything. I didn't."

Holding the boy's shaking frame, the rage drained from Logan. "So am I kid." He pulled the kid in close and attempted to squeeze away both of their pain. "It's okay. It'll be alright."

Getting himself under control, Colton wiped his face across Logan's sleeve. "Do you hate me?"

"Naw." Logan released him. Putting some space between him and the feelings swirling like a hurricane within the room, he gained his feet, rubbed at his face and turned away. "You're a pain in the butt." Only when he was sure that his emotions were under control did he turn back. "Hell, so was I as a kid."

Nodding, Colton absorbed his words. He wiped the moisture from his face with the back of his hand.

Silence stretched between the two of them. Logan leaned against the wall, wondering what he was supposed to do with the boy until Theo and Jaxon arrived.

Colton rubbed the toe of his shoe along the floor in front of him. "I didn't mean to start a fire."

Logan snorted. "Well, that's what happens when you play with lighters." He shoved his hands into his pockets. "What were you doing anyway?"

"I—I—," He snuck a glance up. "I was making a superhero."

"What?" Shocked, Logan blinked rapidly then shook his head. "Who wants a burned superhero?"

"I do." He glanced up and gnawed on his lip before adding. "I want him to look like you."

Physically jolted and speechless, he stared at the kid. He started to speak a couple times but just couldn't get the words out. Finally, he cleared his throat. "Why the hell would you want that?"

"I was making a superhero called the Blue Flame." Leaning forward, Colton's words sped up. "He's forged by fire! That's how he gets his superpowers. He helps people by seeing into the future and preventing them from getting hurt. He can even bring people back to life."

"Getting burned doesn't make you a superhero. It just sucks."

He pulled his hat out of his back pocket, slapped it against his leg and pulled it down tight over his head. "Next time you want to make a superhero come to me first."

"Cool." The kid's gaze glittered with excitement. "Superhero training."

"You're a weird kid." The phone in Logan's pocket buzzed. He lifted it to his ear. "Finally! Where the hell are you guys?" Listening, he watched the kid fiddle with the pencils on Jaxon's desk before spinning around in his chair. "No way. I'm not doing it."

Listening, Colton halted his spinning by dragging the toe of his tennis shoe on the ground. He stared up and tears began welling up in his eyes.

At the sight, Logan closed his eyes and clenched his jaw for a moment before letting out a deep sigh. "Fine. Roger that."

He replaced the cell phone into his jean jacket pocket. "Damn it," he growled.

"What's wrong," Colton whispered. The color had drained from his face and his knuckles were white from squeezing the chair's arms.

"Looks like it's just you and me, kid. Theo, the Fire Marshal and Jaxon will be a while. So, I'm in charge of you."

Colton canted his head all the way back to look Logan in the eye. "Is my sister alright?"

Wondering what the hell he was supposed to do with the kid, Logan absentmindedly answered, "Yeah, she's at the spa with Maddy. Doing girl stuff."

"What are you guys going to do with us? Send us back?" His lower lip trembled.

Logan's heart cracked. *Damn it.* He wanted to scoop the kid up in his arms and squeeze him. Instead, he ruffled his hair and replied. "Nope." He kidded to lighten the mood, "You've got to stay here and work off the damage you did. Theo got you guys a room a few doors down from Maddy's."

Colton turned away and wiped at his eyes with the back of his hand. "I guess that's cool," he mumbled.

"We're pretty much stuck with you guys."

Colton spun back, "You are?" He reigned in his excitement and gave a shrug. "It might take some time to pay it all off. We could be here a long, long time."

Not sure where the boy was heading, Logan replied, "Yep. It might. Years."

"Years," whispered Colton. His face was still streaked black with soot and ash, making his turquoise eyes appear innocent in contrast. "Since the girls are goofing, do you think we can do guy stuff?"

He glanced away from the kid and covered his smile with a cough into his hand, considering the question. Little boys could be tricky. "It's after ten at night. What kind of guy stuff do you want to do?"

Nibbling on his lip, he thought. "Let's go to the hot springs. It's the best after it's closed. No one's there. It glows 'cause there are lights in the bottom. Way cool."

Silently, Colton's expectant face pleaded.

Logan groaned. "I guess I'm stuck with you for the rest of the night. Hell, why not. It's been a good twelve years since I've snuck into the hot springs."

With a loud whoop, Colton jumped from the chair and headed for the door.

But Logan caught him by the back of the collar, "First we've got to get you cleaned up."

"Oh man," he whined. "Isn't that what the pool's for?"

Raising a brow, he considered the kid's comment. "What the hell. Let's go."

The kid in tow, Logan limped through the Grand Lobby and out the doors to the hot springs. He reached up into a crack in the outer wall of the woman's bath house and snagged a key.

"Cool, usually I just climb the fence."

"Stick with me kid and you'll learn all kinds of things." Logan couldn't believe the words that had left his mouth, but it felt good. Right. He pulled the gate closed behind them, tossed his baseball cap into the air and yelled, "Last one in is a rotten egg!" He sprinted toward the pool and jumped in clothes and all.

"This is awesome!" yelled Colton. He ran after him and cannon balled a few feet to his right.

Laughing, they pulled their shoes off and they floated to the surface. Logan had no idea how long they splashed, goofed and raced from one end of the pool to the other, but he was all worn out.

Tired, they sat on one of the long ledges under the water and leaned back. The hot springs water collided with the cold air and created a mist that hovered over the pool. Resting their heads against the edge, they studied the stars twinkling in the night sky. The sound of the water cascading down the big waterfall at the other end of the pool soothed their souls.

The gate squeaked open and they glanced up. In walked JD, barely discernible in her black outfit.

"Pools closed," Colton called out. "Boys only."

"Is that so?" Hands on her hips, she called back, "Well then, I'm sure you don't want to hear a story about the evil spirit who haunts little girls." She turned away and tossed over her shoulder, "That's too bad. Have fun."

"Wait!" Colton called out. He leaned towards Logan and cupped his hand to cover their conversation, but his voice traveled across the water anyway. "Do you think she really knows a story about an evil spirit? Is that like a villain?"

At the sight of JD, Logan's heart pounded in his chest. Selfishly, he replied, "You'll never know if she can't join us."

Brows furrowed, Colton considered his options. "You can come in, if you make a cannon ball big enough to spray us."

"Please," mocked JD. She moved back ten paces, pulled a knife out of her boot and placed it on a white, ladder-back lounger.

Beside the knife she placed a small spiral notebook. She dug into her other boot, took out her cell phone and tossed it beside the other items. Only then, did she tug her feet free from the boots.

"What all does she have in there?" asked Logan before his mouth went completely dry.

For JD had yanked out her rubber band and her hair tumbled down around her shoulders, a glorious mass of red flames. Now those flames, he'd love to have spilling all over his naked body. He cleared his throat before shouting out, "Anything else?"

With a smile, she raced to the pool and cannonballed with enough force that the water sprayed in all directions. Splitting the surface of the water right in front of them, she spit water into their faces.

"Wow!" laughed Colton.

"You can't catch me!" JD shouted and took off swimming towards the waterfall.

With a glance at each other, the boys took chase.

Slowing at the last minute, she allowed Colton to reach the bench hidden under the waterfall first. "You're fast!"

"Too fast for you," replied Colton, his chest heaving. He settled himself on the bench between the two adults. "It's way cool to be inside a waterfall."

Leaning against the mossy rock, Logan couldn't take his eyes off of JD. Her wet hair spilled down her back. Her clothes clung to her in all the best places. And her face was lit up. *Damn it, why didn't I suggest skinny dipping?* Peeling his gaze from the rise and fall of her breasts, he said, "Alright, pay up. Tell us the story."

The falling water enclosing them within a world of their own, JD licked her wet lips and began, "Once upon a time, there was an evil spirit. She could fade in and out of walls and would follow a little girl and her mother from place to place. The mother was a brave woman who would fight off the spirit the best she could. She'd send the little girl away anytime the spirit came. To hide from the evil spirit, they'd run from town to town, criss-crossing the country. But she always found them.

"On the little girl's eighth birthday, she made a wish. A magical wish that the spirit would go away and leave them alone. Her wish was heard and granted, but in a way that she'd never expected. Nor wanted.

"A blaze of fire came and swept the evil spirit away. But her mother was also caught in the fire and taken away. In the end, the mother was freed from being haunted, but she was never able to see her daughter again."

"Wow," Colton absorbed the story. "What about the little girl? Did she escape the spirit too?"

JD watched the falling water. "That tale is for another time."

"Awe." Thinking, Colton kicked at the water. "Sorry I started the fire."

JD trailed her fingers through the water, "Will you ever play with fire again?"

Water dripping from his finger, he crossed his heart. "Never."

Logan thought about earlier. How his anger had overcome him, swept through him like a brush fire. He shouldn't have grabbed her leg and forced her to the ground. He could've hurt her. The idea of causing her pain made him feel physically ill. Clearing his throat, Logan added, "If we're handing out apologies, I'm sorry that I swept your leg and held you down."

Laughter lacing her voice, JD replied, "I'm sorry that I held a knife to your throat."

Colton's gaze swiveled from one adult to the other. "You have to kiss and make up. That's what my mom and dad did when they were truly sorry."

Blood roared in Logan's ears. His mouth was suddenly dry. *Thanks kid,* he thought. *I owe you one.* He leaned over Colton. "Don't want to disappoint the kid."

JD hesitated. "I guess we should set a good example."

She leaned forward and as her eyes closed, her wet lashes

swept down and lay on her smooth skin. For a brief moment, Logan absorbed her beauty and filed it away in his heart. He pressed his lips to hers and fire blazed through him when her lips opened beneath his. He deepened the kiss. Itched to pull her closer.

But Colton squirmed between them.

Reluctantly, he pulled away. "Forgive me?"

She gave a breathy, "Yes."

Later that night, laying between the clean sheets of a king size bed in a suite at Twin Springs, Logan stared up at the ceiling. Colton and his sister were asleep four doors down and a very sexy redhead was on the other side of the wall. He wondered what kind of a nightgown a woman like JD would wear to bed. A thought occurred to him. "She probably sleeps nude."

A stupid smile spread across his face. He felt alive. Human. He repeated Colton's words from earlier. "Yeah, this is awesome."

CHAPTER THIRTY-SIX

*D*ressed in brand spanking new jeans and a Batman t-shirt, Colton shoved his action figures into his new, super-cool backpack. He loved the red lightning bolts, comic book clouds and the red and yellow superman crest with a capital C in the middle. "I can't believe they gave it to me, Christmas isn't until tomorrow."

He thought living at Twin Springs was the best before the fire, but now it was even more awesome. He had permission to go anywhere within the hotel. Except that he'd have to go to school, that kind of sucked. Slinging the backpack over his shoulders, he decided to track down his favorite hero. Using his superhero voice, he declared, "Maybe if the Blue Flame trusts me, he'll give me some of his power." His voice lowered into a whisper. "I'm going to discover the Blue Flame's secrets. Then I can protect everybody."

Rounding the corner from the Grand Lobby to the east wing, Colton could hear the Blue Flame arguing. Pressing a pretend button on his arm, the little boy made a sound deep in his throat and his tennis shoes kicked into super drive. Ducking under the red velvet cord, he ignored the sign saying "Pardon Our Dust." He crouched down and listened, trying to identify the foe of his new hero. A woman. Lying on his stomach, he lifted a corner of the plastic sheeting and low crawled beneath.

The paper-covered floor crinkled as he approached the Blue Flame and JD examining their plans. Logan's blond hair glowed with power under the lighting. Colton knew he hid his identity beneath a clean t-shirt, his cape beneath a blue work shirt and his tights under his jeans. JD wore her superhero suit, clad in black leather pants and a black long sleeve shirt. Her red hair was in a long ponytail that swung down her back. A story built in his head and he inched forward.

"We know you are there, Colton," hollered the Blue Flame.

Springing to his feet, he rushed forward, his pack bouncing on his back. "What gave me away?"

JD reached out and tussled his blond curls with her fingers. "If you're going into stealth mode, you must learn to control your breathing and make no sound. Steady your breathing by inhaling slowly through your nose and back out your mouth. Like this." She demonstrated for him.

His eyes widened with the information, Colton nodded. He hung his mouth open and copied her actions. His mind reveled with a new idea. She might have secret powers, too, that would help him. "Are you the Invisible Woman?" he asked.

"No, but don't worry." JD flicked the tip of his nose with her finger. "The Invisible Woman will never haunt you. I've got her trapped back in time."

Logan rolled his eyes. "What are you doing sneaking around?"

"Theo told me to hang out with you until dinner." Colton's stomach turned with the lie and he waited, watching to see if the Blue Flame guessed his secret.

"Did he now?" Logan's blue gaze pierced Colton to the spot.

Unsure what to do, the little boy stared down at his shoes and waited.

Grunting at the mischievous boy, Logan replied, "Fine. I was just taking JD up to the top of the Tower. Would you like to go?"

The Blue Flame wanted him to go on a mission? With him? The thrill of being the superhero's sidekick bubbled within his chest. *Way cool!* "Yeah!" he shouted, giving a great big whoop. Anticipation rolled through his body and his backpack vibrated with his excitement. Racing through the heavy plastic towards the elevator across the hall, he built on the story growing in his imagination and whispered, "The secret hideout of the Blue Flame."

The two adults followed behind him, Logan lifting a sheet of the plastic for JD to pass through.

Ignoring his action, she lifted her own sheet and dropped the heavy plastic after exiting so that it swung right into Logan's surprised face.

Growling deep in his chest, he limped behind her. "Top floor," he ordered. "Real nice, Diamond," he muttered down to the woman beside him.

Suppressing a smile, she replied, "Call me that again and I'll cut your tongue out."

Logan chuckled down deep in his chest. "Sure, sweetheart. If that's your idea of foreplay."

"Shush," JD punched Logan in the arm. "Not funny. Little ears." And Logan just laughed harder.

Eagerly, Colton pressed the elevator button. Rocking back and forth in his tennis shoes, he watched the numbers move above the elevator door and listened to his superheroes. *Diamond, that was JD's secret name.*

Once the elevator doors slid open, he shot out of the elevator and sped across the newly laid, wide plank flooring. He didn't pay attention to the granite-topped reception desk. Or the eight-foot-wide wall, rocked from ceiling to floor with dark gray rocks, separating the reception desk from the dining room and dance floor. Up lighting reflected off the quietly cascading water as it dribbled a path down the rock's face. The words, Tower Restaurant, were cut out in polished steel and backlit. The swirling words floated in front of the rock wall, with water flowing behind it.

Leading the way, Logan's lopsided cant brought JD around the desk. "Look at those floor to ceiling windows," exclaimed JD. "The plans don't do them justice. They open the room up to the darkened mountain skyline on three sides." Tables sprinkled the outer edges of the room, leaving room for a dance floor. "You did a wonderful job."

Rocking back on his heels, Logan dug his hands into his pockets and gave a crooked grin. "Now that's the kind of sweet talk I like."

Rolling her eyes, JD walked around the room, touching everything.

Keeping tabs on the two adults, Colton zoomed in and out between the tables. He still wasn't sure if Diamond really had super powers or not. From the corner of his eye, he tracked the Blue Flame showing her around the room. "This is where your art show and auction will be," he heard Logan say.

"I see you ignored my suggestion on adding molding to the space."

"I thought long and hard about it. But decided the wooden beams were worth facing the heat of your wrath."

Something in the tone of the Blue Flame's voice was strange and Colton watched them from the corner of his eye.

Diamond tripped but the Blue Flame saved her and held her within his arms. "Sometimes a man has to take matters into his own hands. Think outside the box."

Something sparked between the Blue Flame and Diamond and sent a warm, fuzzy feeling through Colton's heart and down to his tummy. "Let's go up top. Let's go up top!" he shouted, making a beeline for the wrought iron, circular stairs in the corner of the room. Under his breath he repeated the Blue Flames words. "Sometimes a man has to take matters into his own hands."

He left them behind and sped up the stairs. He liked the clanging sound his feet made on the metal treads as he climbed. He exploded out into a glass-enclosed alcove before automatic glass doors swooshed open before him and cold the mountain air surrounded him. "Yes! The Blue Flame's secret hideout."

With the wide-open skyline above, he raced around the square, outer ring of the terrace before getting up on tip toe to peer over the high banister. Even at night, he could see everything from up here. The grounds below glowed with lights. The shimmer of the ice skating rink, the outdoor Hot Springs pool glowed green, the crimson flickers of fire pit where guests made s'mores, the lights of ski range off in the distance. Everything.

Heat radiated from low under the banister and warmed his feet. Colton paused. Gathering saliva within his mouth, he shot the spit out over the banister. Giggling, he looked over to see the results.

"There will be none of that," growled Logan, dragging him back.

Undeterred, Colton continued to race around, dashing between the potted plants and bench seats. Altering course, he disappeared under one of the four, arched pillars holding up a shiny, metal domed roof. Skidding to a stop, he stared up at the underbelly of the dome. Thousands of little lights twinkled like stars from within the copper lining. "Cool."

Drawn to the large water fountain in the center, he sat on the rock ledge and stared into the clear water. From below the glassy surface, pin prick lights glowed in multiple colors lighting up tiny fish swimming around in groups.

"How can it be so warm up here?" asked Diamond.

The Blue Flame's low voice rumbled, "The floors are heated, and we pipe heat up through heating grates around the perimeter."

Colton glanced over, noticing that Diamond was unusually quiet. Glad their attention was on each other, he removed his backpack and rummaged around until he found his Blue Flame action figure. He tugged his sleeve up and reached into the water, pretending the Blue Flame swam beneath the surface. Not noticing he soaked his shirt, he let go of the Blue Flame and stuck his arm further into the water up to his armpit. He tried to catch one of the little golden fish within his fist.

Warmth lined Diamond's voice. "The concept is like what I saw in my visions, but you have improved the terrace and made it even more spectacular."

The water tickling his armpit, the little boy stilled. "Diamond has visions. She is a superhero!"

"Get your hand out of the fountain," she ordered.

Snatching his arm back, Colton glanced at her back. Water dripped from his wet arm and his mouth gaped open. Shaking off the water, he thought in awe, "She must be able to see all around her."

Logan shuffled around the perimeter. "I had quite the challenge because you decided the Tower must have a fountain area and dome complete with clock. First, we had to remove a window and use a crane to lift the steel beams that were needed to support the additional weight. Tore out the ceiling to install the beams." He winked at her with his good eye. "Figured I deserved the wooden beams for that. Then we made a steel ramp from the east wing roofline to bring up all the materials, so we could build the dome and install the fountain. Quite the feat."

"It makes the space though."

"Seeing your eyes light up, I agree."

Again, Colton's tummy tingled. He raced away, out the other side of the archway and climbed up on one of the banisters lining the terrace. With his arms held out at his sides, he walked the thin width.

A great roar penetrated the cold mountain air.

Surprised, Colton teetered and felt his body tip towards open air. Warm arms wrapped around him and the Blue Flame scooped him up around the waist.

Placing him safely on the floor, Logan squatted down and held him by the shoulders. "Fool! You'll do more than crack open your head if you fall. Don't climb up there again."

The phone buzzed in Diamond's boot and she reached down and answered it. "Yeah?" She gave Colton the death stare, promising retribution for his foolish actions. "Sure, I'll be right there." Slipping her phone back into her boot, she said, "I have to go. Ava needs my help with something in her office."

Crouching down before the small boy, her gaze melded with his and she used her mind powers on him. "Don't think your golden curls or cute face will work on me. You need to be more careful. Or I will make you hang out with the Geezers all day long." Bending closer she whispered in his ear. "And I won't let you play with Logan anymore. I don't care what Theo says. Do we understand each other?"

Nodding, Colton's whole body tingled. "Yes, ma'am." That was it. She could read minds too! For the first time in his life, Colton was in love.

Both males watched as the woman of their dreams walked away. "See you later," Logan called out.

"Wow," whispered Colton. "She's the best."

"You said it," replied Logan, appreciating JD's long legs clad in leather. Her long, russet ponytail swayed with her determined stride. "She's a spitfire of a woman. Makes a man feel alive."

Grasping the three fingers of Logan's right hand within his tiny fist, Colton breathed the words, "She's better than Superman."

Staring down at the boy's fingers wrapped around his, Logan swallowed hard before replying. "Well, she does have a way of making men feel like mere mortals." He muttered under his breath, "She makes you question if you are a real man or not."

Leaning his head against Logan's side, Colton sighed, "I'm so glad we came to Twin Springs."

Logan gave a long, hard look at the boy beside him. The stars glittered in the night sky around them and cast them into a storybook world where monsters weren't real. "Me too, kid. Me too."

CHAPTER THIRTY-SEVEN

*W*eaving through the guests in the Grand Lobby, JD breathed in deeply and savored the scent of the huge gingerbread version of Twin Springs on display. She nodded at the two teenagers working the Front Desk. Since she'd discovered Parker's real age, the runaway had seemed to develop a sisterly relationship with Maddy. They bickered and yelled at each other just like the Geezers.

Pulling her cell phone out of her boot, she checked the time. She needed to hurry and find out what Ava wanted. She hoped her business dinner with the doc wouldn't last too long, so she could catch back up with Logan and Colton.

Her boys.

Staggered, she halted in the middle of the Lobby. Somehow, she'd fallen for both of them. Logan's sense of humor and Colton's zest for life. She had the sudden urge to run up to her father and beg to keep them. Like they were two strays.

She couldn't help it. Her heart ached. She yearned for what everyone around her had found. What Isabella discovered with Theo and her idiot brother stumbled across with Ava. That other person who cared and wanted to spend time with you. Loved you.

Even the Woman had found love with Everett. Since the Woman hadn't haunted her since that day, perhaps it was time for her to find someone to share her life with. She wanted to share her life with Logan.

Shaking her head, she crossed to Ava's office and halted in front of the door. She knocked before entering. A new habit for her.

Ava looked gorgeous in a black skirt and a deep purple shirt with wide, sweeping sleeves. Her chin length hair enhanced her features and sensuality flowed around the woman like a silver lined cloud of perfume. Ava had a sense of style. Not only with the clothes she wore, but also in handling the people around her. It astounded JD.

Personally, she detested speaking with anyone over four feet tall. Somehow, Ava enchanted the guests she assisted and created that special experience for them that they were unable to verbalize but secretly wished for. Her sensuality, beauty and ease with others were everything JD could never become. "Hey Ava, I just have a minute. I've got business."

"Oh, you have more time than that," replied Ava.

The door behind JD slammed shut. Turning to confront the danger, she found Isabella barring the door with her small body, looking just a cute as her sister in her chef jacket, jeans and white tennis shoes. JD's hands settled on her hips and her brow arched up, "What are you doing?"

Spreading her arms wide, Isabella leaned back against the doors. "I'm not letting you leave."

"Have you lost it?" JD's phone beeped, and she snagged it out of her boot. "Sniffing too much vanilla or something?"

"Very funny," snorted Isabella, snatching the phone from her hand and slipping it into the pocket of her chef jacket. "We'll have none of that, right now. You have a date."

"No—" Was that what Logan meant when he said see you later? Was the date with Logan? JD's heart thundered against her chest. "Not that I'm aware of."

Ava pulled the chair out from behind her desk and pressed on JD's shoulders until she sat. "Maddy said you've got a date with Dr. Ottoman. We're going to guarantee that you go looking like a woman, not a paratrooper."

Disappointment filled her and her shoulders drooped. The date wasn't with Logan. She surged up. "It's just business."

"It's never just business." With amazing strength, Ava pushed her back. "And we're going to make sure you look your best."

JD crossed her arms. "What's the matter with what I'm wearing?" Since it wasn't Logan, she didn't care. "It works. I'm even color coordinated."

"Nothing," Isabella clasped her hands to her chest. "It's just that men tend to like their women a little," she paused searching for the right word, "softer."

Glancing down at her matching black leather pants, shirt and boots, she frowned at the sisters. Did Logan like his women softer? "Why can't he just like me for who I am?" she asked, thinking of Logan.

Isabella shrugged, "Don't worry, Ava will fix everything."

JD considered the idea of a makeover. After her quick dinner, she'd meet up with Logan and see if his attitude softened with her new, softer appearance. "I'll do it."

Wheeling a serving tray out from behind the couch, Isabella reassured JD. "The doctor won't recognize you."

"I don't really give a damn about the doc," she mumbled. Eyeing the shining metal girl-tools of destruction piled on the serving cart, a chill traveled down her arms. "I've changed my mind." She attempted to surge out of the chair. "No way."

It took both Ava and Isabella to press her back. "You're not going anywhere." Ava sounded like a prison matron, and ripped the rubber band out of JD's hair, tearing a chunk of flaming hair out with the band.

Rubbing her scalp, she shouted, "Fuck me! What the hell, Ava? That hurt like a mother—"

In the corner, Ace squawked and yelled, "Fuck!" He shifted his weight between his two claws and flapped his wings.

Isabella shoved a cookie into JD's mouth and shushed the bird.

She choked back her final words. Frowning at the tiny, womanly form of Isabella, JD munched on the cookie and tossed around the idea of pounding the Fairbanks sisters into dirt. After she'd strung the bird up, of course.

"Seriously, JD," said Isabella, slipping out of her chef's jacket and tossing it on the back of the couch. "You don't have to speak like a debutant here at Twin Springs. Just take it down a notch."

She was surprised at how toned and fit Isabella's arms were beneath the jacket. Maybe there was more to the sisters than she first thought. "What's wrong with the way I talk?" she grumbled around the cookie.

Isabella's lips twisted into a half smile. "Nothing if you are a sailor off ship looking for a booty call in an alleyway."

Both her brother and Lee spoke this way. So did the Geezers. Why couldn't she? "I like the way I talk. It gets the job done and brings results."

Brushing out her hair, Ava asked, "Does saying fuck really bring you the outcome you desire or is it the promise of retribution you give behind the word that brings the right effect?"

Considering Ava's words, she shrugged. "What does it matter?"

Propping herself on the arm of the couch, Isabella broke another cookie in half. "Well, for one, Theo feels your vocabulary is unsuitable for the workplace. And since we live where we work, that pretty much means it's inappropriate all the time. Like it or not, your actions and words reflect upon the Grand Dame."

Allowing JD's mane to flow around her shoulders, Ava added, "All of us strive to make Twin Springs a place where people come to relax, forget about the world outside and enjoy each other's company in the lap of luxury. This hotel is a place where families retreat to make memories. Not to hear gutter talk."

"Besides," bringing out a hot curler, Ava clicked the jaws of the curler open and closed as she spoke, "we want you to stick around and Theo will boot anyone who'll undermine or damage the success of his family and the Grand Dame. Even if that person is a part of his family."

Ava smoothed a long lock of JD's flaming hair and directed her sister to spray the length with hairspray. The air around her filled with a thick cloud.

Choking, she waved her hands in front of herself and bit back the foul words she believed were more than appropriate for this kind of torture.

Ava curled her hair and wrapped the section around a large curler before pinning it to her scalp. She repeated the process, section by section, around her head with Isabella spraying her toxic fumes as she went.

"You're gassing me," she complained. Thankful when they finished, she snuck a quick, covert glance at the Woman in the portrait and grumbled, "What the hell have you gotten me into now?"

Finished pinning her hair, Ava smoothed green muck onto JD's face and hands. "Lean back, close your eyes," she prompted. "You don't have to be tough all the time. It's okay to let down your guard every now and then. You never know what will happen. You might even let a certain guy into your life. Maybe Logan?"

His disfigured face floated behind her closed lids. Inexplicably, the man with half a face drew her to him. Even in her dreams. She sensed the sorrow burned into his soul and a part of her reached out to sooth him. To heal him with her body and her spirit.

Verbally, the man sparred with her at every turn. "I like having to think quickly on my feet around him." He brought her alive. The corner of her lips tilted up, creating little fissures within the mask hardening on her face and her heart picked up pace. "Damn, he's a good fighter. I never expected for him to sweep leg and pin me to the floor."

Over her head, the sisters shared a look.

"I told you so," whispered Ava.

"You know," purred Isabella, "Dr. Ottoman seems like a nice man. He was really concerned about you. It was very brave of him to ask you out in front of everyone. He's been telling Maddy that he helps hurt children, just like you."

"I guess so." She frowned, and cracks formed between her eyebrows. Her mind shifted to the soft-spoken man. "He seems interested," she murmured trying to appease her.

Thinking of her time with Logan in the hot springs, she smiled wide. *But Logan seemed very interested.*

"But," inserted Ava, laying a warm, wet, washcloth over her face. "Logan's a great guy. Before the accident, we used to tease him and call him surfer boy. With his sun kissed blond hair brushed back from his forehead and his sea blue eyes, he melted hearts. And funny! He used to make us all laugh."

"Even Niles," quietly murmured Isabella.

"Yes. Even Niles," agreed Ava, wiping JD's face clean before smoothing on moisturizer and foundation. "Perhaps both men just need a woman to give them a chance."

Remaining mute, she eyed the sisters. Their lives seemed so happy, as if their every desire had been fulfilled. Why were they prattling on about her love life? Or lack of love life. Just like the Woman, sticking their noses in where they didn't belong.

"Let's get you dressed before I apply the makeup and let down your hair. I don't want to mess you up when we slip this dress over your head," ordered Ava.

From the underside of the serving tray, Ava snatched out two wisps of black material. "We will start with these."

"What the f—," swallowing hard, she amended herself. "—heck are those?"

"Your bra and panties, of course," stated Ava. A sultry smile slathered on her face, she dared JD to argue.

"I might as well go without," she growled, holding the scraps of fabric in her hands.

Ava's laughter rang through the room and Ace mimicked the sound. "I'm sure the doctor would appreciate that too." She lowered her voice. "Or Logan."

Growling in the back of her throat, JD stripped down and removed her serviceable white bra and underwear. She replaced them with the black lace. "Now what?" she grumbled.

"Wow!" gasped Isabella. "You have a drop-dead body."

JD felt her face flame and she glared at the sisters.

Holding up her hands, Isabella warded off the angry redhead. "Just saying. Ava, look at her stomach muscles!"

Not sure what all the fuss was about, she glanced down at her stomach and lifted her shoulder in a slight shrug. "Nothing you can't have with a morning ab workout."

"From now on, we'll join you every morning," promised Ava, crossing her heart with her finger, before holding out a midnight black dress. "I decided to stick to your favorite color. Just so that you'd be comfortable. Raise your arms above your head."

Standing on the arm of the couch, Isabella helped Ava slip the dress over the massive amount of curlers attached to JD's head.

The dress slipped into place with a whisper. Ava pulled up the short zipper under JD's arm and the velvet fabric formed itself to each of her curves. Tipped in black satin, the dress dipped low in front but plunged dramatically low in back, baring her soft skin and a daring hint to what was below. The sides of the back of the dress were held together by two wide strips of black satin, tied into a bow under her bared shoulder bones. Sheer black sleeves hinted at the rosy skin beneath and black satin cuffs encircled her wrists.

Ava released JD's glorious mane from the curlers and it floated down her body. Artfully, Ava twisted the thick red hair and captured its flames up above her head.

Caught by the light, a necklace shimmered in Isabella's hands. She draped the necklace around JD's slender neck and diamonds dripped down between the swell of her breasts.

Happy with her canvas, Ava nodded her head. "You're beautiful." She held out sparkling straps of silver for her to slip her feet into.

This was where JD drew the line. Her legs parted in a fighting stance and she argued, "I have to wear the boots." Without her boots, she felt exposed, naked and unprotected.

Arching her elegant brow, Ava asked, "Have you never worn heels before?"

Refusing to answer, she crossed her arms over her chest. "I have to wear the boots."

"Leave the boots," suggested Isabella. "Take the heels. They're a bummer to walk in, but you can do it. Just repeat in your head, heel to toe, heel to toe."

She glared at the sparkling straps dangling from Ava's fingertips and tried to decide if being tough was worth ending up alone. She felt like a fucking fool in the stupid dress but the promise of remaining at Twin Springs, belonging with these women, outweighed the cost of wearing a stupid dress, acting like a girl and softening her hard edges for the night. But, damn it, she felt bare and exposed without her boots.

"Fine," she spit out, snatching the shoes from Ava and sticking them on her feet. "Are you happy now?"

Eyeing the results of the heels on her long legs, Ava nodded, "Immensely."

"*P*lease, please, pleassseee, can I see the parrot," begged Colton. He skipped backward before Logan down the Grand Lobby.

Snatching him up by the straps of his new backpack, Logan prevented the boy from careening into a group of kids in line for a balloon twisted into the shape of their choice. Attempting to ditch the kid and find JD, Logan grumbled down to him, "Don't you want to stand in line with the other kids? Get a balloon bent into a sword or something."

"Nope. Just want to play with Ava's bird." Using the magic phrase that got him anything he wanted at Twin Springs, Colton added, "Theo said," he paused for effect, "I was to stay with you." He peeked up at the Blue Flame.

Logan's brows furrowed into a mean line.

Quickly, he added, "And out of trouble."

The boy's nothing but trouble, thought Logan, dragging the brim of his hat lower in the crowded Lobby. The area brimmed with excited guests, Christmas Eve celebrations in full swing and the promise of meeting the painter, DiWolf, looming. Anxious to get away from all the prying eyes, he crumbled. "Fine, we'll ask Ava if you can play with Ace. But then you need to beat it and let me get some work done."

Letting out a whoop of excitement, Colton shot ahead and plowed into Ava's office.

Grumbling under his breath, Logan followed. His lopsided gate slowed his progress. Slipping through the double doors, he called out, "Sorry, Ava, about crashing in. The boy wants to play with your bird."

Coming to an abrupt halt, he surveyed the scene before him. Isabella sat on the edge of the couch handing shiny instruments from a serving tray to her sister. Ava leaned over someone, blocking his view. All he saw were luscious legs peeking out from behind Ava. "Um, you ladies look busy. We can come back another time." He spied the troublemaker boy reaching up on tip toe to unlatch the parrot's cage. "Let's go, Colton."

"Come on in." Ava gestured them forward. "Let Colton play with Ace. He needs the attention. We're almost done anyway."

Peals of laughter emitted from the corner, as Colton watched Ace hang upside down from his swing with one claw.

Unsure of what to do, Logan worked his way around the group of women. He heard Ava call out "blush brush," and Isabella slapped a stubby, black handled brush into her palm.

Thanking God he wasn't a woman, he stared up at the portrait. Studying Amethyst Fairbanks, a different redhead seeped into his mind. He realized that he'd already moved on from the woman in the portrait. He was no longer content with staring up into the face of a one hundred year old woman, when he longed for the flesh and blood version. He turned when Ava ordered her subject, "Look up!" and shouted out, "Mascara."

Feeling sorry for the woman worked on by the Fairbanks sisters, he glanced over. His heart leapt into his throat. There, sitting in Ava's chair, was JD. She tilted her head back as directed. His hot gaze skimmed the smooth skin of her neck and attempted to dip under the black velvet where her breasts hid. His mouth went dry, his tongue lolled back, and he almost choked. Clearing his throat, he watched as JD's eyelashes were tipped with a magic wand, making them impossibly long and thick.

Sneaking a peek at Logan, Ava's lips curled. "You look great, Logan. Smell good too. What cologne is that?"

Reminded of his new habit of showering, he smacked his own lips together, as Ava lined JD's full lips. His mind raced to catch up. "Whatever soap Twin Springs puts in guest rooms."

"That's right," said Isabella. "You're staying at Twin Springs now."

"Hmmm," replied Logan, his body hardening when JD's lips parted slightly, and a glaze was added to the red tint making her full lips appear even fuller. And wet. When Ava ordered JD to rub her lips together, he groaned deep in his chest and quickly coughed to cover the sound.

"Come help us," requested the dark-haired witch, waiving him over. "I can't decide which perfume to use on her. This one," she spritzed the crook of JD's arm, "has a soft, musky aroma to it." Ava held out the redhead's arm for him to sniff. "Tell me what you think."

Like a moth to a flame, Logan's feet shuffled forward. Bending down, he sniffed the soft skin in the crook of her elbow. Not trusting himself to speak, he gave a noncommittal grunt.

"Or this one," said Ava, lifting a bottle, "has undertones of lavender."

"Not the lavender," JD's husky whisper reached his ears.

"I'm sorry," said Ava. "You're right. Lavender would be a poor choice." She spritzed the base of JD's neck with musk.

Standing stock still, Logan's body vibrated with need. His fingers itched to sink themselves into the flames of her hair that they'd captured high on top of her head. Only Colton's childish laughter, sounding off from the corner of the room, prevented him from falling to his knees and making a complete fool of himself.

"You're finished!" declared Ava. Holding JD's hands, she pulled her up out of the chair.

Logan envied the soft black fabric clinging to her body. She glittered like a diamond beneath the lights.

"Turn around. I want to double check my masterpiece," ordered Ava.

Logan never wanted anyone or anything more in his life than he wanted the diamond before him. For one moment with her, he would stand stripped bare in the town square, for all eyes to stare and laugh at. "Where are you going?" he croaked.

"Tonight, she has a hot date with Dr. Ottoman in the Tasting Room," answered Isabella.

"It's a meeting," grumbled JD.

"That's not what Maddy told us. No one has a meeting in the secluded, Executive Chef room."

The words pierced his heart and a jumble of emotions swarmed within him. He felt like a tank had just run him down. "The doc?"

"Isn't that great!" piped up Isabella.

His eyes swept the diamond before him. The dress skimming the tops of her thighs, his gaze traveled down her long legs before journeying back up along every inch of her and resting on her full lips. He licked his own lips. His tongue touched the scarred skin at the corner of his mouth and reminded him of who he was. What he was. A monster.

The gorgeous woman before him deserved more than a deformed, half human. The real definition of a man dawned on him. A man placed his needs second to the one he loved. Put the well-being of the woman he loved above his own needs. The doctor could give her everything he couldn't. Comfort. Money. Status. Most of all, the doctor could give his Diamond a life outside of the shadows. Somehow, without choking on the lie burning a path up his throat, he forced the words necessary from between his lips. "I hope you have a good time."

CHAPTER THIRTY-NINE

*S*liding a schedule across the granite counter, Parker smiled up at the guest before her. "Santa and Mrs. Clause will be in the Grand Lobby until 8:00 p.m. Then they'll depart back to the North Pole to finish up preparations for Christmas. But starting at 8:30 we are offering hay rides every half hour. The rides begin at the Veranda in front of Twin Springs and take you through the town of Oakton. As you enjoy the festive lights of the season, there will be Christmas carolers and hot chocolate stops along the way. Or, you can drop the little ones off in our KidCare facility and enjoy a horse drawn carriage ride. Just the two of you. Our concierge or I can set that up for you."

While the couple decided, Parker surveyed the evening activities within the Grand Lobby. Families were lined up in their finest to take pictures with Santa. Mrs. Clause oversaw the distribution of the cookies and hot chocolate to children. She wished her family had vacationed at Twin Springs during the holiday season.

She searched the faces of the children for her little brother. She started with the most logical place first—the cookies. Not seeing him, she continued to scan the Lobby. Humming under her breath to the holiday tune playing on the piano, her body swayed.

Her gaze moved over a familiar face. Backdropped by the ever-green branches of the Christmas tree, a woman's white blonde hair glowed like an angel. Parker's body froze. Her gaze snapped back to the woman. "Aunt Vivian."

Vivian's waste length, platinum blonde hair and white pant-suit set her apart from the guests. The sight of her beautiful moth-er's identical twin sister was a shock to her system. Only the cruel twist of her lips, haughty expression and, now, death set the twins apart. Her trance broke when her aunt began elbowing her way through the guests.

Systematically, Vivian worked her way through the line of kids, studying each face as she went. Not caring if she ruined the moment, she plowed a path in front of the photographer snapping a family's picture with Santa.

Her body trembling uncontrollably, Parker's legs gave out from beneath her and she sunk down behind the counter. Her breath came in sharp gasps. She reached out, snatched her back-pack up by the strap, dragged the heavy bag across the floor and hugged it to her heaving chest. She fought the urge to run through the Grand Lobby screaming for help. Help wouldn't come. Seeing her aunt in the Grand Lobby was proof. She couldn't trust anyone, least of all JD.

Her brother poked his head around the corner of the Front Desk. "Whatcha doing?"

She motioned for him to come closer. "Aunt Vivian is here."

Her brother's brow furrowed, and he patted her on the top of her head. "Don't worry. The Blue Flame can take them."

She searched for an avenue of escape. "This isn't the time for your stupid games, Colton. We have to run."

"No!" he shouted.

She sprang forward, grabbing him by the arm and jerking him down beside her. She covered his mouth with her hand and leaned in close. "We have to run. Now!" she whispered.

Colton mumbled behind her hand. She gave him a warning look before releasing his mouth.

Tears filled his eyes and he whispered back, "But I like it here at Twin Springs. I don't want to leave."

"Don't you think I like it here too? But we don't have a choice. Twin Springs isn't safe anymore. She'll make us go back with her. Just like before. Once she's got us back home, she'll keep us under lock and key. You know it and I know it. We might never escape again."

Rubbing his eyes with his still damp sleeve, he grumbled under his breath. "I guess so."

Her breath coming sharp and quick in her chest, Parker ordered, "We'll sneak out the side doors of the Garden Room. You hide in the bushes and I'll drive one of Twin Springs' vans down to pick you up."

Her brother nodded his agreement.

Taking a deep breath, she gathered her strength and waved her brother forward. "Follow me."

Keeping low, she peeked around the corner of the Front Desk and scanned the Lobby for her aunt. Quickly, she spotted her, urgently talking with a tall, well-built black man in tan cargo pants and a skin tight black shirt that molded to his thickly muscled arms. Even his bald head and neck had muscles. Her heart leaped into her chest and she whipped back around. "She brought her boyfriend."

"The Crusher," whispered Colton.

She slung her backpack over her shoulders. "He's just a man. Not a comic book villain." Again, she inched her head out and glanced around the counter. "A very big, strong man," she whispered.

Their backs to them, she saw her chance. Dragging her brother behind her, she ran at a low crouch through the double doors leading to the Garden Room. Their sneakers scarcely made a sound on the slate floors. Reaching the glass doors leading to the

Veranda, she pushed her brother behind the white Christmas tree decorated with candy canes and red glass globes. "Wait here, until I drive up. You'll be warmer."

Escaping through the glass doors, the cold air shocked her. In only her thin, white shirt and black slacks, she made her way up the driveway to the where the hotel vans were stored. Clenching her teeth to keep them from chattering, she waited behind a bush until the valet on duty raced to fetch a guest's vehicle. Then, she snuck in his heated shack and stole a van key from the peg board. Chanting softly, she memorized the number above the hook. "Eighteen, eighteen, eighteen." She weaved her way through Twin Springs' parking lot. Finally, she spotted the number 18 in the front window of a van. Her fingers numb with cold or fear, she didn't know which, she slid behind the wheel, inserted the key into the ignition and twisted. The van sprang to life and relief flooded her body.

Leaning forward, she grasped the gray handle and shifted the engine into drive. Inching forward, the van's tires crunched on the deep snow. Jerking as she went, Parker made her way down the road and around the circular drive. Pressing the breaks too hard, she slid to a stop before the sliding glass doors. Her breath fogged the inside of the van. She waited, expecting her little brother to come sprinting out. But he never did.

CHAPTER FORTY

*T*he look on Logan's face haunted JD. She felt sick to her stomach that he'd misunderstood about meeting with the doc. Obviously everyone had gotten the wrong idea. "It's just a damn dinner meeting," she mumbled.

Isabella speed walked beside her, chattering in her ear, "Heel to toe, heel to toe."

Suddenly, it hit her. She was abandoning Logan. She came to an abrupt halt in the middle of the Promenade. Guests gave her strange looks and moved around her, but she didn't notice. "I have to go back."

Stuttering to a stop, Isabella back tracked. "I know you're scared, but it's too late to bail now." She pulled JD by the arm. "The doctor is already seated and waiting. You can do this. I promise."

"I guess you're right. What's one dinner?" Reluctantly, she followed the petite woman to the Tasting Room, tucked behind the kitchens. Pausing before the heavy oak door, she rolled her shoulders back. Muttered, "Let's get this over with."

Isabella fussed over her hair.

She held up her hand. "I've got this." She yanked open the door, "Women."

The room was long with a heavy oak table occupying the length. Sitting on top of a platform, a hutch was tucked into a corner. The long table was covered with a crisp, white table cloth and intimately set for two, with candles and flowers. Inwardly, she groaned at the romantic scene.

At the sight of her, the doctor pushed away from the long, oak table and rose to his feet. His black suit was only slightly loose in the shoulders, unlike his usual clothing that hung from his large frame. Surprise flickered across his blue eyes as his gaze slid over her. His smile widened across his gaunt, pale face. He rushed forward and with each step, his dress shoes clicked against the wooden floor.

Distracted by the odd sound, she missed the flowers he held out to her.

"For you," he said, his voice just above a whisper.

She glanced down at his gift and the budding smile on her face froze. *Damn it. He does think this is a date.*

His sweaty fist clenched a bouquet of lavender, wrapped with a white satin bow.

What had she gotten herself into? The flowers' fragrance burned her nostrils and made her want to gag. Reaching out, she took them and murmured, "Thank you."

"They made me think of you. Wild, yet soft. Beautiful, but strong."

Maddy entered, appearing professional in a black jacket, slim skirt and crisp, white shirt. She pushed a serving tray with their first course.

Relieved by the distraction, JD tossed the flowers onto one of the many mismatched oak chairs around the table. An uneasy feeling crawled across her skin. She'd made a mistake. She should have told the sisters no.

Pulling out a chair, Clay waited for her to sit so he could assist her.

The teen clasped her hands under her chin. She had a sickly sweet smile on her face and loudly sighed, "How romantic."

Glaring at the teenager, JD didn't notice his chivalrous actions. Instead, she dragged out her own chair. Wood scraped against wood and sent a piercing screech through the room. She flopped into the chair. The dress rode high on her thighs and she tugged it down.

Shifting her attention back, she glanced over at the doctor. Being a girl sucked, but she rallied. "Dr. Ottoman, tell me about how you've helped lost children."

"Please, call me Clay. I'm a pediatric doctor. Recently returned from Africa, after assisting with the many sick children there. I contracted Malaria during my travels and I'm still suffering the after affects."

Maddy sighed, placing two small plate starters between the couple. "That's so sweet. Oh," She gathered herself up into a professional stance. "Crisp Fuji apples wedges, almond slices and Blue Ridge greens paired with a light cranberry vinaigrette. Fall beets and goat cheese on the side. Enjoy."

JD glared at her, but the teen ignored her intense stare and hovered over the tray, listening.

"Don't worry, I'm not contagious." He reached out patting the back of JD's hand. "Tell me, are you having any after affects from your incident in the General's Office?"

Her brows wrinkling, she tugged her hand free and placed it in her lap. "You mean Ava's office? I'm fine. Like I said, just light headed from not eating." She enjoyed her first bite of the salad. "Logan over reacted."

Maddy leaned in, placed two crystal glasses on the table and poured ice water for each of them.

Sipping from his water, he gave her a thoughtful look, pausing before answering. "Yes, Logan. I feel for the man. I've seen many tragic people along my travels, but never someone as deformed as he is."

JD bristled, "Logan's an old Army buddy of my brother's. He was injured on duty, serving our country."

"A true hero," he murmured, tipping his glass. "It was kind of Twin Springs to take pity on him and give him a job."

Maddy slammed the water pitcher down on the table and the lettuce jumped on his plate from the force of the landing.

Frowning up at the girl, JD replied, "From what I understand, Logan's family was the original owners of Twin Springs. He has done an amazing job on the Tower."

He hummed in his throat, before replying, "It must be hard for a man to take, losing his heritage. Must feel like less of a man. From a line of failures."

The delicious flavors of the salad turned within her mouth at his insinuation and she delayed in answering. His attitude annoyed her. But was he right? Did Logan feel like he wasn't a man? "I never thought of it that way. I guess it would be hard for anyone."

She glanced up as Maddy thundered from the room. "I've been working with Logan. He's the strongest man I've ever known. He could have allowed the trauma from his past to twist him on the inside as well as the outside. But he's stronger than that. He's compassionate, driven and loyal."

Mopping his brow with a handkerchief from his pocket, he said, "Forgive me. Sometimes, I still feel the fever. I lost quite a bit of weight from my illness. I was once a mountain of a man, now I am a mere sliver of who I once was. Believe me, I understand Logan's pain."

Sympathetic to the sick man across from her, she shared a warm smile. "I'm glad you're feeling better. Now about the child trafficking—"

Leaning forward, Clay attempted to capture her gaze, "JD, I'm entranced by you. I want to get to know you. I'll stay at Twin Springs as long as it takes."

Her cheeks burned. "I—"

Isabella burst into the room, holding a buzzing cell phone in her hand. "I'm so very sorry to interrupt your dinner, Dr. Ottoman." She handed JD the phone. "I didn't notice it was buzzing until I was in dinner service. Sorry, I need to get back to the kitchens."

Clicking her phone, she noticed seven missed calls. All from Lee. Pushing herself back from the table, she walked over to the old desk in the corner of the room and dialed her cousin.

"Where the hell have you been?" he roared over the phone. "I bust my ass getting you intel and you don't answer the damn phone."

Dipping her head, turning away from the doctor, she murmured low, "Sorry, I'm on a date." She gnashed her teeth, "Um, I mean a dinner meeting."

Silence stretched across the line and disbelief filled Lee's voice. "A date. An actual date. With a real man? You're shitting me."

Knowing it was of no use to correct her cousin or argue, she went with it. "No, I'm not shitting you." She glanced over to Clay, "With a real man. A doctor."

He hooted over the line. "Why didn't someone tell me? What are you wearing? How does the doc like your boots?"

What was it with the way she dressed? "For your information, I'm not wearing my boots. I have a dress and heels on."

His voice low and filled with awe, he repeated, "You're shitting me."

She growled deep in her throat. "Look, Lee, enough. What do you have?"

"Only information on your runaways."

A surge of satisfaction flowed through her. "Tell me."

She heard the shuffling of papers, "The girl didn't lie to you. Parker and Colton Reinhard. Their parents recently passed away."

"I thought it rang true. Her account of finding her parents was so emotional, detailed. Who has custody of them?"

"Their aunt, Vivian Summerland. The mother's sister. I spoke with her this afternoon. She was frantic about their return."

JD snorted, "Right. If she was so frantic about their return, why didn't she report them missing?"

"She'd hired a private investigator on the case. Said they've done it before when they didn't get their way. And the investigator always found them within hours. She didn't expect it to take this long. After they'd been gone for a week she was afraid to call the police. Afraid they'd remove the kids from her custody. So, she trusted the PI. She seemed sincere. Busted out crying over the phone. I could hardly understand her, she was sobbing so hard. Said she finally called the police when the investigator came up empty."

Tears, one of the many weapons in a woman's arsenal to control a man. "I can't believe you fell for tears," she spat out. "If your kids are missing, you'll use all avenues to get them back."

She could hear Lee's fingers thrumming on his desk. Frustration laced his voice, "Well, you can ask her yourself. She should be arriving at your location anytime now."

"What?" she shouted. "You've compromised the kids' location without passing it through me beforehand? What if she's the reason they ran?"

"Shit, you're right. All I can say is I'm sleep deprived from the damn puppies. Sorry."

Her mind raced, trying to remember where she last saw Parker. "I'll take care of it. Gotta go." Quickly, she dialed Logan.

His voice flowed over the line. "You're supposed to be on a hot date." He mocked, "Bored with the doctor already?"

She ignored his comment. "Is Colton still with you?"

"No. He went to hang with Parker. Why?"

"We need to secure the kids. Their aunt is on the way. Don't know if she is on the up and up or not. But we need to be safe."

An uneasy feeling rolled across her spine and she suppressed a shiver. A chill settled into her bones. "I've got an uneasy feeling."

"Wolfe intuition." Without missing a beat, he replied, "I'll get everyone on it. Don't worry, we'll find them."

The strength of his conviction flowed through his voice and warmed her.

The Woman wasn't by her side, pressing her on, but the sick feeling in the pit of her stomach told her something was wrong. She needed to secure the kids' location. Keep them safe. "We have to," she replied and hung up.

She reached down to slip her phone in her boot and found only empty space. For a moment she wondered why they weren't there, then she remembered Ava's insistence. Gnashing her teeth, she considered her choices of where to put her phone. Nowhere else to put it, she jammed the phone into her lacy bra.

Turning, she addressed the thin man standing before her. "I'm sorry. I have to go."

He stood, blocking her exit. "Anything I can help with?"

Her voice hard and sharp, she replied, "No, they're my responsibility."

Not looking back, she headed for the Front Desk, Parker's usual post. Quickly, she discovered that the tall, skinny heels were a waste of effort. Placing a hand against the wall of the Promenade, she kicked off her shoes and abandoned them on a bench without a backward glance. She dodged the guests taking pictures with Santa and scanned the Grand Lobby for her kids.

The Front Desk was empty. The phones rang persistently, and a line of guests waited impatiently. She searched the area behind the desk. No Parker. Even her backpack was gone. "She's running!"

She grabbed a young bellhop up by the front of his jacket and held him firm. "Where's Parker?"

Eyes bulging, he squeaked, "Parker?"

Searching her mind for her girl's fake name, she barked, "Diana. Where's Diana? The young girl working the Front Desk."

"I don't know. She was helping an elderly couple and then took off."

Releasing the boy, she thought for a moment. "Parker wouldn't leave without her brother."

Lavender wafted over her. The Woman strolled past her and walked up the stairs behind the Bellhop Stand. Her pregnant, monochrome form was a stark contrast against the red and white Christmas ribbons draping the handrails. Relief flooded her. The Woman would help find her kids. In her bare feet, she took the stair treads two at a time and raced after her.

Amethyst Fairbanks continued up the steps, pausing only once to clutch at her stomach. The long necklace, from the portrait, draped down over her large belly and glittered.

"Hurry," she prompted the ghost. "The kids need us."

The Woman ignored her.

JD's brows furrowed. "Something isn't right."

The aftermath smell of fire increased as they neared the attics. Realizing where the Woman was taking her, she sped ahead. Her bare feet made soft thuds on the carpeted floor of the canted hallway. Racing through the narrow doorway, she came to an abrupt stop. She searched the room, her gaze flowing over the Christmas tree blackened by fire. Its arms were now just spindly wire and melted plastic. Ashes replaced what were once boxes. The wall and a portion of the ceiling were charred. "They're not here," she whispered.

Confusion and anxiety slammed through her brain. She twirled around, "Where the hell are they?" she demanded. But she spoke to an empty room. The space beside her was empty. Ame was gone.

Surging forward, she swept the attic searching for her. Running back out the door way, she scanned the hallway, and then cleared each room. The Woman was gone. "Ame Fairbanks!

Get back here. Right now!" Her voice vibrated off the walls around her. "All my life, you've been a pain in my ass. Where the hell are you now, when I need you?"

Grasping the charred door frame with both of her hands, she hung her head. It was up to her. She must find the kids without the Woman's help. "Where could they be?"

One terrible scenario after another entered her mind, "What if they've already run? What if they're no longer at Twin Springs?" And the final, terrifying possibility, "What if I've lost them?"

Within the burned room, a new fragrance reached her. Sniffing she raised her head and quickly identified the scent. Fresh pine trees and sap. The smell of Christmas.

A hushed voice sounded from behind her, "Our Father, who art in heaven, Hallowed be thy Name." JD stiffened. Her arms fell to her sides and she slowly turned.

With her movements, her true self fell to the floor and only her ghostly form remained standing, the scorched room fading to gray, replaced by brilliant colors. Instead of darkness, sunlight streamed through the dormer window and glinted off the polished frame of a brass bed, covered by a quilt of multicolored squares. Strung popcorn wound a path around a freshly chopped Christmas tree. The room was spotlessly clean. Tucked into the opposite corner from the tree, a black iron sewing machine sat on top of a slender rectangular table amidst fabric and envelopes. Titled with the banners of Butterick Quarterly, McCall Printed Patterns and Simplicity, the large envelopes had drawings of women dressed in different 1920 outfits. A young woman knelt against the window seat, her midnight black uniform contrasting against the cream walls and bright white lace curtains that framed her.

Even though it was nighttime back in JD's world, golden rays of morning sun kissed the maid's lace cap and created a sunshine halo in the dust particles above her head. A tight bun captured her auburn hair at the nape of her neck. Gabby, Ame Fairbanks personal maid, clutched her wooden cross between her laced fingers and prayed.

"Not now!" JD screamed at the genuflecting woman. "I have to find my kids." Falling to her knees beside her, the light streaming through her translucent gray body, she begged, "Please, not now. They need me. I have to help them. Please, before they're truly lost."

CHAPTER FORTY-ONE

*I*gnoring her own body collapsed on the floor, JD sat cross-legged beside the praying maid. She had no idea how long she'd been concentrating on picturing the attic room as it was in her time. She slowed her breathing and attempted to jump time periods between the thumps of her beating heart. No matter how hard she tried, she could still hear Gabby repeating the Lord's prayer over and over.

Inspiration hit. She struck a classic meditation pose with the backs of her hands resting on her knees and her middle fingers curled in to touch her thumbs. She brought long, deep breaths in through her nose and exhaled through her parted lips. "There's no place like home, there's no place like home." She cracked an eye open to check her surroundings. Nothing had changed. Her hands curled into fists. "Take me home, damn it!"

Trying again, she calmed her breathing, pressed her palms together in front of her chest and mentally pictured the burnt Christmas tree, the blackened boxes, the charred ceiling. But the faces of her kids floated behind her closed lids and distracted her. "I've got to find them."

Gabby's voice grated her nerves, as she continued to pray at a nauseatingly slow pace. "As we forgive them—"

She squeezed her eyes shut and concentrated, tried humming to block out the maid's voice, peered through one eye and checked the results. Exasperated, she sprang up, paced the room, mindlessly kicking at the sleeves of the McCalls dress patterns strewn across the floor next to the sewing machine, even though her foot passed straight through them.

"Forever and ever."

JD threw her hands in the air. "Finally, you're finished."

"Dear Lord, please guide me with your will. I cannot utter out loud the atrocity the Lieutenant is forcing upon me."

Groaning, JD hung her head. "Please, Lord," she begged in her own prayer, "make her stop so I can get back to my kids." But she couldn't help but continue to listen in on the maid's prayers.

"I believed the Lieutenant's soft words at first but now, I know he is evil. The Devil come to life to test me. And I have failed. I succumbed to his whispered lies and his promises of comfort.

"If I do not follow his orders, he will condemn me. Call me out as a harlot. I must think of my brothers and my sisters. They, too, will be tarnished by my stain.

"I beg of You to show me the way. A path off this forsaken mountain and away from the Devil's plans." Gabby paused and raised her eyes to gaze out the window. Lips pressed together, she waited. Her breath came fast within her chest.

"What do you think? God's just going to plop a plan before you? He doesn't do things *for* you, He performs miracles *through* you!" JD growled and continued to pace. "Idiotic woman."

Collapsing across the window seat, Gabby sobbed into her arms. "You have forsaken me. I am not even worthy of Your grace."

She bent over the crying woman, "Use your brain. Think!" Words she never thought would part from her mouth, she added, "Go to Ame, she will help you. Ame. Go to Ame."

Drying her eyes with the hem of her white apron, Gabby brought herself under control. Her head bent, she tucked her cross into her shirt and out of sight. With a great sigh, she rose from the window seat. "I am lost."

Sensing movement in the hallway, JD scrambled to reach the door. Leaning out, she saw the Woman's purple form waddling down the hall, a duck on a mission. "Wait up!" she shouted.

Keeping pace with Ame's short steps, she frowned over at her. "What the hell kind of game are you playing? Send me back, I need to help the kids."

Pausing, Ame leaned her forehead against the wall, her breath coming in short gasps. She huddled over her baby belly, rubbing the mound with the heels of her hands.

Her gray gaze zeroed in on the Woman and she glanced between her face pinched with pain and her belly. "Holy crap, you're ready to pop. Don't move, I'll get help."

Her heart thudding against her ribs, she rushed back down the hallway and waved her hands in front of Gabby's face. Screaming, she jumped up and down. "It's useless," she murmured and sprinted back to Ame, catching the pregnant woman entering the General's Office.

"Father, I need to speak with you," Ame's breaths came in short bursts.

Attired in hunting clothes, his pants tucked into tall, laced up boots, white collared shirt open at the throat, shell vest, tweed button up shooting jacket, the General held a shot gun, cocked open over the crook of his arm.

Ame blinked rapidly, as if she couldn't quite comprehend the sight before her. "Why's your rifle in your office of all places? What are you doing?"

Gradually, the General turned towards his eldest daughter.

"Now Ame, don't go getting yourself all upset. Especially, in your current condition." He gently placed the rifle down on his desk, before propping himself on the edge of it. "I just took Everett hunting. It was past time to teach your husband to be a man."

"He is a man, Father. I think my present condition proves that."

"Yes. Yes," answered the General, unable to meet his daughter's eyes. "It's a male thing, my dear. Don't worry about it. Just take care of my grandson. That is what is most important."

JD yearned to smack the General. How could he treat his daughter like that? "She's not a cow, carrying your prize calf."

Smoothing the fabric of her dress down over her stomach, Ame released a long breath between pursed lips. "Father, you are the most powerful man I know."

He puffed up with his daughter's words.

"Please." JD rolled her eyes. "It's getting deep in here."

Wringing her hands above her belly, Ame addressed her father, "I need your help."

Stepping forward, the General clasped Ame's hands between his. "Naturally, I will help you, anything you need, my dear."

She licked her lips and got to the crux of the situation. "There are two women staying at Twin Springs that need your assistance. One of our employees has been taking advantage of these young ladies."

Releasing her hands, the General stalked the room. He pounded one of his fists into the other. "Taking advantage of our female guests? Give me the name of the man, Ame. I will take care of him. Kick him off the property."

Fanning her face with her hand, "No, Father, not our female guests. This is worse. Women under our protection, Ruby and my personal maids. Gabriella and Betty."

The General stilled, before circling his desk and taking a seat. "My dear, don't worry about those women. We can't get into the personal lives of our employees. Let their own fathers handle it."

Fumbling with the beads on her necklace, Ame implored, "But you don't understand. The man is—"

"No. My dear," interrupted her father. He picked up his rifle and began cleaning it. "You don't understand. These are women's problems. Go upstairs, rest. These things will work themselves out."

Crossing her arms, JD stared down at the General's bent head. "And just how do these things work themselves out?"

Ame had already turned away. She paused at the open door when the General called out, but refused to turn to look in his direction.

"Don't worry yourself, my dearest. The employees' personal lives are none of our business. Go upstairs, get ready for tonight's New Year's Eve Ball."

"Yes, Father," she called over her shoulder, exiting.

"Is that it?" asked JD, walking along beside Ame. "You just walk away?"

Ame paused at the Bellhop Stand and clutched the edges of the wooden desk with her hands. Her knuckles whitened with the ferocity of her vice like grip. Between gritted teeth, she asked the bellhop, "Have you seen my husband?"

"That's it Ame," said JD. "Everett can help. He cares about people."

The tall, thin, black man's brow knit. "I think he's inside the Officers Hall. Do you need assistance, ma'am?"

Ignoring his question, she patted him on the shoulder, turned and shuffled over to the double door entrance. She walked as if she was traversing through deep water, each step a monumental effort.

"Ma'am, you can't go in there. Gentlemen only," he called out.

JD laughed, socking the Bellhop in the arm. Her fist went straight through to his opposite shoulder. "Screw your rules, she's going in."

Opening the doors wide, Ame entered the Officers Hall.

Within the long, smoke-filled room, servants in black pants with white jackets carried trays and served the men lounging in leather chairs or grouped around small tables. Only the men closest to the door glanced up. At her presence, they coughed and gave disapproving glares.

"You can't stay in here long," said JD. "The smoke is bad for the baby." She looked over to Ame and spotted the Lieutenant coming up fast on her six. She shouted, "Watch your back!"

But the Lieutenant was faster. He curled his fingers into Ame's upper arm and she winced with pain.

JD surged forward, but realized she was powerless to help.

Bending his head, the Lieutenant placed his lips close to Ame's ear, while his body blocked the pregnant woman from the other men's eyes.

JD leaned in to hear.

Savagely, he lashed into her. "Keep your filthy mouth shut. My affairs are none of your business. Do you hear me?" His fingers bit in further and Ame's knees gave a little.

"Get your hands off me, Clayton." Ame looked down at his hand, disdain and displeasure written across her face.

He jerked her closer. "You will address me by my rank. I earned it. Something you would know nothing about. This is what you don't understand. I will put my hands anywhere and on anyone I desire and there is nothing you can do about it. After all, whom are you going to go to? The General? You saw how that turned out. To your husband? He's a weak fool," he taunted.

"My husband is smarter than you. Don't discount him as a fool."

"Let me put it in terms you understand." He splayed his free hand over Ame's mound. "Stay out of my affairs, Amethyst Fairbanks. Or those you love will suffer."

Ame gasped, pushing at the Lieutenant's hand as his fingers dung into her stomach. She doubled over in pain and the door behind her opened.

Rushing into the room, Everett bent down beside his wife and pushed his glasses up his nose. "Ame, are you alright? I'm sorry I wasn't here earlier. I didn't know you were looking for me till just now."

Ame glanced between Everett and the Lieutenant standing over them, unable to speak as another contraction spasmed across her belly. Gasping in pain, she clutched at her husband's arm.

Scooping his wife up in his arms, Everett yelled at the Lieutenant, "Open the damn door, and get the hell out of my way."

"You tell him," muttered JD, giving the Lieutenant a death stare. Following the couple, she paused, listening. For a brief moment, she thought she heard her name. Shrugging, she rushed to catch back up. Stopping just as the elevator doors closed before her, she listened. There is was again. She was sure of it. Someone called her name, louder this time. "Diamond."

CHAPTER FORTY-TWO

"Diamond," Logan repeated, louder this time. He checked her pulse. Still strong. "Please, Diamond. Come back." He laid his forehead against her cool, damp one. "Come back to me."

She moved beneath him and he searched her features for a response. "Diamond." Her incredibly long lashes fluttered and he held his breath. Finally, her eyes opened, and he only just stopped himself from breaking in front of her soft green gaze. Words of relief clogged his throat.

She lifted her head and scanned the area around her, then dropped it back down, uncaring that she laid in the dirt and filth of the fire. "I'm back."

"You must stop doing this to me," he said, picking pieces of ash from her hair and brushing it back with his fingers. "Your dress is ruined." Black soot covered her from head to toe. He attempted to lighten the mood and bring his own beating heart back under control. She'd scared another ten years off of his life. "What did you do, roll around?"

She clasped him behind the neck, pulled his lips to hers and branded him with a kiss. "Thank you for calling me back."

He rubbed his lips together and enjoyed the lingering taste of her. "Anytime, sweetheart. Anytime."

Clutching Logan's t-shirt, she asked, "Did you find the kids?"

He shook his head, "No. I came up here looking for them and found you."

She sat up and he admired the length of her leg as the hem of her dress rose high on her thigh.

She asked, "How long have I been out?"

"I'm not sure. I found you a couple minutes ago."

She pulled her cell phone out of her bra.

"You put your things in the most unusual places," he said, watching her.

Her cheeks glowed to a rosy red. "Well, there aren't many places to hide things in this getup."

Logan made a humming noise in the back of his throat and remained silent.

She checked the time stamp on her phone call from her cousin. "I've been out for twenty minutes. We have to get a move on."

He stood and reached down for her.

Ignoring his hand, she sprang up and swayed on her feet.

He wrapped his arms around her and held her tight until her legs firmed up beneath her.

"Whoa," she smiled up sheepishly. "Just a little too fast."

"I've got you." For once, she was soft and leaned in against him.

Pressing her fingertip to her forehead, she let out a breath. "I'm alright." She stepped backward, just outside of his reach. "We've got to find the kids. Where have you all searched?"

She seemed steady enough. But he shifted his weight to his good leg just in case he needed to grab her again before she fell. "Jaxon and Ava are searching the outside of the hotel. Theo and Isabella, the west wing. My brother and father, the east wing. The Geezers are searching the ballrooms and Theatre. I had the attics"

A tear slipped from the corner of her eye, cleansing a path down her dirt streaked face. "No one has seen them?"

Her pain wrenched his heart. But he understood. Those two kids had wormed their way past his defenses and now worry and fear churned his own stomach. Where duty and purpose usually strengthened it. He shook his head and wiped the tear from her chin with the pad of his thumb. "Not yet. But we will find them. I promise."

"I don't know what's gotten into me." She clenched her jaw and brought her emotions under control.

"It's okay to care," he said, just as much for her as for himself. Proudly, he watched her mentally strengthening herself for the mission ahead.

"I care more than you know." Fierce passion lit her gaze. "They're my kids." She swept past him and out the door.

"Lucky kids," he murmured, and tugged his baseball cap from his back pocket. "Wish I was that lucky." He turned, placed the cap on his head, and caught up to her in the hall.

Moving quickly, she replied, "Okay. They'd want to stay out of the common areas to avoid their aunt. Let's check the General's Room. And the secret passageway running behind it."

"You don't think they went down into the tunnels, do you?"

She halted. "What tunnels?"

"There are tunnels that run from beneath the kitchen to an underground river. I figured you knew about them."

Her breath caught. "You don't think they tried to escape down river, do you?"

Thinking of the rushing water, he said, "I hope not, but we will make sure." He picked up the walkie and conveyed their plan to the rest of the searchers.

"Damn it, where is the Woman when I need her?"

He frowned over her strange turn of phrase. "What woman?"

She stalked down the hall. "The Woman. Amethyst Fairbanks. She's been haunting me since I was a little girl. She's the reason why I keep passing out. She's been dragging me back to 1928 for some damn reason."

Things clicked into place for Logan then. Just like Isabella and Ava. Amethyst had been haunting JD. "That's how you've know about Twin Springs. Is she the reason you're able to find lost children?"

"I do the leg and grunt work but she's always been there. Usually, she's a real pain in the ass but this time, I really could use her help. But, damn it, she's having a baby right now."

He didn't reply. Just let the facts percolate in the back of his brain. The ghost was having a baby.

The two of them rounded the base of the stairs and quickly moved between the Front Desk and the Bellhop Stand.

Parker rushed up to them, her eyes wide and frantic. "I knew I couldn't trust you. If something happens to my brother, I'll never forgive you."

He watched JD absorb the body blow of the teen's words and he spoke up in her defense. "It's not her fault."

JD shook her head. "It doesn't matter. Only Colton matters right now." She held Parker by the shoulders. "Where is he?"

Tears filled Parkers eyes. "I don't know. I told him to wait for me to get a van but when I pulled up he never came out."

"You were stealing a van?" questioned Logan, amazed at her ingenuity and stupidity. Mountain roads were tricky but, in the winter, they were downright dangerous for an inexperienced driver. "You're only fourteen. How can you drive?"

"What does it matter now?" Her words hitched on the sobs she held back. "If my aunt finds him, she'll hurt him."

The remaining wall protecting Logan's heart crumbled. He worked to shore it back up, but it was no use. He'd never be able to return to his woods. Not when all he'd think of was JD, the pain in this young girl's eyes and the little boy who looked at him as if he was a real live superhero. "He'll be alright. We'll find him. I promise."

"You promise? Just like she promised?" Parker shouted, drawing the attention of the guests within the Grand Lobby. "My parents promised to be there for us too. But they're dead. I found them. I thought they were sleeping but they weren't. The police said it was carbon monoxide poisoning. My brother and I would be dead too, if we hadn't snuck out to sleep in our new tree house."

"Carbon monoxide poisoning is a terrible way to lose your parents, Parker. A terrible accident, but your parents couldn't have known they were going to die," replied JD. "They didn't leave you on purpose. Is it that bad living with your aunt?"

"You don't understand. She's crazy. Flips out over the littlest thing. And her punishments," she glanced away and licked her lips. "Last time we ran away, she locked me up. The lack of food and loneliness wasn't so bad. It's when she sent her boyfriend in to teach me a lesson..." Her face pinched up to hold back the memories, the tears. "I couldn't walk for a week. The whole back of my body was covered with bruises. I started thinking of places we could escape to. We had to run far away. If we didn't, it would only be a matter of time until her anger would shift to Colton and I wouldn't be able to protect him anymore."

Logan felt physically ill. How someone could hurt two children was beyond his comprehension. He'd be damned if he'd let anything happen to them. "We're combing Twin Springs now. Where do you think he'd hide?"

Parker wiped the tears from her face with the back of her hand. "Did you check the attics?"

"We just came from there."

She hugged herself. "I don't understand it. I told Colton to wait by the Christmas tree," she pointed towards the Garden Room. "He knew how important it was to get away."

JD rubbed Parker's arms, trying to warm her. "Is there anything he would have come back for?"

"No, he had his backpack with all his stuff. We still keep our backpacks ready, just in case we have to run."

She scrunched down to Parker's level and looked directly into her eyes. "Are you sure? Think Parker, what would be important enough for your brother to go back for?"

Parker considered the question. "Only his action figures, but he keeps them in his backpack. So, no nothing."

Thinking of the little boy who trailed behind him everywhere he went, Logan asked, "What if he didn't have all his action figures?"

Parker gasped. "He'd go back for them."

Logan looked at JD, "The Tower. Colton might have left some of his action figures up there."

CHAPTER FORTY-THREE

*G*uests' heads turned to watch the trio rush through the Grand Lobby. A teenager, a burned man and a soot covered woman running barefoot in a black dress.

Reaching the elevator, Logan pushed the button. He grabbed Parker by the arm and pushed her behind the plastic and into the almost finished bottom floor of the Tower. "Stay here. Hide. Take my talkie. Let everyone know where you are and where we are going. If your aunt has Colton in the Tower, we will bring him back."

Parker hugged the walkie to her chest and stared into his eyes. Inwardly, he cringed at the hope shimmering within the tears. "You promise?"

No matter what it took, he wouldn't let this little girl down. Failure wasn't an option. "I promise."

"You know, Colton thinks you're a superhero. He calls you the Blue Flame," she whispered, her throat raw with emotion. "Don't prove him wrong."

Stunned, he nodded. Tears dripped down the teenager's face and he dropped the plastic curtain. Together, he and JD entered the elevator.

"Blue Flame, huh," asked JD.

Staring at the numbers filtering past, he shrugged and grunted.

"That's cool I guess. Not as awesome as Spiderman, but not bad."

"Spiderman's a pansy ass," he replied, exiting the elevator.

Working in tandem, the two of them cleared the restaurant level. Standing at the base of the stairs, he motioned for JD to wait.

Rolling her eyes, she whispered, "Yeah, right." Her face transformed into the face of a warrior on a mission. Soundless in her bare feet, she moved up the circular staircase.

Logan followed behind, appreciating the view above him as he went. None of his teammates ever looked that damn good. Or deadly.

The glass doors whispered open before them. The heat of the floors combating against the cold mountain air created a silver mist around the Tower. Immediately, Colton's voice carried over the night air. "The Blue Flame will stop you."

A woman's shrill voice replied, "Shut up. I don't want to hear about your stupid fantasies."

"The Blue Flame isn't made up. He's real and he is going to stop you."

A resounding slap cut through the mist and Colton began crying.

Logan pushed down at the primal urge to charge forward, grab the woman by the throat and choke her out for hurting Colton. Instead, he motioned for JD to go left and he went right. Closing in on the sound of the voices, he worked his way around the columns.

In a white pant-suit, the aunt glowed from head to toe within the light. Even beneath the twisted hatred, she possessed an angelic beauty. She turned her back and was blind to his approach.

Moving forward, he saw Colton sitting on the rim of the fountain. The sliding colors of the fountain lights glowed around the little boy whose silver blond hair matched his aunt's. A welt in the shape of a hand, blazed on his cheek.

Hugging his action figure close to his chest, he sniffled and wiped his nose on the back of his hand. "You'll never find my sister. She ran."

The woman paced in front of the boy. "Don't bet on it, brat. I found you, didn't I?"

"It doesn't matter. Wolfeman and the Blue Flame will stop you. They'll save me."

She checked her watch. "No one is coming to save you. You belong to me. You're mine as much as my car or house. Nobody takes what's mine away from me. So, shut up."

Even though his chin trembled, Colton raised it and continued. "Then Diamond will put her lasso around you and force you tell the truth about Parker. I know what you did. I know he hurt her because you told him to."

She halted in front of him. "I said, shut up." Her voice rose to a fevered pitch and she swung back her arm to strike him again.

Except, this time, her wrist was grabbed and held in a firm grip. "I wouldn't do that if I was you," Logan's voice was calm. Deadly.

Vivian turned. Horrified, her gaze took in the sight of his burned face and she let out an ear-splitting scream before collapsing into a dead faint at his feet.

"I knew you'd come!" shouted Colton, launching himself into Logan.

Catching the boy, he raised him and hugged him tight.

"Well, shit," said JD. "How come you got to save the day and be the superhero?"

His skinny arms wrapped tight around Logan's neck, Colton whispered, "She said a bad word."

Logan took a moment to absorb the feeling of the boy's hug

and held him tight. It had been so long since someone had voluntarily touched him. Let alone hugged him.

Reluctantly, he placed the boy back on the ground and knelt down until he was eye level. He replied in a stage whisper, "She's working on talking like a lady. Theo said so."

Letting out a sigh, she pulled her cell phone out of her bra, "It's time to call the police."

A huge, dark shape rose behind her, reached out and encircled her neck in a vice grip from behind. "No need to call the cops. The kid belongs to her. She's his legal guardian."

"The Crusher." Fear laced Colton's voice.

Stunned, Logan's gaze traveled up the length of the man, judging him to be just inches shy of seven feet. He swallowed hard and pushed the boy behind him. "Run. Hide."

Holding his hands up in front of himself, Logan moved forward and watched the huge man's movements intently. Searching for a weak spot, he stalked the man. "Let her go and we'll work this out."

His brawny arm tightened like a noose around JD's throat. "What did you do to Vivian?"

Logan stepped over her passed out form. "Nothing. Just a perk of looking like this."

JD's hand snaked down her body, reaching to grab her knife. Instead, her hand found empty space. "Shit, shit, shit," she muttered and gripped the man's muscled forearm with her two hands.

He raised her up until her toes scrapped the floor and shook her like a rag doll. "Hold still."

Unsure what she was about to do, Logan shook his head. "Let's not get excited."

If she pushed the Crusher, he could snap her neck before he could reach her. Her gaze connected with his and he knew he'd be too late. "No!"

"Should've worn the damn boots." She slumped forward.

Logan rushed forward.

Surprised, the man loosened his hold. He shifted his arm across her body and placed his hand under her armpit to support her dead weight. "Don't move. I have no problem killing her."

At the empty look in his gaze, Logan skidded to a stop. Nothing lived within the man. No emotion. He'd break her neck and not think twice.

Coming alive, JD surged up and snapped her head back, smashing his nose with the back of her head. Blood spurted.

Howling in pain, the large man released her and his hands flew to his face.

Whipping around, she stopped cold at the sight of the Crusher. His bald head was like a black bowling ball on top of a mountain of muscle. "Damn, you're a big one." She grabbed him by the groin and squeezed.

In a loud, careening cry, he fell to his knees.

In one fluid motion, she released her hold. Quickly, she grabbed the man by the head and smashed his face over and over into her knee and finished him off with an upper cut punch to the jaw. He crumbled in an unconscious heap at her bare feet.

His blue eyes saucers in his face, Colton whispered in awe, "She grabbed him by the pee pee."

Cringing a little inside, Logan agreed, "Yep."

"She crushed the Crusher."

Logan pressed his lips together and nodded. "That she did."

Scooping her cell phone up from the tiles, an offended look crossed her face at the state of the cracked screen. "Damn it, he broke my phone."

CHAPTER FORTY-FOUR

*H*ours later, Logan heard the thuds of JD's boots ringing out on the metal staircase. Sitting on the edge of the fountain, he watched the woman he desired part the mist and walk towards him. Sporting her boots, but still in the short black dress, his mouth went dry. The boots hugged her bare legs and left a silky expanse of skin that drew his eyes and imagination upward. He dared to wonder what he might find under the dress. Clearing his throat, he said, "I see you have your boots back."

The fountain's rainbow of colors glowed against the smooth, untouched side of his face and left the burnt side in the shadows. She rocked her weight within the boots. "Yep, never taking them off again."

He thought of how she dared to turn the tables on the huge man that she'd smashed. "You were pretty tough barefoot."

She shrugged and leaned against a pillar. "I'm amazed by the warmth up here on the terrace. I like the interesting contrast between the light winter wind and the heat pumping from the floor and grates."

He observed her hovering on the edge of the domed roof. She shifted her weight within her boots and he readied himself for the blast of verbiage that seemed to accompany her like an old, favorite sweater. She had something to say to him and he doubted if his heart would survive.

Her gaze slid away from his. "Is the Sheriff gone?"

Chicken, he thought. *Just say it. Get the pain over with.* "Yes, he's a blow hard but he was willing to listen to our side and let Parker and Colton stay at Twin Springs. At least until the legalities of what happened tonight, and the guardianship of the children, is hashed out."

Taking a deep breath, she stepped within the private world under the curved metal roof of the Tower's dome. She tapped the fountain base with the toe of her boot, delaying the enviable. "We fight and argue on a daily basis. Heck, an hourly basis."

Here it comes. He turned away, protecting his heart from the looming blast of her anger.

Letting out a long breath, she muttered, "Thank you."

Stunned, his head swiveled towards her. "What did you say?"

She lifted a delicate shoulder. "I said, thank you."

His mouth snapped shut and his brain scrambled to catch up. "For what?"

"If you hadn't remembered that Colton had left his action figure up here then we might've been too late."

He pushed away the remembered sticky fear that had clung to him and rubbed his face with the palms of his hands. "We were lucky."

She sunk down and sat on to the ledge of the fountain next to him. "The thought of losing the kids," she paused, rubbing her hands back and forth across the top of her thighs, "makes my knees wobble. I can't lose them."

He understood. Somehow the siblings had touched what was left of his torched heart. He nodded. "They're great kids. Got spunk."

Trailing her fingers through the water, she laughed. "Quite the superpower you have, making women faint at your feet."

He grunted, watching the water caress the tips of her fingers. "Yeah, I'm just full of superpowers."

She flicked water at him. "You know, I didn't need your help with the aunt or her boyfriend. I could've taken them both myself."

Ignoring the droplets, he watched her from the corner of his eye. "Sure, sweetheart. Whatever you want to tell yourself."

Her lips spread into a wide smile and he noticed the cute little freckles splattered across the bridge of her nose and high on her cheeks. He suppressed the urge to press his lips to the little sun spots.

Removing the pins from her hair, she placed them on the ledge beside her. Burying her fingers deep into her glorious red mane, she shook the curls loose and allowed mounds of her thick hair to fall around her shoulders.

He choked back the burning desire her actions stoked within him.

She raised her arms high above her head, stretching out her back and tense shoulders. "I think tonight skinned ten years off me."

The diamond beside him leaned forward and stretched. The flames of her hair fell to her sides, exposing the skin and move-ment of the muscles rippling along her bare back.

Frowning, he noticed blood splatter. "You have blood on your back."

"Do I?" she asked, looking over her shoulder at him. "Must be from the boyfriend's nose. Man, it bled like a mother—" she paused, thinking for a moment, and amended. "A, um, son of a gun."

He removed a work rag from his back pocket and dipped it into the water of the fountain. He couldn't help but smile. "Good job, I know that was painful."

She expelled a long breath. "You have no idea."

He wrung out the cloth. "Let me help you." Sliding the cloth along her skin, he cleansed the length of her back. Goosebumps bloomed along her creamy white skin. The desire within him stretched and expanded, demanding to be fulfilled.

Propping her elbows on her knees, she lifted her hair out of the way and allowed him access. "You called me back."

His voice husky, he asked, "What do you mean?"

"In the attics, I heard you. I was trapped in Ame's world and I heard you calling. It's because of you, I came back."

Not trusting himself to speak, he dipped the cloth again and twisted out the water as she turned towards him.

Unable to stop himself, his eyes traveled her body, noting the soot on her chin and neck. Reaching out, he ran the damp cloth along her chin, exposing the translucent skin beneath. Heartbreakingly slow, the cloth traveled lower, along the curve of her neck and followed the rise and swell of her high breasts. He envied the diamond necklace nestling between the swell of her breasts. Thick desire coated his voice. "You're a mess."

The corner of her mouth lifted in an easy half smile. Eyes hot, her gaze rolled over the man before her. "Am I now?"

"Yes." His body hummed. "I can help you with that."

Her smile widened and stretched his heart, making room for her.

She murmured, "Can you?"

Blue flames burned in his eyes, scalding her where his gaze touched. He groaned deep in his chest, "May I, Diamond?"

Unconsciously leaning in towards the heat he offered, she whispered, "Don't call me Diamond."

"But that is what you are. Right now, you look like a piece of coal, all covered with black ash. But I know, if I take my time, rubbing and polishing your skin, you will shine for me. Just like a diamond."

Entranced by his words, she felt a tug on the bowed ribbon at her back, releasing the fabric holding up her dress. Freed, his lips burned kisses along her shoulders and he slid the sleeves of her gown down.

Close enough to see the freckles peppering her skin, he paid homage to the tiny, golden brown spots with his lips and the tip of his tongue.

Supporting her under the elbows, he lifted her up, until they both stood. The velvet gown slipped from her body and pooled at her boot clad feet. A groan escaped him.

Around the perimeter of the Tower, falling snowflakes glittered. The fountain lights illuminated her naked body in blues, greens, reds, and golds. In the warm glow of the ever-changing colors, his eyes worshiped her.

His gaze ran from her rosy nipples peeping through the black lace of her bra, along the silky length of her body, where it nipped in at her waist, before swelling along her hips. The scrap of black lace was unable to suppress the beauty of her flaming hair at the juncture of her thighs.

Caressing, she ran her hands down his chest until her fingers curled into the waistband of his jeans. She tugged.

Desire flowed through his body and he shuddered with need. For her. Only her.

Logan shed his blue work shirt and spread it out upon the tiles.

She fumbled with the opening of his jeans and he stayed her hands. Capturing her lips with his, he kissed her until both of their chests heaved with unfilled desire. Holding her by the hands, he gently lowered his diamond until she lay upon his shirt. For a moment, he reveled in the sight of her beauty. Her smile welcomed him, and he covered her with his body.

Slipping her hand up behind his neck, she arched her body up to meet his. "The boots stay."

He grinned against her lips, "Anything you want, sweetheart. Anything you want."

Curling her fingers around the hem of his t-shirt, leisurely JD inched the fabric up and over his head before discarding it. The pull of Logan swirled within her and a fire storm had whirled into a ferocious need. Her already burning body was enflamed by the warmth of the tiles below her and the heat of Logan's body above her. The whisper of the cool, December breeze erotically caressed her naked skin.

His tongue licked and his lips teased her nipples through the thin lace and they tightened in response. Her body arched, and the lace was whisked away along with his clothes.

The changing lights of the fountain cast a red glow over his bared skin and he paused, stiffening, waiting for her to decide.

Involuntarily, her breath hissed in at the sight before her. The scarred skin stretched and gathered into hot spots that told of the terror and kiss of death that he'd endured. None of the skin on the right side of his body was spared.

She whimpered below him and tears escaped from the corners of her eyes at the unfairness of his wounds.

Above her, Logan stiffened and started to roll way. "I understand."

The cold air washed over her. "No!" she cried out, gripping his shoulders, dragging him back.

Twisting, she rolled over until he lay beneath her and she straddled him. Bending forward, the thickness of her hair cascaded around them and enclosed them within a private world. His body was a map of pain. Her fingertips traversed the smooth skin of his youth, up over the razed ridges and gorges of his agonizing journey into manhood.

With the softness of her lips, she kissed where fire kissed. The tip of her tongue licked where fire ravaged. All the while, her tears dripped upon his skin and she licked the salty drops, washing away his suffering. Heat combusted between their bodies and built into a fervent need.

Hovering over his manhood, their gazes met, and she knew. She loved Logan. No matter how big of a pain in the ass he was. He was the only man for her.

With one swift movement, she sheathed him with her softness. Rocking in a motion old as time, together they fought the fire burning within. She healed his pain with her love and felt saved in return.

As the flames cooled and she laid tucked into the protection of his arms, the Tower Clock struck midnight. "Merry Christmas," she whispered.

"Merry Christmas," he repeated, kissing her on the top of the nose. Lying back, he pulled her closer and added, "This was the best Christmas present ever."

Her laughter blended with the bongs of the clock. Lights twinkled in the dome above them and their future was filled with hope.

CHAPTER FORTY-FIVE

With her boots firmly back on her feet, JD stood in the corner of Ava's office. Together, she and Ace watched the holiday festivities of Christmas morning. Every time one of the kids squealed with joy, Ace copied the sound.

Two peas in a pod, Maddy and Parker sat on the couch with opened presents and wrapping paper shredded at their feet. Ava sat on the corner of the desk with Jaxon beside her, his armed wrapped around her shoulders. Seated in a chair, with Theo's hands resting on her shoulders, Isabella would reach up and squeeze his hands each time the kids exclaimed over the gifts she gave. JD didn't need to glance up to see where Logan was; she felt his presence within the room.

Plopped down in the middle of the floor, Colton gave a whoop of delight and tore into another of his presents. All the adults around him smiled in tune with his joy. Unconsciously, everyone had come to the same conclusion—taking time to celebrate Christmas with the kids preceded over all other matters.

So far, the young boy's pile of booty had included a small dinner jacket and tie from Theo, a magic kit from Ava, a red apron from Isabella and a box of artist pencils and ink pens with a small sketchbook from JD.

He drug a rather heavy box from Logan closer and ripped at the colored paper. Hooting with excitement, he exclaimed, "Comic books!" He snagged one from the top, held it high above his head and paraded around Ava's office.

"Now, it's your turn," said Ava, giving an encouraging nod to Parker. Even though it was inhumanely early in the morning, she managed to look like a glamorous star.

Colton flopped down on the couch and hugged his comic book.

Ripping the sparkling paper, Parker stared down into the box. A fire engine red sweatshirt with white block lettering read, "Oaktown High School." She lifted out the sweater and revealed a fierce hawk, with talons spread, on the back of it. "Thank you, Logan."

He shrugged, "Once break is over, you'll have to go back to school. Thought this would help you fit in."

Pushing himself away from the door, his uneven gait carried him across the room. His blue eyes burned into JD's and he handed her a gift. "I have something for you too."

Holding the small, rectangular box in her hands, she murmured, "But I didn't get you a Christmas present."

"Oh, but you did," he smiled, his gaze warm.

Flipping around and getting up on his knees, Colton leaned over the back of the couch, facing her. "What did you give the Blue Flame?"

Logan bent down and mock whispered into the boy's ear. "I know her secret power."

Colton's eyes grew wide. "What it is it?"

"She has the power of healing."

Colton's gaze swiveled, taking in JD's flushed face. "She's the Mystical Diamond." Staring at her with even more respect, the boy's lips parted, and he mouthed a silent, "Wow."

He bounced up and down, urging. "Open your present, open it."

Folding back the paper, she snatched the lid off the box revealing a throwing knife in a leather sheath. Sincerely touched, her eyes glowed up at Logan. "Thank you."

Groaning, Jaxon pulled Ava close. "Only Logan would give a beautiful woman a knife. And only my sister would like it."

"Stick a boot in it, Wolfeman," grumbled Logan, lounging back against the fireplace.

"You should've seen her last night," Colton's voice rose with excitement and he took center stage to tell his story.

Her face flushing, JD flipped Logan's gift over and over. Pausing only to gauge the knife's weight and balance in her palm.

Glad everyone's attention was riveted to Colton as he gave a vivid recap of what happened on the Tower's terrace the night before, she slipped the knife away with her own, her gaze meeting the steady stare of Ace. It was as if the bird knew her and Logan's secret. She raised her finger up to her lips and winked.

Munching on a walnut, the bird let out a small squawk in her direction.

Raising one of her brows, she replied, "Just keep eating, pretty boy," and returned her attention to the boy's story.

"And she squeezed," reported Colton, his small fist demonstrating her actions and his face scrunched up into a mean scowl.

"She did, huh?" Theo coughed uncomfortably and gave Isabella's shoulders a slight squeeze when she laughed. "I'm not sure if we should encourage him."

Isabella just laughed harder and wiped at the tears gathering in the corner of her eyes. "That's awesome!"

His eyes wide and intent, Colton breathed, "Yeah, and the Crusher fell to his knees. Then, pow!" he shouted. His skinny arm sliced up through the air. "She dealt the final blow and the Crusher crumbled."

Jaxon laughed appreciatively. "That's my sister."

His story over, Colton quieted down. He lay on his stomach, a comic book spread on the floor in front of him.

Curling her feet up under her, Parker asked, "What happened to my aunt and her boyfriend?"

JD's gaze flittered over to her lover, no longer noticing his burns, just the man beneath. "Logan and the Geezers' waited for the Sheriff to arrive. He took both of them into custody for trespassing."

Parker rubbed the sweatshirt on her lap for a moment, then, slouched down into the couch. "I suppose since you guys now know our aunt is our legal guardian, you'll make us go with them."

Straightening from her spot, JD moved to stand beside Logan. "Never."

Parker sat up straighter. "But the police told me, we have no choice but to live with our aunt. It's the law."

"Your aunt struck Colton," inserted Theo. "And threatened your safety, in front of others. Her boyfriend attacked JD. Those charges should hold them for a while."

JD added, "Don't worry, Parker. I know a woman who I trust. She'll help you. Just like she helped me."

The door swept open, letting in a cool breeze along with the Geezers. "Here now," boomed JD's father's voice. "I hear Santa came last night."

Colton scrambled to his feet. "He did! He did! Look what all I got."

"Well that's fine, son. But the big man's in the Crystal Ballroom handing out more gifts from the North Pole."

Uncle Cliff added, "Mrs. Claus has all the other kids corralled and there's chocolate milk and donuts."

"I'm in," called out Parker, scrambling from the couch.

"Me too." Maddy followed her.

The Geezers herded the kids out of the room. Pausing only to wink at the adults, Milt closed the door behind him.

"The magic of Christmas," sighed Isabella, leaning her head against Theo's arm.

"Alright." said Jaxon, rubbing his hands together and getting down to business. "How are we going to keep the aunt from resuming custody of those kids?"

JD moved closer to Logan, until their arms brushed. "I have a call into Mrs. Malloy." She leaned against the fireplace and crossed her ankles. "She's filing paperwork to give me temporary custody."

"Once Isabella and I are married, we can file for custody of them," said Theo.

"You would do that?" breathed Isabella.

"Certainly, they're great kids," replied Theo.

"Actually, I want to adopt them," said JD.

Stunned, everyone stared at her.

Her brother's jaw dropped. "You? A mom?"

Ava elbowed him in the side and he gave out a whoosh.

"What's so strange about that?" glared JD. "I'd make a great mom."

"Obviously, you would," Jaxon backtracked his comment and rubbed his stomach. "I just didn't think that you wanted to be a mom."

"I didn't want to give birth to my own child." Her eyes met Logan's, before bouncing away. "Didn't want to pass on the insanity of being haunted. For a long time now, the idea of opening a home where children who are in need could go, be safe and thrive, has been a dream of mine.

"Across the street there's a large Victorian building. Almost like a mini Twin Springs. It's a perfect place. With the proceeds from the auction and some money I've saved up, I think now might be the right time to make my dream a reality."

"Wow, sis," awe filled Jaxon's voice. "I had no idea."

Theo moved forward. "I don't know who owns that building. But I can help research it for you."

Logan spoke up, "I know who owns it. If you'd like, I can speak with the owner. See if they're willing to sell or rent it."

She smiled at him. "That would be great."

"Until then, we'll keep the kids safe here," stated Theo.

"Speaking about ghosts, I understand you had another incident with Ame," said Isabella.

Still uncomfortable with sharing so much, she groaned inwardly but added, "Yes, I did." She shared with them her visions.

"The Lieutenant's an evil man," stated Isabella. "He killed both Emma and Ruby."

"Do you think he had something to do with Ame's death and that's why she's haunting me?" asked JD.

"Could be," answered Ava. "I'm not sure what her maid has to do with your visions." She looked at her sister. "Neither of us followed the life of anyone other than Ame's sisters."

"Do you think she was able to tell Everett that the Lieutenant had threatened her and the baby?"

"Since the baby survived, I assume so. We might never know though," answered JD. "The Woman's fickle with her visions."

"On a different subject," said Isabella, slanting a glance at the tall redhead. "The doctor booked another private meal for two in the Tasting Room."

"He did?" Ava sat up straighter.

"Well, he's just going to have to cancel it," muttered JD, linking her fingers with Logan's. "I've decided that safe is boring. Besides, it was supposed to be business. I told you that."

"That's it," said Jaxon, making a beeline for the door. "If we're going to start gossiping and being gooey about romance, I'm heading to the Crystal Ballroom for a donut and to see if the big man has any gifts left over for a boy in a grown man's body. Who's with me?"

Even though her stomach rolled at the thought of donuts, JD said, "I'm in." She tugged Logan's hand. "Hot chocolate?"

"Anything you want."

CHAPTER FORTY-SIX

Colton sped through the attic's crooked hallway with his arms stretched out. The flaming apron Isabella had given him flapped over his backpack as his superhero cape. He pressed imaginary buttons on his wrist and raised his hand to his mouth. "Headquarters, preparing to land. Open bay doors."

Mimicking the sounds of a jet engine, he turned and flew into the charred attic room. He wrinkled his nose at the stink left over by the fire and landed in front of the window.

Since his parents' death, he'd never thought that Christmas would again be a time of celebration. At first, he'd liked having so many adults looking out for him and his sister, but since Christmas, he'd changed his mind. The adults had insisted that he wear a stupid jacket and tie tonight for the art show and keep it on for the wedding following. He couldn't believe that even his best superhero hadn't defended him and kept the others from making him wear the stupid clothes. But Logan had made his opinion clear when he'd said, "Suck it up, kid."

Sitting on the window seat, he shrugged out of his backpack and dragged out the jacket and tie. He frowned down at them in disgust, shook his head and repeated the words he'd heard from the Blue Flame. "Sometimes a man has to take matters into his own hands."

Clicking down an imaginary visor, he scanned the room for a hiding spot. He slid off the cushioned seat to shove the pile under the burnt Christmas tree, but the seat wobbled, making a funny sound. Distracted from his primary mission, he flipped around, lifted the lid of the bench seat and discovered an empty cavern below. "Yes!"

He shoved the jacket into the deep hole and was about to drop in the tie when he heard the soft sound of feet treading on the carpet in the hallway. Startled, he jumped. The wooden lid slipped from his fingers and slammed shut with a bang. He froze. Busted. Beneath his breath he whispered, "It must be the Mystical Diamond. She reads minds. Knows all."

Quickly, he scurried behind an old table. The sewing machine above wobbled and he squeezed his eyes shut, hoping she couldn't see him.

With a soft click and whirl, he turned on his supersonic hearing and waited. Cracking open one eye, he peeked to see if the coast was clear. A large shadow moved past the door and headed down the hall. His brow furrowed and his heart started pounding in his ears. "That's not the Mystical Diamond."

Tie in hand, he crawled forward and peeked around the door-frame and out into the hall. He watched a tall man open the glass door of a box with a hose and axe. The man pushed the axe down and part of the wall moved inward and revealed a hidden room. "A secret lair," he whispered.

Covering himself within the protection of his cape, he whispered into his wrist, "Headquarters, I have the Dark Shadow in my sights."

Within his cocoon, Colton waited until the man left his hiding spot, made his way back and exited down the crooked hallway.

Shooting to his feet, he slid his backpack back on, held his hands out at his sides and flew down the hall. In his mind's eye, shiny red, white and blue armor snapped onto his body, empowering him. He raised his wrist to his mouth, "Headquarters, the Dark Shadow is gone. I'm going in."

He sped down the corridor and repeated the Dark Shadow's movements. Soundlessly, the wall slid open. "Cool."

Sliding through the opening, he used his visor to scan the room. His laser beam focused upon pictures taped to the mirror of a dresser. Pictures of Isabella, Ava, JD, his sister and Maddy. Everyone he loved. The pictures made him feel sick inside. As if the man who'd collected them was hunting his friends. His new family.

His arms dropped to his sides. Something bad lived within this room. Something evil that wanted to prey upon the people he loved. His heart pounded hard inside his chest. He needed help and from the bravest and most powerful superhero he knew.

But first, he removed the magic kit from his backpack. Using his tie and the contents of his magic kit, he set a trap to hold the evil until the Blue Flame could come.

Part Three

CHAPTER FORTY-SEVEN

$\mathcal{D}$ear Journal,
                    They left me to float down the river without a backward glance. I barely escaped the rushing water alive. Soaked to the skin and hiding in the woods, my clothes froze to my body. I almost died.

Did they care? Izzy? Ava? Hell no! Fucking bitches. Yes, they searched for me. Not to save me but to make sure I didn't live.

I crawled back home to Twin Springs and took refuge in the attics. Where it all began. I fought fever, shakes and weakness. Crawling out in the cover of night, I survived by eating the scraps leftover on trays outside the guests' rooms.

Once the fever broke, I woke to find myself a shell of the man I once was. Painstakingly, I nursed myself back to health. When I was able to make it down to the kitchens and raid the fridges, I felt my true strength returning and began watching from the shadows.

It brought me so much pleasure to see that bitch, Ava, brought low by Director Hollingsworth. I didn't want to kill the reporter because her stories destroyed Ava in ways I never could. But, once she snooped in my things, she gave me no choice. Luckily, the

Director had cast himself as the killer, freeing me to continue in my quest to destroy the Fairbanks and Twin Springs.

Until, I saw Justyne Wolfe.

It was as if she'd walked straight out of the portrait. A gift from my great, grandfather and a second chance to belong. With JD by my side and the money from selling moonshine, I'll finally achieve where my ancestor had failed. I'll have Twin Springs and destroy the Fairbanks.

Niles Porter

CHAPTER FORTY-EIGHT

*W*orking just a few feet away from the spot where he'd made love to JD on the heated floor of the Tower Terrace, Logan groaned and attempted to push the visions of her silky skin and long legs from his mind. "Maybe she'll sneak back up here with me late tonight."

He had a busy day before him. The room below was already set up for the art show and he wanted the terrace ready in case the wedding guests wanted to come up and enjoy the view. Blanking out his thoughts, he concentrated on the task before him.

The morning sun beat down on him and the whine of his electric screw driver blended in with the constant ringing of his tinnitus. He inhaled the crisp winter air deep into his lungs. Today was a beautiful day for a wedding. He removed the screws anchoring the metal treads of the temporary bridge to the terrace. Below him, laborers gathered up the last of the building supplies and cleared off the roofline of the east wing. He called out, "Heads up."

Slowly, he released the rope tether and lowered the metal treads down to the roofline below. Only the rope hand rails and the two, long, skinny, metal rails remained of the makeshift bridge. "So, the doc wants another date with JD." His mind chewed on the thought, "That's just too damn bad. She's my girl."

With a whoosh of air two skinny arms encircled his legs. Logan scrambled and grabbed his drill before it fell over the side to the roof line below. Placing the drill safely on the floor, he glanced down at the boy attached to his legs with his red cape flapping in the breeze. "Whoa, watch out Colton. You have to be careful on the job site. Someone could get hurt."

The boy continued to bury his face deep within the fabric of his jeans. Not sure what to do, he rubbed his head awkwardly with his hand. "What's up?"

Squeezing his legs harder, Colton refused to look up, mumbling something into his leg.

Gently, he pried him from his leg and hoisted his small frame into the air. He placed him on the nearest bench and settled down beside him. "What's wrong? If it is girl problems, then you'll need to go to Jaxon. He's almost a girl."

Colton snickered at his joke and shook his head. Hesitating, the little boy glanced around as if to ensure they were alone. Only then did he whisper, "I know you're a superhero."

Throwing back his head and laughing out loud, he brushed the boy's hair. "Good one kid. What made you think that I'm a superhero?"

Colton looked up at him, his turquoise gaze serious. "You can trust me to keep your secret."

Not wanting to crush the only human who seemed to believe there was something good within him, he hesitated. But the kid needed to know the truth. He leaned forward and placed his elbows on his knees. "Look, Colton, I'm not a superhero. I'm the furthest thing from it."

"Yes, you are." His blond head bobbed up and down. "You helped carry Maddy out from the underground cavern. You pushed Jaxon out of the way before the chandelier fell on him."

His voice lowered to a reverent whisper. "You breathed life back into JD."

Logan sighed heavily. "Those things don't make a man a superhero. They are just reactions to incidents."

Balling his hands into fists, Colton's body quivered with the emotions flowing through him. "You are! You are a superhero! You saved me from my aunt with one look. Teach me how to be a superhero." He clutched the sleeve of Logan's t-shirt within his fist. "Please, I just need to know how you get your power. I need super strength to protect my sister. It's not fair for you to keep your power source a secret." He insisted, "I can help."

Growling under his breath, Logan couldn't control the harshness in his voice. "Damn it, kid." He jerked his arm to release Colton's hold. "I'm just a man and a piss poor one at that. Look at me." He jutted his chin out, so the boy wouldn't miss his scars. "People can't stand the sight of me. That's why I mostly work at night and keep away from others. It's not because I'm hiding the secret to my powers. Would a superhero look like this?" He drew an invisible circle around his face with his disfigured finger. "I'm a monster. I scare women and children."

The boy reached up and laid his small hand along his burnt cheek. "All superheroes hide their true identity behind masks." He touched the razed skin on Logan's face with his fingertips, traced the ridges and deep crevices created by fire. "You just can't take yours off."

Stunned, Logan couldn't move. Even his breath was trapped within his chest and a lump formed in his throat. To his horror, tears stung the backs of his eyes.

Colton's fingers burned the flesh they touched, and his young eyes overflowed with emotion. "Teach me how to be a superhero like you, so I can avenge my parents. I want to protect those I love. Just like you." The boy's breath hitched within his small chest and his lower lip quivered. "If you don't, then evil will win. The Dark Shadow will win."

Clearing his throat, he glanced away from the pain in Colton's gaze. How could he make the boy understand? "All the things that you mentioned, that you think make me a superhero. Colton, those actions are what define a man's character." He turned back, facing his emotions head on, and grasped his small hand within his. "They don't make him a superhero, they make him a good man. I didn't help Maddy or push Jaxon out of the way because I wanted to save the day or show how powerful I was. I helped them because their lives are important. They are important. Because they matter, and it was the right thing to do."

Colton sucked in a shuddering breath and caught his bottom lip between his teeth. "How did you know what was the right thing to do?"

He gazed up at the tiny lights blinking on and off within the domed roof of the Tower. What the hell was he supposed to tell the kid? The fountain babbled in the background, mocking his efforts. After a while, he reached out and pressed the tip of his finger on Colton's chest. "You know here, in your heart. Hell, maybe deep in your soul. Everything within you knows it's the right thing to do."

Colton's brows furrowed as he thought about it. He glanced up. "Teach me how to know if it's the right thing to do."

"There's nothing to teach. You already have everything you need within you. You love your sister and you want to help others. You have your secret power." He tapped him on the chest and the burned side of his face struggled to spread into a lopsided smile. "It's the power of love."

The boy bent his shiny head down and watched the swinging of his tennis shoes. Suddenly, he whipped his head up and a bright light gleamed within his turquoise eyes. "What do I do if someone I love is in danger? If there is a great evil stalking them?"

Logan steeled himself and tried not to care about the kid's questions, but the serious flame in the boy's eyes ignited a spark in the leftover ashes that had once been his heart. "I promise that

I'll take care of you and your sister. I won't let your aunt, or her boyfriend hurt you."

Wiping his nose with the back of his hand, Colton replied, "I know. Someone else is in danger."

Confused, he rubbed the back of his neck. "What are you talking about?"

The kid's voice lowered to a conspiratorial whisper. He cupped the sides of his mouth with his chubby hands and leaned forward to protect the information. "I was on a mission. A mission in the attics. And I saw an evil villain go by."

Relief flooded his body and he patted the boy on the shoulder. "Guests take wrong turns all the time and end up in the attics."

Colton's tiny brows furrowed and his hands dropped to his sides. "But—but—" His face fell, disappointed that his hero didn't believe him. "He has secret powers. Can disappear into walls."

Logan sat up and an uneasy feeling slithered down his spine. "What do you mean?"

Scooting his little butt even closer, the boy leaned in and pressed his lips close to Logan's ear. His breath felt hot on the skin shriveled against his skull.

"He walked down the hall," Colton gushed out the information. "And messed with a box on the wall that had an axe in it. A secret door opened up in the wall and he disappeared into the hole. Later, he came out." Finished with his story, he settled back on the bench.

The thundering beat of his heart played back-up base to the tinnitus ringing in his ears. Someone was hiding in the attics? "Did he see you?"

Shaking his head so hard that his white blond curls bounced, Colton thumped his chest with pride. "No, I had on my invisibility cape. I was safe."

He shuddered at the thought of Colton alone in the attics with a stranger. He swallowed back the fear creeping up his throat. "What did you do after he came out?"

"I went into his evil lair."

Logan rubbed his face with his hands. He couldn't help but think of some of the things that could've happened to Colton if some wacko had grabbed him. Did the aunt have someone else working for her? Was someone else hired to snatch the kids? "Next time you see this man, you come straight to me." He stared directly into the little boy's eyes. "Understand?"

A silly, wide grin spread across Colton's face and he bounced up and down on the bench. "Yes!" he shouted. His small fists punched into the air and he wiggled his butt side to side, exclaiming, "I knew it. I knew it. You *are* a superhero!"

Grabbing the kid's hands, Logan held them within his own. "No, Colton. I'm not, but *you* are important. What happens to you matters to me. Just like Maddy, Jaxon and JD." He hugged the boy tight to him, savoring the feeling of love and belief from another human being before he released him. "What did you find in his— what did you call it? Evil lair?"

Face serious, the little boy scanned the area around them before leaning forward and whispering, "He had pictures taped to the wall. Pictures of everybody. Ava, Isabella, Jaxon, JD and you."

"What? I don't understand?" He leaned down. "There were pictures of all of us on the wall?"

His head bobbed up and down. "Yes, but I laid a trap with my magic kit."

"You did what?" he roared, his heart almost exploding from within his chest. "You left evidence that you were there?"

The kid's eyes widened, then misted with tears. Unsure, he added in a small voice, "It was a trap. He might be there, right now, caught."

He patted the boy on the shoulder, "It's okay." He considered the ramifications of the pictures he'd discovered and if the villain, as Colton called him, suspected that the boy knew about his secret space. "Did you see what he looked like? Did you know the man?"

Shaking his head, Colton replied, "Nope. He was just a shadow. An evil shadow."

Logan pulled his phone out of his pocket to call JD, to warn her. Then he remembered that her phone was broken. Instead, he dialed the only man he'd trust not only with his life, but with his most treasured possessions; JD, Colton and Parker. "Wolfeman, we have a problem. I'm coming to you."

CHAPTER FORTY-NINE

"What do you mean, you're dating someone else?" The doc's voice dipped into a low timber that raised the hair on the back of JD's neck.

But, how could she blame him for being upset? From his point of view, he probably felt like she'd led him on. "Hey, I'm sorry." She thought of Logan's hands cupping her breasts as they made love and her face flushed a deep red. "It just happened."

"I understand." The doc straightened until he towered over her from a great height. Displeasure thinned his lips until they disappeared into his face. "It's fine." He turned and strode away from her.

"That went well," she mumbled, watching the doctor storm away through the Grand Lobby.

"What's up with the doc?"

"Nothing he won't get over." JD leaned against the Bellhop Stand and hesitated in telling Isabella that she was an A-Class jerk because she'd just broken a sick man's heart. Her stomach rolled. Even her breakfast wasn't sitting well today. "You're supposed to be all smiles and sunshine. It's your wedding day. What are you doing down here anyway? Shouldn't you be hiding from the groom?"

Pulling her concerned gaze from the doctor's back, Isabella's face lit up with happiness. "I don't know what I'm going to do with myself all day. I wish I had insisted on a morning wedding. It never occurred to me that I'd be missing your art show just because of some bad luck legend of the groom not seeing the bride before the wedding. Maybe holding the show and the wedding on New Year's Eve wasn't the best idea, but we'll make it work."

JD's stomach flipped. Six hours and counting till the art show. What the hell was she thinking, agreeing to the auction of her pieces? Deep down, she understood selling her art, her first born, to fund her dream of a home for children in need was all worth the ill feeling surfacing within her stomach the past couple mornings. "Shoot me now," she whispered.

Isabella laughed. "You'll be fine. I do have a favor to ask of you, though. Could you make sure that Colton wears his jacket for the wedding? I've looked in all his favorite places to play and I can't find him. I have a sneaking suspicion that he might show up without it. You know how Theo likes things," she paused searching for the right word. "Organized."

"Organized?" JD snorted. She glanced up at the stairs leading to the attic. "Yeah, I'll track the little guy down and insure his compliance. Don't you worry about anything. Get back up to your room and out of sight."

Isabella hugged her and for once she didn't feel like cringing from another woman's touch.

"Thanks!" Grinning from ear to ear, Isabella zipped into the elevator.

"Guess I'll find the little guy." She bounded up the stairs to the attic two at a time, swaying at the top step as dizziness overcame her. "Whoa, just a little too fast." She grumbled under her breath, "He'd better be up here."

As she neared his favorite hiding spot, the faint trace of smoke greeted her and churned her usually rock iron stomach. She scanned the room for evidence of a little boy. Her gaze zoned in on the window seat where Gabby had prayed. There was a small gap between the wooden lid and the bench seat. *Did he hide in there? Can he breathe?*

She rushed forward and jerked open the lid. Relief flooded her limbs, when the only evidence of him was a rolled-up jacket shoved into a corner. "Found the jacket." She searched the rest of the room and came up empty. "Damn it. Where all could one little boy hide?"

Leaving the burned room behind, she scanned the crooked hallway. She'd search a little more. If she couldn't find him, then she'd ask Theo to put out an all-points bulletin with the employees. About to leave, she spotted something out of place. A piece of fabric stuck out of the wall beneath a box with an old fire hose and axe.

Striding down the hall, she crouched down and rubbed the thin piece of fabric between her fingers. A tie. Somehow Colton's tie was sticking out of the wall through a hair thin crack. Standing, she ran her fingertips first over the wall, then, the faded orange box hanging there. Opening the glass door, she weaved her fingers in and around the brittle fire hose and searched for a lever. She tugged on the axe. A satisfied grunt left her lips when a portion of the wall silently moved inward and revealed a hidden bedroom.

In front of the doorway, colorful scarves were tied together, creating a tripwire of sorts. Someone had also piled silver cups up to topple over as a warning. "Colton," she whispered. "Are you in here?"

Easily, she stepped over his trap and into a small room. For a moment, she thought she'd stepped back in time. The bed was a match to the one in Gabby's room. A small dresser and crib filled the remaining space. But a high-tech computer and cash sat on the dresser. The evidence was clear. Someone was living up here, but a little boy was nowhere to be seen. "Was this where the kids lived while they were on the run?" She picked up a stack of cash. "Where did they get all this money?"

The hair on the back of her neck tingled and she felt a presence behind her. Leaning slightly, her hand slipped down her side. The very tips of her fingers brushed against her knife, before pain shot through her skull and sparked the world around her in brilliant colors. Everything went black and she collapsed onto the floor.

CHAPTER FIFTY

*L*ogan, Theo and Jaxon took the attic stairs two at a time.

"Boy says there's someone living in the attic." Logan glanced at Colton scrambling to keep up. "There are pictures taped to the walls."

"Pictures of everybody. You guys. Ava, Isabella and JD," piped up Colton. "Plus, lots of other stuff. Loads and loads of money."

The trio moved down the crooked hall and Theo raised an eyebrow, "Sound familiar?"

"There's no way a man could've survived the powerful rushing water that night. Plus, the water was too damn cold." Logan shook his head. "You and Isabella barely survived."

"The Dark Shadow could survive the cold water by becoming a mist," insisted, Colton.

Ignoring the boy, Logan continued, "It couldn't be. He drowned."

"Who drowned?" asked Colton.

"The Sheriff never found a body," Jaxon reminded the two men.

"Niles." Logan's body tensed, readying itself for a fight. Evil had festered and grown within Niles. That evil had stolen a teenage girl, had used her as bait, and had attempted to kill Isabella. "I knew it was too good to be true." Reaching the end of the hall, he waved the kid forward. "Was the Dark Shadow a huge man with shaggy brown hair, a thick brown beard and brown eyes?"

Colton shook his head. "He was a black shadow. Long fingers. Eyes that sparked with hate."

"It's okay," Logan sighed deeply and ruffled the kid's hair. "Just show us how to get in."

Trembling with excitement, Colton reached up and opened the glass door storing a hose and an axe. "I can't believe it! I'm on a secret mission with the Wolfeman and the Blue Flame."

Jaxon addressed Logan over the boy's head. "What the hell is the kid talking about?"

He grunted deep in his chest. "I guess he sees you as a super-hero too."

"Looks like I'm chopped liver," muttered Theo.

Colton tugged on the axe and the wall swung open to reveal a secret bedroom.

Rubbing the stubble on his chin, Jaxon muttered, "I'll be damned."

"Cool, huh," demanded the boy, his eyes lit up with excitement. He flipped around and charged into the room.

Theo grabbed Colton by the shoulder, "Let us go first."

"Look out for my trap."

Logan stepped over a jumble of scarves and cups. Quickly, his eyes swept the room and zoned in on JD stretched out on the single bed. Black rope bound her hands and legs to the simple brass bed frame. Her feet were bare, and her ponytail stuck out the side of her head. Her eyes were wild above a strip of silver duct tape across her mouth and sounds emitted from her as she squirmed.

"JD!" His mind roared. Someone had held his diamond captive. His crooked gate ate up the distance between them and his fingers dug under the edge of the tape. "What the hell happened?"

"Wait!" shouted Jaxon, holding his hand up. "Let me enjoy the peace. Just for a second." He crossed his arms and rocked back on his heels. "My sister's finally quiet."

JD squirmed and shot green daggers at her brother, promising retribution.

"Not funny," growled Logan.

Moving forward, Jaxon begged, "At least let me pull the tape."

Sitting on the side of the bed, Logan glanced down at JD. Growls and grumbles worked their way up her throat and begged to be released. He grasped the edge of the tape and her beautiful eyes widened above.

"No matter what I do, this is going to hurt." He paused. Maybe he should let Jaxon be the one to cause her pain. No, it had to be him. "Sorry." With a flash of movement, he ripped the tape from her mouth.

Pressing her fingers against the reddened skin, she shouted, "That hurt like a mother—"

Knowing the boy was behind him, Logan did the first thing that came to his mind. He pressed his lips against hers and swallowed her curses within his mouth.

"Put the tape back on," Theo stated dryly, stepping through the opening and eyeing the couple.

At the sound of Theo behind him, Logan pressed one last kiss to her lips and lifted his head.

"You guys suck," stated JD, gazing up at him. His kiss had stolen the heat from her words. She attempted to come up on her elbows, but the ropes held her back. She glared at all three men. "Untie me. Untie me now!"

Working on the ropes at her wrists, he asked, "Did you see who did this to you? Can you describe him?"

She shook her head. "No." The band holding her hair in a ponytail snapped and her gorgeous red hair flowed around her shoulders. "He hit me from behind."

Leaning forward, he reached behind her and felt a large lump on the back of her head. At her sharp intake of breath, he asked, "Are you alright?"

She looked up at him, her eyes liquid green. "He hit like Jax. Even a little girl could hit harder than him." Her gaze shifted to her brother's back and she glared at him and Theo examining the contents of the tiny bedroom. She sat up and the room swirled around her. "Actually, I think I'll just lay here for a minute or two."

Colton climbed up on the bed, wiggling between them. "I'm sorry. I didn't think he could hurt you."

Reaching out, she laid her palm along the side of his cheek. "You didn't know. How did you find this room?"

Moving out of the way, Logan listened as the kid filled her in. His story grew, becoming larger and more imaginative.

Turning away from a stack of books on the floor beside the bed, Jaxon asked, "Can you describe the man, Colton? Anything. His hair color. Eye color."

Swinging his arms around, excitement filled his voice. "A thick black fog created him. He moved like a shadow with huge, long arms and his eyes glowed from blue, to green, to red, to brown."

Steadying herself, JD reached down into one of her boots beside the bed. She pulled out her notepad and withdrew the little pencil threaded through the spiral spine. "Can you draw him?"

Eagerly, he grabbed the pencil and bent his shiny head over the notebook. Chewing on his bottom lip, he hastily sketched.

"What do you have there?" asked Theo.

Jaxon tossed a leather-bound book over to him. "Appears to be journals."

Theo tugged at the leather string holding the pages together and glanced down at a stack of similar books leaning against the dresser. "Isabella will want to see these."

"Done!" hollered Colton. He shoved the notebook back towards JD.

"You've got skills, dude." She raised a brow at the picture before turning the pad for the men to see. Colton had sketched a monster, half man and half shadow, hunched as he walked with blood dripping from fangs and his claws raised. "He's scary."

"Well done." Logan scratched at the bristle of his beard. "That's quite a sketch. Do you think if you saw him again, you could point him out to me?"

Bouncing up and down on the bed, Colton exclaimed, "Oh yeah!"

Messing the boy's hair with his three fingers, Logan nodded. "Alright, then you will stick to me like glue." He addressed the adults within the room. "I'll walk around Twin Springs with him. We'll find out who this is."

Holding the leather book within his hands, Theo replied, "I think we already know. It's Niles."

"Niles?" asked JD. "I thought he died, swept downstream."

"Apparently not, if he's sneaking around Twin Springs," said Logan, thinking of his childhood friend. "Now we know who is responsible for the continued accidents within the hotel. It wasn't a little boy with a lighter. Sorry kid."

The little boy shrugged and jumped down off the bed.

Taking his cell phone out of his pocket, Theo added, "I'll let Isabella and Ava know to be on the lookout."

"Don't you have a wedding to get ready for?" asked Jaxon.

"Yes, but we'll need to postpone until we find Niles. I'll contact the Sheriff too."

"No." Logan felt the boys hand slip within his. "We're not going to let Niles control our lives anymore. The wedding will go on tonight as planned. How about the art show?" He searched JD's features. Unconsciously, he brushed a lock of her hair back and tucked it behind her ear. "Are you up for it?"

Carefully, she slipped on her boots and the world remained in place. She swallowed hard. "Of course."

"A little bump on the head can't keep my sister down," said Jaxon proudly. "Believe me, I've tried."

CHAPTER FIFTY-ONE

The Tower Restaurant buzzed around JD. The guests' excitement was tangible in the air. Everyone stared at her and the flashes of their cameras created dark spots within her vision. Her face hurting from smiling, she pumped the palms of one guest after another. She felt a little woozy on her feet. The hit from earlier must've been harder than she thought. Or maybe she was sick and having a hard time shaking the bug.

Ava had outdone herself, staging the room for the art show. Framed with black boards and lit up by lights, her art work dotted the circumference of the room. The lower corner of each piece was numbered with Twin Springs' signature green lettering. A temporary stage had been erected and swathed with gold fabric and rows of white chairs before it. Guests thumbed through brochures and ear marked the pieces that they hoped to attain.

Until now, she hadn't realized just how many pieces she'd created over the years. A lump formed in her throat at parting with her beloved pieces, but she hardened herself. "It's all for the kids."

"Excuse me?" A tall, slender woman stood before her, hand extended.

"Nothing." Slapping a smile back on her face, she shook her hand. The mature woman was a contrast, her understated clothes speaking of elegance, while the roughened palm within JD's grasp told another story all together. Her sandy blonde hair was streaked with silver and she smelled of freshly churned earth. JD parroted the words Ava had taught her and released the woman's hand. "Nice to meet you. Thank you for coming."

Her sky-blue gaze lit with laughter. "It's a pleasure to finally meet the artist DiWolf."

The woman's voice was soft, warm, like sunshine. She reminded her of someone, she just couldn't put her finger on whom. She replied, "Thank you," and added more of Ava's words. "I appreciate you coming and supporting our cause." Even though she tried, the words sounded wooden and flat. "Ninety percent of all sales will go to fund a home for lost children."

Scrunching in the corners, the woman's eyes twinkled at her pained efforts. "I understand that before now, you've rarely placed your pieces up for sale.

She groaned deep inside. The woman wanted to chit-chat. She squashed her first instinct, which was to push the woman away with a foul word or two, just to shock her and get her out of her face. But Ava's instructions to 'play nice' reverberated within her brain. Instead, she chose honesty. After all, she'd never see the woman again. What would it hurt? "Yes, ma'am. Each piece is an outlet of how I felt at a certain time in my life. It's like selling a part of my soul for strangers to examine and critic on a daily basis."

"I can understand how that can be difficult for an artist. It's hard for anyone to bare their scars. You're lucky. Your pain isn't observable from the outside. Some aren't so fortunate."

Thinking of Logan and the pain etched into his skin, she nodded.

"Also, think of the children who'll benefit. Yes, these pieces are a part of you, but they're just ink and paper, not flesh and blood. Have you decided on a place for the home?"

She pictured the Victorian hotel in her mind. "Yes. There's a building nearby, it's old. A Victorian I guess. I looked at it and thought of all the lost children that I'd helped in the past. The building felt lost, searching for someone to care for it and breathe new life into its faded and broken walls." Shaking her head with her foolish words, she shared a small smile with the stranger who had been able to pull so much out of her. "The building has so many rooms just waiting to be filled up."

The woman examined JD, taking an inventory of worth from her hair caught up in a ponytail, down to her scuffed, black leather boots. Judging her, weighing her. "I know about that building. It's in a bad state. It'll take a lot of elbow grease and hard work to get it back into shape for any human to live in. Let alone children."

For some strange reason, she felt as if this stranger's opinion mattered. Thrusting her shoulders back, she lifted her chin up a notch. "I'm not afraid of hard work. I'm not afraid of a challenge. I'm tough."

The crowd gasped, drawing her attention. They pinned their heads together and their murmuring rose to a dull roar. Relieved to have the pressure of their stares averted, if even for a moment, JD's head swiveled to find the cause. Until she saw the reason.

Logan had entered the room, not slowing his rocking canter for the smaller stride of the young boy beside him. Crouching down, he whispered into Colton's ear and the boy shot off across the room, threading a path through the crowd. His little face intent, the kid stopped before each group of guests and stared up at them before moving to the next group.

This was first time she'd observed Logan in public without his hat pulled low over his face. He stood on the fringe of the room, hands on his hips, his jean clad legs spread, daring the guests to approach. Challenging them with the blue storm that brewed in his eyes to say something, anything.

Her attention swiveled back to the guest before her. The woman's eyes brimmed with tears before she blinked them away. "It's okay to be tough. But sometimes, a woman needs to be soft too. Soft enough to soothe old wounds."

The woman's words rolled around in JD's brain and she stared at Logan. The sight of him expanded her heart, until she felt as if it would burst from her chest. She murmured under her breath, "Was that the key to healing Logan? Softness?"

She remembered soothing his wounds with her lips, and with her body. Their time on the Tower Terrace was etched into her brain and secretly sketched onto a page within her notebook. Without thinking, she stepped towards him, her mind made up. Whether he understood it or not, he was the man for her. Remembering her guest, she turned to excuse herself, but the stranger had moved on. Turning back to Logan, she watched Colton run back up to him and shake his head. His little shoulders were slumped. Logan bent down on one knee before the boy and whispered something. They both looked over at her and broke out laughing. Immediately, she bristled. *What did he say?*

The skin on Logan's bad eye stretched and he gave her a barely distinguishable wink. Then he scooped the boy up high on his shoulder and left without looking back.

Ava clapped her hands and mounted the temporary stage.

Groaning inside, JD eyed the microphone on the stage and cringed. She admired Ava, speaking to the crowd without any fear.

"Thank you all for joining us this afternoon for DiWolf's first ever art show and auction.

The room lit up with applause.

"A little quick housekeeping. All bids will be collected at the end of the auction and your pieces will be stored for your convenience. We would like to start the New Year's Eve celebration with a big bang for our cause. As you know from our brochure, eight hundred thousand children are reported lost or stolen each year within the United States. That's two thousand a day. But what you don't know, is that our artist, DiWolf, is not only a talented artist." Her hand made a sweeping gesture through the room. "As you all see. She has another, more important talent. She locates lost children and returns them to their homes."

All eyes swiveled to her and she almost bolted. "Damn it, Ava, just blow everybody's cover while you are at it."

"Sometimes those children don't have a safe home to return to. DiWolf would like to use the sale of her pieces to help those children by providing a loving and safe home for them to live. With that thought in mind, I'd like to begin our auction with piece number one, a watercolor of two children, in school uniforms, chalking on the cobblestones of a courtyard. Notice how DiWolf shows the rain muting their efforts and washing them away almost as fast as the two girls can draw. Their hands and faces are smudged with the colors of the chalk. A large, wooden cross looks down over them as they play in the rain. Named 'Hope'. Opening bid of twenty thousand dollars."

JD almost choked on her tongue at the opening bid. She stepped forward, muttering under her breath, "What the hell, Ava? You're going to scare everyone off. We won't make any money for the kids."

Ava pointed to a couple in the back. "I have twenty thousand. Do I hear thirty thousand? Thirty thousand, do I hear forty."

JD's legs trembled and she grasped the back of a chair as the bidding continued.

"Sold!" shouted Ava. "For eighty thousand dollars, to bidder number one twenty-three."

Sinking bonelessly into the chair, JD prepared herself to watch the rest of the auction. Her mouth hung open at the price her piece had fetched. "It's going to work. I'll have enough money to purchase that old house, fix it up and provide a real home for the lost children. My children."

"Of course it's going to work." Sitting down beside his daughter, Milt stared at the piece that had just sold. The background of the picture, with the two little girls and the cross, tugged at a forgotten memory in the recesses of his mind. "It's beautiful, JD."

"I can't believe the price. I think I'm going to puke." She laughed softly under her breath. "I'll be alright. I've been a little queasy about this show for the past couple mornings. Once this is all over, I'll be good to go."

He searched his daughter's features. Her liquid green eyes stared back at him. Shell shocked, he noticed the yellow tinge under her skin and droplets of sweat dotting her upper lip. Fatigue weighed at the corners of her eyes. "Nothing a good philly cheesesteak sandwich won't cure. With fried onions, garlic and peppers—"

For a second, he thought she'd gag. But she fanned her face with her hands and brought herself under control. The child he'd raised ate anything, at anytime of day. "Are you pregnant?"

"I can't be." Stunned, she spread her fingers over her flat stomach and remembered the kick she'd felt from Ame's baby. "It's not possible," she whispered thinking back over the last week. But all the signs were there. Her iron stomach revolting at smells, her breasts feeling heavy and sore.

Seeing the answer on her face, he shook his head. "When I get my hands on that doctor of yours, I'm going to rip him apart." Moving forward to fulfill his promise, he felt his little girl's hand on his arm and stopped.

For once in her life, JD appeared demure, her eyes downcast and her face sober. "It wasn't the doctor."

He rose out of his seat, and bellowed, "What? Then who the hell was it?"

Ava paused the auction and all eyes turned towards them. Waiving his hand at Ava, he prompted her, "Go on girl. Nothing to see here."

Her laughter filled and air, and Ava continued the bidding. "Do I hear seventeen thousand?"

Calming the feelings raging through him, Milt sat and grumbled low, "Who the hell was it?"

She shared a small smile with her father. "Logan."

Stunned, he sat there for a moment. "Logan? Your brother's Army buddy? Damn it girl, couldn't you have picked a Navy man? I mean, if you were going to decide on a military man, why the hell not Navy?" Agitated, he struggled to keep his voice low and rubbed his hands on his thighs. "My own daughter, turns her back on me. Sides with my brother and the damn Army."

Laughter burst from her lips and she hugged her father, hard. "I love you, Dad," she whispered and kissed him on the cheek.

"Well," mumbled her father, mollified. "Logan's a damn fine man. Even if he enlisted for the wrong branch. But this one," he teasingly poked her belly. "We're going to raise him right. If he decides a life of service is for him—"

"It's Navy all the way." She laughed and gave a little salute, before sobering. "Dad, Logan and I haven't quite figured out our relationship yet."

He harrumphed. "Figured it out enough to have one on the way."

Her cheeks flamed red and she lightly socked her father in the arm. "Let me handle it." She stood up shaking a finger in her father's face. "Do you understand? Mum's the word. I've got this."

Milt watched his daughter march off, just as his brother plopped down into the seat next to him. "I thought you were with the wives."

"They're at the spa. Getting ready for the big shindig tonight."

"Our girl's got a torpedo in the hatch."

His brother gave out a big whoop that drew the gazes of the guests within the room. "That's great! About time we have a grandkid running around. Not so sure about that doctor though. Hoped the girl would choose better than him."

"She did. Logan."

Cliff's mouth lagged open before it spread into a smile as wide as the ocean. Leaning back in his chair, he laced his hands behind his head and stared up at the coffered ceiling. "A man after my own heart."

Growling deep, he warned, "Don't say it."

A humming sounded in the back of his brother's throat. "A man of action, an Army man."

"Shut up." Milt kept an eye on his daughter, smiling at her ever-present boots. "Do you remember when I brought her home? She had on those yellow goulashes."

"They came up to her knees." Cliff chuckled. "Almost swallowed her whole."

Milt glanced back over to the watercolor, at the two little girls bending down on the stones. Then it dawned on him. "The courtyard, the cross."

"What the hell are you talking about?" Cliff sat up and addressed his brother. "A baby swabbie on the way and you've gone senile."

"No, listen to me. The painting. It reminds me of that orphanage. The one at the convent. You know, where I lost the scent on JD's background."

"I remember. You spent years tracking down the ramblings of her mother, then her grandmother. Ended up at a church in the Blue Ridge Mountains."

"That's right. All threads led to that church. But the uptight nuns closed ranks. Assured me that they could account for all of their orphaned girls."

"They praised you for your efforts and sent you away empty handed."

"Everything went cold after that dead end. I didn't have any other strings to pull." He'd felt sick, defeated. The feeling of failure came back to him and flowed over him like black tar. "Damn that mean old nun. Her aged skin had stretched tight across her pinched face when she informed me that I was wasting her time. The old biddy couldn't still be alive. She looked as if death was her shadow when I last saw her."

"Perhaps one of the new, younger nuns would be more willing to help." Cliff sat forward, elbows on his knees. "It wouldn't hurt to check. After all, the church can't be that far from Twin Springs. Send Jaxon and Logan. Between the two of them, they might get better results."

Milt glanced down at the dials on his dive watch. "There'll be plenty of time for the boys to get there and get back." He felt the rush of a fresh hunt. "Things are clicking into place, I feel it."

CHAPTER FIFTY-TWO

*S*upporting his weight against the bookcase, Logan crossed his arms and studied the woman draped in a black habit. Her musty, cubbyhole office was jam packed with bookshelves and filing cabinets. High in the wall behind a desk, the sunlight struggled to enter the room through a rectangular window that was scrubbed clean but fogged with age. Only a small black bible, a plain brown beaded rosary and a yellow pad of paper graced the top of the large, wooden desk where the elderly nun had perched herself on a hard, wooden chair. Like a magpie, she was covered from head to toe in black, except for the stark white around her throat and a white apron like thing pinned to her front. Old enough to be his grandmother, Logan wondered how she breathed under all that material.

Another rosary hung from her hip and jingled as she shifted her slight form on the tall, wooden back chair. With a practiced move, she motioned for the men to take their seats. Jaxon and Sam scrambled to squeeze into the tiny wooden chairs in front of her desk, leaving Logan to lean.

Layering her hands calmly in front of her, Sister Rosemary returned the steady stare of the burnt man. "Many come to our church to hide, young man. But may I suggest, that hiding behind walls is not the way. The pain from your burns will not heal here."

Sam snickered from his chair. "Like my brother would join the church."

Surprised, the nun's brown eyes widened, "You're not here to join the church or to seek sanctuary?"

Shocked, Logan straightened, "Hell no. I mean, no ma'am."

The nun fumbled with a large crucifix hanging from her neck. "Oh, I just assumed."

Bending forward, his elbows on his knees, Jaxon spoke up. "We're trying to track down the family of my adopted sister. We think her grandmother grew up in your orphanage and we'd like to bring peace to my sister. To help her find her roots."

"I'm sorry." Her lips thinned into a straight line and her brown eyes turned to stone. "We don't discuss the children within our orphanage. Their records are sealed for their protection and the mother's protection."

"Please, my sister, and her mother before her, has spent her entire life searching for answers. Do you remember a young girl? I'm sure she had bright red hair, just like my sister and her mother."

"Bright red hair?" repeated the nun, her aged eyes glassing over as she gazed into the distance of the past.

"Yes," replied Logan, stepping forward. His gut was telling him that the nun held the answers that JD needed. "She might've talked to walls. Or people who weren't there."

The nun gasped. She picked up the rosary from the desk and rolled the wooden beads between her aged fingers. "I can't. I can't give you the answers you seek. I must protect the innocent."

Knowing they were on the right track, Jaxon leaned forward and gripped the edge of the desk. "My father came here around twenty years ago. There was a nun much older than you. She promised to tell my father if my sister's family lived here. She promised to help and told him to come back in the morning.

When he did, the other nuns wouldn't allow him to see her. Please, if you know anything, tell us. Give my sister peace."

"Peace?" The nun gazed over their heads and studied an ornate cross above the office door. Her gaze met Logan's. "Maybe it's time," she whispered. "Who could it possibly hurt now?"

Without waiting for an answer, she raised herself out of the chair, opened the bottom drawer of a file cabinet next to Logan and removed a small box, tied with twine.

Settling herself once again, she placed the box on the desk before her. "I, too, was an orphan and grew up here. In the court-yard outside, I played hopscotch, jumped rope and drew chalk pictures with my best friend, Pearl. She and I were inseparable, even through high school. Many times, I caught her talking to thin air. Pearl was never at peace, as you say. Itchy feet she called it. Looking for her place. A place to call home. I joined the church and Pearl went off looking for adventure. She'd often visit me. Until, one day, the visits stopped. I always wondered what happened to her."

Jaxon squeezed the desk so hard his knuckles whitened. "My sister's name is Diamond. Her mother's name was Opal."

"Diamond and Opal." Sadness softened the wrinkles around the nun's eyes. She nudged the box across the desk. "Sister Gabriella spoke to your father. She was an icon within this church and died in her sleep the night before your father returned. But she wrote your father a note and left it in this box."

Outrage filled Logan. "Why didn't the nuns give the box to his father?"

The nun's back straightened and she looked down her nose. "It's not your place to judge. Who are you to think you know better. To know the way."

Afraid she'd grab the box back, Logan gazed down at his feet. "Sorry."

Her shoulders relaxed, and she continued. "I was a young novice at the time. The rest of the nuns at the church felt that

Sister Gabriella had paid her penance. She did great things as a nun. From making clothes for all the children in the orphanage, to food drives. So much more. The nuns didn't want to soil her good deeds by letting the truth get out. That's why they sent your father away without the box or the letter. Just with the news that Sister Gabriella wouldn't see him."

Sam reached across, grabbed the box and moved to pull the string.

Resting his burned hand on his brother's shoulder, Logan said, "It's for JD to open."

With the soft eyes of the young girl that she once was, the nun considered his actions. "I'm glad to see that Pearl's granddaughter found so much love."

The men thanked Sister Rosemary. Quietly, they piled back into Jaxon's jeep and started up the highway towards Twin Springs. Logan stared down at the simple box. "How could something so small, hold so much hope?"

He'd never be able to shed the mask he wore. But once JD found the answers she needed, then perhaps she'd be able to see past the scars to the man beneath. Maybe even see a future with him. "Turn the car around."

"What?" shouted Jaxon. "Theo's going to kill us if we're late."

"It's too late to become a nun," Sam muttered from the back seat.

Logan reached back and smacked his brother in the shoulder. "Men become monks or priests. I have to buy something before we return to Twin Springs."

CHAPTER FIFTY-THREE

"Where are they?" demanded Ava.

Peeking around the reception desk, JD admired the transformation of the Tower Restaurant; all in the few hours since her art show. The temporary stage was now draped with white satins, greenery and white peonies. An emerald green carpet ran between the rows of chairs, bows of white gauze and satin tipping each point along the aisle with more greenery and peonies. Through the panorama of windows, the evening sky with the sun kissing the shoulders of the Blue Ridge Mountains back-dropped the proceedings.

Everyone raced around doing their jobs. Parker, in a gauzy white dress with an emerald sash, and Colton were in charge of seating the guests. Maddy, in an emerald green floor length dress, kept the bride out of sight of the guests and kept an eye out for Isabella's cue to walk down the aisle. Theo, in a dark gray tux, a white tie and a peony bud pinned to his chest, stood still as a statue and alone at the top of the stage, awaiting his bride. Everyone was present and ready, except Jaxon, Logan and Sam.

"I have no idea," stated JD. "But Theo's going to ring their necks when he sees them."

Colton jogged up to the two women, tugging at his tie. "That's the last old person. Everyone's seated." He was breathing hard, with a pained expression on his face. "If one more old lady pinches my cheeks and tells me how cute I am." He left the threat open and rolled his young shoulders within his jacket.

"Stop whining," hissed Parker. "This is a special time for Theo and Isabella. Don't ruin it." She grabbed the small, white ring pillow from the desk and tossed it to her brother. "Hold onto that. When Ava gives you your signal, walk down the aisle. I'll follow you."

Colton caught the pillow and glared down at the two wedding rings tied on with strings. "I'm never getting married."

"Famous last words." Ava's laughter flowed into the room, turning heads.

"You need to stall," said a voice behind them.

JD turned, seeing the female guest that she'd spoken to at the art show.

"Mrs. Oakes," breathed Ava, sweeping up to Logan's mother and kissing her on the cheek. "Thank goodness you're here. Usually, I'd say the show must go on but we're missing the two best men."

Realizing it was Logan's mom, JD snapped her mouth closed. Her mind played back their meeting, checking to see if she'd stuck her foot in her mouth.

"Well, Ava, go do what you do best. Sing for the guests. That will distract them as long as needed."

A sensual smile spread across Ava's face. "Of course. Once the guys are here, flash me my cue and I'll wrap it up."

Ava took the stage. She whispered to Theo and he moved down and gave her center stage. Her beautiful voice blanketed the room and silenced the guests.

JD admired the royal blue, satin dress that hugged Mrs. Oakes curves. She glanced down at her own attire. Black pants, boots and shirt. Dressed more for a funeral than a wedding. "She sings like an angel."

Mrs. Oakes nodded. "Let me tell you, growing up Ava was no angel. She and Logan got themselves into more scrapes than I could count. Can't tell you how many trips to the Principal's office I made because of those two."

"I don't suppose you know where Logan and Jaxon are?"

"No, but I'll jerk those boys up by their earlobes once I find them."

A woman after my own heart. "I say we hang them upside down from the Tower."

"Hook them to the horses and drag them through the streets of Oakton."

Warming to the game, JD's next reply was interrupted by a commotion behind her.

Fighting their way through the doorway, the missing grooms and Sam tumbled in.

She almost swallowed her tongue at the sight of the three men. Sam, dressed in a light gray suit, looked much older than his young years. Her gaze flowed over Jaxon and Logan. It had been a long time since she'd seen her brother in his Army Service Uniform. Their dark blue pants with thick yellow stripe were bloused into the tops of their combat boots. The black jacket broadened their shoulders, and full-dress medals laid in neat rows on their chests. Seeing Mrs. Oakes, the trio's gazes fell, and they shuffled their feet from side to side.

"Sorry we're late, Mom," mumbled Sam.

"Go sit down, Sam. I'm sure you had little to do with it."

She admired Mrs. Oakes. Somehow, she'd balanced strength with softness. She remembered the woman's words. "Sometimes a woman needs to be soft enough to sooth old wounds." Suddenly, everything clicked for her. She didn't have to be tough all the time. Leaning on a man didn't make her weak. It was okay to act like a woman, wear girly clothes and take what you want. And she wanted the man before her. Branded by fire, this man had stolen her heart.

Wearing her heart on her sleeve for all to see, like the Purple Heart hanging from Logan's chest, she strode forward, grabbed his face between her palms and kissed him. Her lips were soft upon his, until his arms wrapped around her added her to the row of medals pinned to his chest. For a moment, he ravaged her softness, filling himself with her warmth.

Parting, he gazed down into her beautiful face. "I have something for you," he whispered against her lips.

"I'm sure you do."

"No, you don't understand."

Theo cleared his throat beside them, breaking the couple apart. "If you don't mind, I'd like to get married sometime this year."

Mrs. Oakes gave Ava a signal and she brought her song to a close. Gracefully, she walked down the aisle and rejoined the group. "It's about time. Where were you guys?"

"We'll explain later," answered Jaxon, kissing her.

"Yuck," muttered Colton, wiping his mouth with the back of his sleeve. "Everyone is sharing spit. If this is what a wedding is like," he rubbed his tongue on his sleeve, "then I'm definitely not interested."

"Go, go," pushed Maddy.

Escorted by Sam, Parker dropped white petals down the aisle. Her brother stomped behind them, a pillow dangling from his fingers.

Logan lifted JD's hand to his lips, "Wait for me after the wedding." He winked at her and turned to escort Maddy down the aisle, behind Ava and Jaxon.

Isabella emerged from the hall, her green eyes sparkling from behind her translucent veil. Her satin dress kissed her curves and swept out into a long train behind her. Lace lay across her chest and covered her arms, leaving her shoulders bare. She held a gorgeous bouquet of eucalyptus and peonies.

"You're beautiful," whispered Mrs. Oakes, wiping tears from her eyes with a small handkerchief. "Give me just moment to take my seat with Dale."

Isabella reached out and grasped JD's hand within hers.

She could feel the bride shaking. "Are you sure?"

Glowing brighter than any star, Isabella replied, "I'm more sure of this than anything else in the world. Theo's my soulmate."

The bridal chorus sounded. Isabella squared her shoulders and opened a fresh page for her and Theo to write their journey on.

Taking a seat, JD looked out over the guests. Her uncle, fit as ever in his generation's dress greens, sat with his wife and, beside them, her mom and dad. Her father, in his dinner dress whites, stood out within the crowd. He nodded at her above his wife's head and mouthed, "Navy."

Sharing a smile with him, her gaze returned to the couple. The sun set in the windows behind them, illuminating their forms in a brilliant glow and darkening the mountains. As the sky darkened and filled with stars, vows were exchanged, while Colton flipped the pillow between his hands in a world of his own.

When the rings were called for, Parker bent down and hissed in Colton's ear. "The rings. Hand over the rings."

Startled, Colton threw the pillow at Theo and the audience laughed. Red faced, the little boy shoved his hands into his pockets.

Pronounced man and wife, fireworks exploded in the skyline above the mountains and Isabella and Theo shared their first kiss as a married couple. The room came alive with applause and the couple made their way down the aisle. The love and commitment they shared for each other was apparent for all eyes to see. Everyone enjoyed the couple's moment.

Everyone except one man. His arms crossed against his chest, his jaw rock hard, he slipped from the back of the room.

CHAPTER FIFTY-FOUR

*A*va herded the guests down to the Lobby, where liquor flowed out of Still Waters Bar and Grill. Standing on the outside of the crowd beside JD, Logan watched Isabella toss her bouquet from the balcony, down to the waiting arms below. A shout sounded, and one woman held up the prize. Men jeered and ribbed another man nearby. He couldn't wait for the reception to end, so he could get JD alone. His lips burned from her earlier kiss.

Vigilant for the signal, in case the kid identified the man who'd hurt JD, he kept his eye on Colton.

JD reached out and linked her hand with his. He stared down at the smooth skin on her hand and compared it to the razed skin on the back of his. Somehow it didn't bother her. He squeezed his eyes shut and made a New Year's Eve resolution. He vowed to protect and care for JD from this day forward. That he'd love and cherish her 'till the day he died.

He opened his eyes, just in time to notice that an elderly woman had wobbled to her feet. He stepped forward to help her, but she seemed determined to move on her own steam, stabbing the ground with her cane as she moved down the Grand Lobby.

Suddenly, he realized that she was making a beeline towards him and glanced around for a place to hide, but JD still had hold of his hand.

The woman came to a stop right before him. He frowned and braced himself to grab her once she looked up and saw his ugly mug. Hunched in the shoulders, she stood before him. Her skin was translucent with blue veins showing through. She smacked her cane on the carpet and shifted it over to her left hand.

Logan released JD's hand and reached out to grab her in case she tipped over.

Instead, she grasped his right hand by the three fingers and shook it with a surprisingly firm grip. "You're a great hero to our country." Her tight gray curls ricocheted around her head with the earnestness of her jerky movements. "My Johnny served in WWII. Thank you for your service."

Shock lit the scars on Logan's face. Encouraged by the elderly woman's actions, a group of guests moved forward and surrounded him, pushing JD away in their exuberance. A panicked look on his face, he called through the crowd to her, "Meet me on the Tower Terrace later tonight. I need to talk with you."

"I need to talk with you too," she replied, stepping out of the way.

A man grasped his hand, pumped it hard and drew his attention away. "I served in Vietnam." He lifted the cuff of his pant leg and revealed a metal post instead of a leg. "Thank you for carrying on when I couldn't."

Logan swallowed hard as his gaze met his fellow veteran's. "It was my pleasure."

The man stepped aside, and a woman grabbed Logan in a bear hug, pressing his medals into his chest. Pulling back but not releasing him, tears dripped from her lashes and she whispered, "I lost my younger brother in Afghanistan. Thank you for your service."

Stunned at how she could thank him, when she'd lost so much, he replied, "I'm sorry for your loss, ma'am. Your brother was a true hero." And he hugged her back.

Across the room, Colton's eyes grew wide. He gave the signal and followed the Dark Shadow.

The crowd of people in front of Logan grew the length of the Grand Lobby as guests lined up to shake the burned man's hand. And thanked him.

CHAPTER FIFTY-FIVE

*E*xiting the elevator to the Tower Restaurant, JD skirted around the receptionist desk and headed for the circular staircase that led up to the terrace. The smell of lavender flowed over her. Hesitating, she paused. Squeezing the handrail, she looked up the spiral staircase. She knew Ame called to her with the fragrance. In the past, she would've flipped her the finger and turned away. But now, with the new life growing within her, she had to find out what Ame wanted and finally put a stop to the haunting of her and her loved ones.

Determinedly, she continued up the staircase. With each step she felt the weight of the life within her belly weighing her down and the sweet scent choked her. Excruciating pain coursed through her abdomen. She leaned heavily against the railing, fell to one knee and rested her sweaty forehead against the cool metal. Pausing, her breath came hot and quick in her chest, and she fought for control of the pain.

Fighting her way to the top, the doors slid open and the fresh air rushed to greet her, cooling her face. The heat from the hot floors collided with the cold mountain air and created a fine mist.

A man walked out of the fog and she gasped, reaching out for him. "Logan."

When he faded into the mist, she realized that her frenzied pain had brought his image to life from the recesses of her mind. She collapsed on the floor and writhed in pain. Realizing her mind had played tricks on her, she ground her back teeth and fought to control another burst of pain that shot across her abdomen. "Fuck that hurts."

The world around her changed. The mist cast the color of her world into black and white and another world slowly gained speed to take its place.

A face loomed over her. Concentrating on holding on to her world, she attempted to bring the pale face into focus. She could make out a man with one blue eye and one brown eye. She frowned, until recognition dawned. "Dr. Ottoman. Oh, thank God." She clutched at his shirt. "Help me. Please. Go get Logan. Please. Our baby, there's something wrong."

Pain coursed through her. The urge to push contracted her muscles and felt heavy upon the floor of her vagina. Her world darkened.

A shrill voice followed her from the end of a long tunnel. "Please," the vile voice penetrated the darkness around her and chanted over and over, "Go get Logan. Please. Pleasssse."

CHAPTER FIFTY-SIX

*L*ying within the sheets of her bed, Ame released a low, long grunt of pain. Using every ounce of her strength she pushed the life within her out into the world. Collapsing back against the pillows, she held her breath and waited for the welcoming cry of her newborn child.

The room was alight with lavender candles. From high above, JD observed the scene.

Gabby helped her remove her dirty nightgown and placed a clean white gown over her head.

Everett swept sweaty strands of Ame's red hair away from her forehead and placed her amethyst and diamond necklace around her neck while the doctor checked the baby. "You look like a queen."

The doctor slapped the baby's bum and a loud wail flowed through the room.

Everett laughed with joy. He kissed his wife and rubbed the back of her hand against his cheek. "I love you, Ame."

Her smile weak, she whispered, "I love you too. Check his fingers and toes. Make sure everything's okay."

The doctor handed the baby to Gabby to wipe clean.

Once swaddled, Everett snatched the baby from the maid's arms and returned to his wife. "Darling, he's beautiful."

Gabby tugged the sheet liner out from under Ame before raising the comforter and tucking it in around her.

Ame lay in the bed, her face glistening with sweat, ringlets of her hair stuck to her face and neck. The rest of her flaming red hair was splayed out around her shoulders.

"But not as beautiful as his mother." Holding his new son in his arms, he leaned in and kissed his wife softly on the lips.

The doctor removed his bloody white apron, rolled it into a ball and finished packing his bag. He clapped Everett on the back, "Did good, son." He winked and smiled at Ame over her husband's bent head. "A fine young man you have there. The General will be proud."

Everett's head popped up at the doctor's comment. His smile broadened, and he pushed his rounded glasses up onto the bridge of his nose. "Yes, he will. Darling, if you'll be alright and if you don't mind, may I have the honor of showing our son to the General?"

Ame's warm gaze flowed over her husband holding their newborn son. He obviously hadn't had time to change into a black tux, like the doctor did. His plaid bowtie was pulled loose and hung at an odd angle. His trousers, suspenders and plain shirt were splattered with oil paint. Still, she wanted him to enjoy the New Year's Eve party that was going on in the Crystal Ballroom below. "You're as giddy as a boy with a new toy." She reached up and fixed his bowtie. "By all means, show my father."

Gabby fluffed her pillows and helped her to sit up higher in the bed. She gasped, "Oh, but, Miss Ame. Perhaps it would be better if you and the baby rested for a while. After all you've been through, you must be tired."

Her husband's face fell, his shiny new toy taken away.

She waved her maid off. "My son can rest in his father's arms.

My husband needs to show off his new son. Is the party still going on?"

The doctor nodded.

"Then go with him. I'll rest until he returns. Enjoy the party." She smiled at Gabby. "Let the men show off their new comrade-in-arms."

A sad expression crossed the maid's face. "If you are sure, Miss Ame."

Hesitating, he bent down to his wife. "You said there was something you needed to tell me."

Laying her palm against his face she replied, "Tomorrow. It can wait until tomorrow. Take care of our son."

He whooped softly, brushed a kiss across his wife's lips and rushed from the room with the baby in his arms and the doctor in tow.

"They'll be back in no time, Gabby. Let's just rest and let the men do their men things." Gratefully, she leaned back against the pillows. "You would've thought my husband had just sweated through hours of labor." She laughed joyfully. "Did you see him almost skip from the room?"

"Yes, Miss." Gabby sat on a corner of the bed. "Do you think they will come back soon?"

"Keep her from the baby!" JD shouted.

"I'm sure, once the baby wants food, they'll rush back here. He wanted to show the General what he had created. How beautiful and right our baby is."

A gasp and low moan escaped from her lips. She clutched her still rounded tummy, surprised to find it tightening once more.

Panting through a contraction, she grabbed Gabby's hand. The pain subsided, and she gasped, "Something's wrong." She grit her teethe in pain as another contraction rolled over her.

"I'll get the doctor." Gabby tried to pull her hand away.

"Stay with me." She felt another gush of fluid between her legs. "I don't think there is time." She whipped back the covers.

A large amount of blood had pooled beneath her mistress. Gabby gasped in horror.

"Go get the doctor!" yelled JD. But the maid stood frozen.

The long nightgown prevented Ame from drawing her knees up into the birthing position. "Rip my nightgown! Hurry, I've got to bear down."

Gabby rushed forward and ripped the bottom of the gown into strips.

Freed, Ame drew her knees up once again, hooked her arms around her legs and pushed through the pain. Strands of her beautiful red hair fell over her face and stuck to the fine sheen of sweat coating her face. Panting with effort and her face pale, she leaned back between contractions before she pushed herself back up and began straining once more. Contraction came on top of contraction.

"So much blood." Shocked, JD watched, unable to help.

Panting like a dog, Ame attempted to catch her breath between the contractions. She felt as if she was being ripped in two. "Help me." She groaned long and deep. Through clenched teeth, she bit back a sob, "Get help. Get Everett. Now!"

"Don't just stand there!" yelled JD. "Help her!"

Wringing her hands, Gabby watched. "Miss Ame, I'll be right back."

Sobbing and out of her mind, Ame dug her fingers into the maid's arm. "Don't leave me." Hunching her shoulders, she gave a great push. The moan came from the depths of her soul and onto the bed plopped a baby girl, feet first. Giving a gusty cry, her bright red hair stuck straight up.

"It's a baby girl, ma'am. A twin," Gabby spoke, softly awed.

JD stared down at the fiery red headed baby and finally understood where she came from and where she belonged.

Exhausted, Ame dropped back against the sweat and blood soaked-bedding. "Now you may get the doctor." Her eyes rolled back into her head and she passed out.

Shocked, Gabby stared down at Amethyst Fairbanks, the woman who had everything she thought she wanted. "So much blood." Babbling out loud, she washed and bundled the baby up as blood continued to seep out of Ame and into the sheets. "The breach birth must have torn up her insides."

Gabby smiled at the perfect baby girl in her arms and then back at her mistress. The smile faded. "Now's my chance. Surely, her husband and the doctor will be back soon with the other baby. They'll take care of your mother."

With one hand, she packed a towel between her mistress' legs to stanch the bleeding and covered her with the quilt. Her heart beating like a trapped bird, Gabby hugged the baby, now sleeping soundly, and glanced about the room. Her gaze fell upon Ame's long amethyst and diamond necklace. A strand of the long necklace was stuck under her body. She wrestled with it, leaned back and pulled hard. Snapping, the necklace broke and she fell backward into the dresser. With the baby in her arms, she slid the pieces into her apron pocket and ran to meet her lover.

In her rush, Gabby didn't even notice that she'd knocked the candles on the dresser back into the curtains. Flames greedily licked and devoured the curtains before moving on to the rest of the Tower room.

"Wait!" shouted JD, calling after the fleeing woman. "Fire!" she screamed. "Fire!"

Flames licking at her body, Ame rose up, pain free. She joined JD's translucent form high above the room. Her gray hair streaming down her face and her body monochrome in the tattered nightgown, Ame had transformed into the Woman from JD's past.

She laced her fingers with her great granddaughter's and patiently watched as the flames ate at her body.

CHAPTER FIFTY-SEVEN

*T*he Tower room now consumed by flames, Ame turned towards JD. "Are you here to take me to heaven? If so, I'm not going. I need to bring my family back together. I must tell Everett he has a baby girl to care for."

JD shook her head. "I think I'm here to help you." She tugged on her hand. "We need to find Everett, he'll help."

Behind her hair, Ame's dark gray lips spread into a smile. "You're right. They are in the Crystal Ballroom."

They floated down to the Crystal Ballroom and arrived just in time to see the General up on stage presenting his new grandson to the audience.

"Wait," called out JD as Ame flew ahead of her.

Sobbing, Ame flung her arms around Everett, only to have them pass straight through his body. Jolted for a moment, she waved her arms in front of the General and her husband. "I gave birth to a girl. Gabby stole her. You must find her. Bring her back to Twin Springs."

The General gazed down at his new grandchild. "You finally did something right, Everett."

In the background the guests and the band began the countdown till the New Year. Huddled around the stage, they shouted, "Ten, nine, eight—" to the beat of the band's drum. The tall feathers on the women's heads bounced with the excitement of their feet.

"I think Ame would've liked to name her own child, sir. Your announcement was premature and in bad form."

Stunned, Ame turned to JD. Her breath hitched in her chest. "He can't see or hear me."

The baby fussed within the General's arms. He moved away from the beating of the drum and the shouting count down of the frenzied guests.

Their shouts rang around him, "—five, four—"

Frowning, the General moved further from the crowd, his anxious son-in-law lagging behind him. "She will come around. It's a fine name. Things are going to change around here, Everett. Let's face facts. You're a wimp. Time to become a man and protect your wife and son, ensure their future and care for them."

"I don't care about the name, Everett." Ame's fingers clutched air instead of her husband's lapel. "Find our daughter!"

"—three, two—" shouted the guests, reaching for the one they wanted to kiss into the New Year or lifting a glass of forbidden Champagne.

Oblivious to the activities around him, Everett removed the baby from his father-in-law's arms. "General, I don't give a damn if you think I'm a man or not. I only care what Ame thinks." He patted the back of his crying son. "Now, I must get back to my wife. She had something important she needed to tell me. She needed my help."

The Tower Clock sounded in the distance. The stench of gun powder permeated the rich perfumes and colognes of the guests as tubes burst and sprayed confetti into the air, sprinkling the stage and crowd with little bits of colored paper and silver tinsel. The new year had arrived and the ground beneath Twin Springs shook. Guests grabbed ahold of each other or anything they could find until the tremors faded. Shocked, they clung to each other and looked around for guidance.

"Did the Tower explode?" asked Ame.

Hating the feeling of helplessness invading her soul, JD watched Everett. He sprinted from the room, his baby safely tucked within his arms. "It's the kitchens. Your sister, Emma, just died."

CHAPTER FIFTY-EIGHT

Slower now, JD followed Ame to the kitchens. The two of them silently witnessed the Lieutenant drag a tall black man by the collar of his chef jacket into the kitchens. He dumped the body next to the huge stoves running across the back wall and then retreated back down the hallway.

"It's Jean Claude." Ame held her hand over her mouth in horror. "Where's Emma?" She rushed toward the hallway to chase after the Lieutenant.

JD gazed down at Jean Claude. His resemblance to Theo was uncanny, only his skin was a few shades darker. "It's too late," JD called out, and Ame returned. "Emma's dead. We need to care for the living."

Ame sobbed into her hands.

"I'm sorry."

Getting control of herself, Ame glanced up. Her eyes glowed like silver sparks of fire from behind the strings of her hair. "My father will kill him for this."

The Lieutenant emerged from the hall with a burlap sack and a large mason jar of clear liquid. His face was bruised and bloodied.

"Looks like Jean Claude gave as good as he got," murmured JD. "Too bad he didn't win."

Dropping the bag next to Jean Claude, he dribbled the liquid along the floor, up over the stoves and across the wooden floor boards.

"Moonshine," Ame whispered.

Finished with his task, he tossed back the last of the home brew, reared his leg back and kicked Jean Claude. "Piece of shit." Squatting down beside the chef's still form, he picked his head up by the hair and admired the results of the beating that he'd given the man. "Emma wouldn't think that you're so pretty now."

"W-w-what have you d-d-done," stuttered Betty, her hands twisting above her massive belly. Unwittingly, she stood beside JD and Ame. "Where's M-m-miss Emma?"

"Run, Betty, run!" screamed Ame. She hovered around the girl, circling her. "Get the General."

"She can't hear you." JD moved closer to the maid and whispered in her ear. "Help. Help. Help."

"Emma?" He rose from his crouched position and threw the mason jar against the wall.

It shattered behind Betty's head and she cringed.

A mad sheen glowed in his gaze. "I killed Emma in the tunnels. Didn't you feel the ground shake with my power?"

Turning, the maid started to run down the hall, passing through JD's transparent body. "Help!"

"Don't bother, Betty," the Lieutenant cackled. "I blew the slut up and the tunnel collapsed around her. The General will never find her."

Skidding to a halt, Betty returned. She rung her white apron between her hands. Her honey brown eyes filled with tears. "W-w-what are you going to do?"

"Why, I'm getting out of this God forsaken place." He opened the burlap sack and revealed stacks of money. "I'm meeting Gabby at the train station and we're going to ransom the General's new grandson. He'll pay handsomely for his heir's return."

"Y-y-you and G-G-Gabby?"

Pressing his face up against Betty's, he taunted, "Y-y-yes, me and Gabby." He kissed her, smearing blood from his cracked lips across hers. "She wasn't stupid enough to get pregnant," he whispered in her ear.

With the back of her hand, Betty wiped the blood from her lips. "B-b-but you promised to make m-m-me the mistress of Twin Springs."

The Lieutenant threw his head back and laughed. "Why the hell would I do that? You were just a warm place to sow my seed. I never intended to keep a retard like you."

She rubbed the mound of her stomach. "And our ch-ch-child?"

He turned the stoves on and lit their pilot lights. Immediately, blue flames danced across the kitchens, licked at the moonshine and spread throughout the room. "Any offspring that comes from you will be tainted by your stuttering stupidness."

Clutching his sleeve, she begged. "You p-p-promised to m-m-marry me."

"M-m-marry you?" he mocked, thrusting her aside. He chuckled when she landed hard. "No way in Hell."

Rubbing her tummy, she moaned deep and low. "Th-th-the baby."

Falling to her knees beside Betty, Ame cupped her hands and shouted, "Help, help, help!"

Turning his back on the mother of his child, the Lieutenant snatched up the sack and left. His boots clicked upon the wooden floors with each of his steps.

Ame sat back and held her head within her hands. "At least help Jean Claude."

Rising up onto her hands and knees, Betty crawled over to the chef and grabbed him by the hand. She dragged him away from the fire, stopping every few feet to bend over and clutch at her stomach. Reaching up, she pulled a tub of water from the counter and threw it over his body.

Sputtering, Jean Claude came to life. "Emma! I must get to her."

"It's too l-l-late. She's dead." Betty cried into her apron. "G-g-gone."

"No, not my Emma." An anguished moan was wrenched from the man. "Not sweet Emma."

Ame rushed up to him. "Jean Claude, I have a baby girl." She fell to her knees beside him, looking like an urchin in her ripped and stained nightgown. "Help me. Gabby took my baby girl." The flames licked closer to Ame.

Fire bells drowned out Ame's pleas, even to JD.

Jumping to his feet, Jean Claude pulled Betty back and away from the flames. He filled and threw buckets of water over the kitchen fire with Ame trailing behind him, shouting in his ear.

"He can't hear you. They can't understand more than one word," said JD. Her heart ached that they weren't able to save Emma. "Maybe we can stop the Lieutenant from killing Ruby."

CHAPTER FIFTY-NINE

*C*atching up to the Lieutenant in the empty Main Dining Room, JD was stunned to see the General confronting the man.

"Lieutenant, where's the fire?" The General's jaw dropped. "What happened to you, man? To your face?"

"Sir, the servant Jean Claude set a fire in the kitchens. The fire must have hit a gas line and shook Twin Springs." He dropped his bag on the floor and grabbed the General's sleeve. "You don't want to go in there, sir. It's grizzly. I had to physically beat the man to stop him. He's gone mad. I put the fire out, but Twin Springs' Chef, didn't fare so well. I think he's dead. Fell and hit his head."

Bending his head, the General clasped his comrade-in-arms on the shoulder. "You've always been loyal to me. You've always stepped up when my family needed help." He cleared his throat, the words he was about to voice sticking as he worked to push them out.

"The time has come for me to take action and secure my daughters' futures. Ruby is strong headed. I feel I must give her hand in marriage to the strongest man I know. You. I would be honored to offer you Ruby's hand in marriage."

Ame moved between the two men. "Father, you can't. He murdered Emma. He's evil."

Reaching through his daughter's body, the General shook his friend's hand. "Welcome to the family, son."

The Lieutenant's face glowed and his chest puffed out. "Where's Ruby, sir?

"Who knows? She's yours to worry about now." The General's booming laugh filled the darkened dining room. "Check the stables, she seems to be hanging out there a lot lately."

"What have you done, Father? You just sold your daughter to the Devil."

The General watched his Army buddy leave, muttering out loud to himself he moved down the Promenade and into the Grand Lobby. "Don't worry my dearest wife. I'll fix this with Ruby in the morning. You'll see. Everything will work out." His loud voice carried through the great hall. "Tonight, we will celebrate. Turn those damn bells off and celebrate 1929." He leaned against a pillar and spoke softly to his wife. Ame hovered at his sleeve. "We did it, my dear. Our little Amethyst gave birth to a boy. I named him after your father. For you, my dear."

Joining Ame, JD said, "Hate to tell you this but your dad is an idiot. I think your best chance is Everett. Go find him. I'll follow the Lieutenant and try to stop him before he kills Ruby."

CHAPTER SIXTY

*A*me followed her father as he made his way back to the Crystal Ballroom. Constantly, she yelled in his ear, "Baby, baby, baby!"

The general flung the doors back and surveyed the room. Guests stood clinging to each other, the music had stopped. Colored papers stuck to their fancy clothes and lay dead at their feet across the polished dance floor.

Gathering himself, the General's voice bellowed out through the ballroom. "Strike up the music. Just a little fire in the kitchens. The Lieutenant handled it."

Gay music filled the ballroom. Awkwardly at first, the guests began to dance, then their feet picked up speed with the beat of the music. Laughter rang out and the servants continued to serve the stashed Champagne.

Sickened, Ame turned to find her husband.

Guy burst into the room. His clothes were disheveled, and his face and arms were streaked with soot. Marching up onto the stage, he shoved the musician and forced the band to stop. "Are you all insane?" He addressed the General. "Your son-in-law is outside battling the fire, while you dance in here. The Tower is on fire people!"

Screams filled the air and guests rushed from the room, pushing and shoving each other in their quest to escape through the French doors.

Seeing another chance, Ame rushed up to Guy. "You have to save Ruby. The Lieutenant's going to kill her."

Exiting with Guy out into the courtyard, the night sky was alight by the fire in the Tower. Her husband, their baby in his arms, pulled on the rope of the fire bell. The flames reflecting in his glasses, he shouted orders and organized teams. Servants and guests alike, battled the flames of the fire. But it was too late. The Tower collapsed inward, onto itself, and there was nothing left to do but smother the remaining flames with water.

His world crashing around him with the Tower, Everett fell to his knees, clutching his son tight to his chest. "I never should have left her."

"Let m-m-me take the baby, Mr. Everett." Betty said, her arms and face streaked with soot.

Ame reached out to take her baby but he passed through her arms and into the awaiting arms of Betty. "No. Please, I haven't held either of my children. Please." Her shoulders shook with emotion.

Stunned with the change of events, the General mumbled, "But the fire was in the kitchens. The Lieutenant told me he took care of it." His face ashen, he shook his head with denial. "Amethyst can't be gone." He pointed at Jean Claude standing beside Betty, his face battered, and lips split. "You started the fire!"

"The Lieutenant has gone mad," replied Jean Claude, holding his hands up as if to stave off the accusation. "He murdered Emma and started a fire in the kitchens. Betty and I extinguished that fire and came to help with the Tower."

His knees shaking beneath him, the General parroted, "He

murdered Emma?" Again, he shook his head. "I don't believe you. She can't be dead. The Lieutenant wouldn't kill her."

"Where is he now?" asked Guy.

"I told him he could marry Ruby. He went to find her."

Guy grabbed him up by the front of his jacket. "You told him what?"

Everett placed a hand on Guy's arm. "Where's Ruby?"

"I left her in the stables when the fire bells rang." His eyes rose to the horizon. The sky above the mountains where the stables stood was ablaze. "Ruby!" he roared, sprinting off towards the stables.

"Everett!" screamed Ame in his ear. "You must save our daughter." A train whistle blew in the distance. "Hurry, we don't have much time. The train has arrived. You must find our daughter before she's gone forever." She watched as the group ran towards the stables. The train tooted its arrival. She gazed after them, before turning towards the train station.

CHAPTER SIXTY-ONE

"The Lieutenant couldn't have that much of a head start on me." JD couldn't understand why she hadn't already caught up with him. Cresting the hill to the stables, she stumbled to a stop. Only woods greeted her. She glanced around. "This isn't right. Damn it, I know the stable are supposed to be here.

"I must have taken a wrong turn." She raced back down the path. "No, something's not right." Above the skyline to the right, she noticed an eerie glow of light rising above the trees. Breaking off into a run, she muttered, "Damn it, the stables now aren't in the same place as in my time."

She skidded to a stop when the trees opened up to a clearing. A large stable and small building were laid out before her. Fire burned from the roof of the stables. Adjusting himself, the Lieutenant walked away from a smaller building. A smile spreading across his face, he headed down the path and passed through her translucent body.

A train whistle sounded in the distance. "Damn Ruby, it's all your fault that I didn't make the train in time to meet Gabby. Fucking bitch." Turning, the Lieutenant stomped back to the stables.

The horses shrieked within the building and JD covered her ears. "Save the horses!" she screamed.

Pausing, he took in the fire's glory. The flames lit the front of his body in an orange glow. His back bowed, the Lieutenant's arms flowed through the air like a conductor directing a symphony of the horses' screams. The heat warmed his efforts.

For a moment, she thought he was going to enter the building.

Instead, he lowered his arms and walked back towards the path.

Shouts sounded in the distance and JD looked back over her shoulder towards the noise. A group of men were charging up the path.

"Fuck, fuck, fuck," muttered the Lieutenant.

Leaning back against a tree, she replied, "Yep, you're pretty much screwed."

Pieces of the building started to fall in. She watched as he kicked a burning timber out of the fire and rolled it around with his boot. Removing his jacket, he folded up his sleeves, bent down and rubbed the charred wood with his jacket. Then he smeared soot across his face and arms, blackening his face and body. He rolled around in the dirt. "I'll tell them that Ruby died in the fire and I tried to save her, but the flames pushed me back." Smiling, his teeth glowed against his blackened skin. "I'll be a hero."

"I hope they beat the crap out of you," she called out. Her fingers itched to reach into her boot for her knife. "I know I would."

The voices grew closer.

He grabbed a bucket, dipped it into a long horse trough and threw the water onto the outer corners of the stables. He practiced out loud, "General, the fire was too big. I tried to save Ruby, my one true love."

CHAPTER SIXTY-TWO

*A*t the train station, Gabby huddled in the corner of a long wooden bench and waited for her lover. At this late hour, she was the only one waiting for the train. "It's okay, baby girl. Doesn't matter if I couldn't take the clothes I made. The Lieutenant will replace them."

The peal of a bell sounded off in the distance. "Fire!" In horror, she looked up at the Tower and saw flames climbing up the sides of its majestic frame towards the clock tower. The sky around it glowed eerily. "Dear Lord," she whispered, unable to look away. "Ame, beautiful Ame. What have we done?"

Her hand shook as she rubbed the baby's back, more to soothe herself than the little girl. She swaddled the baby tighter and tried to stop her crying, unaware that tears flowed down her own face.

"Someone make the bells stop!" she shouted, rocking in her seat. Ignoring the world around her, she checked her watch for the umpteenth time then stood up and began to pace. "Where is he?" she muttered. "He's a stickler for time and really should be here by now."

The train's whistle sounded off and she jumped. Steam shot

out from beneath the train as it slid to a stop before her and she bent her head in shame. "He's not coming," she whispered.

Standing beside her maid, Ame talked close to her ear. "Please, Gabby. Don't take my baby. Go back to Twin Springs, give her to my husband," she begged. "Don't leave Twin Springs. Stay at Twin Springs. Twin Springs."

Shaking her head, Gabby stood up and her wooden cross slipped out from the front of her dress. "There's no turning back now."

Despite Ame's efforts, her maid boarded the train with her little girl. She gazed off towards her home. "I'm sorry, Everett. But I must follow our baby. Somehow, I have to convince Gabby to bring her baby back to Twin Springs. Back to our home."

Seated on the train beside her maid, Ame hummed to the baby quietly sleeping, while Gabby craned her neck, looking out the window for her lover. The whistle blew, three times, signaling its departure and chugged forward. Ame whispered down to the baby, "Don't worry, you'll never be alone. I promise. I'll bring you back home to Twin Springs." She hummed, stopping only to whisper, "*Springs, springs, springs.*"

CHAPTER SIXTY-THREE

Four men crested the ridge and the Lieutenant turned to meet them, bucket in hand. "General, the fire grew too big." He didn't even notice Betty holding the baby.

Pushing through, Guy demanded, "Where's Ruby?"

Dipping his head, the Lieutenant pointed towards the stable. "I tried but my one bucket wasn't enough."

Shoving him aside, Guy rushed to the trough and immersed his body under the water. He grabbed the Lieutenant's wool coat from the dirt and also submerged the fabric. Drawing the dripping fabric out, he covered his head. Opening the stable doors, he plunged into the burning building.

"He's crazy," stated the Lieutenant. "It's a suicide mission."

Everett copied Guy's actions. He dunked himself into the trough and rose up to join in the search.

The ground trembled and horses stampeded through the open doors, pushing Everett back. Their coats were burned raw in places. Some horses collapsed to their knees and snorted, lifting their heads for air. Some horses, too badly burnt, stumbled and fell over dead. The stench of burnt flesh and horse hair penetrated the air as the sides of the building shook.

"It's collapsing in!" called out the General.

Everett ran to help, but the General grabbed him by the arm. "It's too late."

Wrenching free, Everett pushed his glasses up. "It's never too late." He charged forward, reaching the opening just as Guy stumbled free. Pulling the man's body over his shoulders, he yelled, "Back up everyone, it's going to explode!" He and Guy cleared the building moments before it collapsed.

Everyone hit the dirt, as the vehicles inside the stables exploded and sent debris across the area.

Guy crawled across the dirt and grabbed the Lieutenant up by the collar. "You bastard. Where the hell is Ruby?"

"She's in there, I swear."

"No, she wasn't." Guy straddled him and pounded him with his fists. "Tell me where she is." He held his fist poised for another punch. "Now!"

The Lieutenant curled into a ball, sobbing out loud, "I don't know."

"Wrong answer." Gritting his teeth, Guy swung.

But a hand curled around his.

Looking up he gazed into the soft brown eyes of Betty. Her fingers were wrapped around his fist and pressing it backward against her pregnant belly. Jean Claude stood behind her, the man's face beaten and bruised with dried blood cracking across it. He cradled Ame's newborn child in his arms.

"P-p-please don't kill him," she begged.

Disgusted with himself, Guy pushed away from the man and stood. "He's a bad man, Betty. I'm not just talking about running moonshine."

She gazed down at the man sobbing at her feet. "I know. B-b-but he's the f-f-father of my child."

The Lieutenant's sobs morphed into laughter. He rose up. Chin in the air, he scanned the group before him. "Do you really think that I'd take this simpleton to bed?"

"You murdered Emma!" yelled Jean Claude. "And then you set the kitchens on fire to cover your tracks."

"Is that what you did here?" demanded Guy. "Did you kill Ruby and then light the stables on fire?"

The Lieutenant laughed, "Where's your proof?" He turned towards the General. "Whose word are you going to take? The word of a colored man and a half wit or the word of the man who fought by your side?"

"String him up." Guy grabbed a rope from a post near the trough. "If he doesn't tell us where Ruby is, he'll hang."

Handing the child to the General, Jean Claude dragged the Lieutenant to a speckled horse.

Guy looped the rope around the Lieutenant's neck and tied his hands behind his back. Together the men placed him up on the horse and threw the other end of the rope up and over the branch of a sturdy young oak.

Holding his grandson to his chest, the General stated, "I believe Jean Claude. Where's my daughter? Where's Ruby?"

"You believe him over me?" The Lieutenant's blackened face twisted into a mask of rage. "A colored man over me?" Spittle sprayed from his mouth. "Fine! Yes, I killed them. I killed Emma and Ruby." He cackled, his face blacker than the colored man he hated.

The General's face turned ashen and his great body shuddered. "No," he gasped.

A cheshire grin on his face, the Lieutenant cackled at the General. "You'll never find Ruby and Emma's bodies. They're gone. I win, asshole!"

"P-p-please don't kill h-h-him," begged Betty, sinking to her knees beside the horse. She gasped as pains came quick and hard through her body.

JD knelt beside her.

"Shut up woman!" ordered the Lieutenant. Bending over the horse, he spat on her. His insane gaze focused in on Guy. "You can't kill me. You're a law man."

"I'm sure as hell not," ground out Everett.

Guy removed his badge and threw it on the ground. "Not any more. Where's Ruby?"

The Lieutenant's blue gaze pierced the General. "You had everything: power, recognition, women, a family, wealth. But you couldn't share, could you? All I wanted to do was marry Emma. She was sweet and pure." He turned towards Jean Claude, "At least until you fucked her.

"But you couldn't share. Could you, General?" His voice pitched high with insanity. "Just like you couldn't share the glory." His thin lips spread into a smile. He threw back his head, laughing like a loon. "But in the end, I won. I have taken everything from you." He watched the General crumble before his eyes at his words. "I stole your most valuable possessions. Your Gems.

"You all thought you were above me. But I won." He sneered at Guy, "I turned a law man into a criminal, willing to string up a man without a trial." His eyes shifted to Everett, "Made a peace-loving man, a warrior." He raised his nose at Jean Claude, "Stole your one chance for true freedom and bound you without the use of chains." He took the heel of his boot and kicked Betty in the head, shoving her on her back, "Turned virgin into a whore." He dug the heels of his boots into the horse's ribs and it reeled and shot forward.

JD gasped. "He hung himself." She couldn't believe what had unfolded before her.

Betty screamed with pain. The three men rushed forward and knelt in the dirt to help. Through gasps of pain, Betty gave birth under the swinging body of the Lieutenant.

The General babbled in the distance, talking to his grandchild. "I promised Ruby to a monster," he cried into the bundle. "If I just would've listened to my girls, perhaps they'd still be alive. But no, I felt I knew better. In the end, I knew nothing. I brought the enemy home. I failed my girls. I failed my wife. Ruling with an iron fist, I lost the most important war of all, the protection of my family." His shoulders shook, and he collapsed to his knees. Crying into the neck of his bundled up grandson, he begged his dead wife for forgiveness as the Lieutenant's swinging body cast a dark shadow over him.

JD wiped tears dripping down her face.

Jean Claude bundled up the newly born baby within his torn shirt. "It's a boy, Betty."

The General raised his head, his face gray and sunken, etched with loss. He rose and shuffled over to Betty. Pain curled his shoulders forward and hunched his once tall frame. He handed his grandchild to his son-in-law. "Don't worry, Betty. Everett will take care of you and your baby." He paused and gazed at the burning building. "The way I should've taken care of my daughters." Turing away, the General walked down the mountain a broken man, mumbling under his breath. "He'll care for you and Twin Springs."

JD watched as the remaining men made a litter out of horse blankets. Gently, they lifted Betty up and placed her and her baby within.

Everett gazed at the body of the man responsible for killing his wife. "I feel nothing. The man who murdered my Ame is dead and I feel nothing. No relief, no joy, no love, just responsibility. I've wasted my time painting. From now on, I'll provide for my son, for the future generations and for Twin Springs."

"Where's Ame?" asked JD. She glanced around. Three quick toots of the train's whistle sounded off in the distance and she knew. "She followed her daughter. I have stopped nothing."

CHAPTER SIXTY-FOUR

*P*assing between guests, Logan worked his way to the Front Desk. Between the wedding festivities and the count down to the new year, Parker was backing up the concierge with guests' questions. "Have you seen your brother?"

She glanced up from assisting a guest. "Nope, not lately."

"I told him to say where I could see him. But I can't find him anywhere in the Grand Lobby."

"Last time I saw him, he was playing and making up stories. He told me that a dark shadow grabbed the Mystical Diamond. I was supposed to tell the Wolfeman and the Blue Flame that he'd laid a trap for the Dark Shadow until they could come." She shrugged. "His normal made up stuff."

His heart froze. "How long ago did you talk to him?"

"About twenty minutes or so."

"Did you see which way he went?"

"Towards the Tower." She raised her eyes, concern filling them. "Is something wrong?"

"Don't worry, I'll take care of him." His smile pulled at one side of his lips, covering the uptick of his heartbeat. "Tell Jax to meet me in the Tower."

The sea of guests parted for the burned man as he purposefully strode through the Grand Lobby. His blue gaze sparked fires of retribution for anyone who would harm the ones he loved.

Entering the Tower elevator, he prepared himself for a fight. Stopping the elevator one floor shy of the restaurant, he exited and climbed the stairs to the last floor of his journey. His hand on the handle of the stairwell door, something made him pause. Quickly, he turned to confront the danger.

Colton stumbled forward. "You got my signal. I knew you'd come."

"Where is he?" asked Logan.

"On the terrace. He has the Mystical Diamond. She isn't moving, Blue Flame. She needs the kiss of life again."

"Stay here," he commanded, and exited the stairwell. Skirting the receptionist desk, he entered the restaurant. It felt eerie, still decorated for the wedding and illuminated in the soft glow of backlighting. Slowly moving up the circular staircase, he paused close to the top. Peering through the glass enclosure, he saw Dr. Ottoman. His gaunt form paced back and forth, muttering and yelling into the air, as his boots clicked on the tile floor. "Destroy the Tower. Lieutenant's orders. Destroy the Tower and the Fairbanks right along with it." He stacked up artwork between the pillars. JD's artwork.

Logan whispered, "Dr. Ottoman's the Dark Shadow?"

Quietly slipping through the glass doors, he worked his way around to the side of archway, until he found JD. She'd collapsed next to the fountain. From the opposite direction, he noticed a painting shift.

Colton crawled through the opening and gave him a thumbs up.

"Damn it," he muttered. "Why can't that boy stay out of trouble?"

The heavy smell of alcohol wafted over him and he snuck a peek out from behind the pillar. Holding a plastic jug in both hands, Dr. Ottoman drenched the artwork with a clear liquid. Once empty, he threw the jug aside and continued with another. Moonshine cascaded down the artwork and pooled at the doctor's feet. "He intends to burn down the Tower, using JD's artwork as tinder," he said softly.

The doctor shouted, "I gave them a second chance. I remade myself into a man of wealth, and prestige. A doctor no less. Wasn't that what Izzy wanted? A rich man? Isn't that why she picked Theo over me? But no, they still couldn't accept me into their fold."

Knowing his time was short, Logan bent down, leaning forward to crawl between the barricade. The medals on his chest chimed against each other.

Swiftly, Dr. Ottoman turned and scanned the area.

Freezing in place, Logan couldn't believe his eyes. Before him stood both Dr. Ottoman and Niles, combined into one. Sloughing his facade, a dark brown stubble covered his cheeks and peppered the roots of his hair. One eye blue and one eye brown, he could see his childhood friend within the doctor. He whispered, "Niles was alive all along and right under our noses."

Niles continued to pace, dousing the artwork with more and more moonshine.

Waiting for the right moment, he inched forward. When Niles' back was turned, he squeezed between two portraits and knelt next to JD, checking for a pulse.

Colton hunkered beside him, his young eyes serious, lips formed in a strong line. Worry drew at his chubby cheeks and turned him from a little boy into a young man. "Is she alive?"

Her pulse, thready and weak, he nodded. "Barely."

Niles ranted from outside the barricade. "Then in walks JD. It was as if Amethyst Fairbanks had stepped straight out of the portrait and gave me another chance. She could've sent those kids home with their aunt. But no, she kept the kids and the snot nose brat discovered my hiding place. Did Izzy and Ava turn her away?

No! They accepted her. Like a sister! In time, they twisted her to their side. Even she turned away. No matter the gifts I gave her, the love and adoration I showed her. She chose you!" he turned and screamed at Logan.

Logan's gaze met the madness within Niles. He held a blackened lighter in his hand. Raising his left hand up, Logan begged, "Don't do it Niles. We can fix this, I'll help you." The fingers of his other hand rested on JD's wrist. He felt her pulse slow and then stop.

"She picked a mutilated man over me. She and I could've had a future together. Just like Izzy and me. It's time for me to finish what the Lieutenant started. Cleanse with fire." Niles flicked open the lighter with his thumb and threw it into the barricade. With a swoosh of air, flames spread around them, encircling them within a ring of fire. Niles roared with laughter. "Burn, baby burn."

Turning towards JD, Logan bent down. He tilted her chin up, pinched her nose and forced his air into her lungs. No longer feeling a pulse, he added chest compressions between his trio of breaths.

Eyes wild, Niles continued to shout through the flames. The fire spread, using the pools of moonshine as energy. Eagerly, it ate at everything in its way. Consuming the trellises, it spread a path of destruction along the wooden frame of the archways, melting the glass enclosure with its heat, before it inched closer and closer to the madman.

Stepping into a puddle of moonshine, Niles screamed, "Can you feel it, Logan? The power, the beauty. You're going to scream. I guarantee it. Big military hero, you'll scream just like the Director did outside the stables." The flames licked their way up the pant legs of the madman. Niles looked down and shock covered his features, "No, not me. I control you." The puddle ignited. Flames shot up and devoured his body. Niles' screams pierced the air.

Turning away, Logan worked to breathe life into his Diamond. "Shine for me Diamond. Come back and shine for me," he begged.

She coughed and choked. Gasping, she sucked air into her lungs, only to choke again as the smoke of the fire surrounded them. "Dr. Ottoman. His eyes."

"It's okay," he hushed. "We need to move before the whole Tower is consumed."

A wall of fire encircled the trio.

"How are we going to escape?" Tears streamed down Colton's face. He covered his ears to block out the Dark Shadow's screams.

"The fountain," said JD. "We'll use the water from the fountain to douse the flames."

"How?" Logan asked. "We can't splash enough on the fire to stop it."

The flames inched their way up the dome. The clock tower struck midnight and the copper blackened above their heads, while the New Year's Eve fireworks lit the skyline in the distance.

"No, but we might be able to make a path." She removed her boots. "We'll use these as buckets."

Grabbing her by the face, Logan kissed her. "You're ingenious." Taking a boot, he dipped it in the fountain and filled it with water. "Concentrate on one area."

Together, they used the water to clear a small path between the flames.

"What did he use for the kindling? It burns hot and quick."

"Your artwork."

"No," she gasped, seeing her children burn around her. Spreading her hand over the baby inside her, she understood they were just canvas, wood and paint.

Logan kicked the remaining pieces out of the way, clearing a small path. He drenched his uniform jacket in the fountain and draped it over Colton.

"Wait." She scooped water up in her boot, drenching both

Logan and Colton before herself. "Just let me put my boots back on."

"Leave the damn boots."

"I can't."

He held out his hand. "Yes, you can. Trust me. Leave the boots."

JD stared into his blue eyes and knew she trusted this man with her life. She placed her hand inside his. "I trust you."

He lifted the boy onto his hip and together they ran through the gap in the flames. The dome collapsed in a fiery heap behind them. Burning embers and ash sprayed their bodies.

The Tower aflame around them, she pulled back on his hand. Lying before them was Niles, his body blackened, and his clothes melted into his skin. His eyes opened, and he whispered, "Help me."

CHAPTER SIXTY-FIVE

"*We* have to help him."

Immediately, Logan's mind rebelled at the idea. He looked down at the charred body. In many spots, the fire had eaten away the skin and revealed the bones below. Deep down, he knew his childhood friend was moments away from death, but he couldn't leave him to burn. "Okay."

He lowered Colton to the floor and lifted Niles up into his arms, shuttering at the man's screams of agony. Finally, Niles passed out.

Carrying Niles, he ran with JD and Colton towards the glass enclosure. Flames danced on the other side of the glass, darkening it. Heating it.

Stopping short, JD asked, "Do you think we can make it?"

A gust of wind blew across the terrace and flames engulfed the enclosure, blocking their escape.

"No." He turned, "We'll have to use the fire ladder, and climb down to the next level. Maybe even down the whole Tower."

They rushed over to the fire escape ladder but fire blocked their path.

"Can you fly?" Colton stared up at his heroes.

"No, Colton. We can't fly," she answered. Her eyes met Logan's and she knew that they had only moments left. "I love you, Logan. More than anything, more than life."

He lowered Niles to the floor and gathered Colton and JD up in his arms. "I love you, my Diamond." He kissed Colton on top of his head. "I love you too. You're my family and I would give anything to save you."

She considered telling him about their baby but decided to spare him the pain. She tilted her head back and accepted his lips one last time.

They shared a long, parting kiss and separated to the sound of firetrucks calling in the distance. "Do you think they'll make it in time?" she asked.

He glanced around them, the fire illuminating the nighttime sky. "No. They might be able to save the rest of the Tower. If their ladders can stretch up this high, they won't have to use the steep steel bridge that we used to get materials—" He paused and smiled. He gazed into JD's eyes, before continuing, "Up here." He gave out a huge whoop and kissed her hard. "The bridge."

"I thought you removed it."

"Not all the way. There are still two, skinny metal rails, with rope handrails, leading down to the roofline of the east wing. He swung Nile's body up and over his shoulders. "Colton, grab hold of my neck and wrap your legs around my waist," he ordered.

"You can't carry both," argued JD.

"Look, can I at least be the man today?"

"Sure, if acting stupid makes you a man."

"I can do it myself," asserted Colton.

Simultaneously, JD and Logan looked down at the boy, "No!" they answered in unison.

"Alright," agreed Logan, shifting Niles' weight. "You take Colton."

She crouched down and Colton scrambled up on her back and wrapped his arms and legs around her. Together, they skirted the fire to the other side of the terrace and peered over the edge to the steep incline of the bridge.

"How do you think we should do this?"

"Hold onto the ropes and shuffle your feet slowly down on the metal supports. I'll go first." He scrambled up and sat on the edge. Holding the ropes in each hand, he leaned forward in order not to lose Niles. He scooted his butt forward until he felt the metal bars under his feet. With one arm wrapped around Niles and one hand on the rope, he worked his way down.

Watching him for a moment, JD climbed up onto the edge. Reaching down, she pulled off her socks. Sitting there, the mountain breeze cooling her face and the fire heating them from behind, she scooted off the edge. "Hold on tight."

Deliberately, she worked her way down the incline. Every time her bare feet slipped and skidded to a stop against the cold metal, her heart leapt into her throat. "Don't let go."

The fire worked its way across the Tower, devouring everything in its path. It peeked over the edge and licked at the ropes supporting JD and Colton.

Firetrucks screeched to a halt in front of Twin Springs. Immediately, the firemen unfurled their hoses and ladders and guests poured from the front doors. The lights from the trucks illuminated the Tower, silhouetting JD and Logan working their way down the thin metal beams.

Reaching the bottom, Logan lowered Niles to the roof and turned to check their progress. "Over half way there!" he shouted up. "You can do it."

"Hold on tight," she ordered, glancing up to judge the distance left. "We're so close."

Eaten by fire, the ropes gave way and she pitched sideways, her feet scrambled for a foothold but they slipped out from beneath her and they fell.

The crowd screamed with Colton as the ground rushed up to greet them.

Her elbow slammed against one of the metal rails as they descended, sliding against her arm and at the last moment she snagged it within her hand and held firm.

Colton whimpered as he dangled from her neck, his feet kicking against the darkened night. Squeezing tight, the little boy looked down through the blackness towards Logan.

"Hold on!" JD yelled. The boy's hold pinched off her air and his added weight tugged at her fingers where she clutched the metal.

Arms raised, Logan stood below them. "Let go, Colton, I'll catch you."

Immediately, she felt Colton slip from her body. "No!" she cried out and the crowd below gasped.

Logan caught the boy in his arms. His injured hip gave out below him and they collapsed hard onto the roof.

"I knew you were a superhero," said Colton.

Logan squeezed him tight and placed him safely on the ground. He balanced the majority of his weight on one leg and raised his arms up, ready to catch JD. "You're next!" he shouted.

At that moment, Logan's brother, Sam, rushed through an opening in the top of the roof, followed by Theo and Jaxon.

Sam grasped the forearms of his brother and, together, they created a cradle. "Now!" Logan shouted up.

JD's fingers slipped from the metal and she fell into the brothers' arms below.

CHAPTER SIXTY-SIX

*T*hree couples crowed into the General's room, where Niles laid upon the sofa. A paramedic inserted an IV into the burned man's arm and pumped in morphine to dull his pain. Looking up, he wrapped his stethoscope around his neck and shook his head. "All we can do is manage his pain for the few minutes he has left."

His lips forming a thin, firm line, Logan watched his childhood friend die. JD placed her hand in his and leaned against him. He placed his arm around her shoulders and pulled her tight. "No one deserves this."

"Izzy," mumbled Niles.

Leaving Theo's arms, Isabella knelt beside Niles, her wedding dress puddled around them. "I'm here."

"Remember the time we caught fireflies in a jar?" He turned towards her, the blue contact falling from his eye.

"Yes, I remember. They glowed like stars."

"I wish we were kids again." He gazed up at the ceiling. "I feel like millions of fireflies are burning me alive. I love you, Izzy." His lids lowered, and he felt pain no more.

Her head bent, Isabella wept over him, holding his hand within hers. Remembering the boy she'd played with as a child, she whispered back, "I love you too."

CHAPTER SIXTY-SEVEN

*T*he next morning, the sun rose over Twin Springs and shone down upon the smoldering Tower. The top of the Grand Dame's Tower had burned and the people who cared for her most huddled in the General's Office.

Isabella wheeled in a tray with tea and pastries. Her blonde ponytail was askew, but she looked comfortable in black skinny jeans and a t-shirt that said, "Kiss the Chef". She glanced over to the sofa where Niles had passed away only hours ago. "It doesn't seem right, coming in here after Niles died."

Theo, the neckline of his white button up shirt open at the neck, crossed his arms and planted himself on the couch. He spread his jean clad legs wide and leaned back. "I refuse to allow him to affect the people I love anymore."

"I agree," added Jaxon, imitating Theo and sitting beside him. "You three might remember Niles as the boy he once was, but I remember how he almost killed most of the people in this room."

"We have to separate in our minds the Niles we knew as children and the monster he grew up to be," said Ava.

Sam sat at Ava's desk. Maddy and Parker sat cross-legged on

the floor, leaning back against the desk. Colton squirmed in his sister's arms. "Let me go."

"No, you are staying glued to me forever."

Showered and her face scrubbed, JD leaned into Logan. "Why didn't the sprinkler system come on?"

He rubbed the back of his neck. "Niles must have disengaged it. It came on in the restaurant, protecting it and the rest of the Tower. It wasn't until the flames reached that level that the fire alarm rang."

"How did the owners of my artwork react, when they found out the paintings were destroyed?"

"I soothed them over," said Ava, her pant-suit pressed and looking like she hadn't been up all night. "I guess locking the paintings up didn't do any good since Niles had keys to every door in Twin Springs. But, I returned their checks and reassured them that they'd receive first notification of any future artwork."

"It's the least we could do," murmured JD.

"I can't believe he destroyed every piece," wailed Maddy.

"Not every piece," stated JD. "I have a painting of Twin Springs, as it looked in 1928. It's in my room. I'm giving it to Theo and Isabella as a wedding gift."

Logan squeezed her tight. "And I have a penciled drawing that you did of a little girl sitting next to a vending machine. I purchased it years ago."

She leaned back in his arms, remembering that moment in time. "You did? I'll have to tell you the story about that picture sometime."

"JD, what the hell were you doing in the Tower?" asked her brother.

"I was waiting for Logan. I wanted to tell him something."

"What?" asked Colton, sitting up straight. "Is it about your secret powers?"

"I guess it is. I do have a secret power." Her eyes softened, "I'm pregnant."

Logan's jaw dropped. His gaze flicked from her face to her belly and back again. He let out a loud whoop and gathered her up in his arms. "Why didn't you tell me?"

"I tried, but then the guests gathered around to shake your hand and I thought I should tell you in our special place."

The women in the room surged forward to hug the couple while the men shook each other's hands as if they'd achieved something great.

"Well, that's not a secret power I want," muttered Colton.

Laughing, everyone settled down.

"Why were you laying on the floor?" asked Colton. "Did he hurt you?"

"No." She shared with them her journey back in time.

"How sad," whispered Maddy. "So, Ame didn't want to hurt your family all this time. She just wanted to bring her baby back home."

She nodded, "My mother just couldn't handle her presence and turned to drugs and drinking in order to ignore her. Now that I look back at my life, I can see how Ame protected me. She would lead me away from bad situations and led me to the lost children. All said and done, I'm going to miss the Woman hanging around."

Parker shifted, "You don't think she will still visit you?"

Looking into the painted green eyes of Amethyst Fairbanks, she replied, "No, I think she fulfilled her mission and can rest now."

"I guess we know it all now," murmured Isabella.

Shifting his weight from his hurt hip, Logan said, "What I don't understand is how Niles knew so much."

"From the journals," piped up Isabella. "After the fire, I stayed up and read all of them."

Jaxon's teeth gleamed within the black stubble covering his face. "I'm sure Theo loved that on the night of his honeymoon."

"With all that happened, celebrating our wedding was the furthest thing from our minds," replied Theo, shrugging.

Isabella elbowed him, "Be good," she muttered. "The Lieutenant journaled everything and then, when he stopped, Betty continued. Once Niles found the journals, he began writing in them too. I brought the one with the entry that I think added to the poisoning of Niles' young mind."

She untied the leather string and opened to the page she'd bookmarked. "I'll read it to you."

CHAPTER SIXTY-EIGHT

MARCH 25TH, 1929.

*D*ear Journal,
        I have kept an eye on everyone and everything within Twin Springs. The General locked himself in his office for weeks. He came out a different man, gaunt, grief eating at his insides. All the General could do was moan about how Ruby was just like him. That he never gave Everett a chance and turned away when Ame asked for his help. That he was clueless about what was happening with his gentle Emma. He ordered his office to be boarded up and covered over. Then he retreated to a room in the east wing and turned the reigns of Twin Springs over to his son-in-law, a greater man than him in the end.

Guy, Everett and Jean Claude made up a story about how the fires started. They're afraid that if the truth gets out about how they killed a man, being judge, jury and executioners, they'll hang too. They buried my Lieutenant in an unmarked grave but I know where he lies and I visit him daily.

They searched the tunnels and the cavern for Emma and Ruby. But they never found them. So clever was my lover.

In disgrace, Guy went back to DC. He informed his superiors that he was unable to find the still and runners responsible for his wife's death. I guess a little bit of justice was served.

Last I heard, Jean Claude and Guy stumbled across each other. Guy sent back word that Jean Claude is some fancy chef now. Things worked out well for him. Life is so unfair.

After burying the bones of his wife, Everett is raising his son on his own. He's turned into quite a forceful and strong man in the end. A man people can lean on, depend on.

Everett, with his kind way, informed me that I'll always have a place within Twin Springs. They brought a beautifully carved crib up to my room in the attic. I sit and watch my son play with Everett's child. He fulfilled the promise that the Lieutenant made to me, ensuring I am now a part of Twin Springs. In return, I keep an eye on everyone and everything. I sit and wait until the day the rest of my lover's promise is fulfilled and you, my son, are owner of Twin Springs.

Betty Porter

CHAPTER SIXTY-NINE

"I think her mind cracked," stated Theo.

"It was a horrible scene," said JD. "Everything that happened last night has taught me a valuable lesson. Grab happiness and love with both hands when you find it, or it can slip through your fingers." She pulled away from Logan, lowering herself onto one knee.

Maddy gasped behind her.

"I don't have a ring but, Logan, will you marry me?"

He growled deep in his throat and lifted her up. "Can't you let me be the man?" he demanded and plopped her down in the chair. "Don't say anything. Let me do this right."

Holding onto the arms of her chair, he lowered his weight down onto one knee, with his injured leg jutting out awkwardly to the side. Sticking his hand deep into his pocket he withdrew a small, black velvet box. "JD, I cursed the day you entered my life, with your foul mouth, manly ways and your damn boots."

She laughed, tears filling her eyes.

"But you taught me that sometimes beauty can look past the beast and see the man within. That real love is more than skin deep. You have given me everything. My brother back, a full-grown family with these two kids and now one more on the way. Justyne Diamond Wolfe, will you marry me?"

She leaped forward, encircling him with her arms and placing kisses all over his face. "Yes, yes, yes."

Holding her face between his hands, he kissed her back. The room broke into applause around them. She opened the box, revealing a diamond ring flanked by two amethysts.

The women in the room oohed and awed when Logan slipped the engagement ring on her finger.

Standing, he released her as the women surrounded her to get a better look at the ring. "Do you have it?" he asked Sam.

Clearing his throat, Sam replied, "Yep," and tossed his brother a small, rectangular box.

"Getting your ring and this box is why we were so late for your wedding. Sorry."

"You're forgiven," Isabella replied, hugging him tight. "I'm so happy for both of you."

Logan held the box out to JD. "Your father sent us to a church in Charlottesville, where there's an orphanage. He was hoping a nun there would have the answers you needed about your past. The nun he wanted had died but she left this box. From what I understand, there's something inside for you."

The room settled down. JD untied the twine and lifted the lid. She unfolded stationary, yellowed and cracked with time. "A letter," she whispered.

CHAPTER SEVENTY

*T*o my dearest Pearl and her descendants,

  I named you such because I felt it was what the General and your mother would've wanted.

  Many years ago, I committed a crime. A sin against God's laws and mans'. I stole you mere moments after your birth from your mother, Amethyst Fairbanks. I am not sure, but I think when doing so, I started a fire that killed your mother. My shame was so great, that I brought you to a church, said you were mine. I begged the church to take us in and, later, to allow me to serve God as a nun.

  Everyday that I watched you grow, I considered taking you back to your father. But I was afraid and still am to this day. In my weakness, I allowed a man's evil words to fill my soul and control my actions.

  All I wanted was to be free from poverty, to have nice things. I felt cheap and less than the Fairbanks. I didn't want to wither up into a used carcass like the other girls my age, my back bent from hard work and my womb filled with one child after another.

  I craved pretty things. Clothes that swayed as I walked. Sparkling jewels at my ears, long peacock feathers adorning my hair. Soft furs pressing against my chin. I thought wealth and pretty things brought happiness.

I understood what I was about to do was wrong. From the moment I tucked my cross away and hid it beneath my clothes, it burned shame into my soul.

I escaped a grueling life in the mountains for a life of servitude as a nun. I welcomed the pain of paying penance for my sins. I traded a life of poverty and scraping on my knees for others, for another life of poverty, on my knees for God.

I tried to atone for my sins. But no matter how much good I did, I realized it would never be enough.

Tomorrow, a man will come to the convent and this letter will give him proof of your heritage. I hope in doing this, I heal some of the wounds that I caused. Even in my old age, I am afraid and weak. Instead of facing him myself, I'll leave this letter.

I no longer pray for God to release me from my sins and forgive me. Instead, I pray for Him to release His blessings and grace upon you. An innocent, who deserved to grow up within the loving embrace of her mother.

This I pray, in Jesus' name.
Sister Gabriella

CHAPTER SEVENTY-ONE

*J*D folded the letter and looked up at the others.

"That's so sad," said Parker.

Nodding in agreement, JD pulled out a long necklace of amethysts and diamond balls connected by gold links. At the end of the necklace hung a large, wooden cross. She gazed up at the portrait and back to the cross. "It's Ame's necklace. She made a rosary out of it. Gabby separated the links and reconnected them into a rosary with her cross at the end."

The amethysts and diamonds glittered, reflecting the light as the necklace was passed around. "Are you going to change the necklace back to match the portrait?" asked Parker.

"No, I think I'll keep it just the way it is."

"That's not all," chipped in Sam. "Tell her, Logan."

"One thing at a time," he answered, taking a deep breath. "My mom knows you are devastated over the loss of your artwork and even more because the loss of the funds will delay the opening of your home for lost children. I'm sure you didn't know this, but my family owns that Victorian building."

Unable to wait, Sam blurted out. "Mom wants to give it to you both as a wedding gift."

"No shit," burst out JD. Heat flushed her face. "I mean, no way!" She couldn't believe it. Her gaze searched both Logan's and Sam's faces for the truth.

Logan glared at his brother and lifted a brow at his delicate bride to be. "As I was saying, Mom wants you to have the building. Even if you didn't take me. As a gift, to give the lost kids a place to come home to. She just asks that you call it Acorn Grove."

"You're not kidding." JD thought she was going to break down and bawl like a baby. She pressed a hand over her eyes to get herself under control. She rubbed her face and squared her shoulders. "It's all coming true. A home for our lost kids." She hugged Logan, then Sam and back to Logan. "I need to thank her."

"Taking this guy," he pointed his thumb at his big brother, "is thanks enough," joked Sam.

"I just can't believe it." She snuggled into Logan's arms. "I guess my grandmother, Pearl, was the first lost child."

"Mom says, as the kids grow, she'll pay them to work at the farm. If they want to. Builds character to have a job," inserted Sam.

"Or they can have a place here at Twin Springs," added Theo.

Logan scooped up Colton, placing him on his shoulder. "Either way, there'll always be a place, a path and a way for your lost children."

"Once the Tower is fixed from the fire, can we move into it?" asked Maddy.

"No, I think we will leave living in a Tower to the guests," replied her brother.

A ruckus sounded out in the Grand Lobby. With a wiry twist of his lips, Jaxon said, "Sounds like the Geezers are up and moving. Doesn't look like you'll be getting rid of the Wolfe family anytime soon, Theo." He opened the door, allowing Ava to exit before him.

"What do you mean?" asked Theo, the color draining from his face.

Jaxon replied over his shoulder, "The Geezers decided to retire to the mountains of Virginia. Said JD and Logan are going to need help to keep track of all those kids she brings home."

Isabella in tow, Theo rushed out the door behind Jaxon. "When you say retire to the mountains, do you mean here at Twin Springs or nearby?"

Maddy followed her brother out, talking with Sam as she went. "Just call me MJ from now on."

Parker chased after her, "That's just stupid Maddy."

The girls continued arguing in the Grand Lobby with Sam caught in the middle.

"Why so quiet, Colton?" asked JD, following him and Logan out the door.

"I don't know, I guess I feel kind of bad about being so happy without my mom and dad."

Logan flipped the boy over his head and got down on eye level before him. "Your parents will always be here and here." He pointed to Colton's head and heart. "For you to cherish, love and keep alive. They're always with you."

Loving him even more, JD piped up, "He's right. Family never leaves you."

A man halted just ahead of her. She glanced over and he pushed his wire rimmed glasses up on his nose.

Tilting her head to the side, she murmured, "I think I know him."

"Who?" asked Logan.

"Um," she scratched her head. "I'm not sure."

Another man joined him, slapped him on the back and together they walked away. A third man, in a white jacket, jogged by and caught up with the pair. She tracked the three men's progress as they climbed the stairs next to the Bellhop Stand. Following them with her eyes, she glanced up at the balcony.

There stood the three Rockwell sisters. Their men joined them and hugged them from behind. Wrapping her arm around Logan's waist, JD leaned her head against his shoulder and whispered, "Welcome home."

DEAR READER

Now that you've finished Twin Springs: The Mystery of the Three Gems Trilogy, I hope that you loved JD and Logan.

Writing it has been a journey of love. Twin Springs is based on a hotel that I adore and could spend my whole life living at, The Omni Homestead in Hot Springs, Virginia.

It was within the Homestead's halls that the idea of Twin Springs sparked to life. My husband and I used to explore every nook and cranny of the hotel. From it's crooked hallways in the attics, to its lush grounds. Visiting the Homestead was like stepping back in time for me.

I hope that you too, will have a chance to visit this historical landmark, have tea in the Great Room and enjoy the hot springs.

Please take time to leave a review of this book (on Goodreads, Amazon). Share your enjoyment with other readers. Five stars always make an author's heart swell.

I'm working hard plotting and writing more books on JD Wolfe from Haunting Amethyst. Hang with JD before she discovers the secrets of the ghost haunting her.

Thank you for curling up with Isabella, Theo, Ava, Jaxon, JD and Logan. I hope their stories touched your heart like they touched mine. I look forward to hearing from you.

You're the best!

-Dee

♥ Website: www.DeeArmstrong.com
♥ Email: dee@deeArmstrong.com

Ready for your next book? Go to
www.DeeArmstrong.com/shop

:Facebook: facebook.com/DeeArmstrongAuthor

:Twitter: twitter.com/deearmstrongbks

:Instagram: instagram.com/deearmstrongauthor